D1030980

LUCKY CE SOIR

LUCKY CE SOIR

LUCKY O'TOOLE VEGAS ADVENTURE: BOOK 10

DEBORAH COONTS

Published by Chestnut Street Press

eBook ISBN: 978-1-944831-66-0
Paperback ISBN: 978-1-944831-59-2
Hardcover ISBN: 978-1-944831-67-7
Audiobook ISBN: 978-1-944831-53-0
Large Print ISBN: 978-1-944831-44-8

Cover design by Streetlight Graphics
(www.streetlightgraphics.com)

Formatting by Kate Tilton's Author Services, LLC
(www.katetilton.com)

CHAPTER ONE

"*S*HE'LL TURN me to stone." Panic rooted me where I stood as I stared at my nemesis. All four feet and eleven inches of impeccable...Frenchness, she worked her way across the room, stopping periodically, greeting people with a smile, a nod, a quick word. Yet, somehow, she kept the dagger of her attention buried to the hilt between my ribs.

The party in my honor whirled around me—a kaleidoscope of well-heeled French fashion and feigned disinterest. However, the woman headed my way left no doubt I was very much the American *plat du jour*.

Chef Jean-Charles Bouclet, my perfectly presented fiancé in his bespoke tux, cultured manners and delicious accent, pressed close, his shoulder touching mine. His favored cologne, *Eau de Seared Beef and Browned Onions*, wafted around him, telling me he'd been calming his nerves in the kitchen before my last-minute entrance. A single bead of sweat trickled down the side of his face. "What?" He'd been only half-listening.

"Stone. One look from your mother and I'll be a permanent fixture in this ancient ossuary." I made a sweeping gesture that included all the statuary lining the room. Tucked discretely into

1

individual alcoves, they lorded over the festivities. "Maybe that's where all these marble figurines came from, former guests who were found wanting."

He raised an eyebrow. "At least three of them were gifts from various kings. A bit gaudy, but one never says no to a king." Jean-Charles gave me the hint of a smile.

I followed his gaze which was locked onto the oncoming human missile, then I leaned in and whispered, "Don't look her in the eyes."

Sheathed in expensive one-of-a-kind couture that hugged her every curve, she advanced on us with an expression worn by those intent on vanquishing their enemies. Before I looked away, I took a bit of delight in the few extra pounds that expanded the middle of what might have been an hourglass figure. And her shoes were...sensible, a French fashion faux-pas. Her hints of human frailty lent me courage, albeit fleeting, but enough to stiffen my backbone.

Jean-Charles shook his head and finally gave me his attention. "You are making no sense. What do you mean she'll turn you to rock?" His Adam's apple bobbed as he swallowed hard, then ran a finger around the inside of his collar, tugging it to allow blood to get to his brain, apparently without the desired effect.

"Not rock. Stone. Like Medusa." As I braced for the imminent encounter, I let my gaze wander over the gathered throng, looking for friends in the crowded ballroom. No joy. Not a friendly, recognizable face in the lot. In fact, they all looked pinched and judgmental, with a hint of fear, making me feel like I was guest of honor at my own evisceration.

Okay, overly dramatic, but the whole meeting-my-well-heeled-very-French-future-in-laws had me on the verge of apoplexy. Once I did the I-do thing, my options would be gone. How was I supposed to know if I'd picked the right one? God knew Teddie had been an epic fail.

Epic.

My heart still bore the scars, but it had healed. My confidence, not so much.

But who was it I didn't trust exactly? Jean-Charles? Or me?

"Medusa?" Jean-Charles angled his head and looked like he was entertaining my analogy for a moment. Then he dismissed it with a quick shake of his head. "Don't be silly," he said, but he didn't sound convinced. Instead, he adjusted his bow tie and swallowed hard. The usual robin's egg blue of his eyes had turned dark and moody. Emotion pulled the skin tight over his cheekbones. Even still, with his full lips and soft brown hair curling over his collar, and that body hugged by the Italian cut of his tux, he was delish. He could be kind, sensitive, demanding, churlish, enigmatic—a dizzying array, which I currently found endlessly entertaining, but worried might wear me out. Time would tell...if I survived.

Seriously, death-by-mother-in-law is a thing—I know it is.

"You're scared, too," I whispered to Jean-Charles, still unable to focus an unwavering gaze on my future mother-in-law.

"She's my mother." Repeating the obvious was his go-to when avoiding telling me something I didn't want to hear. "And terrified would be more apt."

I swiveled a wide-eyed look at the man I supposedly knew better than anyone.

His eyes caught mine for a fraction of a second before his gaze skittered away. His smile was tight and thin. "You and I, we share difficult mothers."

"*Now* you tell me?" Despite whispering, my voice held a shrill note.

Jean-Charles sidestepped my accusation by focusing on a face in the crowd. Following his gaze, I found myself staring at a balding man, his sneer his only distinguishing feature. Jean-Charles looked a bit surprised and put out at seeing him.

"Who is that?"

"Someone who was not invited."

"Gotta have some steel *cojones* to crash your mother's gig. Personally, I would not tempt death that way."

"He would've been wise to stay away."

Christophe, Jean-Charles's son, moved from clutching his father's leg to tugging on my vintage Bob Mackie gown.

Five years old, blond curls and large baby blues like his father's, he most likely sensed our discomfort and needed reassurance. The kid was an emotional weather vane. My mother, Mona, a new mother to a set of twins, had told me that many things about dealing with children were instinctive. My disbelief had drawn a knowing smile. I hated it when Mona was right. Thankfully, it didn't happen that often.

After carefully disengaging his fingers from the delicate fabric, I squatted as much as I dared in the tight sheath, then lifted him. "Ooof! You've been eating too many happy-face pancakes." Christophe still fit on one hip, but he would soon outgrow that perch, and my ability to fly him there. I nuzzled his hair which smelled of baby soap and warm memories.

"*Grand-mère*, she looks...different," he whispered, one hand fisted in my hair.

"A woman on the warpath," I muttered, then braced for the elbow to the ribs I knew would be coming. Jean-Charles didn't disappoint. A soft nudge of displeasure which I ignored. "Girding her loins for battle to protect her sole and sainted son," I explained to my future stepson despite his father's glare. The hint of laughter in Jean-Charles's eyes told me I was on safe ground. The laughter dimmed when I turned on him. "I thought your mother lived on a farm and named the cows." Even with my limited functionality at the moment, I distinctly remembered that was how he'd described his mother—a charming story about his father's irritation at not being able to butcher and serve the cows which, in the naming, had become pets. The woman advancing on us with the purpose of a bullet fired from a rifle could have killed the cows with her bare hands and thought nothing of it. My opinion, but the look on her face did little to convince me otherwise.

Jean-Charles shrugged. "The vineyard. The farm is more of a hobby. How do you say it, their men's farm?"

"Gentleman's farm?" Usually his trouble with American idioms, which I had a strong suspicion was slightly feigned for my benefit, charmed me. Today, not so much.

"*Oui.* This." He seemed far too pleased with himself.

I resisted the urge to wipe the smug off his face. Probably bad form at a fancy French *soirée.* Instead, I narrowed my eyes. "Lying by omission." Was that a capital offense? Punishable by death or just slow, delicious torture? Either way, it was still a big check in the "con" column.

Yep, I was straddling the commitment fence. Uncomfortable to say the least.

And Jean-Charles's mother was just more of what I didn't need.

As she drew closer, the partiers formed a circle of interest, their intensity wafting off them like cheap cologne. Activity and conversation stopped.

My future mother-in-law, Madame Jeanne Marchand Bouclet, stepped into my space. I resisted the urge to step back, reestablishing my boundary. The more I traveled, the more I realized the American concept of personal space translated about as seamlessly as our humor. The English were equally amused and appalled by it, the Italians ignored it, the French invaded it, and the Asians missed the concept entirely.

I held my ground as Madame Bouclet gave me a rheumy-eyed once over. The pale bow of her mouth scrunched in only slight distaste—I took that as a win. Her brown hair, the color softened by invading gray, was cut in a stylish bob. Her gown, a golden chenille that changed hues where it wrinkled and flowed, was fitted and tasteful, yet provocative in its off-the-shoulder design. A long cocktail length, the dress exposed her ankles and the color-coordinated ballet slippers adorning her feet.

My shoes were French, but my gown shouted American chutzpah and not a little bit of Vegas showmanship, no doubt considered a bit bourgeois by this crowd. I envied the effortless style with which French women carried themselves. I also envied their figures. Of course, they didn't have to ignore the Siren call of In-N-Out Burger, animal style, every day.

Jean-Charles's mother said nothing, so I clamped my mouth shut, too, thinking then it would be impossible to stuff my foot in it. We faced off, her appraisal and my fear a chasm of silence between us.

Jean-Charles leaped into the breach. "*Maman,* may I present Miss Lucky O'Toole."

She flicked one stenciled eyebrow skyward and extended a hand, palm down.

I hadn't a clue what to do with it. Kiss it? Not a chance.

"*Maman!*"

Using his exalted-son status, Jean-Charles competed with the raised eyebrow thing. I could beat them both but now was probably not the time. The crowd eased even closer. I felt certain they'd drawn a collective breath and held it. The air didn't move, hanging instead thick and stifling with emotion.

"Jesus," I sighed, the dregs of my patience dried on the bottom of my empty flagon previously filled with the Milk of Human Kindness. I took her hand in both of mine. "It's a pleasure to meet you. The men in your family have been singing your praises nonstop. Thank you so much for inviting me to your lovely home and having this amazing party. I am incredibly honored." What can I say? Suck-up is my best thing—a skill well-honed through years in customer service at the Babylon, Las Vegas's most over the top strip resort. And before that, at lesser properties in the wild and wooly parts of Vegas most well-heeled folks never see. When I began life at a whorehouse in Pahrump, who knew I'd end up here, in Paris, feted by those at the upper end of the upper crust? Certainly not me. This was so far from my normal that all I could do was make it up as I went…and apparently use too many superlatives.

Madame Bouclet inclined her head slightly.

The room filled with expelled air. The mood brightened. The fear skittered to hide in the corners. Jean-Charles visibly relaxed, and the lady in front of me gave me a smile. "My dear, please ignore my son's lack of manners. I've been looking forward to meeting you. You have captured my son's heart and have enraptured my grandson—both challenging tasks. I must learn how you have done such a thing." Her English was flawless —infinitely better than my high-school French, which I had yet to trot out. In this crowd, being six feet tall, curvy, and American was enough of an embarrassment. "Let me introduce you to my friends." She turned on her heel.

Jean-Charles motioned for me to follow, then fell in behind me. Christophe gladly rode my hip, bobbing along high above the fray. Being tall was my cross to bear, but I figured it was infinitely better than staring at everybody's thighs. So I took pity on him, and on me, and let him ride into the fray, a human shield as it were…but he didn't need to know that.

"Where's Desiree?" I tossed the words over my shoulder as I followed in Madame Bouclet's wake.

Jean-Charles rested a hand lightly on my shoulder as he leaned closer to catch my words. "*Pardon?*"

"Your sister?" I was counting on her to be my wingman. Her absence left me flying solo. Of course, I'd been complicit in the death of her estranged husband, Adone Giovanni, who, with his mistress had conspired to steal Desiree's business. So maybe expecting her to greet me with a buss on both cheeks might be overshooting.

Frankly, I thought my assistance in taking him out of the

gene pool was a good thing, but love could be super-complicated. Maybe Desiree was planning to plant a dagger between my shoulder blades. To be honest, I didn't have a clue what transpired between her ears, nor what she held in her heart.

"She would not miss Mother's party." Jean-Charles made the prospect sound like doing so would mean the guillotine.

"Hope she's okay."

"*Pffft,*" he puffed in French derision. "It will be a man. It is always a man."

"Rather evolved of you. Your man card is in trouble. Don't you Y-chromosome types always blame bad things on women?"

"I am not saying she is not at fault. She chooses the men." He tugged a bit with the hand still on my shoulder. "What is this man card?"

"Only thing that keeps you guys in the game."

Madame Bouclet yanked my attention back to the terror at hand. I so should've brushed up on the rules of French decorum. Vaguely, I remembered something about not touching anyone, and for sure not smiling very much—the French think it makes Americans look like fools, and perhaps a bit insincere. Spot on, in my book.

She stopped in front of a couple waiting with expectant expressions. Tiny, perfectly turned-out, they gave her a thin smile. "This is Miss Lucky O'Toole, Jean-Charles's fiancée."

I painted on what I hoped was a pleasant expression that wasn't a smile and tried to remember my fancy manners.

The names, unusual in their pronunciation, faded as one overwrote the one before on my mental hard drive. Christophe wriggled on my hip and my arms ached from corralling his weight as a starched and unctuous liveried member of the staff hurried to Madame Bouclet's side. If the interruption bothered her, I couldn't tell. Composure was something I strove for, failed at, and consequently strongly admired. Jean-Charles's mother's was impeccable. I wondered if she also had the royal wave down.

As the man bent and whispered in her ear, Madame Bouclet's hand moved to her throat, her fingers intertwining with her pearls, twisting them like expensive worry beads. Her face paled. Her jaw slackened, revealing her age and her worry. The man stepped back, and Madame Bouclet motioned to her son with a fluttering hand held close to her side, a subtle move to not draw attention.

Jean-Charles touched my elbow with a gesture of understanding, and I relinquished his son, my arms screaming their thanks. In one fluid movement, Jean-Charles took his son, lifting him high, then dropping him on his shoulders. "What is it, *Maman?*"

"It's Papa." She wilted as her knees buckled slightly. With a flawless segue, Jean-Charles caught her arm, steadying her. "He's not well. His heart."

Jean-Charles skewered the butler with an unmistakable look. The man turned on his heel and disappeared through the doorway. Jean-Charles, now holding his mother's elbow and his son, inclined his head, indicating I should follow him. I dug in my heels. "I should stay here."

"*Non!*" His tone brooked no argument.

This was not the place to make a scene—I could feel the heat of the partygoers' stares.

Jean-Charles ushered us through a doorway hidden in the paneling of the front hall, then down a hallway with multiple intersections with other corridors. The back of the house. As a hotelier, I was familiar. As a gal from Pahrump, this was home.

Worry propelled Jean-Charles. I had to hurry to keep up.

At the third intersection, he turned right, then burst through swinging double doors. I followed, catching the doors on the backswing. Blinking at the light, I found myself in a cavernous, white and stainless kitchen, the workstations spotlighted by commercial-grade overhead lights. Delicious aromas wafted from ovens and bubbling pots. My stomach growled. I cringed as the family clustered around me, afraid they might have heard.

But something was wrong.

Jean-Charles pushed into the kitchen. "What is going on here?" He kicked at a pot rolling on the floor. Utensils were scattered on the tile like grown-up Pick-Up Stix. A pool of something that smelled drool-worthy oozed from under a prep table. "Where's my father?"

"Over here." A voice, indignant but weak, answered in a timbre that held hints of his son's.

Jean-Charles kicked at a pot as he hurried toward the voice. His staff remained rooted. In full French bluster, he turned and shouted at them. "Back to work. And clean this up, now!"

They all jumped. Hell, Jean-Charles's imperious tone had me wanting to reach for a spatula. Instead, I followed him while the others held back. While food sizzled and steamed, they clustered together, staring at the man slouched in a chair someone had pulled into the center of the kitchen. Long, lean, all angles and anger, he pushed away a young man pressing a cloth to his head, pressing it to his head himself. When he lifted it slightly, I gasped at the long, red gash in his forehead. The man let loose a long stream of French I didn't understand yet understood perfectly. His other hand drifted to the center of his chest where he pushed, then winced in discomfort—from the gash or his heart, it was hard to tell.

I glanced at Jean-Charles, then again at the man in the chair. That apple hadn't fallen far.

Jean-Charles shifted Christophe to his hip as he knelt by his father's chair. Christophe, his eyes glistening, patted his grandfather's face. Children and their empathy.

Why do we lose that as we grow?

"The pain? Is it bad?" Jean-Charles asked his father in a whisper.

Looking at his father, I could answer that one. The man was so pale his skin held a hint of blue. His cheeks hollowed below too-wide eyes. He panted as if running a race, perhaps against Death himself. My father, with a bullet in his chest and blood leaking out so fast, had been as close to death as one could get without stepping into the afterlife. Jean-Charles's father was right there, toes curled over the edge of the abyss, his features donning a death mask as he sank into himself, his life force depleted. The man was way past "not well."

"Should I call the doctor?" Jean-Charles had seen the same as I had. Without waiting for permission, he nodded at his mother who eased away to summon help. "Did you take the nitroglycerin?"

He pushed his son's concerns aside. "It will go away."

With two fingers, Jean-Charles fished around in his father's breast pocket extracting a small tin. With a thumb, he popped it open and extracted a tiny white pill. "Take this."

One of the kitchen staff appeared with a glass of red wine. "It is the Lafite."

Jean-Charles nodded his thanks as he took the glass, waving it under his father's nose. As ammonia does for a fainter, the wine brought back the elder Bouclet, focusing him. "That's the '82," he gasped, then sucked in more air. "One of the best vintages," another gasp then pull-in of air, "a rare cult wine. We set aside a case for a special day. We wanted to toast your engagement," a gasp, a wince, then a deep breath, "with something special."

"And that is very special." Jean-Charles held the glass to his father's lips. "Take a sip. See if it is aging well." Christophe, his eyes wide with worry, clung to his father.

A little nitro with your rare Bordeaux. Not a great pairing but a terrific bribe. One that worked as the old man did as his son insisted. Jean-Charles's mother returned. Her slight nod let her son know she'd found the doctor. I assumed he was on his way since no one made any move to relocate the elder Bouclet.

"How is it?" Jean-Charles asked after his father had taken a few sips, savoring each of them. A touch of color returned to his cheeks. He breathed easier now, easing the force with which he pressed on his chest. "It helps. The pain is lessening."

"The wine?" Jean-Charles asked as if that was what he'd meant. "How's the wine?"

A smile passed between them. His father bestowed a look of love. "Not as special as you, but it is very good."

"Papa? What has happened?" Jean-Charles used a soft, measured tone. "Are you sure you're okay?"

"The pain is almost gone." His father waved his hand, a human flag of surrender. Jean-Charles had his father's hands, long and narrow—artist's hands that could concoct a variety of delights.

Jean-Charles pushed his father's hand away from the cloth he held to his head. "Permit me." A demand framed as a question, one of his best things...and most irritating. He snuck a peek under the now-red cloth, then let loose a stream of low, guttural French.

Madame Bouclet swooped in, snatching her grandson to her chest. "Jean-Charles!"

Her offense was justified. If I were more of a lady, the bit I caught would have made me blush. One of the staff rushed to do his bidding, returning quickly with a first-aid kit. Jean-Charles set to work. His hard expression brooked no argument. His father sat motionless, as if carved from stone, his hands on his knees, his back erect, his face flushed with emotion. "The wine," he gasped.

His son brushed the comment aside. "Who did this?" He dabbed at the cut with cotton soaked in alcohol drawing a few epithets from his father, which he ignored. A quick glance around the kitchen. "Did you fight with someone? Who was here?"

Most of the staff turned from his question—apparently, they knew what happens to the messenger.

"Laurent." The word sounded like an epithet.

"Here? In our home? What did he want?"

"The wine," his father repeated.

"He wanted the wine?" Jean-Charles closed the cut with two butterfly closures.

"He had a crazy story. I didn't listen. I didn't let him finish," his father managed, then convulsed into a fit of racking coughs that he caught with a white napkin pressed over his mouth. His skin turned an alarming shade of red. "Uninvited in our home," he managed between coughs and gasps.

Still a bit iffy on French protocol, I assumed from his inflection that was almost as grave a sin as disrespecting the women of the household, maybe more.

"Easy, Papa. Slowly." Jean-Charles helped his father take a few more sips of the Lafite between spasms.

This stress, both physical and clearly emotional, only put more pressure on a bad heart.

"Enzo did this to you?" A hint of incredulity subtexted the question.

From Jean-Charles's inflection, I took it Enzo Laurent might be scum, but he was no blackguard, and as an honorable man he wouldn't ever do such a thing. Men came in all types and sometimes shifted from one to the other with the proper motivation. I guessed we all could. My mother often had me seriously considering homicide. I mean, the idea of three-squares, a cot, and no Mona was almost irresistible at times. But jail would probably be incompatible with my serious authority issues, so I'd restrained myself...so far.

"No. A man. In the tunnels. I surprised him. He ran out through the kitchen. I couldn't catch him. The swine ran right by Enzo. At my shout, he tried to stop him as well. His jaw may be broken for his efforts."

"What did the man in the tunnel look like?"

"Young. Dark hair. I never saw his face. He and Enzo tussled, and then he was gone."

"Where is Enzo?"

"I threw him out!" The elder Bouclet seemed offended at the question that, in its asking, suggested there was another course of action. "The wine," he gasped as he grabbed his son's lapel.

"What about the wine?" Jean-Charles asked again, looking at his mother who bracketed his father on the other side. Holding his hand in one of hers while securing her grandson with the other, she eyed her son, her eyes dark with worry.

Monsieur Bouclet sat up straighter, his face clearing as he stared at his son with a look of pain and disbelief. "The wine, it is gone."

This time it was Jean-Charles's turn with the raised eyebrow trick. "What do you mean it is gone? The cellar is full. We even transported the entire winery library from the winery to show our guests. I checked it myself last evening."

The truth in his father's stare could not be denied. "It's all gone."

CHAPTER TWO

$\mathcal{J}$EAN-CHARLES ROCKED back on his heels and sprang to his feet. As he passed by, he said, "Come." It wasn't an invitation. He snagged his son from his mother, then handed him to me.

"It's okay, sweetie," I whispered as the boy tucked in close, wrapping his legs around my waist and fisting a hand in my hair.

"Mother, stay with Father," he ordered in a head-of-family tone.

As I turned to follow Jean-Charles, his sister Desiree, the one I'd been waiting for, burst into the room, making an entrance more impressive than welcome. I was the only one who smiled. Jean-Charles ground to a stop, glaring at his sister. I narrowly avoided plowing into him. All this stopping and starting was making me goofy. Or maybe it was the fact that I barely dared to breathe in my very fitted sheath. Either way, not much oxygen filtered into my brain.

"I thought this was a party, not a funeral." Desiree, resplendent in her own sparkly sheath, her matching shoes dusted with dirt, stopped in front of her mother. She reflexively bussed the air near each cheek while she kept her eyes on her father.

Her mother looked happy to see her but angry as well. "You're late."

Self-consciously Desiree brushed down her dress and patted at her hair—a female reflex that connected us even though a vast culture separated us. Even the French had taught their daughters that, if the exterior is found pleasing, then you have a chance of being found pleasing as well.

She needn't have bothered. Any daughter could read her mother's look—her displeasure lurking under the smile.

A man, Jean-Charles had said. The last one in Desiree's life was dead. Could there be another so soon? She was stunning, no question. With that tiny yet lush figure, tousled curls, inviting mouth and a hint of haughty, she was the kind of package men wouldn't be able to resist trying to unwrap...even though they knew they should. If recent history was any indication, she liked the bad boys. Another bit of personal synchronicity—this one I was even less comfortable with.

Desiree brushed aside her family's disapproval, but worry doused her hint of jaunty. "What is going on? Why is everyone in here?" She hooked her thumb over her shoulder. "You do know we have a roomful of guests, *oui?*"

Everyone used English in my honor for which I was profoundly grateful. Being a fish out of water, I was glad they didn't leave me at sea as well.

Her light brown hair that matched her brother's was piled high on her head with a few tendrils tickling her cheeks adding softness but unable to hide her concern. "*Papa?*"

"Tend to him. The doctor is on his way." Jean-Charles dismissed his sister with an order. "He always brightens when he sees you." Spoken like a true older brother.

Jean-Charles lifted his chin in my direction then turned and disappeared down the hallway. I hurried to keep up. "Where are we going?"

"Shhh."

I hated being shushed. Halfway back to the party, he paused in front of a heavy wooden door on his right. "My father's study." Ushering us inside, he secured the door behind us. A button in the top right-hand drawer of the massive desk released one of the beautiful burled wall panels on the side wall to swing open a few inches. A hushed rush of air ruffled my hair and raised goosebumps. "What is this?"

Jean-Charles pushed the door open wider. "The wine cellar."

For some reason, I was thrilled he didn't say the dungeon. "Must be some kind of special wine down here."

"Indeed. The wine cellar is very private. A secret of only our family. The wine is very precious. Be careful here. The steps are steep." Leaving me feeling like I'd just stepped back in time— way back in time—he bounded down the stone steps.

My eyes needed time to adjust from the glare of the kitchen, so I took the steps slowly, balancing Christophe, who held tight. His hand fisted in my hair tugged, but I ignored it as I concentrated on placing my feet on the narrow stairs. With one hand holding him and the other hiking my skirt to keep it from tangling with my feet, I worked my way step by step. Almost down, I tripped. Reaching out, I caught the railing. But the momentum, with Christophe's weight added to mine, was too much. My hand slipped.

Christophe jerked my hair as he held tight. I bit down on a yelp, sucking air and holding it.

Jean-Charles bolted up the stairs, catching me around the waist. His other hand found the railing. He held tight, using his body to block my fall. "Steady."

I think all three of us held our breath until conscious thought registered the danger had passed.

I felt the press of someone behind me. Perhaps I heard a

gasp, but something made me realize Desiree and her mother must have followed.

Jean-Charles backed down a step but still held me. "You okay?" I nodded. He held out his arms for his son, but Christophe held tight to me. He wrapped both arms around my neck. His breath was warm on my cheek when he said, "It's okay. I have you."

Jean-Charles caught my eye as he helped me down the last couple of steps. We both smiled, and the tension eased. Later, the could-have-beens would haunt me. Tripping and hurting myself was one thing...

As my foot found the sandy floor, he let go of my waist and extended a hand. I took it, and he led me down a narrow stone tunnel. Sconces dotted the wall providing enough light to navigate, though Jean-Charles seemed to know exactly where he was going.

"Who is Enzo Laurent?"

"Our sworn enemy."

I almost laughed. "You mean like dueling pistols, twenty paces, dawn, all of that stupidity?"

He threw an irritated look over his shoulder. "Same emotion, but the battles today are fought differently."

"Swords? Sabers?" I hurried to keep up as he increased his pace. "Oh wait, fake news, Russian interference, reputation assassination, hours of forced listening to techno-pop to see who screams in pain first, Pez dispensers, swizzle sticks, arm wrestling."

"Lucky, stop. You are making this worse. We are gentlemen." The hint of a laugh undercut the indignation. "Swizzle what? I do not know this."

"The plastic things you stick in drinks to stir them."

"An odd weapon."

"An odd battle. You may be gentlemen, but you need to grow

18

up." Here I was offering advice, and I had no idea what the fight was about.

"Your words will not change history. We fight. It is what we do. By any means appropriate. There is a code, defined rules—boundaries, if you will. The wounds go deep, but you've made your point."

I was running short of sarcasm. Rather horrifying, to be honest. Without the shield of a clever quip, I'd have to pretend to be a grown-up. "How quaint. The Rules of Engagement and the Geneva Convention are curious bits of arcana, so gutted they've been left as beyond resuscitation on the battlefield of life."

I let him have his little bit of fantasy. Nobody played fair these days, and he was a fool to think this Enzo Laurent would be the exception. "What is this place? Where are we going?" The air was dank and cold and smelled of centuries long past.

"A series of tunnels built centuries ago." He dropped my hand and grabbed one of the torches from the wall.

"Seems more like a dungeon." Ancient screams whispered from the shadows, raising goosebumps.

"Your imagination is racing with you."

"Running away," I corrected reflexively. My toe connected with something hard. A bone? I shivered still under the spell of my imaginings.

The rustle of the people who followed mingled with imagined sounds of wraiths whispering past.

"What?" he asked, his question gutted by distraction.

"My imagination is running away with me."

"This is what I said."

"Lost in the translation." I shook off the ghosts. "I still think this place was a dungeon."

"Feel the air? It is a perfect wine cellar." His words filtered back to me on the coolness as he rounded a corner and disappeared.

So, it was *a dungeon.*

I stepped up my pace and followed him. The narrow tunnel opened into a slightly larger room. Racks upon racks lined the stone walls.

All of them empty.

Jean-Charles stood like stone. I recognized his look. Thinly veiled homicide.

The thieves had left one bottle which must've fallen and lay forgotten and half-covered in the loose dirt on the floor. Jean-Charles bent and picked it up. A tic worked in his cheek as he brushed the dirt from the label. I shifted Christophe to my back, securing him by hooking my arms under his thighs. "How much was here?"

He held the bottle for me to see. "It's not how much was here, but what was here."

Even though I recognized the label, I bent down to catch the year, then gave a low whistle. "Chateaux d'Yquem 1996. Pricy stuff."

He handed the bottle to his mother. Desiree peeked over her shoulder. When he turned back to me, his face was calmer, but the hardness remained in his eyes. He turned up the gas to the lit sconce and the flame jumped, flickering light into the shadows. "The Chateau d'Yquem was one of the lesser bottles. We had one of the Chateau Margeaux Thomas Jefferson bottles. A Chateaux Lafitte 1869. My father purchased one bottle from a gentleman who had bought a triplet for over six hundred thousand U.S. dollars. Then there was our vineyard library collection—one bottle from each vintage ever produced." He shrugged. "It is priceless and irreplaceable. This collection, our bottles and the others, was my father's work of a lifetime." He turned slowly in a circle. "And now it is gone." He leveled a gaze at me. "This could kill him."

I had nothing to say, so I squeezed his arm then stepped aside, leaving him to wrestle with his emotions. Madame

Bouclet seemed to wilt as she watched from the doorway. "The wine! All the wine!" She twisted her pearls like a tourniquet—they'd either break or she'd faint dead away.

"Stay there, please," I said as I focused on the small space, taking in as many details as I could. "Jean-Charles, don't disturb any footprints." Christophe breathed in my ear but kept quiet. I pulled at his arms, loosening them. "Not quite so tight, okay? I won't drop you."

"I know. You keep me safe." His shiver echoed through me.

Misplaced confidence, but I didn't argue, preferring instead to try to live up to his opinion.

Jean-Charles shot me a glare, but he did as I asked, carefully placing his feet as he moved along the shelving. I worked my way around the other side looking for anything that would give a hint as to who and how. "I take it the only exit would be back the way we came?"

"*Oui.* Yes." He seemed irritated at his French.

"But they didn't carry all this wine out through the house under the noses of the family and staff," I muttered, thinking aloud as I walked slowly along the wine racks, staring at the sand. They'd been in a hurry. And, from the scuffle of footprints, there had been several of them.

I'd gone about a third of the way around when I saw it—gouge marks in the sand as if someone had dragged something heavy. Desiree had shouldered in next to her mother and now watched me intently from the entrance. "Here, would you?" I lifted Christophe slightly.

Desiree followed my footsteps as she walked carefully to me. I lifted the boy. "Go with your aunt, okay?" Christophe leaned into his aunt's open arms. Unburdened, I returned to the lines in the sand. They corresponded with the legs of the racks. Someone had tried to obscure one of the gouges in the sand as if attempting to cover their tracks. But the other one was clear.

And no scores marred the sand for the sections on either side— just this one.

I bent to look closer. Yes, someone had moved this section. I was sure of it.

I tugged on one of the uprights of the rack. Built of solid wood, at first it didn't move. Then I threw a bit more of my bulk against it. An inch. Another tug. Six inches. Jean-Charles, having noticed my efforts, joined in. Together, we moved the rack enough for me to wiggle behind it, while Jean-Charles kept tugging the rack away from the wall inches at a time. His anger fueled him, giving him leverage I didn't have in heels.

White tears of deposits left by water seepage scored the bricks like chalk marks left by an inmate counting the days. Cool to my touch, the bricks were dry as I patted them. The mortar flaked as I ran my hands slowly over sections of the wall. Starting at the top—with my height reaching the ceiling was easy—I worked my hands back and forth as I went down the wall to the sandy floor. Then I started on the next section. Three-quarters of the way down the second section of wall, a mere foot and a half above the floor, I felt it. A cool whisper of air leaking through a chink in the mortar. I inched my hand back across the path traveled. Closing my eyes, I concentrated. Yes, I was right. I held my hand in the slight stream, my finger on the hole in the mortar.

Movement was a challenge in the Mackie. Squatting on my haunches strained the seams. With only threads to hold my dignity intact, I tried not to breathe as I angled my head to look at the section of the wall where I'd felt the air. Curious. The mortar was darker than the rest.

With a fingernail, I scratched at it. Wet, it flaked off easily.

The brick that let in the air had no mortar at all holding it.

With Christophe riding her back, Desiree leaned over me like a vulture. Jean-Charles watched from the side.

The brick extended just enough so I could get a decent hold

on it with my fingertips. Rocking it back and forth, I worked it loose. I handed it to Jean-Charles and went to work on the next brick. Able to get my fingers behind it, I had more leverage. I pulled it loose easily. Same with the third and fourth. Working my way up, I kept glancing at Jean-Charles.

If looks could kill.

His face flushed crimson. "The bastards."

"Rather clever actually." I know, not exactly a good strategy to diffuse the homicide suffusing his scowl, but I never could resist admiring a good job, even if the goal was not so good. And this heist had been spectacular in the planning and pretty impressive in the execution. "What is back here?" Another brick broke away.

"I haven't any idea."

"The catacombs? Do they come this far? Aren't they really on the south side of the river?"

"Yes. I don't know of any that extend this far, but Paris is a maze below the surface. In the past, whole neighborhoods would sink into the tunnel below. One of the kings financed repair of the supports, but that was a long time ago."

In the U.S., the whole city would be some sort of Superfund site to protect people from their history. "Are there any maps?" I wiggled another brick free.

"Many, but none of them accurate," Jean-Charles said. "It is forbidden to explore. The routes are very old, very dangerous. Many collapses in the tunnels. It is so easy to get lost."

This time two bricks came together. I set to work on the row above to enlarge the opening. "Well, someone not only got in; but they also managed to get out. And with a lot of heavy wine bottles. I find it impossible to believe no one saw them."

"Perhaps," Desiree joined the game. "We must determine where they entered and exited the catacombs or whatever tunnel this is."

"And that would be impossible," Jean-Charles announced.

"We could follow their tracks," his sister argued.

"Finding an accomplice would be easier." Their heads swiveled my direction as I worked on a particularly tough brick. "Someone had to know exactly where all this wine was. And exactly how this chamber was walled off from the tunnel beyond." With both hands, I grasped the bricks and put my weight against this section of the wall.

The wall gave way. Surprised, I landed on my ass.

From the darkness beyond, a form fell through the opening.

Unable to move in my tight sheath, I raised my arms.

A man. Dark hair, dark eyes, wicked grin, landed in my lap.

"Lucky! You cut it rather close, old girl. Just a bit longer and I would've been a goner."

CHAPTER THREE

I FELT the burn of intensity as all eyes turned my direction.

And just when I thought the day couldn't get much worse. *Some days the bear eats you.* Apparently, today was my day to be gobbled by a cliché.

And to be implicated in a theft by a liar from my past.

Desiree gasped, but unlike everyone else, she wasn't looking at me. Her cheeks colored.

"You know this man?" The question, cloaked in haughty, came from Jean-Charles's mother and hit me right between the shoulder blades. "You know this man who stole our wine and put my husband closer to the grave!"

Now I knew where Jean-Charles got his overly dramatic flair.

My hands full, I blew the bangs off my forehead as I stared down at a nightmare, manifest in flesh and blood. Yes, I knew him. That fact alone made me suspect. I took my time to formulate a response.

"If I kill him now, I'd be doing us all a huge favor." I glanced at Jean-Charles, who looked at me with a mixture of disbelief and fury. "Ah, I can see innocent until proven guilty isn't a thing on this side of the pond, the protections of American jurisprudence tossed on their ass. Haven't you heard, leaping to conclusions can be bad for your health?" And your sex life, I thought as I gazed at my future former fiancé. Yes, he was toast if he kept up this sort of ass-hattery. Surely, he knew he already skated on thin ice? But cluelessness was one of the worst aspects of the Curse of the Y-chromosome, so as an unafflicted female it was best not to expect too much.

"Who is this man? He seems to be expecting you," Jean-Charles asked in feigned amusement. The cold tone, a dead giveaway, made it sound like he'd caught us both naked in his bed.

"Sinjin Smythe-Gordon. A Hong Kong financier, self-styled Robin Hood, and a man for whom the truth is at best a suggestion and always an inconvenience. He's also an opportunist, and right now he's taking advantage of an interesting turn of coincidence."

Sinjin lay on his back half across my lap, his hands presumably bound behind him with the rope that circled his shoulders several turns, then trailed off toward his feet, which still extended into darkness through the hole in the wall. A gag that he'd worked loose circled his neck. Oh, how I itched to tighten it like a garrote.

Since I'd last seen him in Macau, he'd let his dark hair grow even longer. Now it fanned out behind his head, framing his flawless combination of Asian and Caucasian. He flashed his patented smile. "Lucky, if you would?" He moved a bit against the rope. "I've loosened it, but I could use some help." His gaze flicked to Desiree who had kept her position at the front of the crowd. He gave her a slight shake of the head, then rekindled his smile for my benefit. "Really, just a few ticks longer. You do love to push a man to his breaking point." His tone was seductively familiar.

"Oh, for God's sake, cut the crap. And I wouldn't loosen one of those ropes even if you were turning blue."

"Blue is not my best color." He didn't seem put off by my vitriol.

"I agree. I'm thinking prison orange *would* enhance your coloring nicely. And, if you're nice, I'd consider loosening the rope around your hands if I could wrap it around your neck and throw it over a beam."

Jean-Charles stepped between the two of us as if I might be tempted to follow through. Please! Mr. Smythe-Gordon wouldn't be worth the trouble. Besides, all I really had to do was give him enough metaphorical rope and he'd eventually hang himself, figuratively speaking. Regardless, the result would be gratifying.

"I'd quit before she completely buries you." Jean-Charles grabbed Sinjin by the lapels, lifting him off me. "Did you hurt my father?" His voice dropped an octave or two and held more than a little lethal.

"Do I look to be in any position to hurt anyone?" Sinjin worked against his ropes with no success.

As I said, Mr. Smythe-Gordon was generally inconvenienced by the truth.

Jean-Charles fisted a hand and reared back.

"Don't!" For once my bark matched my bite. "He's not worth it. And you won't get the truth out of him. At least not without pulling a few fingernails followed by a few hours of water-boarding. And, frankly, I don't have the time for all of that." Nor the stomach, but I was channeling all the badass I could muster. Madame Bouclet and her son still hung in the balance teetering between my side and excommunication, or drawing and quartering, or tarring and feathering, or whatever they considered an appropriate substitute for banishment in these parts.

Jean-Charles straightened at my verbal cattle prod. He dropped Sinjin, who landed in a rush of breath. I extended a hand, an invitation. Jean-Charles accepted, pulling me to my feet. After a feeble attempt to brush the sand from my behind, I realized it had found a home in the intricate beadwork of the gown.

"Torture would be beneath you," Sinjin said, but his voice had lost its swagger.

His uncertainty made me smile—I tried for my best evil grin. "Would it?" I crossed my hands behind my back as I loomed over him, as close as I dared. "Let's put this in context, shall we? In Macau, you were more than willing to leave me responsible for the loss of millions of dollars' worth of rare watches. Now you're using your not insignificant charm to convince my fiancé and his family that I am a partner in your petty criminal enterprise which has cost them dearly, both in real value and in emotional currency. Don't push me, Sinjin. I can give as well as you take."

The flicker of mutual understanding lit his eyes. "What do you want?"

"Who did this? Who are you working for or with? Tell me, does the name Enzo Laurent ring a bell?"

"Who?" The word substituted for a "no."

"The wine distributor?" Jean-Charles added.

Sinjin's eyes widened slightly.

I'd learned to look for that tell when our paths had crossed before. If he wasn't overtly lying, he was lying by omission. If he didn't know him personally, he knew of him. Another cat- and-mouse game. Another bit of out-foxing him so he would show his hand. A game I'd won before. A stroke of luck and a good guess. Would I be as lucky this time? Sinjin Symthe-Gordon was a man of many resources, great intellect, and the ego that came with it—an ego I'd done damage to. If I had to guess, I'd say Mr. Smythe-Gordon carried a grudge behind the self-effacing bullshit.

I'd bested him once. Now he was wise to my act. Surprise and his underestimation wouldn't work this time.

"Lucky, seriously, what is going on?" Jean-Charles vibrated with anger—the frustration of a fight with no one to hit. I got it. "You were supposed to free him by an appointed time?" He'd softened his tone, but he hadn't removed the barb of accusation.

With his shuck and jive, Sinjin Smythe-Gordon brought out the worst in me. Jean-Charles and his inability to leap to my defense sealed the deal. I hated games almost as much as I hated overblown egos. I wondered if the French, by birthright, qualified. "Of course not. His presence here is a curious coincidence which he's spinning in his favor. A classic technique. The magician who throws down a smoke bomb then disappears while the audience's attention is focused on the smoke."

He seemed unappreciative of the analogy which I thought was one of my better ones. Tough crowd.

"How do you know him?"

We'd been through that. "I don't *know* him. We crossed swords in Macau as I said. He kidnapped Romeo then thought he'd get the drop on me and leave me holding the bag."

"Such vitriol," Sinjin tsked. If I could've slapped him without relinquishing the upper hand, I would've. "I gave Romeo back to you." He acted like that was deserving of lifetime allegiance.

"After you used him as bait to lure me into China illegally. And not to gloss over the fact you took him in the first place." I clamped my mouth shut and held up my hand. "Smoke and mirrors. I am not going to argue facts. You would've been more than happy to leave me taking the fall for those watches."

Jean-Charles looked at Sinjin in a new light, although exactly what light remained a bit murky. When he looked back at me, his expression remained a bit too conflicted for my taste. Where was my knight in shining armor, the man who would defend my honor to the death? "You didn't tell me someone stole all those watches."

"They didn't. Specifically, *he* didn't. Romeo and I pulled a switch." I nudged Sinjin with my foot. "Are you back for revenge?"

"Well, if I am, I'm making a mess of it now, aren't I?"

"At least you're consistent. Your kidnapping skills are pretty stellar, but your B and E could use some refining." His smile lost some wattage as I bent to grab his elbow.

He scrambled out of the hole as I tugged him to his feet. The rope secured his hands behind his back, as I suspected, then made a turn around his neck, then a couple of turns around his chest before snaking down to capture his ankles, binding them together. He could stand, but only if he bent at the waist. If he stood tall, the rope would tighten, cutting off his air. He looked disheveled, dirty and more than a little uncomfortable which was fine by me. Perfect, actually.

"Where does the hole lead?" I thought about poking my head in for a look but then figured he'd put a shoulder to my ass and push me through, so I resisted.

"I believe to a part of the sewer system."

"Lovely." Well, at least one of my decisions this evening had been a good one—I was happy to have resisted diving through that hole. "The tux is a rather odd choice, all things considered. I'm sure your little gathering was an invitation-only affair. So, who crashed the party? You?"

"I don't know what you mean." He tried for jaunty but missed by a mile as he shot a veiled glance at Desiree.

"Someone blew your cover. That's the only explanation— well the only reasonable explanation—as to how you came to be trussed up like a turkey at the holidays."

He cocked his head. "What's the other explanation?"

"That your friends used your pretty-boy-with-country-club manners act, then threw you over like last week's girlfriend. Now that I think about it, that one sounds pretty good."

"Cute." His smile dimmed. Nothing like running out of ammo to take the fun out of the verbal skirmishing.

And his down-in-the-mouth act told me all I needed to know…well, almost. It told me his role, but it didn't confirm which team he played for.

"The ropes? Would you? I can't feel my hands." He gave me a petulant look that I'm sure had melted lesser women.

"Not a chance. Not until you tell me how you arrived at this point, dressed like a prince but trussed up and bricked behind a wall like a common criminal." Well, an uncommon criminal, but I wasn't going to give him even that.

"Please," he huffed. "I'm anything but common."

"Opinions differ. But you clearly ran afoul of someone with a serious Edgar Allan Poe fetish."

"Lucky, he can't feel his hands," Desiree whispered.

I ignored her. Too many looks had passed between the two of them. Sinjin had roped her in somehow, and I really didn't want to face the prospect now. If a woman made bad choices when it came to males, was she doomed to repeat that mistake over and over?

Sinjin gave the gathered throng a once-over. I marveled at how he could look haughty and resplendent covered in dust and with his hands and feet tied. He paused when he saw the bottle Jean-Charles's mother held. "May I see that?"

Looking like she'd rather hit him with it than hand it to him, Madame Bouclet gave the bottle to her daughter who, in turn, passed it to me.

I shielded the bottle. "What is it?" I don't know why I asked. Maybe I wished he could give me something, anything, that would let me believe him. Like I'd said, an accomplice who I could turn to the side of good would be a massive help in getting the wine back and my life back on track.

"Chateaux d'Yquem 1996. I left it here."

I held the bottle where he could see it. "Why?"

"Things were going south. I knew if I didn't make it out alive at least, with that bottle, maybe someone would start asking questions."

"Why?"

"It's a fake."

A murmur rippled through the crowd behind me.

"It most certainly is not!" The accusation ruffled Jean-Charles's French feathers.

"You don't believe me? Look closely."

The printing wasn't quite right, but only someone familiar with such a bottle would notice. And the label showed signs of a quick dousing in coffee or something to try to age it. A bit of the original cream color showed through.

A fake. A careless one at that. Quick and dirty. Nothing about this passed the smell test, and my gut was clanging a warning bell big-time. But who was the bad guy here? Sinjin was a self-styled Robin Hood, employing less-than-savory tactics for a noble end. But what was the endgame?

I stuck my nose in Sinjin's face. "Tell me what's going on." Asking him to give it to me straight would be a waste of energy and emotion. He'd spin it so he came out smelling like a rose. My job would be to separate the truth from the bald-assed lies.

Oh, and find the wine. Preferably before my future father-in-law expired and my life imploded.

Sinjin took a moment as he surveyed his audience, no doubt reaching for just the right note that would be music to their ears. "Recently a wine counterfeiting ring came to light. The perpetrators followed a similar pattern to this heist. They identify a worthy target—priceless wine that the owners have talked about and put on display."

"So, they know the exact makeup of the collection," I said, stealing his thunder and stating what I considered to be obvious. This one was hard to stomach but easy to follow and his stringing me along pissed me off. Not hard to do, actually, hard-wired as I was.

"Precisely. Then they create a counterfeit collection and replace the originals with the fakes. Many times, it takes months, even years, before the collectors discover they've been swindled."

"They target collections to be admired but not necessarily opened and enjoyed." I eyed him looking for a tick, a hint of nervousness, a tell that would highlight a lie, but I saw nothing. "Three of them have been in France. Bordeaux, actually—three of the *Premier Cru* houses. This is the fourth."

"I've heard nothing of any thefts," Jean-Charles huffed. "The wine world is small, especially at the top."

"Would you want your competitors to know of this theft?" Sinjin asked, his smile indicating he already knew the answer.

"No." Jean-Charles didn't say any more, but the red in his face stayed.

"Why didn't they replace this collection with fakes?" I lifted the bottle of Chateau d'Yquem I still held. "They clearly came prepared."

"Yes, but someone must've blown my cover. They got spooked."

"And this bottle?"

"Things were not going my way." He flashed a grin. "I didn't know what else to do. I thought maybe someone might find it."

"And do what?"

He shrugged. "Keep looking?"

Plausible. I narrowed my eyes as if looking at him through slits would disclose an aura of untruth or something. Nothing. He looked delicious like he always did. Lies and truth, deception and straight-shooting all looked the same on him. Damn. I could see his captive audience was buying his bullshit. "You really should think about giving up a life of crime. You're not very good at it."

"Somehow, I'm okay with that." Sinjin's soul didn't run as black as he'd like us all to believe, not that he didn't suffer from a serious Robin Hood complex. One of his eyes was swelling.

"The bad guys didn't much care for your extracurricular activity, did they? That's going to be quite a shiner."

"Hard to blame them. To guys like that, the world is pretty black and white."

"So says the man who makes a living in the gray areas. Did you know any of them? Could you ID them?"

"No, they were very careful." He shifted from foot to foot. From nerves or pain, it was hard to tell.

"What did they need from you?"

"Charm." He flashed a bit for our benefit.

With a growl, Jean-Charles advanced on Sinjin. "How dare you!"

I grabbed his elbow and held him back. In his anger, he missed the look of relief that washed over his sister's face. "Stand in line, my love. We'll have our shot." I resumed my grilling of Sinjin who had not yet shown even a sheen of sweat. "Charm. That's a good one. Maybe you'd be a good front man, but I don't think that's the angle you've taken in all of this. Care to enlighten me as to your real role? I can help you…or not. Up to you. I need a bit of quid pro quo."

"Undercover investigator." He didn't even choke on the words.

I almost did, though. "Really? You expect me to believe that after the egg you laid with the local authorities, the Chinese government, and the FBI? You're telling me you have now seen the light, turned over a new leaf, and any other applicable cliché that doesn't spring readily to mind." My eyes went all slitty. "Seriously, you expect me to believe you've gone legit?"

He made unwavering eye contact. "I have full backing."

A tap dance worthy of Fred Astaire. Impressive. "Of the Hong Kong Police? The FBI? The CIA? The Mossad?"

His stare shifted to something over my shoulder. "A very powerful man."

I couldn't stifle an exaggerated eye roll. "You're a mercenary hired to recover a stolen collection." Not his normal gig but stepping out on the slippery slope with a bit of larceny, it wasn't hard to fall all the way. Sinjin was best at operating under the color of the law but running just outside of it. His slipping more toward greed would be a fall from grace, if you will. And, for some reason, I believed Sinjin to be a man of principle, much like the wise guys of mob days long past. Kill your competition, but their families were off-limits. Like I said, this whole gambit stunk to high heaven and was oddly disappointing. One had to care to be disappointed...

"Is he on our side?" Desiree asked.

I didn't know *we* had a side. "As long as it benefits him."

Sinjin looked wounded at my assessment, but he didn't quibble.

"So, who are these folks and why, this time, did they not replace the wine but decided instead to flee?"

Sinjin slowly turned and gave Desiree the fullness of his undivided attention. "You should ask her."

Everything stopped. No one breathed. Even the air itself seemed to hang motionless.

Then Jean-Charles muttered a string of epithets. I leaned into him. "I call and raise." I turned back to Sinjin, the fun gone from the repartee. "Explain."

"I can explain," Jean-Charles said through gritted teeth as he whirled on his sister. "It was Victor, wasn't it? I saw him at the party."

Desiree, pale, her eyes wide and glistening, stood tall under the assault. "*Oui.* He"—she squirmed—"he broke it off with me. Then, as I arrived tonight, I saw him leaving. I didn't invite him. He wasn't supposed to be here. Angry, hurt, intending to do what, I don't know, I followed him."

"Who is Victor?" I asked.

"One of the dogs sniffing after my sister."

"Jean-Charles!" his mother admonished. "Please. Not tonight."

So, they'd had a difference of opinion about Victor? Older brother protectionism or something else? "You knew him as well?" I asked Jean-Charles.

"No. We had words one day at the winery. I caught him spying around in areas he wasn't allowed. After that, he stayed out of my way."

"Where was he?"

The light dawned as my intended's eyes widened. "In the restricted area."

"What was he doing there? I assume he didn't tell you he was casing the collection."

"We keep the wine in a special room. Only invited guests are allowed in. He was not in there. He was in the office that is adjacent to the lab. He was looking for trade secrets."

"He tell you that?"

"Of course not! He said he was lost and looking for Desiree."

Although not very good at leaping to my defense, Jean-Charles sure showed a talent for jumping to conclusions. "You followed Victor from the party?" I asked Desiree. She nodded. "To the entrance to whatever tunnel lies through that hole?" I asked. She started to waffle then noticed my pointed stare at her shoes, still covered with fine sand. Of course, she had an excuse now—the sand she currently stood in most likely matched the sand she'd found at the other entrance. I held up my finger to silence the answer I saw forming. "Has anyone called the police?"

COMMISSAIRE EMMA MOREAU WAS NOT WHAT I WAS EXPECTING.

Of course, my expectations had been obliterated the minute the wine disappeared, and the thieves left Sinjin Smythe-Gordon as a calling card.

Madame Bouclet, carrying her grandson with her, left to check on her husband. Desiree, Jean-Charles, and I worked to avoid each other as we surrounded Sinjin, still trussed up and trying to maintain a James Bond level of composure in light of his...predicament.

The *commissaire*, stylish in her slacks, white shirt, and Hermès scarf knotted around her neck, breezed in, breathed an introduction—no flash of the badge needed apparently—then greeted Jean-Charles warmly. "Jean-Charles."

He took her hands and kissed her on each cheek, slowly and with intention. "Emma. Thank you for coming." Still holding one of her hands, he swept an arm my direction. "Miss Lucky O'Toole, from America. My fiancée."

The Commissaire raised a perfectly arched eyebrow above a startling blue eye and nodded in my direction. The other eye was brown. Odd, that. But her alabaster skin and so-black-it-almost-looked-blue hair added enough perfection to make the color difference exotic rather than a curiosity. Apparently, capturing all of me in a quick once-over, she turned to give a bear hug to Desiree. "What is this? The wine is missing?" she said in flawless, impeccably accented English. "And Enzo..."

A look passed between them, riding on an understood history—a history I'd need to delve into at an appropriate time.

"Are you here in your official capacity?" I asked, doubting the affection was a by-the-book police procedure, even in France. Yes, my deductive powers are impressive.

"Of course. Our families have known each other for many years." There was more there in her thinly-veiled smoldering glance at Jean-Charles.

And Enzo Laurent made a nice little threesome.

Great. I was the odd man out before the game even started.

Cooperation from the local constabulary would be grudging at best. What else was new? I needed an ace up my sleeve like Detective Romeo back home. I'd have to work on that.

"I see. Well, friendship or no, don't there need to be a couple of lawyers here before you question Desiree or Mr. Smythe-Gordon?" As an American, I practically had the Fifth Amendment tattooed on a hidden body part, available for easy reference.

Commissaire Moreau gave me a fleeting smile. "We don't do that here. In France, one must tell the truth, even if you are guilty."

A totally foreign concept. "The truth? That would never fly in the U.S."

"*Non.*"

There was so much more than a tad bit of disdain stuffed in the single syllable that I chose to ignore it. Now was not the time to disassemble the merits and shortfalls of the Napoleonic Code versus the American/English Common Law approach to justice. Unfortunately, the American way often ran right over the truth and left it for dead. Gamesmanship rather than justice —one huge, life-altering sideshow. So much broken and no one with any idea how to fix it.

As they said in Vegas, the fix was in—there and, from the looks of it, here also. So much they all knew, so much they weren't saying as they went through the motions. How could they be so sure someone told the truth if nobody knew what it was? The only way to get the truth out of Jean-Charles would be to get him alone where he wasn't playing to his hometown reputation.

I stepped back to watch and to learn—hard to win at a game if you didn't know the rules. Good thing I was a quick study. If I'd learned anything from my years in Vegas, it was sleight of hand—how to recognize it and how to employ it.

Sinjin remained against the wall where we had propped him.

He wore a half grin as he shared my amusement at the show. For a man bound, but unfortunately not gagged, and looking like a primo suspect in more than a few felonies, if they called them that here, he looked remarkably at ease. And I had no doubt he also was absorbing the rules. But he would be working on ways to tap dance through the loopholes while I was bound and shackled by a need to stay out of prison. With my authority issue, I didn't do well in enclosed spaces where someone else made the rules. Truth be told, I hated rules—but they held back anarchy most days. And, despite assumptions to the contrary, the Gaming Commission was reluctant to grant gaming licenses to anyone other than a rule follower. And without a gaming license, I wouldn't have a job. And without a job, I'd just be Jean-Charles's wife with no way to be me.

And there it was. *Shit.* I so needed to so get over myself.

I refocused.

Yeah, the fix was in, for sure. Sinjin acted like he held all the cards. I couldn't wait until he turned them over for all to see.

The *commissaire* now turned her attention to him, taking in all the details both as a *commissaire* and a female. Appreciation for his obvious attributes pinkened her cheeks.

Great.

The stink of sexual attraction permeated the small space. Rational thought and logical investigation were doomed, at least where Sinjin Smythe-Gordon was concerned. Of course, to expect any different would've been stupid, even for me. But, seriously, could this go any better? Everybody here knew a whole lot of backstory I wasn't privy to. Sinjin smirked like a poor poker player with a trump card. A fortune of wine had disappeared. And the *commissaire* should recuse herself as too close to the investigation, but she clearly had no intention to do so.

And I was the kid with her nose pressed to the glass, looking, salivating, but not allowed in. And I was okay with that.

I took a moment to process that. Problems that needed solving. Problems that involved someone I cared about. And the need to find the solution and save the day for Truth, Justice and the American Way didn't poke or prod me.

I felt nothing. No irresistible urge to fling myself off a cliff. No need to take up a sword and slay the dragons of evil.

I wanted a drink and bed.

Whoa. Was I sick? What had happened to the me I used to be? Maybe I'd shed that skin like a snake that had grown too large. Interesting metaphor. I didn't try to overanalyze. And I didn't panic at the new me. "I'm very tired. May I go to the hotel now?" I felt like a kid asking for a hall pass.

"Not yet." Commissaire Moreau pulled out a pad and produced a pencil from somewhere, which she held poised over a notepad. "Who goes first?"

Desiree volunteered. "I will tell you about Victor—Victor Martin. I met him at the winery. He worked for one of the local *négociants*. The last time I was there, he came by asking if we would have any excess grapes to sell after the harvest."

"You sell the excess grapes from your vineyards?" That would be like Patek Enzo discounting watches they don't sell at full price. And they never do that. Instead, they destroy them all —a fact that still stopped my heart when I thought about it.

"No. Of course not." She gave one of the patented French *boofs*, with a puff of air and roll of the eyes in case I hadn't gotten the message that what I had just suggested was beyond ignorant.

She'd have to do better to put me off the chase. "If he worked for the local crusher, shouldn't he have known that?"

Desiree shrugged as if to say, *Men!* I told him we did not sell any grapes. The next day, he came back. He was charming, disarming. We struck up a friendship."

The *commissaire* finished her notes, then looked up. "Did you tell him about this wine cellar, about the party?"

"The party, yes. The wine cellar?" Her delicate features crumpled with thought. "No, we don't talk about it. It's a curiosity, but not one that is well-known."

Well, he'd invited himself to the party. I wondered if that invitation also extended to the wine. "Who did he say he worked for?"

"Paul Bay. They are just down the road from our main vineyard in Bordeaux. They make very good wine under their own label."

"They should." Now it was Jean-Charles's turn to get huffy. "Good grapes make good wine. And the local grapes are the best. The *terroir* is unparalleled."

"Funny. Recent studies have proven that is a bunch of hooey." The ladies of the family gasped. Jean-Charles turned a color of purple I'd not seen before. Sinjin laughed.

I didn't care.

Had Desiree been the rube, the one they used and tossed aside? Not beyond belief. While she and I suffered from the same disease when it came to men, I'd never known her to lie... only to make abysmal choices. Too trusting, by far. Was there an antidote for that, other than cynicism?

How did one remain a skeptic without becoming a cynic?

Like a drunk negotiating a sobriety test, I'd never managed to walk that fine line.

Anyway, if she didn't tell him, how had the information become common criminal knowledge. An inside job, it had to be. But who was the insider?

"How do you know Mr. Smythe-Gordon?" I pushed myself off the wall I'd been holding up and inserted myself into the conversation.

"What makes you think we know each other?" Sinjin leaped to Desiree's defense a bit too quickly. He noticed his mistake and tempered his response. "We are not acquainted."

"I asked Desiree." I turned to my future sister-in-law. "Fish or cut bait time."

She gave me a blank look.

"Sorry. Is he worth jail time?"

Her moxie wilted. "We met...once."

"Recently?"

She nodded. "At a party. The wine, it flowed freely. I don't remember much. But I remember him."

I bet. "Do you remember what you talked about?"

A delicate shoulder rose then fell. "Wine, of course."

"Details?" the *commissaire* asked.

Desiree shook her head.

"Okay, you met him at the party," I said, keeping the questioning on track. "When did you see him next?"

"Tonight." She gave him a steady look.

"Where?"

"He stopped me when I was following Victor. He told me to get away, to go back to the party. He'd take care of it."

I bet. My inner snark was getting repetitive. "What did you do?"

"I came back here and found everyone in the kitchen."

"You gave up that easily?"

"Really, Lucky, what was I going to do? I was in a ball gown chasing after some man I hardly knew. There would be a better time and place."

"That was it?" Commissaire Moreau asked, saving me from a very difficult question. "You had no knowledge of what Victor was doing, what Mr. Smythe-Gordon had in mind?"

Desiree crossed her arms, hugging herself. "You have to believe me. I didn't tell anyone. I had no idea!" Her voice rose in a desperate plea.

"Then how did they know the wine would be here?" Commissaire Moreau pushed. "I know your family. They do not share that kind of information."

"I don't know." Desiree crumpled in defeat.

I believed her. From the looks of Jean-Charles's face and even the *commissaire's*, we all believed her...we just couldn't prove her innocence.

I whirled on Sinjin. "Aren't you going to ride to the lady's rescue?"

"I have nothing to add to her story. I don't recall speaking with her at any party recently. I've been following these thieves across the continent since I first caught wind of them in Hong Kong. But" –he paused for effect as all eyes turned hope on him –"I do have a photo of Victor Martin."

"Why?" I eyed him, not wanting history to hold together.

"He caught my attention."

"Part of the group who departed with the wine and left you holding the bag." The divine justice of it all made me all warm inside. Normally setting someone up as the fall guy was Sinjin's M.O. "Text it to me?"

With the ropes binding his arms, he gave me a pleading look.

This was a guy who would make a mile out of a millimeter. "Which pocket?"

"Inside jacket."

He watched me with those eyes as I stepped closer and burrowed a hand in next to his chest. The corner of his mouth lifted as my skin brushed against his with only a thin shirt between.

Far from a playful mood, I ignored him, which was hard to do. I found his phone. "Password?"

"Lucky."

"What?"

"That is the word: Lucky."

He hadn't forgotten I'd bested him. Instead, he'd kept me as a constant reminder. No, we weren't friends. Enemies and perhaps grudging allies, but only when it suited us. I tapped in the letters. He hadn't been joking.

I held the phone so he could see as I scrolled through the photos. "That one there."

A grainy image of a man turning to look over his shoulder where the camera caught him. The date-stamp indicated tonight, a few hours earlier. I forwarded it to myself, then caught the *commissaire's* eye. I raised my eyebrow in question.

"Please." She extended her card. "My email is there."

I took a moment to scroll through the rest of the recent photos. Nothing of interest in the few he'd left on the camera. Emma held out her hand for the phone. I redeposited it in Sinjin's pocket. I could rifle through his belongings, but, without more, the police's hands were tied...at least in the U.S. Cultivating the friendship of criminals and the enmity of the constabulary probably wasn't wise, but I had lines I wouldn't cross. And I'd learned it could be very bad for my future freedom to assume the good guys were good and the bad guys bad.

I glanced up into Sinjin's blue eyes. "And how were you put onto them, exactly?" I asked, knowing I wouldn't get the truth, or at least not all of it, but only something that sounded like it. "My employer. His wine was...replaced. An inside job—one of the kitchen staff, identified as Jai Ling Ping. Through him, I was able to track them, although they did give me the slip in Jaipur. I picked up their trail again here in Paris."

"How?"

"If you recall, I have a great many...resources...at my disposal. Let's just say some information as to Mr. Ping's whereabouts came to my attention."

Two uniformed officers stuck their heads through the doorway. "Ah, there you are *Commissaire*. Forensics is here."

"Very well. Would you take Ms. Bouclet and Mr. Smythe-Gordon back for further questioning, please?"

"Emma!" Desiree sounded desperate.

"I have to. I'm sorry." Commissaire Moreau looked to Jean-

Charles who gave her a nod indicating his understanding if not his happiness.

"Come." She extended an arm to herd us all toward the opening. "Step carefully, but let's leave this to the experts."

I positioned myself behind Desiree with Jean-Charles and the *commissaire* trailing a bit behind as we trooped back through the hallway and up the stairs. Jean-Charles and the *commissaire*, engaged in hushed conversation, fell back a bit and I seized my opening. I leaned forward. "Where is the entrance to the tunnel?" I hissed, hoping only Desiree could hear.

"What?" She started to turn.

"Don't turn around. Tell me where you last saw Victor. I can help you, but you have to trust me. We've been through this drill before." Reminding her of Adone and his demise could cut either way, but it was the only card I had so I played it.

"The Metro. There is a door. Look for the Picasso. But watch your back."

CHAPTER FOUR

"*L*ET ME drop you at the hotel," Jean-Charles said as he focused on his phone. A text had dinged.

"Aren't you coming with me?" I watched Commissaire Moreau usher Desiree and Sinjin, whose ropes had been loosened but not removed per my warning, into the back of a black SUV. A young man in kitchen whites motioned to her from the door. Securing Desiree and Sinjin, she glanced around then heeded the summons.

"I need to see after my father. The doctor is with him at the hospital. He wants to talk with us." The furrow between his eyebrows told me all I needed to know. There would be decisions to make and, as the eldest, they would fall to him. When my father had been ill, or at least more ill than now—a worry niggled at me—the responsibility for such decisions had been mine. The responsibility had weighed heavy. No doubt it would with Jean-Charles as well.

"Thanks, I'll walk. It's only a couple of blocks, and the fresh air will help clear my head." I pulled my wrap tighter around my shoulders against the chill in the freshening wind. "I hope he is better soon."

"He will not get better. His heart is weak, damaged by several heart attacks. There's nothing more they can do other than help him with the pain."

"I'm sorry."

"He has had a good life." As he said the words, I could see him trying on the loss in anticipation of the inevitable.

I wanted to fix it, make it better, but I didn't have any answers. The right words evaded me...if there even were any. Life and loss, neither could exist without the other.

With a hand on each shoulder, he turned me into him and made a point of adding warmth to what could've been a perfunctory kiss. I kissed him back. Snaking my hands around his waist, I squeezed him hard.

He touched my cheek, then slipped into the back of a waiting car. I turned my screaming, heel-shod feet toward the refuge of the Hotel Raphael, my sanctuary of choice whenever in Paris.

But first a slight detour.

Under one of the iconic "Metropolitan" signs, the entrance beckoned, less than a block away. I grabbed my dress, lifting it slightly, as I hurried down the stairs. Stares followed me. You'd think in this swank neighborhood a lady in a gown would be commonplace. With a car and driver, perhaps, but apparently not in the Metro. With no way to make myself less of a stand-out, I held my head high and conjured a French insouciance. I arrived at the platform just as one of the green-and-white trains blew by, the wind of its passing pulling at me. The narrow strip of concrete didn't strike me as a great place for a Picasso.

At the far end, just as the darkness of the tunnel pulled all the light inside, I found it. Not a Picasso exactly, but a poster advertising an upcoming exhibit at the Picasso Museum. A doorway cut in the concrete wall and painted a matching white hid in plain sight, the gleam of a silver-toned handle the only real clue as to its existence. The platform was relatively empty.

A couple, arm-in-arm, nuzzled at the opposite end. A man in fancy European jeans, a polo shirt under a leather jacket, and with black curls slicked back, smoked as he leaned against the wall and focused on his phone.

I moved near the door. The handle moved easily when I pressed it down. The door clicked open. Air, damp, fetid, cool, filtered through the opening liked ghosts released from the bounds of Hell. The metal was cold to the touch when I pushed the door open wider. A quick glance behind me. No one looked in my direction.

My heart hammered as I debated my next move. Alone, with no idea who or what lurked in the darkness, I knew it would be foolish at best to press on. Not to mention Bob Mackie and Christian Louboutin weren't exactly the appropriate gear for spelunking in the sewer.

I stepped over the transom. Nobody would claim me as their fool—I was in a class by myself. I knew it, but I couldn't stop myself. Pausing in the doorway to let my eyes adjust to the gloom, I felt cool whispers brush past. Sand gritted between my toes. Thankfully it was dry. Wet and sewer were two words I did *not* want to experience together.

I closed my eyes and took a deep breath for courage.

A hand grabbed my arm.

I yelped—I couldn't help it.

"You shouldn't be in here." The voice male, foreign, unknown and unhappy.

I turned and found myself looking into dark, angry eyes.

"Very illegal to be here. Big fines." A funny square box hat. The blue shirt. The combat boots.

Le Flic.

The breath I'd been holding escaped in a whoosh. "Are you the police?"

His mouth puckered in distaste. "*Oui.* You should be happy I found you first. My partner would put you in jail." He sounded as if all American tourists, dressed smartly or not, should be incarcerated for being stupid and irritating.

I couldn't blame him. In Vegas the roles were reversed, but the sentiment the same.

He was most likely overstating for my benefit—if I'd been in his shoes, I would've done the same...and have...but there was a hint of truth. Perhaps they'd throw me in the same cell as Desiree and Sinjin—what a party *that* would be.

"What are you doing here?" He looked ready to reach for the handcuffs.

Think, Lucky. Think. "Scavenger hunt. I must've taken the wrong turn."

His face cleared. I'm sure he was used to drunk patrons, silly games, probably even more things than I could imagine. On second thought, doubtful. A lot went down every night at the Babylon. "Go back to the party."

I gathered my dignity along with a handful of my skirt and hurried away. This might be how the thieves got down to the tunnel behind the Bouclets' wine cellar, but it didn't explain how they got out. Not with cameras and cops everywhere.

Not unless they had help.

At the top of the stairs, I paused, drinking in the fresh air and allowing my heart rate to settle.

I'd learned one thing: the thieves may have gone in that way, but no way they carried a bunch of wine out the same way.

Commissaire Moreau took my call, listening without interrupting as I filled her in. "And you are there why?"

"Curiosity."

A pause as she mulled that over or considered her response. "It is best if you stay out of the way."

Maybe, maybe not. As an American, a wait-and-see attitude wasn't my birthright. I didn't respond; instead, I let the silence stretch between us. So much to say...no words.

The *commissaire* tired of the game first. "If the wine is still down there, we will find it." She rang off with a perfunctory, *"Merci."*

I tucked my phone back into the silk side pocket inside my bag. The night slipped around me like a comforting blanket.

Standing in the middle of the beautiful Avenue Kléber, a boulevard in this particular section, with the *L'Étoile* and the *Arc de Triomphe* shining brightly at one end and the *Trocadéro* with its spectacular view of the Eiffel Tower across the river, staking the other end, I sagged with fatigue as the beauty sucked the adrenaline right out of me.

I'd done all I could.

And I didn't know what to make of any of it.

But I did know I needed a bath, food, Champagne, sex and rest...not necessarily in that order. I thought through the probabilities.

Four out of five.

Better than normal.

~

FOR THE PAMPERING PARIS PROMISED, MANY HEADED TO THE more talked about five-stars, but I preferred the Hotel Raphael —the quiet elegance, the homage to its refined and sumptuous beginnings, the attentive care and the personal touch. Not to mention the unrivaled rooftop bar that offered a three hundred and sixty degree view of Paris...and Champagne, in season, of course. With the bar closed for the winter there was no Champagne, but the view was always available.

The bellman greeted me, key in hand. "Miss O'Toole. We have prepared your room. It's so lovely to have you back."

"Thank you. My things?" I took the key, exchanging it for a twenty-Euro note I pulled from my evening bag.

He bowed slightly. "Unpacked and pressed."

"Thank you."

"Miss?" He stopped me in the doorway. "A gentleman is waiting. He's in the bar."

My adrenaline had trickled away with each tick after midnight and now was so low I could hardly express any surprise. *Who could it be?* I realized I didn't really care—probably just another problem to solve. I acknowledged the information with a nod.

Once through the door, I turned left, up a couple of steps, then stopped in the narrow lobby that extended from the concierge desk along the front of the building, in a long, wide hallway toward the rear. Two young ladies at the ready behind the burnished front desk nodded and smiled their eagerness to assist should I need something. I didn't—at least not anything they could help me with.

My heels clicked on the alternating black and white tiled corridor. A man, dark, mysterious and impeccable in an Italian-cut suit, French cuffs clasped with Hermès cufflinks, crisp shirt, open collar, carefully manicured facial hair, and thick, wavy, black hair brushed back from his face, looked up from his phone as I passed. He gave me an appreciative smile—the lone bright spot in what had started as a hopeful evening. Why did most endings fall short of the promise of most beginnings?

The bar was just beyond the front room where breakfast would be served—I glanced at my watch—in a few short hours. The curtained opening to the bar evoked a secret warren, a Kasbah, although disappointingly lacking any overt iniquity. The overstuffed couches and chairs, the dark wood, the bottles of various weird and wonderful healing waters behind the heavy bar, the yellowed and cracked artwork that reeked of importance completed the ambiance.

Where many of the newer properties had succumbed to the shift toward a clean, contemporary—a style I found rather cold, especially when it came to spaces that should exude a warm collegiality—again the Raphael made the right choice. Their bar, comfortable in the permanence of good taste, invited all to come, relax, enjoy, and stay awhile.

Only the barest necessity of light glowed from the lamps and wall sconces. Couples clustered in the dotted gatherings of wingback chairs. The music selection made me smile—a soft smattering of American oldies from the '80s. Someday I'd figure out what exactly the French loved about that particular era, especially when they had iconic café ballads sung by the likes of Edith Piaf.

I dropped the handful of fabric I still clutched, smoothed my skirt, and drifted my cloak off my shoulders while still holding it closed in the front—a poor attempt to fit in with the local fashion glitterati. Or perhaps a vain attempt to reassert my femininity. France wasn't Vegas. In fact, it was hard to imagine two more different places. Here, I didn't know the rules and couldn't fathom the expectations. I wanted to fit in, to be found acceptable, but I had a feeling I'd failed miserably. Fashion faux pas. Social missteps. Each of them taunted, telling me I'd been found wanting. The sand in my shoes didn't help.

I strolled through the collection of tables, chairs, and revelers, looking for someone familiar.

"Lucky!"

It can't be! My heart tripped then fell.

I turned toward the voice. He'd risen from his hiding place, deep in the fold of a high-backed, fully-winged chair.

His smile. His voice. The blue eyes, the tight ass I couldn't see but could imagine without any effort at all—in fact, the memory came to me completely unbidden, which did little to improve my mood.

Great. Feeling as bucked with life and confidence as I was, the last thing I needed was the man who stole my heart then dumped me for a younger model. "Teddie. What are you doing here?"

His face fell. "I thought you'd need some moral support."

If he expected open arms and the warmth of old friends reunited, he was even better at self-delusion than I was. His kind of help was exactly what I didn't need. That piece of parchment from Harvard that hung on his wall was testament to the fact he was smart enough to know that. I tried not to drink him in. "Funny, the doorman told me a gentleman waited for me."

"Well," Jordan Marsh breezed into the awkwardness bearing two flutes of Champagne. He held one out to me. "He was right. One gentleman. Two of us. You decide which one he referred to." Jordan gave me a wink, then lifted the flute slightly higher. "Pink. Your favorite." My stomach growled, widening his grin. "And perhaps some food? Come. Sit. We come in peace."

All dark and mysterious with a perpetual tan and a white-toothed grin, Jordan was female fantasy personified—well, if the tabloids and his rabid, poorly behaved fans could be believed. Attention followed him wherever he went. Tonight was no exception. I caught the veiled looks from the rest of the patrons in the bar. "Please, Rosé. Hanging with such oenological lightweights could seriously impair my rep around here." The verbal hanging curveball over the plate was for my benefit—he knew how much I loved a good game of verbal ping-pong...and mixed sports metaphors. And he knew me well enough to know when I was dragging my tail, despite my best attempts to paint on a smile.

Teddie held out a chair.

A moment of weakness, then I succumbed to my shortcomings and gladly sank into it, snagging the Champagne as I did so. "You do know that just being seen with you will be considered an act of war?"

"Speaking of which," Teddie glanced around me, "*où est le chef parfait?*"

"Handling a problem." I swiveled to skewer Jordan with a feigned frown. "How do you tolerate such childish behavior? The Perfect Chef? Seriously?"

"Truth fits. I've never seen the guy with even one hair out of place."

For sure I'd witnessed Jean-Charles in various states of *dishabille*, but I didn't think this audience would be receptive, so I didn't regale them with that little confidence.

"But of course. *Le Chef* is *le boss.*" Teddie's accent sounded more Inspector Clouseau than he intended, I felt certain.

Jordan held his flute to the light. "Why does everything, especially Champagne, taste better in Paris?"

The bubbles tickled my nose as I lifted my flute to my lips. I held the liquid happiness in my mouth, savoring the pop of the captured bubbles, and imagining the tiny bits of happiness they released for me to capture. The bubbles tickled all the way down where they settled with a pleasant warmth in the hollow of my empty stomach. "Because we expect everything to be exceptional here. It's Paris."

His eyes held mine. "Exactly. The key to enjoying life is having appropriate expectations."

The subtext irritated me. His eyes flicked to Teddie, his implication that somehow I'd been at fault! I resisted tossing the bubbles in his face. First, it would be a waste of bubbles. And second, as tired and confused as I was, it was entirely possible I was misinterpreting. But, expecting a lover who had professed exclusive and undying fealty to be faithful was appropriate. Teddie had not met that expectation.

"Seriously, what are you doing here?" Frankly, friendly faces added a comfort I so needed right now—but I wished they could have been different friendly faces. Teddie was a complication I didn't think I could handle. And Jordan Marsh would attract attention I didn't need. Both men would lead to whispers I couldn't counter.

"Our show?" Teddie had his own beverage of choice that looked like single malt. He swirled the liquid in the glass, the lone ice cube tinkling like a Salvation Army bell at Christmas.

Their show! I'd forgotten! "Are you in rehearsals?"

"Show opens tomorrow. While you were traipsing around London leaving destruction in your wake, we were working." Jordan set his flute on the round bar table. The bartender leaped to refill it, almost without pause, then vanished.

"That's amazing," I said as I marveled at Jordan's full flute. "That's like that movie. You know the one? Where Cary Grant played the angel?"

"*The Bishop's Wife?*" Teddie said, abandoning the childish act. The look he gave me was anything but. One of our favorite routines was Tuesday night movie night. He'd favored Rogers and Hammerstein so he could sing along. Juilliard-Trained, he had a warm, sensuous tenor that could make just about any woman I knew willing to disrobe. He'd learned to use it to perfection.

"That's it. The professor's glass kept refilling as if by magic, but Cary Grant did it. He was the angel." I knew he'd know. But I didn't know that his knowing would make me sad. The worst loss of our breakup had not been the love, but rather, the friendship, the shared history, the intimate knowing. And he'd known me well.

While I'd worked my way through the Kubler-Ross five stages of grief, clawing my way to acceptance, every now and again I regressed to pissed off. Miss P, my right-hand man and epic sounding board, had told me that sort of boomerang thing was normal and would diminish with time. I'd neglected to ask her how much time would be required. Clearly more than suited my lack of patience.

The bartender appeared at my side about the same time I thought of summoning him. I leaned into Jordan. "Do you find him a bit...disconcerting?"

Jordan rolled his eyes.

Apparently not. I graced the bartender with my best smile. "Would it be possible to get something to eat?"

"It's quite late. The kitchen is closed."

"Is it?" Time could slip by when one wasn't having any fun as well; something I'd proven too many times recently. I needed to fix that. "I haven't eaten since London."

A grimace replaced the bartender's smile. "English cuisine is an oxymoron. That must've been wretched."

I think he even shuddered, but I may have imagined it. I didn't quibble over his assessment of British fare. The Brits' culinary skills had improved significantly, especially with the influx of amazing Indian chefs. But, outside of Indian, it would never rival the French preparations...especially to the French. "I *am* a bit famished."

"We wouldn't want you expiring right here. That would be such a waste. I will try to find *something*."

Was he flirting with me? I watched him wiggle through the tangle of tables.

"Only a Frenchman would consider the possibility of a woman who has to shop in the transvestite section to be on the verge of expiring from lack of sustenance. The Oscar committee should take note of his brilliant turn of implied sincerity." I relaxed back into the embrace of my chair. "I do love France."

"And Frenchmen," Jordan added, salt to Teddie's wound, which did little to abate my sadness, even though, from his squeeze of my hand, that was Jordan's intent.

"How are rehearsals going?" I asked both of them. "Forgive me, but I've forgotten where you will be performing."

Jordan pulled a pair of tickets from his breast pocket and slid them across the table. "We'd love for you and Jean-Charles to come. Opening night, tomorrow, fourth row, center. The entire run sold out within an hour of announcing it."

For a moment I thought about refusing, then decided that would be hurtful. I doubted we could attend, but I'd deal with that later...tomorrow...I glanced at my watch...today. "Thank you."

"I know it will be hard for you to fit it in your schedule." Teddie's words lacked the sarcasm I expected. Maybe we could get beyond all the hurt.

He'd said he wanted to be friends. I had no idea how to do that.

I drained the last bit of happiness from my flute. After seriously considering licking the last delicate drops clinging to the crystal, I set it back on the table and waited for it to replenish magically. But the bartender had disappeared.

I swiveled, looking for him and avoiding Teddie's gaze that followed me. On the verge of losing hope, I spied him weaving his way across the room, a platter held high on one hand. With a flourish, he presented the tray for my inspection. "The kitchen, they make a special present for you." He slid the plate in front of me, saving me from near-starvation and small talk with my tablemates.

"A blessing on you and your family," I managed to stutter as I took in the most perfect sandwich I had ever seen. Hugged delicately between lightly toasted triangles of white bread, three tiers of chicken salad with egg in all of its sublime gooeyness awaited my pleasure. Next to it, a tiny cup of roasted almonds. Next to that, three plump strawberries and a square of dark chocolate.

Oh, to be French. The Art of Eating—one more peak French experience.

"Would you like some?" I asked Jordan and Teddie—a perfunctory bit of politeness. I'd just as soon lop off a limb than give them a morsel of this exquisite example of culinary perfection.

Despite eyeing the sandwich with lust, both shook their heads. "You've got to be kidding," Teddie said. "You look like a lioness guarding her kill. I wouldn't dare."

"Wise man," I managed through a mouthful of deliciousness. I closed my eyes and groaned in delight, then dove in for the next bite.

"Lucky! *Mon Deux!* We have a problem. I am so glad I found you."

The voice, unexpected and terrifying stopped me mid-chew. As I looked up into the worried face of Madame Bouclet, I felt a glob of chicken salad dribble down my chin.

With a bemused expression, Jordan held out a napkin like a white flag in a lopsided skirmish.

I snagged it, swiped at the offending chicken salad, then swallowed the large bite I'd not yet finished chewing. The gag reflex kicked in. The Champagne chaser killed it, and I could breathe. I dabbed at the tears and tried for some cultured composure. All I managed was a pained smile. "Madame Bouclet! What are you doing here? Where is Christophe?" She'd taken the boy when the police had taken Sinjin, and the *commissaire* had kept Desiree for questioning, and dismissed the rest of us. I pushed up out of my chair like a jack-in-the-box.

Teddie and Jordan followed suit, but with a tad more decorum.

Although seriously back on my heels, I managed some manners. "May I present Theodore Kowalski and Jordan Marsh?"

She acknowledged both men with a nod. Jordan got a second, surprised look, and then Madame Bouclet pinned me with her pained look. She breached French social mores and grabbed my arm. "You must come!"

I dropped the napkin in my chair. "What has happened?"

"It is Victor." She dropped her voice as she noticed the interest her arrival and her emotion had garnered.

"Desiree's Victor?"

She nodded. "He is dead."

CHAPTER FIVE

J HELPED Madame Bouclet into the back of the waiting sedan, then squeezed my bulk in beside her. Jordan had folded the rest of my sandwich into the napkin and forced me to take it. "You'll need this. Eat," he'd said. Uncharacteristically, I took his words to heart.

Unfolding the package on my lap, I tried to remember my manners in the face of still gnawing hunger. "Where are we going? I need to let Jean-Charles know where I am."

"And who you were with?" She gave me a frown. "That blond man looked at you with familiarity." She lobbed that little stink bomb, then waved me to silence.

Professing my innocence would only make me look guilty, so I instead focused on my sandwich. I motioned to the untouched quarter and raised an eyebrow. Madame Bouclet wrinkled her nose and pinned me with a disapproving look. Please, my mother was an expert at the guilt trip. After years of dealing with her, I no longer got on that train. Madame Bouclet would have to do better...much better. "How is your husband?"

"He is dying." There was resignation there, and sadness, too.

Long goodbyes—everyone professed to want one. I thought they sucked. "Aren't we all?"

She smoothed her dress and maneuvered for a glance in the rearview to check her hair. Perhaps she found that calming, arranging the things she could, but it came off as self-absorbed —the Queen waiting in the wings to assume her rightful place.

"Some more quickly than others." She kept her tone bland which left me wondering whether she was stating a fact or making a threat, not that it mattered. Most of the time we got the wars we'd failed to prepare for. This one I'd seen coming and had spent months girding my loins. So, I took false comfort in the hope it would not be the battle I had to fight.

Apparently satisfied, she settled back, still not looking at me. "Jean-Louis doesn't have long. I need Jean-Charles here. I cannot run the business by myself. His help is essential."

What did the woman expect me to do? Leap to my feigned death like Lana Turner in *Madame X* so as not to hinder my future husband's career? That hadn't turned out well for anyone. My trust issues reared their ugly heads, hissing and snapping like a three-headed Hydra. "How long has Jean-Louis been ill?" Had Jean-Charles been holding out on me, luring me in only to spring the you-are-the-wife-you-must-stay-by-my-side trap? Now and then I glimpsed a high-handed manner in my betrothed. Was that merely French or corrosively misogy-nistic—not that the two were mutually exclusive.

"The last years have taken their toll, but the heart condition is new. Congestive heart failure, the doctors say."

Okay, not as bad as I feared, but still some tough decisions to be made. "I won't stand in the way between Jean-Charles and his family, but the decision is his. I will honor his choice." I shifted, angling toward her. I waited until her eyes met mine. "But you must do the same."

"You don't understand."

Okay, different rules for different folks. I put a hand on her arm forcing her attention back to me. "I understand better than anyone. You forget I run a multi-billion-dollar family enterprise. My father, too, is in ill health."

"That is not a woman's place." Her gaze shifted forward as she said it.

I retreated out of her personal space—invading it had been a breach of French etiquette. I didn't care. I had no doubt the woman had been running the Bouclet Family Vineyards for a long time. Or, if not overtly running them, she was the steel in her husband's backbone. "Don't bullshit a bullshitter," I said, taking off the verbal kid gloves.

That got a fleeting smile. "You are my son's problem."

Okay, upping her game and lowering her standards. "If I can't be a problem, then I'm not doing my job."

That got a straight-on hard look, which I met with my own. Then she pursed her lips and nodded once. I had no idea whether I'd passed muster or started a war.

"Jean-Charles asked me to come get you. He tried to call, but you didn't answer. I understand why. Jordan Marsh!" She let his name ride on one long, awe-inspired breath.

"He's gay." No secret. I thought the scandal when Jordan announced he would marry his longtime and heretofore secret partner, Rudy Gillespie, had traveled around the world twice, shattering hopes and dreams of females everywhere. Apparently, Madame Bouclet wasn't tapped into the celebrity gossip hotline. I sorta liked her for that.

She didn't even flinch. In fact, she gave me a dainty version of the classic Gallic shrug. "He is still a very handsome man. The attention of a man like that..."

"Would be feigned."

"It is all a game, the dance between a man and a woman. It is what the man likes—the thrill of the game."

"Thrill of the chase," I corrected without thinking, just as I did with her son. But game or chase, it didn't matter. Both required an artifice I lacked. If that's what would keep Jean-Charles interested, then I might as well take myself out of the lineup right now. The thought defeated me. "Will you tell me where we are going?"

"You will see. I cannot explain. Jean-Charles asked me to bring you. That is all I know."

"That, and that Victor is dead." The lady was stonewalling me! "I'll ask again: why am I here?"

"I said—"

"I know, Jean-Charles wants me there. Why?"

She plucked at an invisible speck on her perfect gown as she adjusted the mink stole wrapped around her shoulders, letting loose a cloud of *Joy* perfume. Then she turned her attention out the window. Her emotions marched across her face. At war with herself—boy, I could identify. She wanted to be rid of me, but she needed me…or at least she needed to play along to keep her son in the fold.

We were all caught playing some sort of game. Who won, who lost, and who threw in the towel would keep even a tough audience on the edge of their seats. The waiting had my stomach in knots, that was for sure.

Food might help—whether it did or not, it was a go-to when comfort was a matter of life or death. I eyed my sandwich, measuring the next spot.

"He said you know about these things," she admitted, her face still turned away.

"Murder? I've contemplated it a time or two." I took the next bite, stifling a groan. "This is manna from Heaven." The words found their way around the chicken salad.

I glanced in the rearview. The chauffeur glanced back, blue eyes crinkled at the corners. I lifted my lips in a smile.

Madame Bouclet didn't join in, not that I expected her to. But hope springs eternal and all that. "And you are good at solving…crimes."

As the Chief Problem Solver at a large Vegas hotel, the Babylon, I was responsible for all the mischief that occurred there. Murder was a part of that. Not a part I enjoyed, but one I'd learn to deal with—with the help of friends. "I run a hotel or two. I have good friends in the local police department. They do the heavy lifting."

"What is this, heavy lifting?"

"Work. They do the work."

"And you do the thinking." She settled back and stared straight ahead. Conversation over.

Taking the hint, I did the same, making short work of the rest of my sandwich as the car eased from the curb. The driver glanced again at me in the rearview. In the lights of an oncoming car, I could see the blue eyes, curiosity replacing the humor, but nothing more. Somebody had put a bug in my future mother-in-law's ear. While I couldn't quibble with their characterization, I chafed under the competence it implied.

I was lucky, that was all. At some point, my luck would run out.

The driver accelerated toward the *L'Étoile*. Tonight, bathed in light, the *Arc de Triomphe* stood in regal majesty, a testament to resiliency. Each cut in the marble stood in stark relief in the crisp, clean winter air. January chased off the hordes of tourists that generally ringed the edifice. Unfortunately, winter did little to thin the traffic that careened in a demolition derby around the Arc. No lane markers, multiple streets pouring traffic in and siphoning it out, and French irritation, combined into a consistent life-before-my-eyes moment. Thankfully, we peeled off quickly, so we didn't need to venture too far into the melee from the curb.

I blew out a breath and tried to relax and drink in Paris as it rolled past the windows. We accelerated down the long stretch of the *Champs-Élysées*, leading to the *Place de la Concorde* at the far end. At this time of night, the retail shops had long since shuttered. A few bundled-up couples strode arm in arm, but I still felt as if we had the avenue to ourselves—a rare thing. A few blocks of high-end everything gave way to a few trees, then the crosshatch intersection near the Grand Palais. We turned right, heading toward the river and my favorite bridge, the Alexander III with its gilded horses and lighted lanterns. I leaned forward and pressed my nose to the window. I couldn't help it. Paris, with its art and architecture, its emphasis on beauty and time-lessness, stood as a testament to the best that we could be.

Even the Nazis, in their horror and hate, hadn't laid waste to Paris, proving, at least to me, there was a spark of goodness in even one or two of the most evil of us—in that case, one lone general who defied Hitler's orders. But it was incumbent on each of us to find the good that lived within, nurture it, grow it, express it, and live it. Far too few made the effort, preferring instead to hide in their ignorance and fear.

Our speed slowed as the driver maneuvered the car through the narrow streets of the 7th Arrondissement. This was my favorite part of the city with its gaggle of students who studied at the cluster of universities and the professors who taught there, to the tourists who wandered through from *Les Invalides* on one side to the *Champ de Mars* and the Eiffel Tower on the other. *Rue Cler*, with its restaurants, boulangeries, fruit stands, meat merchants and fromageries, lent the neighborhood that lovely, livable feel. When I was in school, I'd spent a year of study here in a flat just off *Rue St. Dominique*. I barely fit in the bathroom, and the bed was too short, but I hadn't cared.

Lost in the gossamer tangle of memories, I didn't notice the car slowing until we'd stopped at the curb.

A familiar black SUV hunkered at the curb. The sign above the door was dark, but lights shone inside. Displays of wine blocked a clear view inside. "Fabrice Wines? I thought we were going to the restaurant."

The driver leaped from the car and opened the door for

Madame Bouclet. Offering a hand, he helped her out, then steadied her up the curb, finally relinquishing her at the door. He moved to help me, and I waved him off with a smile. At the door, I took Madame Bouclet's elbow, caring not a whit whether I would offend her or not. Manners were manners, even to a priggish old lady who jealously guarded her only son.

"Are you ready for what's inside?" I wouldn't insult her by suggesting she might not be able to stomach it. Women were warriors and anyone who thought otherwise risked being a casualty.

We pushed through the door, a bell cheerily announcing our arrival. "Jean-Charles," I called, my voice echoing in the crowded space. Bottles and cases rose in chaotic towers and low hedgerows of knee-knockers created a maze of spectacular wine. St. Émilion. Chateau Margeaux. Petrus. Domain Romani Conti. Screaming Eagle as a stellar nod to Napa. None of it behind lock and key, some of it old, all of it stupid expensive. The musty smell of dust, history, and alcohol lent a comforting familiarity. My father's wine cellar smelled the same.

Wine thieves went to great lengths to steal Jean-Charles's family's wine when this veritable treasure trove was ripe for a smash and grab. Why? Yes, it screamed "personal" but who had a beef with the family that big? Who was this Enzo Laurent everyone seemed to suspect in hushed tones and veiled looks? Clearly some questions were in order. "Jean-Charles?" I called again.

"Sorry." His head appeared through a doorway leading from the back of the store. "Here." He looked a bit haunted as he ducked back out of sight.

Murder could do that. I was assuming. Victor could've stroked out, but then I wouldn't be here, and Jean-Charles wouldn't have his knickers in a twist.

Guiding Madame Bouclet by the elbow, I moved her in

front of me as we both joined the gathering in what appeared to be a back room filled with inventory and cooled to keep it fresh.

Jean-Charles motioned for us to join him and *Commissaire* Moreau gathered around a wine barrel, on its end, the lid removed. A bad penny, that *commissaire*. And she was getting under my skin. Jean-Charles nodded toward another man standing back from the barrel and looking a little green. "This is Monsieur Fabrice. He is the proprietor of this shop."

I acknowledged him without a smile. He shifted from foot to foot, looking antsy and out of sorts. Murder could do that, I guessed, although I'd grown used to it.

As I moved closer to the barrel, my foot connected with a bottle on the floor. Empty, it skittered across the concrete, careening off others that littered the area. All empty.

Jean-Charles stepped to the side, making room for his mother. With an arm around her shoulders, he held her as if with one jostle, she would shatter. "You shouldn't see this, *Maman.*"

She ignored him. "I have seen much worse than this," said the lady who'd named the cows then refused to serve them for dinner. A brave show so as not to be excluded.

Personally, I'd be delighted to be excluded. I could be in bed, at the Raphael, snuggled between luxurious sheets and under a down duvet with visions of sugarplums in my head. But here I was, suffering from a serious sugar plum deficiency, and not feeling quite as confident as my fiancé's mother.

Murder made me twitchy.

I stepped in beside Madame Bouclet to my right, my shoulders touching those of *Commissaire* Moreau to my left. Taking a deep breath, I summoned a calm stomach—no matter how you spun it, death was an ugly business—and then peered into the barrel.

A man, presumably Victor, had been stuffed into the cask,

his neck at an odd angle, his eyes unseeing as they stared upward.

The killer had emptied the bottles of wine on top of him, filling the empty spaces and staining his white shirt a blood red —a nice contrast to the blue of his skin. Victor hadn't been a handsome man. I felt panic rising along with a strong gag reflex. I swallowed hard. "Now that's a full-bodied wine."

I think even the faint beating of the angel's wings stopped.

I looked up to meet the wide-eyed stare of my intended. "I said that, didn't I?"

Jean-Charles nodded, his eyes tearing up as he bit down on his lip.

I felt the *commissaire's* shoulders twitch. I gave her a side-eye. She covered her mouth and refused to look at me.

M. Fabrice had turned his back and hidden his face.

Madame Bouclet looked at her son, then at me. I pressed my lips together as my eyes grew wide. She broke first. Gales of laughter discretely hidden behind a tiny hand. Unable to resist, the *commissaire* and Jean-Charles joined in. Unsure as to whether they were laughing at me or with me, my chuckles weren't quite so robust. But the laughter broke the tension. *Commissaire* Moreau sagged against me as she sucked in great gulps of air and swiped at her eyes with the back of a hand. Jean-Charles held his mother tight.

I set *Commissaire* Moreau back on her feet. "Did your officers find the wine in the sewer space behind the wine cellar at the Bouclets'?"

She brushed down her slacks then tugged her police-issued jacket into place. "*Non.* No wine. No other way out. And no footprints."

No way they carried it out through the kitchen. And no way they carried it out through the Metro. Not unless someone, somewhere was in on it. I kept circling back to that. An inside job. The police? Everybody was a suspect.

"Who found the...Victor?" I asked since no one else stepped up.

"I did," M. Fabrice said in heavily-accented English, the two words taking a toll—or something else was making him sweat in the January coolness. A heavyset man, his face florid, his clothes sloppy—his suit nice but his shirt untucked, his collar open. He mopped his face with a crumpled and stained handkerchief as he switched to French. Jean-Charles translated as Emma took notes. "Whoever did this wasn't expecting me. We have some of the bottles alarmed. Especially the expensive ones. If they are moved and not replaced within thirty seconds, a silent alarm is triggered. The system alerts me through my phone."

"They didn't know about the alarm," the *commissaire* said as she jotted notes.

"I surprised them." He gently touched the back of his head. "They hit me. When I awoke, they were gone."

"Did they come by car?"

"I noticed a sedan in back. It shouldn't have been here." He reached into a pocket and pulled out a slip of paper which he handed to the *commissaire*. "I made note of the license number. Clearly, they did not think someone would take notice. It is very late."

Or they didn't care. One hundred Euros the car was stolen.

"What time was the first notification?" Apparently, Jean-Charles's interpretation of my investigative skills made everyone willing to concede the floor to me—or, maybe I made a good patsy. It was far too late for me to care.

He glanced at his phone. "Oh one hundred, oh seven."

It was two o'clock now. "You live close?"

"Three blocks." He looked down at his clothing. "I had fallen asleep in my chair. I am alone." He paused, a flash of pain.

Jean-Charles turned to me. "His wife died just before Christmas."

"I'm so sorry."

M. Fabrice nodded as tears brightened his eyes.

"You are friends?" I asked Jean-Charles.

"M. Fabrice is a friend of all the French winemakers." A bit of a non-answer giving me the feeling he was dodging my question.

"His wife was my sister," Madame Bouclet said, her matter-of-fact tone covering a hint of hurt lurking beneath.

"I'm so sorry. I didn't know." I shot a look at Jean-Charles. Why hadn't he told me? "Family then."

"M. Fabrice, what did you do when you awakened?" He listened while Jean-Charles repeated my question making it sound so much more beautiful in the fluid French intonations.

He shifted uneasily and cast a veiled glance at Jean-Charles who encouraged him with a nod. "I called Jean-Charles. It was his wine, you see."

"Why not the police?"

"I called them next."

"Did you move or hide anything?"

His eyes grew wide with guilt. He pursed his lips and shook his head. He didn't trust himself to speak.

Totally lying.

The *commissaire*, her head bent over her notes, hadn't seen.

Jean-Charles and his mother both pinned me with looks. Easy to read, they threw me on the horns of a dilemma. I let M. Fabrice off for the moment.

Secrets.

But soon, very soon, I'd have M. Fabrice on a spit over a hot fire to sweat the truth out of him.

My foot nudged one of the empty bottles causing it to roll across the concrete floor. I retrieved it. Then I picked up another. The same wine. Then another. All the same. And they looked like they'd come from a broken wooden crate tossed in the corner. Chateau Shasay, the imprint read. My arms full of bottles, I proffered them to Jean-Charles. "Your wine." It wasn't a question. "All the same vintage. Estate Laurent, the '94."

His eyebrows shot toward his hairline. "The '94? You're sure?"

I handed him the bottle. "What's special about the '94?"

"It is very old, nicely aged, and one of those rare vintages that took on cult status. It is highly prized."

"How much inventory is left?"

"None. The vintage sold out almost immediately." He turned a serious look on M. Fabrice, who cowered back into the shadows. "Where did you get this wine?"

"From a buyer in Singapore. He had collected it over the years and asked me to sell it slowly to get the highest price."

"This is a lot of wine." Jean-Charles clenched and unclenched his fists, a sure sign he was looking for some crockery to throw. With none available, I jumped in to try to defuse the situation. "I don't need to tell you this is personal. All of it. Any idea who might carry a grudge so big they'd go to these lengths?"

Jean-Charles reached out and took one of the bottles off the cache I held. A tic worked in his cheek as he ran a thumb over the label, a personal, almost loving gesture. He flicked a glance at his mother. "It's time."

She read his thoughts. She grabbed his arm with a white-knuckled grip. "No. It will kill your father."

"One way or the other, that is their intent." He threw the bottle down, shattering it. "Hate begets hate. One wrong. Another. One lie. More hate. It stops now."

"You know what all this is about?" I couldn't hide my amazement. "How could you let whatever it is, a misunderstanding, whatever, escalate to murder?"

"You don't understand. My father..." At the pained look his mother sent his way, he stopped. He patted her hand that still clutched his arm. "It has to stop, *Maman*. Now. Before someone else dies."

His eyes lifted as his gaze locked with mine. "It is an old feud."

"How can you be sure?" his mother whispered.

He showed her one of the empty bottles.

She paled as a hand drifted to her throat to twist her pearls.

THIS TIME, THE WARM, TIMELESS EMBRACE OF THE HOTEL Raphael felt even sweeter. But it would take a darn sight more to dispel the specter of death. "A bottle of Nicholas Feuillatte, on ice, my room. *S'il vous plâis.*" I tossed the words at the young lady behind the front desk as I breezed by.

"*Oui, madame.*"

Almost to the bar, I stopped and turned on my heel. Arriving back in front of the young woman, I said, "*Je suis desolée.*" I pulled out another twenty-Euro note. Too tired for anymore French...anymore anything, I pushed the note toward her. "Thank you."

She pushed the note back. "You have had a bad day; I can see this. The pleasure is mine."

"Your name?" I left the note on the desk.

"Pauline." She pronounced the first syllable as Americans would say "pow."

"Of course, it is. I shall call you my French Miss P, if you don't mind."

"Not at all."

"Big shoes to fill." I patted the desk with both hands; then filled with a longing for home and its familiar insanity, I gave her a smile and took my leave. Another thought struck me, and I turned. "My room?" I had no idea where it was.

"Our best suite. Fifth floor. You and Mr. Marsh are the only two on the floor. You will need the key in the elevator..."

I held up my hand. "I know the drill. Thank you...Miss P."

Somehow that bit of silliness made me feel better.

THE BATH, BUBBLED AND SCENTED, WOULD MAKE ME FEEL EVEN better, almost human even. Of course, it would take a while. Five minutes and I'd managed one flute of Champagne and up to mid-thigh. When I'd said scalding, the butler had taken me at my word.

Pausing, breathing in the steam, I worked my shoulders trying to keep them from ossifying somewhere near my ears. As I took a sip, Jean-Charles strode through the doorway. Then, catching sight of me, he stopped mid-stride.

His eyes grew warm and his mouth curled into a smile as he crossed his arms.

Immediately, I sucked in my stomach.

"Don't do that. You are a vision."

"You need glasses." I sunk into the steam, hovering over the water. Burning one's choochillala would be totally self-defeating—especially since I was hoping for mind-blowing sex in the very near future. If my mind was blown, I couldn't remember anything about today. Hey, as theories went, it held water. Besides, it was the only one I had, and even I could see the potential serious upside.

"I know every curve. You are a woman as a woman should be. Not some branch person."

"Stick figure."

He gave me a complicit smile. "May I join you?"

"Only if you order another bottle."

"Already done. The young lady at the front desk..."

"My French Miss P." Flicking my fingers in the water, I determined it was choochillala-safe, so I eased in all the way.

"Yes." He looked like he understood.

"How is your father?"

"Resting." He didn't say more. Perhaps there wasn't anything else to say.

"Join me." I splashed my feet. "There's room for two. But you must share all your secrets." I leveled my best serious look. "Jean-Charles, it is time to come clean."

I didn't smile at the pun.

CHAPTER SIX

$\mathcal{T}$HE WATER was tepid, and my patience stretched so tight I could pluck it and hit a high C by the time Jean-Charles had killed the second bottle of bubbly and appeared ready to talk. Okay, maybe not ready *ready*, per se, but unable to keep secrets any longer. Like aliens accidentally ingested, they pushed at his skin, bugging his eyes, exploding to be out in the open.

Frankly, I wished he'd hurry. The warmth slipped away, and my skin had pruned to the point of no return. But I wasn't going to push. Frankly, I wasn't sure I wanted to know. Sharing would make it my secret too.

Secrets. So deadly. Who knew? Up to this point, the worst secret I knew was in ninth grade, Julie Best kissed Jake Wallace while he was still going out with her best friend. An ugly scene, for sure, but no real blood was let...well, only a little. And everyone recovered...I think.

I held the first bottle high so the dregs could drip into his flute, then I stuffed it neck-first into the ice. *One dead soldier.* I could see my father's smile as he buried many a previous bottle in its own ice coffin. The thought tugged at me. His health wasn't good. The last time I'd spoken with my mother, yesterday or the day before—fatigue had muddled time—she'd been worried and trying to hide it for my benefit.

I needed to go home. "When I rode over to M. Fabrice's shop with your mother, we had a bit of a chat."

Jean-Charles knew me well enough to know what was coming. His shoulders slumped further as if my unspoken question was the last stone in an already too heavy load. The thought made me feel bad, but I had as much on my plate...well, almost...and I needed to offload some uncertainty. Barring that, I'd like to get at least an indication of the direction he leaned. In my world, preparation was the key to survival.

"I can't give you the answer you want, not now." He brushed my question aside with the flick of a wrist. "There is so much to fix, and I am the only one who can pick up the gun, as you say."

"Sword."

He shrugged but didn't smile.

"I understand. Even though I know you know this, I want to make it clear. Marriage is a partnership. I will not anoint you as my Lord and Master, should I decide to go through with it."

"Should *we* decide."

"Fair."

"And, neither will you be installed on a throne."

"Pedestal." I felt a fight coming on, just when we needed it the least. "We both are under a great deal of pressure. My responsibilities, which are as important as your own, are in Vegas. Yours are here. How we manage that..."

"Time will tell. For now, will you help me solve Victor's murder, get my sister from under suspicion, and put my family's business back to right?"

"Piece of cake."

A smile split his face and broke the tension. As if he really thought I might say no. I still might—to a different question. But this one I couldn't resist if I'd wanted to. "You need to be honest with me, though. Don't leave anything out. No spinning to make your family appear to all be dressed in shining armor."

"I am always honest with you."

"Always is difficult to achieve. I will agree that you are honest in the words you say but hide a bit of subterfuge in the words you don't."

He accepted that. "Sometimes I am not ready to say things."

I let it go, writing the whole thing off to semantics. An easy explanation, but a thin excuse. "Was M. Fabrice's explanation as to how he came by so much very expensive, very rare wine reasonable?"

Jean-Charles shrugged, grateful for an easy entry into a hard discussion. "Collectors can fall on hard times. From time to time, they will divest themselves of their collections. It is best to do it as M. Fabrice said, a bit at a time, to not lower the price by increasing the supply dramatically."

With one hand I found the light controls and lowered the level to "intimate." As he had drawn my bath, the butler had also lighted several candles that now hissed and sizzled as they danced in the almost indiscernible wafting of the cool air. I shivered. Had I opened one of the large French doors in my room? I couldn't remember, but it sounded like something I would do—even when the temp hovered a tick above freezing. Maybe, especially then. As a Vegas rat, I had a fascination with cold air. I'd gotten the words flowing, and now I waited for Jean-Charles to join in. If I had to wait long, the physical complications could be numbing. With the water lapping at my chin and my toes tickling Jean-Charles in places that made him squirm, I leaned my head back on the rim of the tub and closed my eyes.

"This is a very bad thing," Jean-Charles started.

I eased one eye open to make sure he wasn't talking about the tickling. He wasn't. *No shit, Sherlock!* I thought. "Seems to be quite the pickle" is what I said.

"Pickle?"

I needed to shelve my fascination with clichés and puns for the rest of the evening. "Problem."

"Yes, this pickle it is. It goes back to 1855, maybe a bit before."

I lifted my head. "1855? As in too many years ago for my limited math skills, but enough to be irrelevant, and well beyond just about any statute of limitations. Well, unless it involved a murder back then. But, really, after all this time, both parties to the murder would be dead." Yes, I was blathering. But, seriously, was America even America in 1855? I didn't think so —the war that would solidify the country was still to come. In 1855, France had been France many times over. "Why is it that getting things done here in the Old Country always requires a history lesson?"

"History is who we are." He seemed incredulous that I didn't know this.

"No, history is who we were."

"Americans do have a disregard for what came before."

"Doomed to repeat it, are we?"

He shrugged, but the tension in his shoulders relaxed a bit. "This history between our families, while a man died, it is much worse than murder. It is the death of the heart."

Death of the heart. What did that involve? Death and dismemberment? Or a counseling session with Dr. Ruth? Where was Google Translate when I needed it? I wondered if it had a subtlety function.

"Worse than murder? Oh good." I replaced my head on the lip of the bath and resealed my eyelids. Maybe, when I opened them again, this would all have been a bad dream. "But you can't be serious. 1855?"

"Yes, that is when the *Premier cru* vineyards received their designations. Time erased many details, but the hate remains."

"With most long-lasting feuds and wars, often most of those

fighting can't remember why they are fighting. Hating their enemy becomes a way of life. Nobody remembers the why."

"Oh, in this case, they remember."

"Who is *they?*" And we came to the sixty-four-thousand-dollar question. And so soon. Maybe I'd get out of the bath before I caught pneumonia...and shriveled into a raisin. Before he answered, I held up my hand. "Let me guess. The Laurents."

"*Oui.* My great-grandfather and the elder Enzo Laurent were friends. They both came from immigrant families from Hungary, I think. By that time, they were Frenchmen, and land-holders of some stature. They owned farms next to one another, many hectares apiece and in the heart of Bordeaux. Vineyards, not farms. Our families have been making wine since Cabernet Franc and Sauvignon Blanc, both very popular Bordeaux grapes, cross-pollinated to create Cabernet Sauvignon in the seventeenth century. By 1855, the classic Bordeaux, a blended wine, was considered the best in the world."

While I wasn't much of a straight Cabernet fan, I did enjoy a fine Bordeaux with its blend of Merlot, maybe some Petit Verdot, Cab Franc or, *gasp*, Malbec, with the base of Cabernet. The other grapes cut the heaviness and tannic influences of the Cab. Still, I found it so interesting that what most considered to be the best wine in the world was a blend, while Americans remained fascinated with single varietals. "So why is 1855 such a seminal date?"

"Two things happened to create our horrible history. M. Laurent came under severe financial pressure. His family asserts that my family somehow ruined his harvest several years before, or we tainted his wine. No one knows exactly. But they blame what came next on my great-grandfather and all his progeny."

"A bit of business hanky-panky? That's what all this is about?"

Jean-Charles drained the last bit from his flute, then reached over to set the delicate crystal on the floor. The heat of the water had flushed his skin a delectable color of pink. The steam curled his hair even more. The story and the memories sharpened his features. "Are you familiar with the Bordeaux Wine Official Classification of 1855?"

I bit my lip, stifling an almost overwhelming urge to kiss him, to make him forget this awful thing he carried, as I shook my head.

"Napoleon III wanted a classification of the best Bordeaux wines, long considered the best wines in the world. He wanted to take it a step further listing the best of the best."

I always considered "expert opinion" to be somewhat of an oxymoron, if not a complete fallacy. Of course, most days I spent a lot of energy hacking my own path through the forest, so I was never shocked when my opinions were not widely adopted. "Why?"

"It's not important. A big show in Paris. The world would come. Nobody thought a great deal about it. The wine merchants complied with the Emperor's wishes. They compiled a list of the best wineries, the *Premier cru*, or the first growth, based on the Chateau's reputation and the price their wine commanded in the open market. Back then, reputation and the price someone would pay were directly related to quality. Today, with all the marketing and the influencers, the perception of quality is just that, only a perception...in most cases."

"Real quality is a curious bit of arcana?"

"Of course not. It is just harder to find." Stretching his arms across the lip of the oval tub, he invited me into an embrace.

It'd be tight, but that was an invitation I wouldn't turn down. The buoyancy of the water let me lie half-on Jean-Charles as I knifed my body in beside him without feeling I might be squashing him.

He curled an arm around me, his fingers finding tendrils of my hair to worry. "The designations actually had five levels, but the *premier*, the first, is the only relevant one for our discussion."

"And your Chateau is a *Premier cru.* That much I know. And I'd bet my reputation, such as it is, that M. Laurent's was not given that designation."

"He was placed in the third *cru.* A very big insult, and one he took umbrage with stating my family had too much influence in the designations and his wine, which had a high reputation and commanded a good price at market, had only suffered from a couple of years of lesser quality. Unfortunately, those years had eroded both the price and the reputation."

His fingers playing in my hair sent shivers through me. A simple gesture, a powerful response. Was it lust or love? And why was I disdainful of one and scared of the other? "This happened a long time ago. How is it important enough now to kill over?"

"The designations have remained through the years. They are immovable. No one is taken off the list. Chateaux Margaux fell under rather suspect management at one point that caused a severe decline in quality for fifteen years or more. They have since recovered beautifully, but they remained a *Premier cru* despite the lack of quality expected of such a designation. This is bad but worse, no one is added."

"Not ever?"

"Only once and not since 1973. And only because the wine was a Rothschild. They are the most powerful family in all of Bordeaux wine. Mouton-Rothschild was promoted from the second classification."

"Ah, the splinter that has caused a huge abscess in the Laurent family." I shifted to move my arm that was bent under me and tingling with lack of circulation.

"You cannot underestimate the importance of the designation. The *Premier cru châteaus* grew in prominence and wealth spanning the globe, vast wealth and power."

"And the others did not."

"And when the vineyards are neighbors." The pieces were

falling into place for me. The love of money truly was the root of all evil.

"The Laurents lost their vineyard."

The way he said it made my heart fall. "Your family owns it now?"

"My great-grandfather, he was very clever. The Laurents would rather have burned all their vines, destroying the vineyard, than see it fall under my family's control. When you have power, there are ways to hide a purchase. When the deal was done and the new owner made known, M. Laurent killed himself."

"Oh." My words disappeared as I contemplated the Laurents' pain, piling on misery, piling on insult, creating an injury to last millennia. "If that story is even half-true, I can see why you might think the Laurents are behind the wine theft and Victor's death."

"I am not yet sure, but I know in here," he tapped his heart. "Enzo Laurent was there, in the kitchen...in my family's home!" His indignation increased with each assertion.

"Which makes me wonder if he is stupid."

Jean-Charles gave me a *boof*, one of those irritating French mannerisms to exert their superiority, which did nothing but make me smile, oddly enough. Arrogance normally was one of my buttons. "He is very smart."

"Then why would he traipse through your parents' kitchen, putting himself at the scene of the crime?"

"He was at the scene of the crime. Yes?" Jean-Charles wasn't yet willing to accept that the Laurents might not have been behind the evening's activities.

They were still on the suspect list, for sure. But why be so stupid? A question for Enzo Laurent. "What happened to the Laurents?"

"Oh, they are very powerful, too. They may not make wine,

although, according to my father, one of the younger ones has a talent for it, but they control it."

"How so?" Controlling it sounded way better than making it. But I was a gauche American, so what did I know?

"They are the most powerful wine distributor in all of Europe. The exclusive representative of some of the world's finest wines."

"I thought I recognized the name. Of course, I am many levels removed from wine purchasing for the Babylon and its multitude of bars and restaurants, as well as those of the many other properties we own and manage, but, well, you know my love of fine wine."

"Especially Champagne." He smiled then a flash of irritation thinned his lips.

"What is it?"

"For a very long time, we had an agreement with the Laurents. They had our exclusive; in return, they would not represent any of the other *Premier Cru Châteaus*. For all of my lifetime, the renewal of the agreement occurred automatically. Recently, they said they would not renew. They even took on three of the other *châteaus*, three who were always unwilling to attach themselves to a distributor so closely aligned with our family."

"They found a way to carve out their pound of flesh."

"Emma, Commissaire Moreau…" He cleared his throat as if her name had stuck somewhere. "She always called it an uneasy alliance. Without either of us, we both would fail."

I wondered what the Emma thing was about. "You wouldn't fail, but you wouldn't thrive quite as much. But are you going to accuse the Laurents based solely on a minor misunderstanding?" I wondered who the non-renewal hurt more. Now, with Jean-Charles laying his heart open, would not be the time to dive down that rat hole. But I had a feeling the answer, whether comfortable or not, would provide an interesting piece to the puzzle.

"It is far from minor, but there is more. Our wine, the wine they poured over Victor? It was a special vintage, an estate wine as they call it in the U.S., from one particular growth block."

"Let me guess. The growth block that was formerly the Laurents' vineyard." Hence the name. Even in my wilted state I could string those two tidbits of logic together. "Laurent had the exclusive on that as well?"

"Yes, but my father gave it to M. Fabrice."

"I'm sure that didn't help the bad blood between the families."

"*Non.*" His blue eyes, dark and serious, met mine. "There is one other...hurt." I waited, holding my breath. "My wife. Christophe's mother. She was a Laurent, the product of some...indiscretion. When they discovered our alliance, they sent her to Brazil with her mother, but she was still family. They blame me for her death."

JEAN-CHARLES HELPED ME OUT OF THE TUB, WRAPPED ME IN A sumptuous robe, then left me to process while he ordered some more medicinal pink bubbles. "Some food, maybe?" I called after him, hoping my voice carried into the next room. More bubbles without food could get ugly.

"Already ordered."

Avoiding conflict, or the specter of a lost love, I took my time. My manic brushing reduced my scalp to the verge of rawness when I finally came out of my reverie. To bolster my confidence, I donned a lovely silk negligee rimmed with lace. The lace peeked provocatively when I pulled the robe tight and cinched it, armor for a battle of the heart.

Candles in tall silver candleholders burned brightly, book-

ending a beautiful spread on a white-clothed round table—
room service had been prompt. Jean-Charles occupied one of
the two wingback chairs and stared into the fire banked in the
fireplace, which burned with a brightness that managed to push
back the heaviness I felt.

When he saw me, he rose, a smile lighting his eyes. "You are
lovely. I am so sorry to bring you into this mess." He swirled the
bottle in its ice-bucket bath, then lifted it, cradling it in a white
napkin as he held it out for me to see.

He'd waited for me—an appreciated thoughtfulness. "Nice.
Thank you." He'd sprung for the epic stuff. A pleasure to offset
the pain.

"Let's eat; then perhaps talk will be easier."

An interesting theory that I wasn't above trying to prove.

Jean-Charles waited until I'd fed the beast in my stomach
and calmed the one in my head. The detritus of a feast littered
the plates between us. I leaned back in my chair and waved
away any more Champagne.

"Who in the Laurent family carries this Hatfield and McCoy
sort of hate?"

"Hatfield and McCoy?" His French accent lent beauty to the
ugliness.

"An American version of the Capulets and Montagues?
Romeo and Juliet?" I raised an eyebrow in question.

"Enzo is the head of the family. My wife and I, we had been
together since we were children, sneaking through the vineyards in defiance of our families. Then we reconnected when I
found her in Paris, studying the art of cooking. The attraction
was still there." He rubbed a hand over his eyes. "Fuel to a
generations-old hatred. So easy to see that now. Maybe being
the Forbidden Fruit brought us together. Time dulls passion,
changes memories."

Unable to bear witness to his pain without doing something,

I reached across and found his hand. "Your hearts were bigger than that."

"For a bit, it seemed we had helped to heal the wound. The families were talking."

"With such a minefield between the families, how did you do business together?"

"Business is business. It is of the head, not the heart." Without letting go of my hand, he poured himself more Champagne. "My father was teaching one of the younger Laurents, Enzo's second cousin, I think. Things were...better."

"Better, but far from ideal. I met Juliet's sister, your sister-in-law, remember?" My path had crossed Chitza's in Vegas. She'd teamed up with Desiree's then-husband to take what they could from not only Desiree but Jean-Charles as well. They'd worked to take the one thing he had...his reputation. Now I got the why, which had eluded me before.

"She was only a half-sister, but the bond with Juliet was very strong." Jean-Charles sighed. "Juliet had that effect on many. She was the light, the joy, and the glue. Maybe, we just wanted it to be better, so we believed it was. And when Juliet—"

"Juliet." I shook my head at the irony.

He gave me a weak smile. "When Juliet died..." His voice cracked.

I squeezed harder. She'd been a part of his heart since childhood. I couldn't imagine the hole her loss would leave. And every day looking at and loving a child who, by my guess, looked a lot like his mother. "What happened then?"

"Grief let loose the hate anew."

"Who led the charge?" I got up, rounded the table, then crawled into his lap. "I'm assuming Chitza is still behind bars in Nevada?"

"As far as I know. Even thought of her is painful."

Tomorrow I'd touch base with Detective Romeo back home

to make sure. "Okay, we'll assume she's not the brains behind the wine theft. Who would be your number one suspect? Enzo?"

"He is the family head, and he and Juliet were very close."

"One thing bothers me." Afraid my bulk had cut off blood flow to his legs and knowing he wouldn't say a word, I pushed myself off his lap. The robe gapped open and I retied it, securing my dignity if not my comfort. Something was off here. "They went to great lengths to pull off an incredible heist. If not for your father, they might have replaced the wine with clever fakes, and we'd be none the wiser."

He straightened in offense. "Not notice inferior wine?"

"I'm sure I deserve a firing squad for suggesting such a thing, but, Jean-Charles, it was a party for us. How much attention were you giving to the wine?"

"My father was giving a great deal. Because of my family's status in the industry, each move we make, each wine we serve, is scrutinized. With him especially it is more than just a matter of pride, it is everything."

Worth killing for, I wondered? "Okay, so let's say I'm wrong and everyone would've noticed the substitution with the fakes. Assuming you are right and the Laurents, educated oenophiles in their own right, would know that as well. If they went to so much trouble to employ such sleight of hand, then why did they stuff Victor in a barrel and pour wine that points to themselves over his body?"

"To make a point."

"Yes, but don't you think that getting yourself thrown in the slammer would hand the victory to your opponent?"

"Well, it also brings doubt on my family." Jean-Charles clearly had mulled that over. His assertion held little emotion.

"So, if either of you had any brains, neither of you would steep poor Victor in that particular vintage, would you?"

"You are speculating."

"True. And assuming a whole lot. Common sense doesn't

often play a big part in deaths of the heart. Tell me about the wine merchant."

"That vintage is a small run, very few cases, but very exceptional. M. Fabrice is the only one who sells it."

"He's family. Makes sense."

Jean-Charles's glance told me there was more to the story—more that he wasn't sharing.

"And the Laurents?" I had to ask, but they seemed to have their fingers in all the pies, which was interesting even without murder and theft to add spice to the mix.

"They place all our wine." He seemed like that sort of thing was a normal game played in the local wine scene. But something in his tone didn't ring true.

"But this wine was different. Something happened?" A total fishing expedition, but I couldn't shake the feeling there was something Jean-Charles didn't want to tell me. I wondered how he would play it. Was I in or was I out?

"Enzo, he came to my father. Even though the wine is a very small run, it is exceptional. Laurent, in his role as distributor, he has many, many good customers who should have been rewarded with an allotment. It is how the game works. As you Americans say, you itch my back..."

"Scratch. And I'll scratch yours."

"Yes, this." He didn't say it with his normal *joie de vivre*, not that I expected him too.

I wasn't feeling it either. "Who made the call to give it all, the entire run, to M. Fabrice and leave the Laurents with no placement with which to favor their best customers?"

"My father. We had quite a disagreement over it, but he is sick and there is only so far I will push." Jean-Charles shifted underneath me.

I put a foot on the floor, levering a bit of my bulk off of him. "Am I hurting you?"

"Of course not." He unwrapped my arms and shifted my

weight to his other thigh. The man was a gentleman through and through, lying to protect my feelings. I unfolded myself from his lap then took a chair that I had pulled close, so I could still touch him. With the backs of my fingers, I casually stroked his thigh where the robe failed to close.

"Did your father give any explanation?" He shook his head. "And Enzo Laurent, how did he feel about your father's decision?"

"He was livid."

"Livid enough not to renew your exclusive agreement?" Which was the cart, and which was the horse? I had a feeling that changed with the telling.

Jean-Charles pursed his lips. "It would be like him. Revenge is a motivator for him. As head of the family, he must protect the family's reputation."

"That's one of those odd things where you can go only so far before you end up destroying it rather than protecting it."

"A lesson the French have never learned." At least Jean-Charles had enough perspective to see at least some of the fallacies of the whole duel-to-the-death ridiculousness. Like mutually-assured destruction, it worked so long as no one stuck a toe across the line thereby triggering a cascade that would leave no man...or woman...standing.

"Did your father give any reason for his choice to favor M. Fabrice over all the others?"

"He said it was his choice. They are old friends. M. Fabrice didn't want the exclusive...something about too much confidence in him."

"But he took it anyway." With one man dead and two families choosing pistols, I'd like to talk with him, get his insight into this twisted, incestuous arrangement.

CHAPTER SEVEN

*L*IGHT PINKENED the horizon when I finally gave in and ordered a pot of American coffee and as many croissants as they thought my self-respect could handle. The "Yes, Miss" that came back, confident words full of uncertainty, made me smile. His interpretation of my request would be amusing, a bit of light in a dismal day.

A peek into the bedroom confirmed Jean-Charles still slept. He'd fallen into an uneasy sleep in my arms. Sleep, uneasy or not, had not been quite so kind to me. A couple of hours at best, but enough to run on for a bit.

From years of being so slighted, I'd learned a copious amount of caffeine was the only antidote. The odds of getting my Don Francisco's Vanilla Nut here in Paris, even at the Hotel Raphael where the staff made it a matter of pride to meet all expectations, were slim enough I didn't ask. Way too early to make a random staff member in the kitchen feel as if they'd fallen short.

My next call would be to my mother.

With seven hours of time difference yawning between us, the hour in Vegas was acceptable, if marginally so. Not yet midnight. In my 24/7 home, the night would just be gearing up. My mother, Mona, with her new twins, might have a different take, but I'd risk it.

My father wasn't doing well. Last time we'd talked, she hadn't said as much, but I heard her worry lurking between her feigned interest in my love life. Okay, her interest wasn't feigned, it was super irritating, but, well...mothers.

She answered on the fourth ring. "Lucky!" Now her enthusiasm, that for sure was feigned. A thin blanket to mask her worry.

I knew better than to ask directly—that just put her guard up. "How are you? You sound tired."

"Oh," she deflated like a balloon letting all its air leak out. "Between the girls' schedules being all upside-down and visiting your father in the hospital, I'm beat. You know, I think those little heathens can tell when something's not right."

"The hospital?" I kept my tone light. Any bark from me would scare her quiet.

"I wasn't supposed to tell you." She didn't sound all broken up about having done so. In fact, she sounded desperate for a shoulder to lean on.

And here I'd been hoping she'd give me good news to save my ass from road rash. God knows I'd been dragging it around long enough. "How is he?"

"He puts on a brave face, but the doctors are worried."

"Where are you?"

"In front of your window. I loved watching you and your father, shoulder to shoulder, staring out at your city as you plotted and planned some corporate assault on the unsuspecting public."

"Unsuspecting yet appreciative public," I reminded her, hoping to lighten the load.

"It won't be the same without you both."

I could see her, in her threadbare peach robe—her favorite

despite a closetful of expensive boudoir ensembles. The robe had something to do with me as a child. I couldn't remember the details, but I remembered the feeling of warmth when she told me. She would've pulled her hair up, leaving a few tendrils to soften the passage of time. Her eyes would be round with fear, her face drawn with worry. Still, her beauty would take a man's breath and my confidence.

"Father and I are not going anywhere."

"Yes, you will stay in France and your father, he is older. He will...leave, someday."

"Today is not the day. And I have a business in Vegas. It is where I belong. My Frenchman will accept that, or he is not the right man for me."

"Compromise, Lucky."

"That implies both parties come to the table willing to deal." I had no idea whether I wanted to or not, nor how Jean-Charles was feeling about everything right now.

"How's it going?"

"Fine, just fine." No way would I add more to my mother's plate right now. "Any idea what is going on with Father? What do the doctors say?"

"He's anemic. They don't know why."

"Bleeding?"

"They've looked but can't find anything." She stopped, perhaps drawing strength from the carpet of lights unrolling at her feet—the Las Vegas Strip, in all its glory and promise. I'd pulled wattage from that view more times than I could remember.

"He'll be okay, Mom. He's fought through worse."

"Right. Right." She drew a breath. "Of course he will. We have to fight."

Life. To win you couldn't drop your shield, not for a moment.

"I'll call the doctors, see if I can coerce anything more from them. Call me if anything changes." I almost rang off, then thought of one more thing. "Mom?"

"Yeah?"

"Call me if you need anything, anything at all." Normally making that sort of an open offer to Mona would have me doubting my sanity and looking over my shoulder. But lately I felt we both were clawing our way to a more adult relationship. I could be wrong. If so, I'd regret those words more than I could imagine. Mona could exact a price for a promise better than anyone I knew, although Jean-Charles's mother might give her a run for her spot atop the Most Irritating list.

This time I did terminate the connection.

My stock was a little down with Detective Romeo, so I decided to text. He could be home...with Brandy, my assistant... in bed...naked. A nauseating shudder ripped through me, and I almost pitched my phone across the room. A FaceTime mistake right now would be terminal.

Are you awake?

I waited, staring at the device as the bubbles popped up giving me a clue.

Seriously? Aren't you supposed to be the belle of the ball or something?

Yes, well, there's been a hitch. I need your help. May I call?

You're asking? I know this is Lucky's phone, but what did you do with my friend?

Cute. I hit his speed dial number.

"Lucky? Is that really you?" Music played in the background, soft, Rat Pack oldies. "Travel actually changes you. Who knew?"

And, for the record, I knew. Travel as a personal growth tactic was one of my oldies but goodies. "Funny. You working?" I wanted his answer to be no. I knew that playlist—I'd put it together...for my new hotel.

"Yep, curious you should call at this precise moment. It's like telepathy."

"You're at Cielo." While I worked at the Babylon as their Chief Scapegoat, I actually owned Cielo, a boutique hotel that, as a gambling-free oasis, flew in the face of Vegas tradition. My chance to test my ideas. And it was working beautifully...until now. The presence of the police in my sanctuary hadn't featured anywhere in my business fantasy.

"Somebody told you." Romeo sounded guarded.

"Where you are at this precise moment? Highly unlikely."

"Even Brandy doesn't know so she couldn't have told you." He seemed genuinely bothered by all this like I'd planted a GPS transmitter on him or something. "You know, Lucky, sometimes you creep me out."

"Sometimes? I must be slipping." I stared into the fire and allowed myself a nanosecond of self-pity. How did life get so fucked-up? Or was this what all the adults were working so hard to keep from us kids? "Kid, the music? Listen for a second." I waited, letting silence fill the distance between us. "I put together that playlist and paid through the nose for it." I didn't point out that triangulating his whereabouts on a snippet of Sinatra approached a superpower—the kid seemed to be toting a large enough load. "Do I want to know why you are at my hotel?"

"Well, that's a good question." The arrival of the elevator dinged in the background.

Okay, he was going up. I stifled my curiosity with limited success. Knowing would make the problem mine. Wondering would make the worry mine. I'd take the former over the latter, although, just once, I'd love to turn down both invitations. In an effort to do just that, I kept quiet.

"You see," Romeo continued with the bland intonation of a bored professor, "the owner of this hotel and an avowed unrepentant problem solver would want to know." The music now echoed a bit, pinging off the walls of the enclosed elevator. "But the woman, dressed to the max, with a dishy fiancé—Brandy's opinion, not mine—who is probably having mind-blowing sex in the City of Love would not want to go near what I'm dealing with."

"Lights."

"What?"

"City of Lights. It can be singular or plural, and I favor the plural as more evocative and accurate. And it actually is a reference to enlightened thought, not illumination." Mind-blowing sex was so far from my reality I wouldn't—no couldn't—admit. Life was so much more than merely complicated—a Gordian knot with not a string to tug. "Give it to me."

"There's a big brouhaha over some wine."

"Really?" Sensing a common theme, I drew the word out. "By the way, that's redundant. And, aren't you a bit young for a brouhaha?"

"As the man said, when you get the chance to use that word, you should seize it."

As an avowed logophile, I wasn't going to argue. "What sort of brouhaha are we dealing with?"

"You're irritating. And, by the way, Paris is also known as the City of Love. I Googled it."

"Ah, irritating is better." I shrugged on my comfortable Vegas skin. "Much better. And I'm willing to embrace the City of Love angle." In this new age of enlightenment and conjuring could I bring love to my door by merely accepting it and inviting it in? Was it that simple? A choice?

"I bet." Somehow, his blush infused his words. "Anyway, some customer, a big wig and one of those snotty, asshat wine know-it-alls, is claiming a very expensive bottle of wine is not what it says it is." He sounded as if he'd made up his mind.

"Careful, your bias is showing. Remember, open mind, Detective." Secretly I agreed with him—I hated dealing with the folks who knew just enough to make your life miserable. I hated it even worse when the blowhards were most likely right. "Let me guess; he says the wine has been substituted—mediocre wine in a high-priced bottle with no overt signs of tampering."

A long, uneasy pause told me I'd hit the bullseye.

"Jesus. You creep me out, you know?"

"One of my superpowers. I'm taking it creeping you out means I'm right?"

"That's what they tell me, but I'm just getting there." The elevator dinged his arrival at the top floor, the home of JC Prime, Jean-Charles's eponymous restaurant. Five-star, über expensive, and beyond reproach, it was the perfect target for whoever was targeting the Bouclet family. "You going to tell me why you called at exactly this moment? How'd you know I was on my way to JC Prime, looking forward to a bottle of bad wine and an irate customer?"

"Why exactly were you called? Bad wine is a bit outside of Metro's purview."

"Guess a refund wasn't enough. The unhappy customer has gone on a bit of a rampage. He started this thing last night. Seems he can't let it go. Two media vans out front already. I can only assume the camera crews are already recording the chaos and taking eyewitness accounts."

"Shit." The word came out as a sigh riding on the tiny bit of fight I had left. In this day of guilty-until-proven-innocent, where the Court of Public Opinion routinely shredded reputations, Jean-Charles would be sliced and diced like a cut of prime beef.

"Miss P is on top of it. Running interference like a pro. Let her do her job. You focus on you, for a change. Life's got to have balance, Lucky."

Maybe I didn't want to hear it. Maybe I knew it was true and wanted to avoid it. Either way, I shifted to problem-solving spin mode and gave him the Cliff Notes version of my recent fun and frivolity in the City of Lights, leaving out the personal parts.

"You think all this is related?" Romeo asked one of those questions that would make even the most patient and tolerant reassess the assertion that there is no such thing as a stupid question.

I was far from patient and only marginally tolerant of stupidity. "Blaming all this on coincidence would be the easy way out, and—"

"The easy way out is always wrong; I know." He finished one of my truisms by rote. "I got that tattooed on my ass as you suggested like a million times."

I shut down that visual. "I can't tie anything to anything, but give me time—"

"And you'll hang the bastard."

This time I heard the smile in Romeo's verbal poking. One thing I did know—I was getting a bit too consistent for my own comfort level. Was I really that pedantic? Man, I'd so lost my edge, my mojo. "Can you keep the line open while you wade through the bullshit being thrown around my fiancé's restaurant? His ass is on the line." And his family under attack, but I chose not to shovel it quite so deep.

"Not exactly protocol, but half the world will be watching anyway."

Something muffled the sound on his end—still audible but not as crisp.

He must've dropped me in his pocket. I hoped it was his shirt pocket. Anything else would seem like a violation, an odd twist on pocket pool that was most likely illegal in several states.

Intensely happy no one could read my thoughts, I buried my face in my free hand. I should be embarrassed, or, at the minimum, alarmed. Good thing minimums were still way over my head.

Caught in the visuals of catastrophe at JC Prime, I bolted out of my chair at the knock at the door, soft as it was. I rushed to greet the waiter before he could knock again. At least Jean-

Charles was getting some sleep. Between the two of us, if one was functional, we had a fighting chance…or at least a slight running start. I opened the door wide.

A young man tended a white-clothed cart on which a myriad of silver domed plates, napkin-covered baskets, and gleaming silver coffeepots tempted. "May I come in, Miss?" he whispered. At this time of morning when the sun was barely yawning awake, most at a hotel like the Raphael slumbered on.

Lucky them.

Putting a finger to my lips, I motioned him inside.

"Detective Romeo, Metropolitan Police. Everyone stand down." Romeo's bark transmitted through the distance to the device I still clutched in my hand. His voice echoed as if he was standing at my shoulder. I jumped. The waiter stopped, half in, half out. His mouth open, his smile frozen, his eyes wide as he stared at me.

"Come, come." I waved him inside then, after a quick glance to make sure the hall was clear, I secured the door.

He gave me a wide berth as he wheeled the small cart around me, then began offloading baskets, plates, and pots onto the table, recently cleared, in front of the embers in the fireplace.

"What the hell is going on here?" When had Romeo's voice changed to Dirty Harry menace? A man had replaced the kid while I wasn't looking.

The waiter knocked the silver covers together as he revealed the plates as quickly as he could.

A shout. An angry bellow. The pop and sizzle of a Taser. A stuck-pig scream of pain.

The waiter gave me some side-eye. "Should I pour the coffee, Miss?" His voice quavered, and he cleared his throat. He clasped his hands in front, a trick I often employed to keep shaking hands still.

I waved the phone at him. "Movie. Couldn't sleep."

More shouting.

"Little wonder," the waiter said as, mollified, he reached for the pot of coffee.

A shot. Then another.

The waiter's head swiveled. Coffee overfilled the cup, spilling onto the table.

My heart tripped. "Romeo?" Even though I wanted to shout, I managed to modulate my voice.

The waiter slammed the pot down and began mopping with a napkin. "I'm so sorry."

Shouts. Furniture breaking. Glass shattering.

"Romeo!" I hissed through gritted teeth, trying for quiet, for calm. He'd be okay. This sort of thing was a one-hand-behind-his-back adventure.

Pulling the door open, I motioned with my head for the waiter to beat it. "Thank you," I mouthed. I don't think he saw.

Pushing his cart, he bolted past, careened around the corner and out of sight.

Emotion overrode decorum. "Romeo!" I shouted, trying to be heard above the distant melee. Impossible, but I didn't know what else to do from a whole other universe, light-years away.

Jean-Charles, mussed, worried, and somehow diminished in a robe that hung off him, wandered barefooted, bed-headed and sleepy-eyed from the bedroom. Like a tractor beam, the aroma of fresh coffee pulled him toward the table. One look at me, and he stopped. "What's happened? Why are you shouting? Is the young detective here?"

I covered the tiny speaker on my phone, muting the destruction happening at his prized restaurant—we couldn't hear the shredding of his reputation, but I feared that might be happening as well, and would deal a more lethal blow. With great effort, I settled my features into a benign expression—or at least one that felt benign. "May I have some coffee, please?"

He narrowed his eyes. "You look...tired. Did you sleep?"

I shook my head. Yes, I needed coffee in the worst way.

And I needed Romeo to answer me.

"What happened? There's coffee all over here." He frowned at the mess on the table. "And who are you shouting at?"

"Phone rang." I left it at that. "I called Romeo. Checking on your former sister-in-law's whereabouts as I said I would."

Romeo. He still hadn't answered. Of course, I'd covered the speaker. I moved my thumb but stayed at the ready in case I needed to cover it again.

My heart hammered but there was nothing I could do but listen and wait. I couldn't shout. I couldn't panic. I couldn't fall apart. Launching Jean-Charles's temper to the heavens would only bring destruction to this side of the pond.

My mercurial fiancé, who liked to sling crockery when angry, doctored the coffee to my liking—enough cream to turn it to light brown, but no sweetener. The first sip, as were all first sips of magnificent beverages, was a religious experience. A groan of pleasure escaped driving a bit of the worry out of my man's eyes. Good, I needed him calm. He wasn't about to touch the plates until I'd had a shot at the breakfast feast calling to me.

"You still haven't told me why you are shouting. What is wrong?" Instead of pouring himself some coffee, he focused on the fire. Adding logs, some paper underneath, he lit a match, then blew softly, flaring the flame until the logs crackled and popped.

Since I didn't know what was going on—well, not exactly—I deflected. "Impressive. You've been hiding your pyrotechnic skills."

He rubbed his arms as he stared into the fire. "Not valued in Vegas. But necessary in the winter here."

"Please, I'm thermally challenged. Anytime the temps fall below seventy, I'm game for a fire."

"And you have the French doors, both sets, standing wide open because?" He closed them without waiting for my answer.

"I like fresh air."

He left them closed. "Now, for some coffee...if it's still warm."

The noise of the major scuffle in Vegas had settled to the point I felt I could talk. "Romeo? You there?" I tried for casual, but even I heard the edge of panic in my voice.

Jean-Charles did as well. His look sharpened as he focused on me. Turning my back to him, with the phone pressed to my ear so he couldn't hear Romeo's side of things, I stepped in front of the fire. For the first time tonight, I realized how cold I was. How very, very cold.

"Romeo," I hissed, willing him to answer.

Fumbling noises. Then the voice I wanted to hear. "Sorry. Man, touchy European arrogance and Nevada concealed-carry laws sure can make a rather mundane evening pretty damned exciting."

I took a few deep breaths and felt calm return. I put my phone against my chest and mouthed, "He's okay," to Jean-Charles.

"I didn't know he might not be. What is going on?"

With me, most of the time calm was a perspective thing, sorta relative, too. Tonight was no different. Despite the disaster at JC Prime, played out tomorrow in most of the world's major papers no doubt, Romeo still walked and talked, so I was cool.

"Anybody leaking blood?" I asked as if this was a normal question.

Jean-Charles cocked his head at me, his features crumpled with worry.

"Bullets through the ceiling like some goddamn Western saloon brawl. I broke the shooter's nose after my guys reached out and touched him with a Taser."

"I hope you used your elbow."

"Felt a bit sissy doing it."

"Good. No broken hand that way." I'd taught him that trick.

"Yeah, but a few black marks on my man card, for sure."

I laughed at his serious tone. "You want to talk with Jean-Charles? Maybe it's better you tell him what's going on. I'd rather not be the messenger—you know what happens to them."

Romeo shifted the phone to his other ear. I could see him holding it there with a shoulder as he flipped open his notebook. "I got names of the players and the accusations. We've secured the wine in question—the guy took the bottle last night after making a fuss. Came back tonight shouting the stuff was fake. The shooter, the wine asshat I told you about before, was way overplaying. Makes me wonder. Perhaps J.C.'s take on this would be helpful. But if you've got any plates around, I'd run for cover."

Once I turned over the conversation to J.C. as my bougie American friends called him, I figured I had maybe three minutes before the china would be in danger of taking flight. Pausing before starting the time clock by handing over the phone, I plotted my assault on breakfast.

Eggs first. Needed protein. Coffee in silver urns would be safe. Ditto the croissants—they were nestled in baskets. Three minutes was more than enough. Even a rookie chowhound could handle this challenge—and when it came to calorie consumption, I had serious trough skills.

But the china was logoed and expensive.

That could be a hitch. Jean-Charles would need an anger intervention. Oh joy.

"Here." I thrust the phone at him. "Romeo needs your help."

With a questioning look, Jean-Charles accepted the phone.

"And the plates are china, high-quality, and custom."

"What?"

"Just remember. It may be important later." I grabbed a fork and started shoveling eggs.

"Detective?" Jean-Charles took my former stance—back to me, front to the fire.

I bent over the plate of now lukewarm yet still amazing eggs but kept a close watch on Jean-Charles as I shoveled. His expression hardened, his color rose from mildly pink, through various shades of pissed, to a stroke-threatening fuchsia or maybe crimson—I'd never memorized the Crayola thing when I was young and periodically felt supremely inadequate. This morning, I just felt scarified, my personal mashup of scared and terrified.

Like a mushroom cloud, life was expanding and exploding, threatening to incinerate all vestiges of my existence—and all in a foreign language. Over my head, out of ideas, and somewhat at a personal relationship loss, I didn't know what to do but eat.

Yep, I was the poster child for stress eating. It never helped, but it made me feel better—until I could no longer writhe on the bed like an orgasmic porn star way overplaying it and end up sausaged into my skinny jeans. That was my self-respect metric—simple, but brutal and unassailable. Either they snapped, and I could still breathe, or I keeled over. Of course, my other rule was never, ever bring skinny jeans to Paris.

Romeo's voice came out muffled and unintelligible as Jean-Charles pressed the phone tightly to his ear. He nodded as he listened as if Romeo could see his response. We all did it out of habit, but that didn't make it any less silly. "Who?" he asked, murder infusing the one syllable.

Romeo's response solidified his fury. His color rose and his voice with it. "Nigel Wilde?" He breathed heavily as if the name carried a weight of history. "The pompous ass. He's a dead man."

I cringed—never a good thing to test the Fates and their sense of morbid humor. Threats said in anger tended to come back to haunt you. Trust me on that one. Gripping Jean-Charles's arm didn't get the moment of attention I wanted. He shrugged off my hand. "What wine was he saying was...inferior." He listened as a tic worked in his cheek. "Okay, he said it was counterfeit, that I had substituted inferior wine, packaging it as the very best, to charge a premium and pocket the difference. I understand." All that came out on a one breath rush, leaving him winded. He sucked in air, closing his eyes for a moment to capture elusive control. "What wine?" he asked, his voice was low, modulated, mimicking control.

Like the rest of his side of the conversation, Romeo's answer was unintelligible to this eavesdropper.

An evil smile stretched Jean-Charles's full lips, thinning them. "My own wine? The best of Burgundy? Why would I do that?"

Romeo's muffled voice sounded firm. Even though I couldn't make out the words, I could answer the question.

He'd do it because it would be easy.

After finishing the eggs, I collected the plates and put them on the lower shelf of the cart where they would be hidden from view by the drape of the white cloth.

"That, of course, is imbecilic. Thank you, Detective. Let me know if you actually come up with a viable theory."

Jean-Charles turned, his hand raised to hurl my phone across the room. I bolted to my feet. Grasping his hand with both of mine, I rescued the device. "If anyone is going to have the pleasure of shattering this tether, it'll be me. But, for now, we need information, and unfortunately, this is how I get it." I slipped it into the pocket of my robe.

Jean-Charles sank into a chair and idly held his hands to the warmth of the fire. "Why would they think I would counterfeit my own wine?"

"Oh, any number of reasons." He fired a warning scowl across my bow. Frankly, asking a question and not wanting an answer was disingenuous, so I continued. "Money. You said so yourself at M. Fabrice's; for some of your wines there is almost no supply and huge demand. Each bottle is worth a fortune." With my explanation, his eyes narrowed further, and his color rose.

"You are insinuating I am willing to ruin my family's reputation, our future income, for a few bottles?" He spit the words.

I held up my hands. "I'm insinuating nothing. You asked; I answered. I am not saying any of it is true."

"It is untrue, and it is said by someone who knows nothing about fine wine."

Boy, this guy was going to give me saddle sores riding to my own defense. This time, I let it go. "Which of your wines is the wine in question?"

That took a bit of starch out of him. He slumped deeper into the embrace of the chair, the anger leaving his posture. The flames from the fire licked his face with tongues of orange and red light. His silence told me everything. And despite his... disappointing behavior, I still wanted nothing more than to give him a big hug.

I didn't.

The fire drew my attention, and I too stared into it. The ancients used to divine the future in the flames. I stared and stared until the flames danced in my sight even when I closed my eyes. If a hint of the future lurked in there, it was now burned onto my eyeballs, yet still avoided detection. I'd start with what I knew. "Let me guess. The same wine somebody marinated poor Victor in, the '94 Estate Laurent?"

"That wine is making a statement. Not one the family intended, I can assure you."

"Curious bit of coincidence, don't you think?"

He straightened. "What are you saying?"

"Is that wine normally available in your restaurant? As I understand it, it is a small vintage and highly sought after with most of the bottles pre-ordered by your best customers."

"That is true, but I always like to keep a few bottles at my restaurants for special guests."

"And Nigel Wilde would qualify?"

"He is a wart on the ass of every winemaker. Through the years he has developed quite a following among would-be oenophiles. His reviews can often affect the price and the distribution of a vintage."

"So, everyone plays nice with him?"

"When we can. For us it is not quite so important with our pedigree. But we will accommodate him when possible."

"Could you check on where the bottle of wine in question tonight came from, if it was part of your private inventory or perhaps had a different origin?"

"Of course."

Tendrils of the chill air prodded me to add a log to the fire then poke at it to encourage heat. Blowing on it did the trick. I half listened as Jean-Charles barked into the phone. One side of the conversation wouldn't give me the complete picture, so I warmed myself and waited.

"I cannot believe it!" Jean-Charles sent his phone flying into the couch.

"Not your inventory?" I cocked an eyebrow at him in mock amusement.

"No! It was one of two bottles sent, special delivery. They arrived two days ago. My sommelier assumed I sent them as the shipment originated in France."

"But not with you."

Vibrating with anger, he raked a hand through his hair as he glared at me. "You are not going to believe who sent it."

"Enzo Laurent."

Jean-Charles crossed his arms and nodded. "It's all circling back to the Laurents."

"Or someone wants you to think so."

He didn't respond, preferring instead to focus his anger on a known enemy. It was time I got up-close and personal with the head of the Laurent family.

A house call would be in order, even though that sort of thing was frowned upon in these parts.

Good thing I'm not much for rules.

CHAPTER EIGHT

Y MEETING with Enzo Laurent was set for ten a.m.

He'd taken my call without question. One of the perks of teetering on a high rung of the Babylon International's corporate ladder. With a handshake, I could buy enough expensive wine to make a wine distributor have kittens.

But first a hot shower. Then armor designed by some of the locals—Dior sprang to mind, with a dash of Chanel confidence. Walking into a wolf's lair required some planning and strategy. As a child, I'd lapped up the message that sheep trusted wolves in sheep's clothing.

Problem was, I couldn't figure out whether I was the sheep or the wolf. However, I did know that, to keep from being eaten alive, I would need all my skills.

Too bad thumb screws weren't part of my executive utility belt.

Without so much as a kiss or a smile, Jean-Charles had launched off to do battle. Not that I blamed him. Murder and reputation assassination could extinguish even the most ardent libido. Trust me on that one, too. But it was better this way—

Jean-Charles leaving me to find trouble all by myself. Well, not for my libido, but Enzo Laurent would clam up tighter than a snitch on the hot seat if Jean-Charles walked into the room.

Maybe I could catch him off guard and charm a confession out of him—Perry Mason in *haute couture*.

Right.

RUNNING LATE, AS USUAL, AND OF COURSE, THE TRAFFIC WOULD tangle in the narrow streets. I paid the taxi driver and stepped into the fray two blocks from the address the concierge had given me. My long strides ate up the distance, far outpacing the cars. Well, some cars did catch up when the delectables in the window of an ancient patisserie slowed me down. The baker had twisted and turned, rolled, pressed flattened and plumped the dough, and then baked it into fabulous things—trees and shells and leaves and alligators—all of them wearing the glaze of an egg wash. Walking in Paris wasn't a choice; it was a necessity if one wished to avoid a serious case of dun-lop disease, or its second cousin, muffin-topitis. Although, with gastronomic temptation in every block, walking could also be considered a health hazard. It was as if the entire country wanted to be confounding.

Stuck in glacial traffic, the cabbies honked and yelled, gesturing wildly—a common bond that connected all of us, no matter where we lived. And I took reassurance in the fact that the sense of French decorum didn't extend to expressive cabbies. Not big on decorum myself, I felt a momentary kinship that would disappear the next time I crawled into the back of a cab and the driver pretended not to understand a word I said.

The building, on Rue St. Dominique in the Seventh Arrondissement not far from M. Fabrice's wine store, was curiously minimalistic in the European way of dispensing with ornate inanities, preferring to leave them to embellish the historically significant. Large, smooth blocks of stone comprised the façade, with a simple sign—LAURENT—spelled in individual silver letters affixed to the stone. Intent on the addresses and dodging pedestrians gnawing on baguettes and hurrying as I was, I almost missed it. The glass door was unmarked. I couldn't decide whether everyone knew the office location or the Laurents eschewed walk-in riff-raff.

The lobby was cold, austere, but for the large wooden table in the center under a crystal chandelier. An explosion of long-stemmed, blood-red roses in an antique vase added a splash of life, a beating heart in a lifeless vessel.

Security hid behind the fish-eyed camera lenses stuck discretely in not-so-hidden places. Guards watching prisoners. Vegas casinos wrote the book. Even so, I'd never gotten used to the vague bit of Big Brotherism.

As I rode the elevator to the top floor, the fifth, I flipped my phone to silent mode and dropped it back into my Birkin. Enzo Laurent's office was at the far end to my right. He'd told me so —that was the only way I knew. No signs. No arrows in multiple languages. And no unctuous staff to greet me once I'd pushed through the heavy glass doors. Well, not if you didn't count the impeccably styled, sunken-cheeked older woman who looked up from her computer and stood as I approached.

She greeted me with a frown as if I was an expected but unwelcome annoyance. A wide gray swatch swooped through her mousy brown hair that she wore parted in the middle and bobbed at her shoulders. Her style was inimitably Parisian-professional: a simple starched white shirt and a single piece of adornment—a gold heart-shaped locket like the one the Big Boss had gifted to Mona upon my birth. As a bit of self-expression, she wore her Hermes scarf as a sash, threaded through the belt loops of her black slacks and knotted in front. One lone photo added a hint of personality to her workspace. A boy. A teenager, maybe. Pale skin, eyes dark and too large, thin wisps of blond hair. "Ms. O'Toole." A statement, not a question. So very French.

Even though I wanted to say no just to see her head explode, I nodded.

Why was it, even the cold and uglies still had melodious French accents?

She pressed a button under her desk and the large set of double wooden doors to my left hissed open like the secret passage to an inner sanctum, where, if you dared trespass, they locked the doors behind you. And nobody knew where I was...

I leaned around one of the doors trying to get a good look into the room beyond.

"He's expecting you." I jumped, which amused her. "Coffee?"

"Please." Straightening my shoulders, I marshaled all the badass I could. My position as a valued customer opened the door to this little fishing expedition. But I'd better get my corporate on if my bluff had any chance of working.

"American?" Enzo Laurent's personal assistant asked, a slight sneer in her voice.

"Espresso." I tossed off the request as if slightly insulted. "Make it a double, thank you."

With a slight arch of surprise to both eyebrows, her look of disdain faded...slightly. Actually, I hated espresso—a bold imposter that promised more jolt in return for enduring a muddy tar that tasted like last night's indiscretions...all of them. In fact, my frou-frou brew packed a bigger punch, but being American was enough of a disadvantage on this side of the pond. I wasn't going to erode my already evaporating respect any further, so espresso it was.

As I stood there, she gave me a slightly curious grimace. "Will there be anything else?"

Sure, take that stick out of your butt, you'll feel better. Come to think of it, so will I, I thought, then smiled sweetly. "No. Thank you."

I took a deep breath and brushed down my skirt—I'd settled on Versace. The Dior seemed just too...arrogant. I'd shouldered my Birkin—a bit of Hermes wizardry that separated women from vast sums of money for a rather mundane bag. Some years ago, my father had thought it the perfect gift for me. I'd wondered about that until I realized the bag was an entry card into exalted social circles. Not that I aspired to be accepted— such rarified air was way too high octane for this simple showman—but sometimes it behooved me to be seen as belonging.

Like now.

Just inside the doors I stopped, rooted by a Dorothy-in-Oz moment. I'd left Kansas and arrived in Oz. Where the vestibule had been all marble and cold, Enzo Laurent's office was all wood and warmth. The whole thing felt like a British library in a grand country manor. High ceilings. Walls of bookcases that held actual books and ladders to reach the top rows. And these were not books to impress, arranged by color or importance or whatever suited the decorator. But books to be read arranged at the whim of their owner. The most loved, with their broken spines and faded covers stood within easy reach on the lower shelves. A few pieces of art, well lit, graced the walls. A Caravaggio, maybe, but I wasn't sure. And a David Hockney—that one I was sure of. Enzo Laurent presented himself as a man of varied tastes and boundless curiosity, an interesting and formidable combination.

Backlit by a wall of windows, the man himself, I presumed, rose to greet me. Tall and carrying a paunch, still he moved around his desk with the grace of an athlete, and the slight limp of a former footballer or maybe his sport had been rugby. The mashed features and the hint of a droop in his left eye told me I was close. His thick mane of salt-and-pepper hair drifted past his collar in the back and hung thick and full in the front giving him an Albert Finney allure. As if he knew it and wanted to further the comparison, M. Laurent favored rumpled tweed, khakis, an open collar, and short sleeves despite the January weather. He shrugged into his jacket as he stuck out a hand.

I took it, bracing for the robust pump I knew would be coming.

He didn't disappoint. "Ms. O'Toole. Such an unexpected pleasure." He pulled around a heavy, ornately carved wooden chair. "Please." He motioned me into it, then, once I'd settled, took an identical one next to mine. Close enough to be collegial, but not so close as to be intimidating or inappropriate. Comfortable in his skin, oozing confidence and...maleness...the guy had his game down, making all the right moves.

Was that assessment cynical or merely safely skeptical?

Was he a man to be bedded or beheaded?

Were those the only two options my brain now considered?

Was I losing my mind?

Even I didn't know, but I found comfort in my ability to ask the question.

"What brings you to Paris?" He had an interesting way of speaking. The accent was French but the cadence and word choice much more British. I almost expected an "old girl" tacked on the end of his question.

A bruise bloomed on his jaw. Jean-Charles's father had mentioned Enzo taking one for the opposition. Feud or no feud, I liked him for that.

Conflicted for sure, but it's where I live.

And nothing like a difficult question to make me refocus.

I inhaled through my nose and settled back. "What brings me to Paris?" I had a lot of answers to that one, some spun, some not, but something told me Enzo Laurent already knew. "Business and pleasure." Suddenly uncomfortable, I arranged my rather tight skirt, so it managed to cover the important parts. That left me with perhaps a hint of dignity but left my legs exposed. Wearing clothes designed for a much smaller person demanded attention and a good bit of confidence, neither of which were in plentiful supply at the moment.

He leaned on the arm of the chair closest to me. "How is Jean-Charles?"

The question, not unexpected, came a bit more bluntly and quickly than I expected. "Fine." I kept my voice calm, conversational. "I'm enjoying meeting his family."

Enzo snorted. "Then you are a better man than I. Granted, Jean-Louis is a kind man. But he is an old fool. His wife is the warrior. Jean-Charles is a combination of both, sometimes to his benefit..."

"Other times not?" I smiled. "Perfection isn't my thing. Far too difficult to live up to."

With a nod, he ceded the point. "And Desiree is a bit lost."

I couldn't disagree. "And Emma Moreau?"

"You've met the good *commissaire*?" He seemed surprised.

"The three of you go back a long way?"

He eased back, increasing the distance between us. "If you expect me to tell secrets, cast aspersions, or create friction where there shouldn't be any, I'll not be a party to that."

Yep, he totally had the whole younger, roguish Albert Finney thing going on.

Secrets. That word was first. And that word always got my attention.

But secrets, like distant stars, hid from sight when examined directly.

"I would never put you on the spot. I can handle my personal life." A total lie, but it sounded so grown up. *Be it until you become it as Mona would say.* "I just was wondering if she was a straight shooter in her capacity as police *commissaire* or is there some conflict of interest I should know about?"

"History creates a layered fabric."

How he said that with a straight face... If he'd prefaced that with a "me thinks" I would've snorted, and I probably wouldn't have been horrified either. Regardless, his mastery of Old English cadence left me a bit slack-jawed. "Okay, I'll watch my back." I tugged on my skirt, but the fabric wouldn't budge. I leveled a gaze. "Look, I'm new to the whole centuries of bad blood hatred thing. Americans, our attention span lasts fifteen minutes, max. So, help me out here. Can I hear, not so much the story—history being immutable and all of that—but where you stand on all of this? Your jaw must be quite sore. Never heard of an avowed enemy taking a shot to save a rival."

He gently touched his jaw, wincing as pressure found pain.

"Who popped you there?"

"I didn't get a good look. Dressed nicely. He'd knocked Jean-Louis down. I was more concerned about that."

"Why? To hear people tell it, you two are at odds these days. Serious odds."

He shook his head as if fighting an internal battle. "We are not enemies, although Jean-Louis has taken up the sword with more vigilance than those of us left. He and my father sparred, but, unbeknownst to most of the family, they met over very fine sauterne and brokered peace through business. Both our families have benefitted from the alliance."

"Jean-Louis. Jean-Charles's father?"

"You have not been formally introduced." The thought seemed to amuse him.

"Last night did get away from all of us." I tried to circle him back to my original question. "Did you get a look at the man you scuffled with?"

"I've already given Emma my statement. I didn't get much of a look. He burst into the kitchen throwing punches and generally flailing about until he bolted out the back."

"Where did you go after you left the kitchen?"

We both paused as his assistant interrupted. "The file you

asked for." She fingered a manila envelope she clutched, then she put it on his desk, lingering.

Enzo ignored her. Instead, he gave me a derisive smile. "If I didn't know any better, I'd say I was being interrogated."

"He came back here." The assistant jumped in. "We both worked late."

Enzo gave her a startled glance but recovered quickly. "It was late here but still early in the U.S., and I had to return some calls from our retail partners there. Is Jean-Louis alright? I know his heart is weak and I believe he took a glancing blow."

"Glancing or not, it still split his skin. He's weak, but recovering, according to the warrior." He eyed his assistant who still hovered. "Daria, the coffee please?"

He didn't watch her go. Instead, he eyed me like a prized heifer at the state fair. "Madame Bouclet, she doesn't scare you?"

"No, she terrifies me. But I'll never show it. And if you breathe a word, I'll deny it."

He threw back his head and roared with laughter.

Thankfully, the comedienne masquerading as a distant and cold assistant and working on her straight-man skills interrupted my mental walkabout and saved me from my dubious making-friends-and winning-people personality. "Your coffee."

I accepted the tiny saucer with the thimble of coffee. Not a hint of steam. If she'd touched it, she'd probably turned it to ice. The dollhouse accessories had looming disaster written all over them. "Thank you. Please let me know when Barbie and Ken arrive. They'll be driving a pink Cadillac. Her skirt will be inappropriately short." I was one to talk.

Silence.

I glanced up as I pretended to blow on the icy brew. Both of them stared at me, poised in their respective activities.

Damn! I'd said that out loud.

"Are you expecting others?" Enzo asked as he continued with doctoring his coffee. American. With cream.

Damn.

"Don't mind me. I haven't had more than ten winks of sleep in two days." I pretended that my outburst was normal. Which, unfortunately, it was. "Jean-Charles received an order of two bottles of Estate Laurent three days ago at his restaurant in my hotel in Vegas. The manifest indicated they came from you."

Even though he kept a slight smile, a tic flared in his cheek. "Really?" He shot a nervous glance at his assistant.

She returned it with a flat stare.

His hands paused over the coffee mug. "I can assure you, I initiated no such order."

"Curious, don't you think?" What was it with these two?

He continued with his coffee ministrations.

"Especially since the wine was counterfeit." Nothing like goading the tiger with a lie. Okay, a suspected but as yet unproven bit of truth. Is that the same as a lie? I chose to think not.

He didn't even flinch. "Who says?"

"Nigel Wilde."

That bit of news pushed him back in his chair. As he lifted his coffee mug and breathed deeply, he waved the name away. "He is a *poseur.* A know-nothing who the uninitiated pay tens of thousands to offer unfounded opinions. If you dig, you will find he authenticated a lot that a collector bought for over a million Euros. The lot turned out to be fake. Nigel Wilde paid handsomely to have his participation covered up."

His assistant, with one corner of her mouth lifted in an odd expression of I-told-you-so, backed out of the room. Either he'd demanded regal subservience, or she thought I might do something rash and needed to not turn the other cheek. Always nice to make an impression.

"She knows Nigel Wilde?" I watched her slip through the door, leaving it open a crack.

"I have no idea, but everyone in the wine world knows of him."

"So you didn't send the wine to Jean-Charles?"

"Of course not. He has better access than I do." He said that without a hint of vitriol. "I'm sorry about your sleep-deprivation." Enzo circled back to pick up the conversation at the point at which he'd lost control. "It can make you see problems where there are none." He took a sip of his coffee and watched me over the rim of his mug as if I might miss his point. "You'd be best to leave this muddle to the professionals." His word choice was cute, his tone light, but the hint of a threat lurked in the banter.

"Funny. Usually sleep deprivation just has me walking into walls and making outlandish connections. I guess you haven't heard about the dust-up at M. Fabrice's wine shop in the wee hours this morning?"

"Yes, I've heard. He just phoned."

He phoned. Every one of the players so far had a history with the others—a history they could use to obfuscate or clarify, depending. "Why did he phone?"

"We are business associates. The wine was...unique. He wanted to explain."

I felt like I was riding a pony who ran away with me and now wanted to stop. I dug in my heels. "And?"

"He said he bought it from someone in Hong Kong, a collector who wanted it sold a bottle at a time so as not to diminish value."

"Like a hedge fund dumping its portfolio."

He flashed a tight smile. "Similar."

I'd sure like to know who this mysterious man in Hong Kong was. I'd bet my next year's salary that Sinjin Smythe-Gordon was up to his baby blues in this mess. "Your thoughts? Did you know this Victor Martin?"

"Not that I'm aware of." He angled a thoughtful look my

direction, but he didn't hold my gaze for long. "You're rather inquisitive, for a fiancée."

I took a moment to frame my answer. Being passed off as a mere fiancée was a pisser. But righteous indignation would get me nowhere. "I am the head of problem management for a very large hotel conglomerate. I can help you both if you let me."

"Problem management?" He flashed a smile. "Is that a degree path?"

"The University of Life offers an advanced degree." I quit worrying about playing a game and got down to business. "He claimed to have worked for Paul Bay."

"The *negociant?*" Enzo seemed genuinely surprised. "If he did, he was unknown to me. And I make it my business to know all who are producing wine in Bordeaux."

"Even the mediocre stuff?" I hid my smile.

He put a hand to his chest in mock insult. "Please, mediocre is not an adjective we use in Bordeaux."

"Perhaps you should, when appropriate. Arrogance breeds mediocrity." Before he could counter, I hurried on. "Why would they choose the wine from what was formerly your family's vineyard? Perhaps pointing a finger?"

"That certainly would lead to the conclusion that whoever it was might have an issue with us. But we were not responsible. We would not point a finger at ourselves." He leaned forward and moved a paperweight slightly, angling it just so.

I knew that drill. My paperweight that I repositioned when I needed to wrest a bit of control back from a situation that was spiraling the opposite direction was Lucite and contained a cockroach. A gift from my employees as a thank you for containing a rather odious client and his many thousand Palmetto bugs. The memory shivered through me. "If you knew about the murder and the Bouclets' interest, then why were you surprised I'd met *Commissaire* Moreau?"

"I hadn't realized you'd been brought into that bit of ugliness. By implication and assumption, I thought you'd met Emma at the Bouclets' party."

"And that surprised you?"

"Yes. It is considered rather bad form to include one's former wives at a party to present one's future wife."

"Wife?" I swallowed hard. The thimble of coffee clattered on the saucer. For the first time, I could understand Jean-Charles's predilection for throwing breakable things. Oh, how I'd love to see the tiny bits of porcelain shatter off the stone facing around the fireplace. How I hated things ill-designed for their intended purpose, in this case, caffeination. And how I hated men who kept secrets, important secrets.

Enzo waved a hand. "I'm not sure they ever managed to get officially married. They'd run off, both of them very young. The families were apoplectic. Jean-Louis and his father caught the kids somewhere near the Italian border. I never knew the whole of it. She was the daughter of the winemaker. Which in and of itself is unimportant. But the families found her unfit."

Unfit. The daughter of a winemaker. I'd love to see his reaction and then punish him for it when I trotted out my lineage. "I thought everyone revered winemakers."

"Yes, we all work in partnership for the wine."

"But as a winemaker's daughter, Emma was unfit."

Enzo rested an ankle across one knee. His foot jiggled up and down. "You misunderstand. She was not unfit because of her family. She was unfit because of her personality. Her father has been the head winemaker for the Bouclets for decades. The Moreaus are like family."

"He's still the winemaker?" I guess business did trump emotion around these parts—at least when it came to wine.

"And very important, as you might imagine."

"Tell me about Emma. What was the Bouclets' objection?"

"She..." He bit his lip as he worked for the words. "She was a bit hot-tempered, wanted what she wanted. You understand.

She would always push too hard, take one step too far. And in our business, maintaining our reputations, being seen as stewards not only of the wine and its history but also of the land and the people who work for us. It takes a soft touch and a kind heart."

"I see." Emma was a damn-the-torpedoes kind of gal. Glad he'd sounded the alarm and given me fair warning. Now perhaps I had a chance not to be broadsided. Of course, like any good journalist, before a fact became a fact, it had to be corroborated by two independent, trustworthy sources.

If the story was true about Emma and Jean-Charles, Enzo Laurent had gotten what he wanted. Now he knew Jean-Charles kept me in the dark about important things. My anger flared, but I tamped it down. Wrong recipient. I'd learned something about Enzo Laurent that would be just cause for a case of red-ass, but as I said, self-restraint would win this day.

With studied care, I set the saucer on Enzo's desk as I let a thick cloak of composure settle back over me. Nothing like a good case of fury to make me go stone-cold and deadly. I gave him a long steady stare. He finally looked away, and I bit down on a gloat. "How did you come to be in the Bouclets' kitchen last night? Jean-Louis said you had quite the story."

He shifted to look out the window. I didn't blame him. The view of *Les Invalides*, the sunlight sparkling off the golden dome giving Napoleon the luminescent resting place he thought fitting, was magnificent. "It's not so much a story really, as much as it is a gut feeling."

"And Jean-Louis wouldn't listen."

"No. He didn't want to hear what I think." Enzo swiveled to spear me with an intense gaze. "I know someone is working to drive a stake in between us, to torpedo our business alliance."

"You all hate each other. How hard would it be?"

"That is personal. The other is business. It is wine." He said that last bit with a reverence that transcended petty centuries-old feuds. "And personal never comes in the way of wine."

Not that I totally got it or anything, but I was beginning to understand. And I also understood they'd all have to be super-human not to let the personal boil over no matter how good the wine. "You didn't have anything to do with stealing the wine?" I watched for a response.

He wasn't surprised. "No, shocked to hear about it. Very clever, but all that lovely wine! This will make things worse."

"You knew about the wine?" My turn, but I was actually surprised.

"No, I knew about the wine cellar. Jean-Louis and I met there often to hash out our business arrangements, go over the vintages and the production, work on pricing and distribution allotments. It is a very special wine with a long lineage that gives it much prestige. But I had no idea he planned on bringing his library of wine there for the party. I have no idea what he was thinking."

"Perhaps he thought it might be time to share the bounty of his life's work with those he holds dear."

"Sentimental to the last." Enzo seemed envious.

"You met in the wine cellar at the Bouclets'?"

He nodded, knowing how it must look.

"The one place the two of you could be assured of privacy." I nodded as more pieces of the puzzle presented themselves. Problem was, I didn't know where they fit. "Did anyone else in your family or circle of close acquaintances know the location and inventory in the cellar?"

He pursed his lips and shook his head. "No one. That was the point."

"Not even Miss Hathaway out there?" I tilted my head toward the vestibule.

"Who?"

"*Beverly Hillbillies*? Mr. Drysdale's secretary? Absolutely no expression of emotion ever?" I said to a blank look. "Your assistant?"

He ran a hand through his hair, his attention turning toward the window and the view beyond. "We made it a point to keep things on the down low. No one knew."

I wanted to point out what he said bordered on the impossible, but, in my past dealings with men of his stature, telling them they are stupid and naïve rarely is a good strategy unless your goal is to be tossed out on your ass. "What about the staff?"

"We met when no one was about. None of them are allowed in Jean-Louis's office. It is his sanctuary. And, as you must know, the entrance to the cellar is quite hidden."

"No one saw you?"

"No. We have a very public family battle. If word got out we were meeting in a clandestine fashion…"

"People might think you were plotting to keep the Frank Lius of the world out and the old fusty folks in."

He shifted uncomfortably. "People are always ready to vilify those at the top of the heap. Even when their *facts* are only suppositions and their claims unfounded."

No argument there. "Something we Americans are great at. So, something you said earlier I didn't understand. You said the theft of the Bouclets' wine will make things so much worse. What things?"

"My grandfather worked in the fields. He tended every vine as if they were his children. He used to tell me that wine is for the people. They are what makes the wine great. So now we have wine that sells for much more than an average man can pay. It is no longer for the people. When this happens, the wine will not be great anymore. If no one drinks it, no families share it at their table, then what is it for? Now people collect it as if it is fine china or a silly toy that catches fire. The price goes up and up. Now we have wine auctions. This is not what wine is for. And when they took a man's wine like that, they stole Jean-Louis's heart. And they are driving the price of that wine up as it becomes more scarce. The thieves will sell it on the black market, so, where Jean-Louis would share it with family and friends, now it will be on a shelf, behind glass, as a prize to show how important and how ignorant its owner is."

"You think that's why they stole the wine? To sell it?"

"Money. Greed. It drives men to do many bad things."

"Indeed. Why would someone care about your business alliance with the Bouclets?"

"Together we are very strong."

"You know, in the States, the Hunt brothers darn near went bankrupt trying to corner the silver market in defiance of the Powers That Be."

He shook his head and sighed, a teacher with a specifically dense student. He drained the American coffee I would've killed for, then set his mug down next to my playset before answering. "It is not this. It is about quality in a time where every rich textile manufacturer from North Carolina, or retired sports figure, or rich Chinese can buy a beautiful vineyard in Bordeaux and call himself a winemaker. It is about keeping our heritage, about being true to the wine."

Easy to say sitting in the catbird seat, but he had a point. If you paid attention to your product, took care of your people, and operated with a clear set of rules imbued with integrity, success had a chance to flourish. My father had taught me the same lesson. "I see. And someone got to Jean-Louis, and he refused to give you the exclusive on the wine from what was formerly your family's vineyard." I watched the red climb his neck and then pop on his cheeks. Bull's-eye.

"That agreement had been in place for two centuries. My family considered it a bit of payment if you will."

"Blood money."

"Crass but accurate, I suppose. When Jean-Louis backed out

of our deal, it was like pulling out the dagger; then all the blood rushes out after it."

"So you canceled the exclusive distribution agreement."

He raked a hand through his truly magnificent mane. "I am old and not as in control of my emotions as I once was."

"I thought it worked the other way around, hot-headed youth and all of that. But, I'll give you that excuse if you need it. Who was it, do you think, who got to Jean-Louis?"

"I don't think; I know. I just can't prove it."

"I am so used to that; trust me." I waited for a name. Pushing him wouldn't help.

"Frank Liu."

Not a name I expected. "Tell me about him."

"He bought one of the venerable *châteaus, Château Shasay*. A third *cru*, but very nice wine and quite successful. We offered him distribution on several of his labels. It's been profitable for both of us."

There was so much subtext there the words were practically floating on it. "So, what's his beef?"

"He is convinced his wine is worthy of a higher classification." He left the implication hanging.

Jean-Charles had given me the history here, thank God. "And that never happens."

"No."

"Just because something used to be great doesn't mean it always will be."

"I would agree." He softened his look. "Except for when you are in France and speaking about wine. If the *Grands crus* are not immutable, then the…"

"There will be no keepers of the flame and the wine world would shift on its axis." I reached over and busted through all bounds of social interaction by giving him a pat on the knee. "I'm an expert in an overblown sense of self-importance. I think we've got a bit of that going on here." I held up a hand to stop his counter-argument. "But I also understand. The past deserves its reverence. But that doesn't mean new blood can't appreciate the weight of history and their place in it." I paused as I considered all the options. "Any idea what little *bon mot* he might have whispered in Jean-Louis's ear?"

Enzo shifted uneasily. "According to Jean-Louis, Frank told him that we were undercutting his price on the Bouclet vintages, offering his wine at a discount or as an incentive for our clients to buy other *Grand Cru* wines."

"Were you?"

He shifted uneasily. "Sometimes. The market is very competitive."

"And selling at a discount, for whatever the reason, undercuts the Bouclets' perception of quality."

"Precisely."

I raised an eyebrow.

"Oxford." His lips curled slightly. "Everyone asks."

"And giving the exclusive for Estate Laurent to M. Fabrice?"

"A knife to the heart."

"He was family."

"They were never close." He wanted to say more; I could see it in his eyes. Instead he pressed his lips together.

For each question answered, thousands more lurked in the wings like understudies waiting to take center stage. "Why?"

He pursed his lips, unwilling to speak.

I'd have to try that question on my fiancé. "What do you think Frank Liu's plan is exactly?"

"I've thought this through, and, as I said, I only have a gut instinct. But he wishes to break our alliance. The classifications are less protected that way. Not in reality, but in his way of thinking. He called here recently and said he was going to make a formal complaint to the ruling body and perhaps file a lawsuit claiming Jean-Louis and myself, personally, have exerted influence to keep the Bouclet vineyards as *Premier Cru*."

"And to keep Frank Liu's out." I didn't have to remind him he'd planted the seeds of his own business demise with Jean-Louis by cutting prices.

"It just wouldn't be right. You cannot buy yourself a *Grand Cru* classification."

Ah, a hint to the snobbery underscoring this whole silly business. Wouldn't be right for someone to buy his way in? Wouldn't be right for that someone to be a non-Frenchman? One worse than the other, but both unpalatable. This classification system was supposed to be about the wine, not the winemakers.

But when had absolute power not corrupted absolutely, as Lord Acton said? And too much inbreeding results in serious issues. That one was from me, not Lord Acton.

"Is there any validity to his claims?" Of course, to an American, the whole system sounded rigged. I struggled to accept the French way.

"Of course not."

"Well, grounded in fact or not, I'm sure the bad publicity will not help either of you. The wine world is terribly small, terribly snotty, and filled with people just waiting to tear someone else down." Much like the world at large, but that was cause for a drinking binge at a later date.

"Yes, it will hurt us. A man's reputation is all he has."

That wasn't limited to the penis-bestowed set, but I didn't quibble. "Assassination by implication, it's a national pastime in the States."

He seemed to deflate.

"The problem is Frank Liu's plan seems to be working, doesn't it?"

CHAPTER NINE

$\mathcal{T}$HE DAY had turned cloudy, and a cold wind kicked up, rushing up my short skirt like a groper copping a feel. And I had nobody to slap for the indignity.

Something caused me to glance back at the building. High on the top floor in the corner, a thin figure stood in the window watching me. When I turned her way, she stepped back, letting the shadows hide her.

Odd.

In fact, the whole visit with Enzo Laurent had left me feeling a bit off-kilter. Like a trapper luring his prey to the trap, M. Laurent meted out tidbits, urging me along the path he'd chosen. Not that I bought any of it. But it was interesting he felt the need.

While I buckled the belt on my coat, cinching it tight, I took a moment to survey the area. Trying to avoid myself and my problems, and with no one desperate for my opinion, I was at a loss.

I needed a target, something to do. Shopping would be too easy. Drinking too hard.

I watched the people flowing past, admiring the men, and

wishing for a bit of the women's sense of style and ease with which they carried it. A man on the other side of the street caught my attention, maybe because, unlike everyone else, he wasn't moving. Instead, he stared into the window of a *boulangerie*. Just imagining the eatables in the window made my stomach growl. Like a spoiled child, my stomach constantly complained. I'd fed it eggs and croissants, but was that enough? No.

How could I be a better me when each body part conspired against me?

Dressed in a dark overcoat, a hat pulled low, his hands clasped behind his back, he stared. I let my glance drift past him another time. He stared all right.

At me. Or more correctly, at my reflection in the slightly mirrored glass.

I couldn't imagine having attracted anyone's attention, but his stare held more than casual interest. Either someone had put him onto me, or he'd misread me thinking I'd be interested in a flash of his junk at some point—I knew the type, they slithered around Vegas from time to time. He had the perfect coat for it, and the crazy fascination of a creeper identifying a mark. He looked a little on the young side for that sort of debauchery, but this was France. Maybe they grew them younger here. Either way, he bore looking into.

Semi-familiar with the area, I chose a direction and, matching my speed to the crowd's, I blended in. The guy peeled himself from the window and followed me, keeping his distance. But in the windows lining Rue St. Dominique, he was easy to keeps tabs on. Now, I was no expert, but his tailing technique seemed a bit unschooled, or perhaps rusty...if I gave him the benefit of being Parisian. Not feeling particularly magnanimous toward the locals at the moment, I chose to hold him to a higher standard.

I strolled as if I hadn't a care in the world. The wind was

cold, the clouds scudding as the humidity rose. My short skirt had been the perfect costume for my performance at Laurent Wines, but it was a poor choice for this sort of cat-and-mouse game. Thin-blooded, I shivered and tried to marshal my thoughts. Who had sent this ding-dong? The aromas of fresh-baked bread lured me into a boulangerie about halfway down the block. I made a fuss of the whole ordering and paying thing, acting the dumb American. All the while, I watched the man following me in the many mirrors slanted around the space.

He was nervous. I took my time, playing to his curiosity to bring him closer.

As I was counting out the money with the numbing stupidity of an arrogant tourist, I caught him peeking in the window directly. This game I could play. Gnawing on the baguette like a local, I exited the store, hung a left, and kept heading toward the Eiffel Tower. I didn't so much as toss a hint of interest at my stalker, hoping my feigned ignorance would make him even sloppier.

It did.

As I strolled without a care, he eased closer, using the unsuspecting pedestrians between us to shield him. Nice try. In this well-turned-out crowd, he stuck out like a cheap hood.

And I was itching to know who had stuck him on me.

At the next intersection, I dipped to my left, disappearing around the corner. Immediately, I flattened myself to the wall on my left, tucking into a shallow doorway, and waited. If memory served, this was a narrow alley with little foot traffic. A glance to my left confirmed it. Now, to be patient—not my best thing, especially on a bad day.

But recent events had me hardwired to pissed off, and somebody had to pay.

Coiled for a confrontation, I fisted my hands at my sides and tried to breathe. I set my bag at my feet but off to the side so as not to interfere. I was ready.

I didn't have to wait long. I caught a whiff of cheap cologne before I heard him. Then came the halting steps as he'd inch forward, then stop to listen. If I could've silenced my heartbeat, I would have as I froze, waiting. I could hear him closer now, quick, excited breaths. He was unsure. His boldness betrayed him. I knew his thoughts. I was a woman, not a formidable opponent, he thought. Weak and stupid. Let's get this over with.

Bring it on, asshat.

I braced my weight on my left foot, my elbow cocked, my body coiled. For the first time today, I was thankful my coat was thin.

He was close. Close enough to know he'd had garlic in his morning eggs. My thoughts settled, my vision telescoped, and I focused all my energy into listening and translating what I heard into a picture of what he was doing. He eased toward the corner, wondering if he should take a peek.

I willed him to do just that.

The soft scraping of cloth on the bricks of the building.

He took a chance.

Tucked out of sight, I pressed back. More soft rustling as he leaned farther. The shuffle of a shoe as he stepped and leaned, bolder now.

I breathed.

One more step.

Come on. Do it.

A few interminable silent seconds. Then I heard it. Another step, this time exposing himself further. I could picture him leaning, his weight moving forward.

I counted to three.

Then I launched myself out of my hiding place. Surprise froze him momentarily, but long enough. His weight on his front foot, he couldn't dodge easily. With my entire bulk behind it, my elbow arced toward his nose, connecting with a satisfying crunch of cartilage. He grunted as his hands flew to his face. His eyes wide, he recoiled in surprise and pain.

As he retreated, I moved in. With both hands to his chest, I shoved...hard. He stumbled as he tried to back away. Blood seeped through the cup of his fingers. He muttered in French, fast and unintelligible.

"Who sent you?" I pushed him again.

This time he fell, landing with a thud as his elbow broke his fall. He rolled onto his back.

Anticipating—this wasn't my first schoolyard brawl—I fell on him, a knee to his chest, my hands holding his arms to the ground. He probably had a view right up my Versace, but I didn't care. In a fight, vanity could get you killed. First win, then feel bad about it.

If I had one more hand it would be around his throat. "Who sent you?" I asked again, refraining from the American habit of shouting repetitively when faced with a non-English speaker.

At his blank look, I struggled to find the words in French. I failed. Using my other knee to hold an arm down and free one of my hands, I pulled open his coat and searched his pockets. Blood dripped from one nostril, and his nose listed to one side. Recently I'd sworn off guilt, so I ignored the pangs, with marginal success.

He remained calm as he watched me, his gaze never leaving mine as I felt for a wallet or any other identification. Most of these guys were smart enough to make the guessing game at least a bit of a challenge.

This one wasn't.

My fingers found a thin leather fold-over in his inside breast pocket. I flipped it open, and my heart fell. "The police? Shit. Why didn't you tell me?"

As I backed off him, scraping together the shards of my dignity, he gave me a slight shrug. "I am not so good at this. It is

—how do you say it—an embarrassment? To be beaten by a woman."

Okay, the guilt was kicking in. He was a kid like Detective Romeo back home. But with a touch of exotic. "What's your name?"

"Sam. Sam Desai." In no rush to jump to his feet, he sat cross-legged and pressed a handkerchief to his nose, pinching it into line.

I couldn't watch—it must've hurt like hell. "Indian?" I tugged my skirt so that it at least marginally satisfied the fashion police even if it still brushed the boundaries of common decency.

"On my father's side."

I brushed back my hair then tightened the belt of my coat. A run laddered down one shin from a tear in my stocking on the knee. A splash of blood on the elbow of my coat was drying to a dark brown. Without a mirror, I couldn't see any more damage, so I pretended that's all there was. "Well, following an American citizen is a bit outside your legal boundaries, isn't it?"

"I am with the Judicial Police. We have been asked to investigate the murder of Victor Martin." With his nose looking more like it did when he walked into my elbow, although bloody, bruised and a bit soft, he levered himself to his feet. He brushed down his coat, but, other than that cursory straightening, he seemed disinterested in his appearance.

Even though he pulled himself to his fullest height, I still had him by a few inches. "And how am I related to the investigation? Did your presiding judge order my surveillance?" A judge presided over criminal investigations in Paris with the investigations themselves handled by the Judicial Police under the supervision and at the direction of the presiding judge. To an American, the term "judge" was a bit of a misnomer—these judges were more akin to Chief Detectives. My opinion, but the only way I could really make sense of it all.

My new friend Sam scuffed a toe. "No."

"Your boss, then?"

"What is boss?" His eyes were blue, so clear and bright with youth and naiveté. Also, just like Romeo. Or like Romeo had been when he started out.

I'd shown Romeo the ropes, but I wasn't sure I'd done him any favors. "The person who tells you what to do."

"Ah, *la patron*, she..." He stopped. An appealing pink flushed his cheeks.

"Say no more." I slapped his identification into his chest. His *boss* had some answering to do. Was her curiosity personal? Or was it about murder? If I committed one, as I felt inclined to do at the moment, then the distinction would blur. But, I couldn't give her that satisfaction, could I? "I won't say a word about your nose. The story is up to you. What did your chief want with me?"

"Only to know where you went and who you talked with."

"Only." He had the decency to look away. "You tell her..." I looked up at the Eiffel Tower, the top third visible above the buildings. "Never mind. I'll tell her myself."

COMMISSAIRE EMMA MOREAU HAD SHOT TO THE TOP OF MY SHIT list. What sort of bullshit stunt was that, siccing a wet-behind-the-ears junior cop on my tail? That could've gotten him killed and me thrown in the slammer, in a foreign country, with my in-country friends dwindling by the day.

Well, if I was going to die on Devil's Island, I'd be damned if it would be for busting some kid's nose. No, I would earn it. And I would enjoy it. For a moment, I wallowed in the feeling of my hands around Emma Moreau's throat. Okay, way over-fantasizing. And my Versace and Dior would never translate to Devil's Island. Better keep my nose clean...but that didn't mean I had to be nice.

I'd sent the young *commissaire* off to report whatever he wanted to whoever expected to hear it. As far as his nose went, mum would be the word on my end. No use making the kid suffer before he was even old enough for long pants. Wrong country, I know, but I liked the analogy.

As I walked, thoughts pinged around in my head. With no destination, I wandered, keeping an eye out for another fool deciding to stick to my ass. Two in one day would be pushing it. But still switched to my serious anger mode and with no one to punish, I'd almost welcome it...almost. To be honest, for some time now, the whole life-and-death thing had been wearing me down like a pumice stone on a callus. I was down to the raw.

I needed answers. And I needed to go home.

Home.

My father had always told me, when looking for answers, the best path began at the beginning. But where was the beginning in this whole mess?

If not the exact beginning, which remained shrouded in the distant past, the murder of Victor Martin certainly changed the game we all had been playing. I'd encountered Victor in M. Fabrice's wine shop, as good a place to start as any. I stepped back out of the pedestrian flow to check my bearings. Only a few blocks, no more. Funny how my subconscious had led me where I needed to go.

As I pushed through the door, a familiar smell wafted over me. Wine. Old wine. Exceptional wine. And death. A bell announced my arrival with a merry tinkle. M. Fabrice appeared from the back. Despite the smile, he looked as bad as I felt.

"It is bad, *non?*"

I had no idea exactly what he referred to but, since really everything was pretty dismal, I nodded and shrugged, fighting tears. Death dogged my every move and worried my every thought. Still too early to call home. Would I find Death had visited there as well? Someday I would have to face life without the Big Boss. Please, not today.

Using the theory that no news is good news, I summoned a wan smile.

"Come." M. Fabrice touched my elbow, then turned, expecting me to follow.

Thankfully, the police had removed the barrel holding Victor Martin. The bottles were gone, the wine mopped up. Still with a case of redass ignited by the *commissaire* who didn't miss a beat letting me know how much she'd like me out of the way, I wondered if Jean-Charles could use his *connections* to find out what they might have found.

That was cynical *and* sarcastic. Funny how quickly my defense mechanisms kicked in. Once burned...

Feeling like a sad, angry child, I followed him into a back room, turning right into a small office. While he stepped behind the desk to a fancy bar, I stood in awe in the middle of the small room. What was it they said about smart people? Their work-spaces were super messy? By that metric M. Fabrice left Einstein in the dust.

End plates from the wooden boxes wine often shipped in covered one entire wall. The logos represented the best châteaus in Bordeaux, many in Burgundy, two of my faves in St. Émilion, which technically was Bordeaux but treated differently. Only one American winery made the cut—Screaming Eagle, of course. Actual corks wallpapered the rear wall, which was adjacent to the first. A ring of red on one end of each cork indicated they'd each been pulled from presumably an exquisite bottle of wine. M. Fabrice had a great gig, but, if I was him, I'd hide the evidence. Although he didn't seem worried about a potential overindulgence issue like yours truly. Of course, all I'd done was worry about it, so how bad could it be?

Papers drifted off the piles on his desk like large snowflakes on a windless evening. I angled a look—mostly handwritten notes in an illegible scrawl and printed invoices, some red-stamped as paid.

M. Fabrice looked up from the bottle he'd chosen from the diamond-shaped cubbies above the bar that lined the remaining wall. "Perhaps we should leave Bordeaux alone for a bit," he said, lofting a bottle for my distant inspection.

"I'll leave the choice to the expert. Quite the office you have here."

He seemed unconcerned by the chaos. "I know where most things are. My wife, she believed in filing things in drawers. She never understood my piles. But it is messier than usual. Last night..." His voice hitched as he turned and focused with renewed intensity on relieving the bottle of its cork. "I can't bring myself to replace her," he whispered as if her ghost lurked nearby and would be offended at the thought.

Unfamiliar with personal loss of that magnitude, I didn't know what to say. People had told me you never get over loss; you just figure out how to live around it. M. Fabrice had yet to figure that part out. No need to belabor the point—time and its healing powers. "M. Fabrice, your English is very good." I forced a smile and a bit of levity, I hoped. Two sad sacks and racks of wine were a recipe for serious humiliation and a blistering headache. "Are you holding out on me?" Last night he'd used Jean-Charles to interpret.

"The words come more easily when I am not afraid." The cork gave with a satisfying pop. M. Fabrice poured a thin stream of blood-red liquid into a curled decanter constructed like glass spring with coils nesting on top of each other.

Watching the wine swirl through the rings was mesmerizing.

"We won't take time to properly decant. This makes it more quick." He made a fuss over choosing the proper wine glass. Warming to his English practice, he chattered as he fussed and puttered. "This is a nice wine from St. Émilion. Much age, so it will be nice to drink. But still, with a little air, it will rise nicely."

Rise? Despite the malapropism, I liked the visual. "Open?"

"Yes, open." He gave me a quick glance with bright eyes. "My wife, she teased me about this as well. I miss this word always. I don't know why." Once the wine had reached the vessel at the bottom of the coil, he collected a healthy pour for each of us in his chosen glass. "Open," he whispered as he touched a napkin to a drop of wine that had the audacity to linger on the lip of the decanter.

He handed me a glass, keeping the other for himself. He held it by the stem with the reverence of a small child cradling a baby bird. With a practiced movement almost too small to see, he swirled the liquid, watched the legs trickle down, then held the glass to the light. "You know the glass is very important. The wrong one can ruin a brilliant wine."

"I didn't know."

"You must come back. I will make your brain blow with Champagne in a series of different glasses. It offers something different in each one."

I let that idiom go. "I would love that."

After taking a sip, savoring it, then swallowing with a relish I totally got, M. Fabrice gave me a questioning glance.

Enraptured by his whole show, I'd forgotten to take a sip of my own wine. My mimicry of his routine, unskilled and awkward, drew a smile. I gave him a shrug and returned his grin.

"There. You are especially beautiful when you smile."

An old man who had recently lost his wife was flirting with me? I considered my rhetorical question and decided the unwanted answer was no—he was just being French. Either way, I felt my blues brighten. Being in the company of a nice man always made life better. Thoughts turned to my father. Very early in the morning in Vegas yet, but, still, the silence from his doctors had me worried. My mother made a science out of being a drama queen, so her histrionics, muted as they were, weren't sufficient incentive to go to general quarters. But I sure would like to talk with the doctors...

"You look unhappy." M. Fabrice watched me as he took another sip of his wine. His joy in the vintage added a bit of sparkle absent before. "It is nice, isn't it?"

"Exceptional."

"So why are you sad?"

"Worried more than sad." A flick upward of his eyebrows told me he saw through the ruse, but he was too much of a gentleman to press the issue. "We have a blood feud, a dead man, some stolen wine, and my fiancé and his family in the middle of it. Targets or merely foils? I'd love to figure that out. Any insight you might have would be most appreciated."

He replenished his glass. After checking the level in my still-full glass, he added a bit more to his own. The broken capillaries scattered across his nose and cheeks hinted at a love of the grape. A perfect job for an aficionado but filled with pitfalls. One misstep. One serious blow...like a wife dying... Not long ago, a winemaker came to the hotel to persuade us to buy his wine. As a recovering alcoholic, he couldn't taste it, couldn't risk falling down that hole again. Nevertheless, he'd sworn it was sublime. He'd been right.

Love created its own kind of crazy.

I wondered whether M. Fabrice had fallen down the hole or was still teetering on the edge, peering into the depths. Either way, I was pretty sure he heard Bacchus calling. Mired in the pull and tug myself, who was I to judge? Besides, judging wasn't my thing. In fact, I thought it should feature prominently on the list of Seven Deadly Sins.

"My father is seriously ill. I should be home." Maybe a bit of shared pain might open him up. Besides, it helped to talk about it even though right here, right now, I was powerless to alter my father's trajectory.

"Heart?" A good guess.

I took a gulp of wine, praying for the comfort. Exploding in a nice warm ball in my stomach, it didn't disappoint. "A bullet."

M. Fabrice's shock reminded me that the rest of the world often considered normal Vegas to be very abnormal. Like Shangri La, Vegas cast a spell on those who stayed too long. An alternate reality where sex and silliness were commonplace, and given our Mob background, bullets and baseball bats were expected. The bullet to my father's chest because he was an important man and stepped on toes occasionally dovetailed into the whole Mob mystique.

"He is a powerful man, then."

"He's considered so." The Big Boss had wielded sufficient power to shape the city. Some agreed with his ideas; others took offense. Decisions favored some and hurt others—a fact I currently struggled with. "Sometimes people want to change that."

M. Fabrice nodded and took a bit more of a slurp than a true oenophile would. "This is so even here."

With the wine taking effect, he seemed sufficiently mellow for me to hit him with more difficult questions. "You mentioned earlier that last night you were afraid."

"I did?" He squinted into the shadows over my shoulder as if trying to once again see last night, the dance of the various players as the horror unfolded. His attention flicked toward the backdoor. With his free hand, he probed the back of his head, wincing as his fingers found a sensitive spot. The pain seemed to confirm the memories.

"Who do you see?"

This time when he added wine to his glass, his hands shook. Splatters of red splashed from his glass. He ignored the mess, focusing on guiding the glass to his mouth and inhaling the liquid. "No one." He answered too quickly. "It was dark. He attacked me from behind."

"Nothing you remember about him?"

"I can't say."

"Can't? Or won't?"

He pulled a scrap of dirty cloth out of his inside pocket and mopped his brow. Guilt always took a huge toll, and I had no doubt he was guilty of something, something bad. I just didn't know what. Or, even worse, maybe, the guilt was by association. The very worst kind. No authority to change anything yet all the responsibility for what had happened.

"Was all that wine, the '94 Laurent, part of your inventory?"

"A special shipment from an investor."

"Who?"

"I don't have a name, only wiring instructions. My business is very sensitive. Discretion is highly valued."

"He wants you to sell it?"

"Yes. This is not unusual."

I had to take his word for it…for now. "Can you give me any insights into what is going on and why poor Victor was marinated in some rather unique and expensive wine?"

"It is bad business." He poured a bit more liquid courage.

"The families hate each other." I offered the bait, praying he would take it. Out of patience, I took a deep breath and tried to still myself. What I really needed was somebody to hit, or arrest, or yell at, or something. I was a ball of frustration ready to explode. Everything in France frustrated me at each turn. God knew my country had a ton of problems, but there were things I missed—In-N-Out, ice in my drinks, more sugar in my chocolate, dinner at six, and a more direct path to the point. But, in inimitable French fashion, M. Fabrice seemed determined to lead me down the path and through the woods before we got to Grandmother's house. And the Big Bad Wolf lurked somewhere in all of this. I hoped I at least saw him coming before he got his shot.

M. Fabrice waved a hand in dismissal. A bit unsteady, he sank into the desk chair. Wine, not just for breakfast anymore. "People like to talk about this, but the families are in business together. In spite of past bad blood, they have made money together. Much, much money."

"Why did Jean-Louis give you the exclusive to retail Estate Laurent?"

"Perhaps it was guilt." He wilted like he'd said too much.

"Even though you married into the family, you weren't close." I needed to tread lightly here—the wounds were raw.

"No. My family was very poor. We had no land, no reputation...nothing. Jean-Louis thought his sister-in-law could make a better choice." He leaned forward, his hands on the desktop. "I did, too. But a miracle happened. She chose me, and we were very happy. But my wife, she missed seeing her sister. Jean-Louis made it very difficult."

"Even though you did business together?"

M. Fabrice shrugged. "That is business."

"And this is family. So, you think that now, facing his Maker, Jean-Louis is trying to make amends."

"He should not have such faith in me. I am a small merchant." Suddenly uncomfortable, M. Fabrice paled. "Perhaps he was right in the beginning."

"I'm sure that's not true." I patted his clasped hands. "Have you eaten?"

His eyes glazed a bit—with wine or tears, hard to tell. Perhaps one eased the other. But he didn't answer. I took that as an invitation to try to find something to force feed the man. Under a pile of papers in the corner, a fridge wheezed under its load. Curiously, a nice round of Brie and a hard cheese, both fresh, nestled in the cool interior. Three boxes of crackers, two of them still unopened, hid behind a half-full box of a lesser

Burgundy on the table against the side wall. On a paper napkin, I fashioned a rather nice little repast. M. Fabrice didn't seem much interested or to care.

"You must eat." I carved off a bite-sized bit of cheese. Placing it on a water cracker, I picked up his hand and placed it in it. "Eat this. It's good."

He looked at me, then did as I asked. His wife had taught him well. After several more crackers, he perked up a bit.

"So, the families aren't at war?"

"It makes a good story." Not a denial, but a bit of an explanation, spun for full effect...or to divert inspection.

"But somebody wants to break up their business alliance." Brushing my pride aside, I made a cheese cracker for myself. Popping a bit in my mouth, I groaned in delight. Just another example of how everything tasted better, sounded better, felt better in Paris. I washed it down with the St. Émilion, which could qualify as an elixir for the gods. Were there more bottles where this one had come from? Of course, I'd have to arm-wrestle M. Fabrice for it. Given his current state, I felt reasonably up to the challenge.

"Break up the business?" He mulled that over as if he hadn't thought of it before. Seemed obvious to me, but I was standing outside the forest, and he was nose-to-nose with the trees. "That is an interesting idea." This time he actually reached for one of the cheese crackers I'd assembled and placed in front of him. "I have seen the man in the barrel before. I have tried to remember where, but I can't." He shook his head. "I know it is important."

"He said he worked for Paul Bay, the *négociant.*"

He chewed on the cracker and cheese, some light and focus returning to his eyes. "No. This is not it. He was from somewhere else. He represented someone important. You must find out."

"Okay." Given my lack of facility with the language, my lack of understanding how things worked around here, and the shaky ground I trod with the local authorities, I wouldn't give myself better than one-in-ten odds, or worse, but he didn't need to know all my shortcomings. "I will." Something niggled at me. No, someone. Someone who didn't fit. "Do you know Nigel Wilde?"

M. Fabrice rolled his neck as if all the muscles had tightened at once. "He is an American wine critic." His words sounded as if he was reading from a bio.

"So I hear. How's his nose? His palate? Any sophistication?"

"He is like most Americans."

I took that as a "not much." "Looking for their fifteen minutes of fame?"

He gave me an affirmative shrug but didn't elaborate further.

"What do you remember about the man who assaulted you?" Circling back was worth a shot, although chances of success were low.

"Nothing. I never saw him." He wouldn't meet my eyes, focusing instead on pouring more wine into his glass.

"Yes, you said that before." The window for getting a straight answer out of him was closing. "But you know something. He left something behind?" A dart in the dark.

For a moment he seemed pained, straddling the fence. Then he reached down and shuffled through some of the papers. He pushed several aside, grabbed one, squinted at it, then tossed it aside and rooted some more. Finally, he found what he was looking for. Still unsure, he held the paper close to his chest. "I hid it in with the others. The police would never think to look there."

"They would never think to look for a paper at all." I resisted the urge to rip the thing from his grasp, but I was pretty sure it wouldn't help—not that that had ever stopped me before.

"You must promise not to tell anyone. Not the police. Not Jean-Charles." Curiously, he left out Enzo Laurent.

"But if it will help?"

"It only begs more questions. You must find the answers."

I leaned back, putting as much distance between me and that paper as possible. Bad business for sure! Throughout my life, I'd never been able to resist the call of Trouble. With all that history, we were now on a first-name basis.

Of course, just because I could recognize it didn't mean I could resist it. "Deal. What does the paper say?" My fingers itched to snatch the bit of paper. I sat on my hands.

"It is an invoice, in French, so let me read it to you." He relinquished his now empty glass, but not without a bit of remorse. Then he donned a pair of reading glasses and shook the paper open. "It is for two bottles of the '94 Laurent, dated four days ago. My stamp is on the invoice reflecting the wine shipped three days ago."

I'd stopped on the point he'd made before. "The Bouclets know the customers and communicate with them personally?"

"But of course. It is common practice." He looked at me over the top of his cheaters. "What are you implying?"

"Nothing." To be honest, I didn't know what to think or who to impale on the petard of my suspicion. Whether I liked it or not, everyone was a suspect. Well, except for me. I knew I didn't do it...at least I was pretty sure. But the pinball game of my life flashed "tilt" in big red letters, so nothing appeared quite as it was. "Who ordered the wine, and where was it shipped? Frank Liu?"

He reared back in surprise, a look of distaste puckering his lips. "Frank Liu? He is not sophisticated enough to appreciate such a vintage." M. Fabrice was jumping to conclusions—there was an epidemic of that around here. "Even if Frank Liu had ordered the wine, I would not sell it to him. It is too good for the likes of him."

"But what about the empty wooden case?"

"What case?"

"The empty one in the corner the night we found Victor. I assume the bottles of the Laurent '94 were in that case."

He swallowed hard and focused on a wine opener on his desk. He flicked open the curved knife used to cut the foil. "They could've been. We all reuse the crates when shipping wine."

"That one was from Chateau Shasay. That's Frank Liu's outfit, right?"

M. Fabrice didn't feel the need to tell me what he could see I already knew.

Mr. Liu had made friends far and wide. I had to meet this guy. "He doesn't want to play by the old rules?"

"He doesn't want to earn his way in."

As an upstart foreigner, I got that. But there were ways to curry favor in any crowd. Clearly, Mr. Liu wasn't inclined to take the nuanced route. "I heard he was threatening legal action claiming the Laurents and the Bouclets conspired to keep his wine at a lower classification and theirs at a higher."

"That is not the way here."

I wasn't exactly sure what he referred to, but it didn't matter —conspiring or complaining clearly weren't part of the Oenophilic Code, or whatever.

"I need to know where the two bottles on that invoice went."

M. Fabrice paused, shifting under the burden of knowledge. He didn't want to tell me; that I could see. "You must not leap to conclusions."

One with his date stamp and a matching entry in a shipping manifest would be hard to fake, but I nodded. How many times had I told Romeo that making up one's mind before all the facts were in sent you after the wrong suspect more times than not? I needed to drink my own poison. Damn hard to do. "Was it from the same batch, the case that came from the man in Hong Kong, the wine used to bathe Victor?"

He waffled about a bit. "I checked the bottle numbers against the manifest. It is the same wine."

"After the police cleaned up, were all of the bottles accounted for?"

"Yes, including the two that I shipped out just before."

I raised an eyebrow and pressed harder. "Who ordered them?"

"Enzo Laurent." He deflated with a heavy sigh. "Enzo Laurent ordered the wine."

"And was it delivered to him?"

"Yes, to his offices here in Paris. Four days ago."

With M. Fabrice on the ropes, I leaned forward, pressing my advantage—not terribly sporting, but effective. "And the black sedan behind your store?"

"Laurent's." He mopped his brow, the perspiration beading quickly now.

"You told this to the police?"

M. Fabrice squirmed a bit before answering, taking great care with his words. "Emma knows."

Emma. The woman clearly was running her own game. Protecting her friends for sure. But was she also hiding a killer? When I'd caught killers before, the police had been on my side. Not knowing whether the good guys were really bad guys upped the ante way beyond my risk-comfort level.

"She's a friend of Enzo's?"

"And of Jean-Charles."

I didn't care much for his implication.

M. Fabrice eyed the paper he still clutched in his fist. "Enzo didn't leave this. He was looking for it."

"Covering his tracks."

M. Fabrice didn't disagree. Instead, he stared into his wine looking as if his faithful dog had turned on him and bitten him in the butt. I knew that look. Disappointment.

How the mighty can tumble.

"You think he killed poor Victor?" Victor who nobody appeared to know. A non-participant and he's the one who winds up dead? That made no sense. Why? Did he walk into the shop to find Enzo Laurent rifling M. Fabrice's office? Hardly something to kill over. What then? Who the hell was he, and why was he important enough to kill?

Important enough to who? Whom? Who? I shook my head. When I didn't even have a grasp on my own language, how could I expect to function in another?

If Enzo Laurent was covering his tracks, I bet he'd like to get his hands on those two bottles shipped out.

Could those be the two that ended up in Jean-Charles's restaurant?

Why would Enzo Laurent send them?

Nothing was adding up.

And the wine that ended up in Jean-Charles's restaurant.

Nigel Wilde claimed it was fake.

CHAPTER TEN

*B*Y THE time I'd buttoned up M. Fabrice, walking him home and stopping short of tucking him in, the day had turned dark and colder. In January this far north, daylight was a fleeting thing. As a child of the lights of Vegas, most of the time I liked that. This afternoon, as I walked, I tried to absorb the tiny residuals of holiday cheer that lurked in the colored lights, the festive displays, the gifts now on sale. Holidays were like that—timing was everything. One day a toy was worth a hundred Euros; two days later, the store slashed the price to half.

Supply versus demand.

And now a prime vintage of an epic wine was down to one single bottle.

Who would benefit from that? The Bouclets, for sure. The Laurents, not so much. As wine distributors they looked for that sweet spot where supply fell just short of demand, thereby causing the price to soar. But the profit on one bottle, no matter the price, wouldn't be enough to keep the doors open for long. Probably longer than I thought—the prices single bottles demanded at auction these days were insane. But wholesalers didn't usually participate in the auction market as a business strategy. Distributors catered to consumers, auctions to collectors. Two completely different markets.

Until they weren't.

I needed more information about this particular vintage of Estate Laurent.

As I stepped back into the shelter of the door to a restaurant still hours away from opening for the evening, I snagged my phone then hit Romeo's speed-dial. I pressed the thing to my ear, counting the rings. Why did they sound so different one country to another? You'd think a ring was a ring.

Three weird hollow rings, and he picked up. "You're doing it again, creeping me out," he said without preamble, his voice clear and strong as if he was standing at my shoulder.

"You couldn't possibly be talking about me." To be honest, being considered creepy wouldn't ruffle my feathers. Teddie always had said a bad review is almost the same as a good one—both meant you inspired strong emotion. While I didn't consider myself up to the task, I knew who was. "Have you been talking with my mother?"

"Yes." Romeo breathed out the word like an accomplice planted in a magician's audience. "How did you know?"

"I recognized the licking-your-wounds tone. And?"

"She's..." He gave a shaky sigh as words failed, which was often the case when describing an encounter with Mona.

"Yep, and then some. What did she say?" I knew Romeo cared about my father almost as much as I did.

"The Big Boss is better. Still not out of the woods, though. They still haven't found the bleeder they suspect is causing his low iron levels."

My turn to breathe out slowly, letting in the buoyancy of hope.

"I didn't know she'd named the twins."

"She told you?" I whispered.

"Yeah, Frankie and Sammie. Pretty perfect, if you ask me. I'm too young to be a part of that crowd, but even I got the reference."

"Francesca and Samantha, when they want to escape the reference. But are names supposed to be burdened by history?"

"Your mother thinks so. Something about the standard-bearers of the past carrying it into the future, so no one forgets."

Man, I was sensing a theme in all this craziness. At what age exactly did one's view become obsessed with legacy?

"But that's not what's creepy." His voice had settled to its normal timber. "Shit, Lucky, you have got to stop calling at the exact moment I'm thinking about you."

"At least I save you the trouble and the embarrassment of having to guess what sort of… situation…I might be in." I could almost hear his blush as it flushed his cheeks. "What did you need me for?"

He cleared his throat. "You wanted to know what Nigel Wilde had to say?"

My irritation flared. "No, I wanted to be in on his questioning."

Romeo chuckled. "Well then, you're in luck." A few clicks and pings, a moment of silence that drew on to the point I thought we'd been cut off, then he came back on the line.

I listened while he went through all the procedural bits. "Lucky, you there?"

"Still here." The noise of the traffic increased as the day dimmed toward night and the knot of cars thickened. I stuck a finger in my ear to block the noise. I wondered about the legalities of conducting an interrogation while huddled in a doorway in Paris, but for once I figured I didn't rule the world. If Romeo got it wrong, it'd be his problem. At this point, I'd bust a kneecap or two to break open this case, so I wasn't about to argue.

"Why don't you start since your questions have little to do with the charges against Mr. Wilde?"

"Then why the hell would I answer them?" A male voice, low and ugly, resonated with a lack of cooperative spirit. "I'm still going to file a complaint for the broken nose. Police brutality."

"Knock yourself out," Romeo said in his best Mickey Spillane imitation.

"You will answer, Mr. Wilde, because you might very well be implicated in crimes far more serious than Conversion of Property, Assault, and Making a General Ass Out of Yourself." I liked that last one the best.

"That's not a crime."

"Sure it is, a crime against humanity." I heard him groan. Maybe he'd be an easier nut to crack than I thought. "You haven't been paying much attention, have you?"

Another sound of discomfort. "Kid, you don't have any Alka-Seltzer or anything? My stomach is on the fritz." I suspected he was addressing Romeo with that bit as I heard his muffled voice say something about Wilde answering the questions and then they'd talk about his stomach. Romeo was growing into his role as a Junior Bad-ass.

"You're not scaring me," Nigel said with a growl and a belch.

This I believed was tossed my way, so I hit it back. "I love when folks say stuff like that. It means just the opposite. But, on the off chance you might be as tough as you think, let me try a bit harder." Nothing like a veiled threat to grab a man by the short hairs. Most bullies took it as an affront to their manhood. Mr. Wilde ran with that pack.

He breathed into the phone, heavy and labored. I bet he was sweating like a pig, too—the bullies always were the first to break when they got some serious pushback. I could imagine his knuckles whitening as he squeezed the juice out of the thing. "Give me your best shot."

"Murder."

"What?" he squealed like a pig being chased by a horde of rednecks at the state fair.

I gave him enough of the details to worry him but retained enough to be irritatingly oblique. "How did you come to be in Jean-Charles's restaurant last night?"

"I was there by invitation. The card I received led me to believe Jean-Charles had extended the offer to join him for a special tasting dinner. Imagine my pique when I arrived to find there was no Jean-Charles, no tasting dinner." He covered the phone with his hand, but I could still hear. "Kid, something for my stomach. I'm dying here."

"But you did have a reservation?"

"Yes. And Jean-Charles had arranged for a bottle of Estate Laurent, the '94, a rare exquisite thing, to be presented to me. One of the rarest wines, the gift was most appreciated."

"For that, you tore up the place."

"After I obtained proof the wine was fake. I had it tested."

"So you came back with the media in tow. Did you do anything before that?"

"I called Enzo Laurent to let him know he's shipping fake wine." Gloat buoyed Mr. Wilde's voice. He definitely had an ax to grind.

"What did he say?"

"He wasn't there. I left a message. Nobody makes a fool out of Nigel Wilde."

No, you don't need any help there. Somehow, I refrained from letting that thought loose in the verbal world to boomerang back.

"When was this?"

"Couple of nights ago."

I made a mental note. "Have you received any threats lately?" A shot in the dark. I mean, they ask this all the time on TV, so I thought why not?

"People threaten to kill me all the time. It's a badge of pride

—means I'm doing my job, stepping on toes. But no one sets me up."

That little bon mot diverted me to a side track. "Kill you? Anybody recently?"

He belched again. "I wouldn't know. To pay attention gives them credence. They don't scare me." I could almost hear his shrug.

"Not ever?" Not my business, but if someone threatened to deprive my family and friends of my bullshit, I'd at least maybe look under a rock or two.

"Nope."

Only a fool is never afraid. "Sounds like you're having some stomach trouble. Didn't you eat anything last night, or have you eaten since?"

"Not a morsel. After the wine insult, I didn't have the stomach for it."

"How was inviting you to share in a very special bottle an affront?"

"It was a joke. I'd been writing about it, talking it up, since the invitation arrived the day before yesterday. So everyone wanted to know what the wine was like."

"But it wasn't what you thought?"

"It was swill." He launched into full bluster. "A cheap wine. Even the *négociants* make better wine than the thin, weak, unremarkable juice in that bottle."

"But the bottle, I'm sure you examined it?" Sinjin mentioned a counterfeiter. I'd half-written off his explanation as smoke and mirrors. But at the core of the best lies is usually a kernel of truth.

"Of course, there were no signs of tampering. The label, the printing, the aging, nothing raised an alarm."

"It was good, then?"

"No, I've told you, the wine was horrid. Undrinkable!"

"Not the wine, but the counterfeiting job."

"This was no cheap Chinese fake. Jean-Charles was behind the whole thing. He substituted the wine to make me the fool." His confidence returned as he warmed to his story. Magical thinking is such a safe place. "In some circles, I am considered an expert in wines of the Bordeaux region. Many call on me to authenticate their bottles. Some still trade on my provenance. If this was a forgery, it was brilliant. Way beyond anything I've seen before."

"You've seen labels like the one on the bottle last night?"

"Of course." We both arrived at the same conclusion at the same instant. I could hear it in the way his indignation trailed off. He'd been duped. Enzo Laurent had been telling the truth about Nigel Wilde. "But you've been fooled before."

A hollowness echoed across the ether as he considered how to play me. I'd met so many like him before, all bluster and bite and low opinions of women's capabilities outside the bedroom or the kitchen.

"Once. But no one knows." He actually moaned. "My stomach is killing me. Must be the stomach flu that's going around. It's that time of year. My sister had it last week."

"I'm sorry. Twenty-four hours of hell, but you'll be better." Personally, I thought twenty-four hours was letting him off light, the pompous ass. "I think you're lying. I think someone knows about your misstep, and that someone is whispering it strong and clear on the grapevine, as it were. Anybody help you cover it up?"

He belched again. "Some fixer from Hong Kong. Looked like a fucking pirate."

"Dark hair, blue eyes, really smooth bullshit."

"Sounds like the one."

Mr. Smythe-Gordon had some answering to do. "How'd he get put onto you?"

"Hell if I know. My back was against the wall. No way would I turn down an offer to make it all go away." His income rode on an impeccable palate, nose, and reputation. Without all three, he would be looking for another job. Mr. Wilde sounded like he had a very limited skill set and was lacking in basic social skills. Not good for future income prospects.

"Did he make it all go away?"

"Until now."

"How do wine buyers satisfy themselves a wine is not a fake but indeed the real thing?"

"Now, for the high-end wine at the prestigious auctions, they require a provenance."

"Like art?"

"It's more like a chain of evidence," Romeo chimed in.

Had the kid gone all highbrow on me and started using his meager funds to buy rare wine?

"Brandy is studying to be a sommelier," he said, as if he could read my mind.

Sounded like I was going to lose a very able assistant.

"The kid is right," Mr. Wilde confirmed. "The black market is a bit looser."

"But the consequences more severe." I'd lived in Vegas long enough to know the quickest path to a shallow grave in the desert was to try to con a bad guy. "How was Jean-Charles's invitation communicated to you?"

"A woman called my office. My secretary took the call. Jesus, kid, don't you have anything to help me?"

"I would suggest referring to him as Detective might help." If he could talk to two people in the same conversation, so could I. "Let me guess; the woman who called didn't leave her name."

"No. Men like Jean-Charles and myself, we have staff. This is not unusual and no cause to take notice."

There was so much wrong with that I could teach a whole course on the subject. Something told me Nigel Wilde would not be a stellar student, so I didn't waste the breath.

"Romeo, you still there?"

"Hang on." His voice faded, then returned, the echo in the background missing. "I took you off speaker."

"Did you get him something for his stomach? Sounds like he's about to hurl."

"I got something coming. He doesn't look too good."

The vision of Victor Martin steeping in wine danced in my head like sugarplums or something. "You know, one guy has been killed in this mess already. I don't know that much about wine, but when important reputations are on the line, fortunes hang in the balance, and folks start dying, that makes me get all twitchy and start looking over my shoulder. Take the guy to the hospital. Have him checked out. Have them run a poison panel for kicks and grins."

"Seriously? The guy has the stomach flu. Caught it from his sister. You heard him. He has us all feeling a bit queasy."

"Just do it. If I'm wrong, I'll pay for it."

"Your hunches have never let me down."

That made one of us. "There should be one more bottle of the wine your walking egomaniac, Mr. Wilde, sampled."

"I've got it, and the empty one as well."

"Are they evidence?" If he had to impound them, that would complicate things.

"Not of any charges pending."

I let out a breath. While not sure what that bottle would tell me, I had a feeling it hid lots of secrets—secrets that could help crack this case wide open. "Overnight them to me."

"I can bring them both to you."

"I'm in Paris."

"I know."

Well, okay. "How soon can you leave?"

"As soon as you can get that fancy bit of iron you guys own ready to fly."

"Arm-twisting me for a ride in the G-650." The kid had upped his game. "That's beneath you."

"I learned it from you." He paused to let that sink in. "Besides, as a servant of the people, that sort of thing is way beyond my reach unless I strong-arm my important friends."

A line to cozy up to but never to cross. That lecture was in Romeo's future. For now, I could make his dream come true with no *quid pro quo*. "I'm on it. But, before you head this way, check on Mr. Wilde's death threat boast. I'd like to know if he's been particularly irritating to anybody recently."

"Got it. I know that tone. You sound like you're playing an angle."

"Hardly. But I think I will sit down for a peek behind the curtain of the fine wine scene."

THE SAME BUTLER WHO HAD ESCORTED ME TO THE "entertainment level" yesterday opened the door at the Bouclets' little *pied-à-terre* and gave me the same look of forced resignation. Had it only been less than twenty-four hours? I'd aged a decade or more, felt it for sure and probably looked it as well.

"*Oui?*" he asked as if I was a Girl Scout selling cookies and acting as aloof as if he'd never laid eyes on me.

That part of the whole French thing left me cold. I stepped through the door, brushing him back as I moved past. In the middle of the foyer, I turned. "Please tell Jean-Louis I'd like a moment."

"He's not feeling well."

"It's important." With my shoulders back, I forced myself to every millimeter of my full six feet. "Please let him know I'm here. I'll wait in the library." I strode toward a room lined with bookshelves I'd spied in the middle of my act. I hoped it was the library. "And hot tea would be nice. With lemon, no milk." Champagne would've been far better, but I thought maybe that would be pushing the bounds of decorum too far, even for me.

"Yes, miss." His words crackled like dry ice.

A good bluff works in any language. I allowed myself a moment of concealed gloat. An invisible member of the staff had banked a fire. Its warmth beckoned me like a fly to sugar.

I had only a few moments to gather myself before Madame Bouclet flew into the room like she'd been shot from the cannon at Circus-Circus. As her husband's first line of defense, she didn't miss a beat, as I knew she wouldn't.

"My husband is very ill. The doctors have left strict orders. No guests."

Christophe careened around the corner, hot on his *grand-mère's* heels. "Lucky!" Dodging around his grandmother, he didn't even slow down before launching himself into the air.

A game we often played, I was prepared and swooped down to snag him mid-flight. Using his momentum, I twirled him around until I could slow us both down. We ended with his arms bear-hugged around my neck and his legs ensnaring my waist. "You are getting too big!"

"Then you must grow too!" He nuzzled in. "I've missed you."

"I've missed you, too." I glanced at Madame Bouclet who had stayed back, out of the range of a flying five-year-old. "Will Desiree be joining us?"

"She is not here."

"Still at the police station?"

"No, Emma let her go. She came flying in here, changed clothes, then left again."

Oh, that was a bad idea. "Any idea where she went?" I kept my tone light, without the hint of future incarceration in it.

"She didn't say." Madame Bouclet's mouth puckered into a tiny bow.

"Aunt Desiree is gone," Christophe whined as if he was entitled to a constant stream of adult playmates. I could tell him that was way overrated. "*Papa* is never here. When he is, he is angry. *Grand-père* is sick. You can make everything better." He twisted around to look at his grandmother. "Isn't that right, *Grand-mère?* Isn't that what you told me?"

As our eyes met, some of her indignation faded into a guilty smile, small but it was there. The first hint of a truce.

"I really am trying to help." Not that anything I said would convince her, but I felt the need to reiterate, more for me than her. Sometimes I needed to reassure myself, take stock of my motivations. Nothing ulterior here. Just a crime to solve, wine to recover—then the playing field would be back to level. Well, as level as it could be considering I was on their turf and far outnumbered and outgunned. Romeo couldn't get here fast enough.

"Your tea, miss." The butler oiled his way across the floor to set an exquisite tea service on a low table between two chairs. "I brought some for you as well, Madame." He eyed me. "Two lumps and milk, no lemon." Then he turned on his heel and slipped out of the room as noiselessly as he'd arrived.

My turn to smile. "Looks as if I've been given my orders." I gestured to a chair. "Tea?"

With a weary sigh, Madame Bouclet sagged into the chair. Still impeccably put together, she frayed at the edges a bit. All of this must have taken an incredible toll.

I lowered Christophe to his feet. "Grab one of the settees over there. Pull it close. It looks like we might have some choco-late milk for you."

"And cookies!"

"Go on." I shooed him away. "It's not polite to drool on the pastries."

We all settled down, and both of my tea guests waited until I had served everyone. Christophe reached for the cookies but stopped at my raised eyebrow. "Your grandmother first." She graciously took one, and then he put the plate on his lap as if laying claim. "Now me."

He eyed the cookies, mentally counting. Then, his eyes wide

with reluctance, he offered me the plate. I felt like scraping off most of them into my napkin, but I was above punishing his largess. "I'm fine, thank you."

He seemed stunned. After all, the kid had born witness to my appetites many, many times. Not a proud moment, but a real one. I felt an urge to eat spinach in an odd kinship with Popeye. *I yam what I yam.*

Self-acceptance, a large step on the path to maturity.

Not that I was in any hurry. But at some point, life would become untenable if I didn't grow a pair and get on with it. With Madame Bouclet eyeing me as she cradled her teacup and with Christophe hanging on my every move, I was closer to fish-or-cut-bait time than I realized. With both Teddie and Jean-Charles waiting for a falter—one to run, the other to pounce—bullshitting my way was no longer working. Jordan had warned me. Hell, everybody had.

The worst thing about all of it was I'd disappoint somebody.

In a blinding flash of that self-awareness I struggled with, I realized the only person I couldn't disappoint was me. If I did, I'd lose myself altogether.

"Lucky?" Worry softened Madame Bouclet's voice.

"Sorry." With a slight nod, I gave Christophe the go-ahead to dive into the cookies, then I joined Madame Bouclet in enjoying our tea.

"Where did you go?" she asked.

I gave a self-conscious shrug. "Life." Both an ineffective and apt explanation.

"It is a bit much these days, isn't it?"

"How is Jean-Louis?" I caught myself. "I'm sorry. How is M. Bouclet?" In France, using given names was by invitation only. So far, mine hadn't been delivered.

She waved a hand. "Please. No formality. You are family."

An elegant upgrade. Christophe beamed. "Jean-Charles and I have much to work out."

"With time, all is possible." She fussed with her grandson, moving his plate closer and his mug of hot chocolate back from the table's edge.

Sure signs I needed to change the subject. "And Jean-Louis?"

"Resting comfortably. He is home from the hospital only now, so he is very tired. I told him you were here. He is weak but excited to see you." Her cup clattered against the saucer as she replaced it. "If you could, please keep that in mind."

"Of course. Toward that end, perhaps you could give me some insight."

She puffed up like a little bird perched on the edge of the chair, pleased that I'd asked. "I'll try, but the wine business is Jean-Louis's work."

I didn't believe it for a minute, but I played along. "What can you share about Enzo Laurent? He and your husband met regularly in the wine cellar here, but for the world, they pretended to be adversaries."

She gave me some shrewd side-eye. "Most of business is a game, is it not?"

"Indeed. I see how a perception of antagonism would drive the price up. The two families could start shooting at each other any moment, so grab the wine while you can. The producers gain from the higher prices, but the distributor not so much."

"Correct. Make no mistake, the wine, it is very good. But there are many good wines and wine drinkers can be...how do you say it?"

"Fickle?"

"Yes, fickle." She focused on pouring some more tea. At the raised pot, I extended my cup.

"Thank you."

She didn't look at me as she placed the pot with measured care on the silver tray. "You think Enzo is behind the theft?" She tucked her hand in her lap to hide its shaking.

"No."

That shot her eyebrows toward her hairline.

"You want him to be guilty?" I thought about shooing Christophe out of the conversation—he was riveted—but it wasn't my place to do so.

Crumpling a bit, she wilted. "I don't know what I want. That's not true. I want my husband to be well, the wine restored to our cellar, and for the fault to rest outside of our family and our friends." She let me see her worry. "The Laurents and the Bouclets, there is much history between our families. This is a precious, priceless gift."

"But Jean-Louis canceled the contract."

"He is sick and not thinking well. An old sick man is not a good businessman. I tried to speak with Enzo. I knew he would be angry, but I can usually talk to him, make him see things as they are."

"But he wouldn't listen?"

"I never got the chance. His assistant wouldn't let me in, nor would she put my calls through. She said he'd told her to do that." Hurt glistened in her eyes.

"I'm sorry."

She straightened, anger now pushing back the worry and sadness. The warrior was back. "He would never do such a thing! We have been...friends...for a long time." Her intonation was turgid with subtext. She glanced at her grandson, and then added a bit of pleading in the look she gave me.

With great effort, I kept my expression bland. "The assistant kept you from seeing him? What is that woman's name anyway?"

"Daria. You don't like her?" A smile ticked up one corner of Madame Bouclet's mouth.

"Cold and calculating."

"You read people well."

"Only when they don't matter to me. Does she have a history that might be interesting?"

"I have no idea. Frankly, all of us were confused that Enzo kept her on."

"Not exactly the person I would want interacting with my customers." I abandoned my tea. When it was hot, it was marginally interesting. Now that it was tepid, it tasted and looked like dirty dishwater.

Madame Bouclet's intensity dimmed, and her features softened. "This time is very difficult for her. Her son, you see, he is very sick. I saw them at the hospital. The boy didn't look well, even thinner than I remembered him, and so pale."

Sympathy welled. The photo on her desk. Her son. *Damn.* "What is he fighting?"

"Something he's been battling his whole life. I'm not really sure exactly what. They didn't expect him to live. It's a miracle he's lasted this long. A mother's will is very strong. I think she's willed him to live, but the time is running short, I fear." She stroked her grandson's hair. "The boy, he used to play here all the time. Remember, Christophe? You used to play hide and seek. You both knew all the best places to hide."

"No. I'm sorry." The boy looked sad at disappointing his grandmother.

"It's not important. You were so young."

"May I be excused?" Christophe had polished off the cookies and reached his tall-people tolerance limit.

"Sure, but could you wait for me in the kitchen? Ask the cook to get you a few more cookies." I ignored Madame Bouclet's pinched mouth of disapproval. "Family." I shot her a smile.

That got a laugh. Making progress.

Once Christophe was out of earshot, I resumed the conversation. "Enzo Laurent. Any family?"

"The tea doesn't seem to be to your liking." Madame Bouclet's smile wavered.

"No matter how hard I try, I'll never be a tea person." In the

U.S., my confession usually earned a nod of, if not agreement, then for sure sympathy. Here it could earn me five to ten without parole.

"Perhaps it is late enough for something a bit more refreshing." She moved her foot to the right and pressed. Somewhere in the bowels of the building a bell chimed.

My sentence had been commuted! And by the least likely judge.

Lurch appeared like magic. The long neck of a bottle of bubbly peeked from the silver ice bucket he carried.

"Would you like to try some of the *crémant* we are experimenting with? It's not the right season for rosé, or we'd critique that." Either she'd been briefed as to my proclivities, or she was a woman after my own heart.

"Rather forward-thinking for a House of Bordeaux." A satisfying pop, muffled by good technique, heralded happy hour.

"The wine industry is changing. So much competition from all corners of the globe. Sparkling wine and rosé are the two fastest growing segments. Other, more eclectic varietals are catching on as well, although only in small numbers at this point. But it is wise not to be complacent."

Lurch removed the tea service, replacing it with two tulip flutes filled with light golden liquid sparkling with tiny bubbles. Madame Bouclet held it to the light. "It is ready for market."

I tasted it and agreed. "Very nice. Now about M. Laurent."

"He has no family. No siblings. His older brother died when he was young, a genetic disorder of some sort. It was all very sad. As the oldest and the only, Enzo didn't want to accept the responsibility for the family's legacy. He ran away to Oxford. Earned a D-Phil in Philosophy. He wanted to change the world." She got a little wistful at that last bit.

The light dawned. "You two...?"

"Yes. We were in love and wanted to be married. Our families, while reluctant at first, accepted our wishes, but they

163

wanted us to wait. We were very young. Then Enzo's brother died, and then Enzo went away. The world changed. My father forbade me to follow him." She twisted her pearls as she talked. "I've always wondered if I should have defied him." Her eyes misted. She blinked away the tears.

"And you married Jean-Louis instead."

"Enzo wasn't coming back, or so he said. He was in a very bad state of mind. He was happy in Oxford. It was his place. My place was here and in the vineyards. My family was not wealthy. My father was one of the leading *négociants*, but that is not the same as a landed family."

"Then Enzo came back."

"Yes. It is a very Catholic country. There was nothing we could do." She finally gave her pearls a rest and accepted a freshening of her bubbles by Lurch.

"Enzo never married?"

"No."

"No children?"

"None claimed. Like most wealthy, powerful men, he had mistresses, and there were rumors of a love child, but only that and it was a long time ago."

The whole thing broke my heart.

No wonder Jean-Louis took up the sword against Enzo Laurent. Despite common perception, the battle had nothing to do with wine.

As usual, when men go to battle, there's a woman at the center of it.

On one level, it was nice to be reminded that not everything was about money, despite the Americans' single-minded dogged pursuit of filthy lucre.

"Jean-Louis has been carrying this for his life. We all have. I've done my best to be a good wife, to bear his children and support him."

She gave him everything but the most important thing, her

heart. Not that it was her fault—we love who we love. Sometimes, in doing so, we sow the seeds of our own destruction. Or at least, we construct our own prisons.

And love was supposed to be this glorious, euphoric thing.

Nothing about this story made me want to sidle off the fence. But the old Vegas adage echoed in my ear: you limit the downside; you limit the upside. I could trot out probably ten clichés along the same line, but in the interest of growing up, I resisted. "When Frank Liu told Jean-Louis that Enzo was undercutting his price, selling his wine on the cheap, Jean-Louis was locked and loaded for a fight to the death."

"He hasn't said so, but I think, before he dies, he wants to punish Enzo, to make him pay. He is dying. This was his chance. But the whole thing was really my fault. I should pay."

"And you have. Early on, your husband could have released you. He could have told the Church and had your union annulled."

She looked surprised as if the thought hadn't occurred to her. "That would've been scandalous. We all would have suffered."

"Until the public's attention turned to the next salacious tidbit."

"Perhaps. But Jean-Louis is a proud man. His son is much like him."

Was there a veiled warning in there? Or was I reading something I wanted to hear in her words? If overthinking was a professional sport, I'd be world champion. I shelved my insecurities for the moment. "Is Jean-Louis strong enough for a few questions? I'll try to be quick."

"He would be most upset if you didn't see him. But finish your *crémant*. He will be desperate to know what you think. It is his *pièce de résistance,* or so he says."

I was happy to do as she asked. "Bordeaux far outshines *crémant* on the wine snobbery scale."

"But it is his creation. The family wine he says was created centuries ago. All he does is quality control. And winemakers are remembered for what they create."

Maybe they aren't remembered as much as celebrated through the product they leave behind. A nuance only a weak ego would worry about.

"If Jean-Louis is expecting us, let's not disappoint him."

CHAPTER ELEVEN

*T*HE ROOM was warm; too warm, with a fire flaming in the corner grate. Yet Jean-Louis huddled under a pile of blankets six inches thick. The outline of his emaciated frame was barely visible. The blankets were tucked just under his chin, leaving his face exposed. In the few intervening hours since I'd seen him last, his cheeks had hollowed. His eyes had disappeared into dark caverns. Sutures closed the gash on his forehead, but nothing covered the wound other than a film of medicine. Blood underneath the skin purpled the area around the wound—a garish insult to an old face. His bones formed an even sharper scaffolding to hold the drape of his translucent skin that exposed the latticework of blue veins underneath, the mask of the very old who were losing the battle. I'd seen it before. I never wanted to see it again.

"Has Jean-Charles been by?" I asked as I pulled a chair close so he didn't have to strain to see me.

"Yes, just a bit ago." Effort rasped his voice, roughing it up like coarse grit sandpaper. His cough, deep and determined, had a phlegmy rattle. "He is chasing the wrong bit of hate."

Hate. "He hates Enzo Laurent that much?"

"No, Enzo can be a boil on his ass, and mine, from time to time. But together we all are stronger. The hate is not his. But he must tell you, not me. He loves you." Jean-Louis's look told me he saw the difficulties, felt the conflict, prayed for the resolution. "We need him. The House of Bouclet needs him here."

"We all know some choices are impossible. Despite the American advertising machine, it is impossible to have it all."

"Yes, but there is responsibility." He wheezed at the effort.

"To whom? We owe it to ourselves, yes. And perhaps our families when much is at stake, and there are no other choices. But don't we owe it to the ones we love as well? What is the priority that results in the happiest, most productive balance? To force someone into a life he doesn't want? To force him to give up a love he needs? Will he be the best choice to serve your needs?"

To answer honestly would kill him. It would vilify his choices, especially regarding those he loved. His decision not to release his wife had doomed him to a life of suffering. Hadn't he learned anything?

"You are saying I should let Jean-Charles go be with you."

"Not at all. I'm saying you should let him choose."

"If he chooses to stay, you are willing to live with that?"

"Of course. I love him. I'm not saying it would be easy. But, if you love somebody, you want the best for them. And they get to decide what that is. That's how this gig works."

"You are a better man than me." The idea deflated him further.

"On the contrary, I only talk a better game. I know what's right. So do you. Doing it is a whole other level of sacrifice. The jury is out as to whether I can handle it or not. I've been accused of being a tad controlling. Not my best thing, but it's part of me."

"You are wise and kind to an old man who has made many mistakes."

"The *crémant* is not one of them. It's lovely." I wanted desperately to lighten his load.

But a lifetime in the making, it was a boulder too heavy to shift. He pushed himself higher in the bed, an effort that had him breathing as if he'd sprinted all the way here. "If Jean-Charles turns his back on all that he is, then he will live with the consequences for the rest of his life." He glanced at his wife. His pain was clear.

It wasn't that she didn't love him. She did—that much was evident. But her love sprang from a duty, not a passion. A world of difference. One brought joy, the other only pain and regret. And, not to make the whole thing about me, but he might be overplaying this entire scenario just a wee bit.

"That's how this whole thing works. Each choice carries a consequence. Hate carries the worst of all."

"I cannot tell you what you want to know. Jean-Charles will have to." The rattle of illness punctuated his words.

"Then it's a good thing I've not come to talk about hate, but rather about wine instead."

That relieved his pallor a bit. Now it was just gray rather than the unhealthy blue-gray when we had arrived. I'd always thought that it took years of abusing one's health to achieve such a bilious color. Apparently not. It seemed like dying also did that. Duly noted and filed with all the other things I've told myself not to do, but routinely ignored.

"Wine." He said the word with a reverence normally reserved for saints, if you believed in that sort of thing, and sainted relatives if you didn't. "She is a jealous mistress, I warn you."

"Vices and passions share that quality. But that's not why I'm here. I'm trying to figure out two things: why someone marinated Victor Martin in the last of your best vintage of Estate Laurent and then why someone stole all the wine from your cellar. The motivations seem the same: money. I understand the first—the smaller the supply and the higher the demand, the greater the profit. Assuming Enzo Laurent is our prime suspect." He started to argue. I raised a finger, and he stopped. "Just a theory. You'll like where it leads. Enzo would not gain anything by destroying all the wine he had to sell. But one damning bit of information—he knew about your wine cellar."

"He wouldn't disclose its location. I often stored wine for him. There are not many safe places to keep very valuable wines. They need to be kept at the right temperature, of course, which often makes it difficult to find discrete places. You understand?"

"Of course. But someone else had to know."

"The family, of course. No one else that I know of." He glanced at his wife. "No, no one."

They were naïve. Maybe the staff was forbidden to go down those stairs, but as sure as I knew human nature, I was sure someone had put a modern twist on the Eve-and-the-Apple story. The question was who?

"Okay, so, assuming Enzo kept the info to himself. That leaves him out. Who else would dump all that wine, and why?"

"Collectors." A coughing fit seized Jean-Louis, and it was several minutes before he could continue. He hacked and wheezed, and turned red as he fought for air until I thought he'd surely expire before he could answer. But slowly, the fit relinquished him. "You know about all of the counterfeiting and the new reliance not on appraisers who are too easily fooled but on a provenance, a trail, if you will, of the wine from the winery to the ultimate consumer?"

"I know it's big business and centered mainly in China. So far, they've targeted only the best, most prestigious wines."

Jean-Louis, warming to the story, tried to push himself higher, but his strength failed. His wife grabbed one arm. She nodded to me to grab the other. Together we lifted him higher, then she tucked pillows around him to hold him comfortably.

"The prices the proven wines are bringing at auction have increased tenfold, sometimes more over a few short months. Too many collectors are holding wine they paid millions for that are now being proven worthless. Yet, they want the wines. Now they are willing to pay much more to get the authentic wine."

Another one of the forces acting on supply and demand. "Okay, I get that. But the wines in your cellar weren't marked; there were no papers that passed with them to prove their authenticity."

"On the contrary. We'd chipped the bottles that we had produced with a RFID chip that recorded every movement of that wine from bottling to consumption."

Whoa. I loved it when Old World met New World with great consequences. That gave me hope for the future. No more battles, only collaborations for the betterment of both. "Can they not then trace the bottles to you and your ownership?"

"Not easily. When we finally embrace blockchain, then we can track all that information. Right now, the chips only collect lot and bottling date numbers on them with a unique code particular to each winery, each vintage. Rudimentary, but it is all we have right now. They are like chips in dogs—they can give you the ownership info, and a bit more, but that's it. Wine is a bit of a commodity. Each bottle is not a unique work of art in its own right, so they are indistinguishable. What gives them value are the lot and vintage, so that's what we use to identify them."

"And destroying the rest of a vintage raises the value even more."

"Yes, although there were many other wines in my cellar besides my own, not all of them chipped."

"Maybe they were after different bottles for different purposes."

He cocked his head as if he hadn't considered that.

"And M. Fabrice? Why did you take the exclusive from Laurent for the Estate Laurent and give it to M. Fabrice?" Curious as to how he'd shade it, I decided to leave out the whole family angle.

"To punish Enzo, perhaps? I was angry. Fabrice and Enzo do business, but don't see eye-to-eye."

"How so?"

"Laurent is our wholesaler. Fabrice retails wine all over the world."

"You chose Fabrice to make a point."

"That, and Emma suggested it. Her father and Fabrice have been longtime friends. And, to be honest, I felt a bit sorry for him, losing his wife so recently."

"Do you have any idea who Victor Martin was?"

Another glance toward his wife. She nodded.

"He was an undercover investigator, or so he said. He flashed a badge of some sort. He was looking into Frank Liu's allegations of collusion between Enzo Laurent and me to keep our wines elevated and his not."

"He was a cop?"

"So he said."

Funny, he'd told Desiree he was a winemaker. "And he was looking into your business practices with Laurent?"

"I'm afraid so." Jean-Louis smoothed the blanket covering him.

"Was there anything you wouldn't want him to find?"

Color rose in his cheeks as his voice choked down to a whisper. "May I have some water please?" he asked his wife.

A stall tactic that gave me the answer I didn't want. "What have you two done?"

His hand shook. Some water escaped to dribble down his chin. He ignored it as his body went rigid. A coughing fit seized him. Just like before, he hacked and wheezed, desperate for breath. This time the fit didn't ease.

"Call the doctor!" Madame Bouclet yelled at a staff member who came running. They hurried to do her bidding.

"Some water perhaps?" Helpless, I could only watch as he turned bright red, then blue, as his oxygen plummeted.

She stroked his cheek with the back of her fingers and whispered into his ear. The words hummed, a mere murmur I couldn't make out, not that I would understand if I could. But they seemed to help. Soon he gulped air, his color fading a bit to a more normal pink.

"Go now. He'll be okay. The doctor is close by, and he will calm him. This is very stressful. We will talk more soon."

"Should I get Jean-Charles?"

"No, he and his father have made their peace. There is nothing he can do."

I turned to go.

Her voice stopped me. "There is one thing *you* can do, though. Find the wine and catch the killer. Absolve my family... quickly." She turned back to her husband. "Please," she whispered.

That was three things, all of them impossible.

And, for a fleeting moment, I wondered if they intended for me to play the role of the sacrificial lamb thrown to the wolves.

CHRISTOPHE WAITED FOR ME, HIS LEGS SWINGING FROM HIS PERCH on a three-legged stool. Red and green icing ringed his mouth. When he saw me, he hopped down and rushed over. "Lucky!"

I grabbed him before he could transfer any of that icing to my coat. "Hey, big guy. Thanks for waiting."

"I am so glad you have come," one of the chefs, a young woman in her whites, said. "He has eaten almost all of the cookies. I am making more. Madame Bouclet must have her cookies."

I clucked at Christophe, alarmed at how much of my mother I channeled. If my luck held, only the good parts would come through, not that I counted on being that lucky, of course. "You should not have eaten so many. You'll ruin your dinner." I patted Christophe's rounded belly. "You look like Winnie the Pooh after draining the honey pot."

"I think I feel like him, too." The boy did look a bit green.

"I need your help." I drew him away from the kitchen staff, who weren't paying attention to us, at least not overtly. But one could never be too careful.

That seemed to restore a bounce to his step. "Me?" He sounded slightly incredulous.

"Yes, but it's a secret between you and me, okay?"

"What about *Papa?*"

He would cut right to the hard part. "Maybe later, but for right now, just you and me. Promise?"

His lips pinched into a straight line as he considered keeping his sainted father on the outside. He weighed my request for so long I began to doubt my status. Finally, he came to a decision. *"Oui."* He nodded solemnly. "Pinky swear. We must do this, *non?"*

Explaining that it probably wasn't necessary wasn't worth the time, so we did that bit, and I figured that was as good as a five-year-old could do. I squatted so we were eye-to-eye. "You spend a lot of time hanging out in the kitchen, don't you?"

His face clouded. "Am I in trouble?"

"Of course not. This is as much your kitchen as anybody's. If you like it here, then hang here."

"Sara, she lets me help, just like you do. I really like that."

Whether his father wanted him to or not, young Christophe Bouclet was already stuffing his feet into his father's shoes. A hard life, but a good one. Vices and passions. The Bouclet men embraced both with vigor, so to do so was in Christophe's DNA. "Sara? The pretty cookie-maker?"

"*Oui.* Yes," he quickly corrected.

"*Oui* I got. Relax, this is not so important. It is like a treasure hunt. You like treasure hunts, yes?" He nodded, looking far too serious. I glanced over his shoulder to see if anyone seemed interested in our conversation. The dishwasher kept glancing our way. He looked familiar, but he didn't look overly concerned, only vaguely angry and foreign, like so many faces I'd seen, especially on our staff in London. The world was mixing, disturbing some. Not me. I thought it good for all of us to have to deal with each other. According to the news, I seemed to be in the minority. I turned back to Christophe, who eyed me with a serious frown. "You know the door we all went through last night?" Was it only last night? It seemed an eternity. Of course, with no sleep and little food, everything seemed a struggle at the moment.

"The one in *Grand-père's'* room?" He nodded toward the hall-way, somehow remembering that people with bad manners pointed while the rest gestured, a distinction still lost on the vulgar American. But for now, I was grateful he remembered.

"Yes. It's supposed to be a secret door." I lowered my voice to a whisper to emphasize my point.

"Aunt Desiree told me."

"Really?"

"I saw her coming through the door one day. She asked me not to tell, but I don't think she meant not to tell you or Papa."

I wondered at his reasoning but decided not to delve into it now. "Why did she not want you to tell?"

"There was a man with her. She said *Grand-père* would be angry."

Parading some of the family jewels, so like a Bouclet, although her brother was a bit more discrete, or so I hoped. "Did you know the man?"

His face pinched in fear. He nodded once.

"Is he in the kitchen now?"

175

"No."

That was not altogether unexpected. "Can you describe him?"

He turned and raised his arm, pointing at one of the prep cooks dicing vegetables with a large knife. He paused mid-dice as Christophe whispered in my ear, "He looks like that man there."

"Asian?"

"Yes, but not as much. He looked a lot like the man in the wine cellar last night. The one tied up."

Sinjin. Desiree. I knew it.

Feeling eyes on me, I glanced up. The dishwasher's face froze in fear.

The man turned and ran. Pans clattered as he knocked over a colleague in his rush to the back door.

I dropped my head. "Don't run," I muttered, knowing he couldn't hear me. "If you do, then I have to follow you." And he had a knife.

I grabbed Christophe by the shoulders. "Stay here. I need to talk to him." I scanned the room. At all the ruckus, everyone had stopped. In the group, I found the pastry chef who stared at us with wide eyes. "Sara? Will you, please?"

At her nod, I turned and ran.

I caught the backdoor on the bounce-back, so I wasn't too far behind. But, unfamiliar with the rabbit warren behind the buildings, I was at a loss. I was in luck—there was only one way out, a short alley leading down the block toward the river. My feet screamed as I ran. Last time I would don heels as part of a daytime ensemble. I should know better. Wearing the things invited the Fates to visit abuse. They'd been particularly munificent today. A slight uneven patch in the concrete rolled my ankle slightly. Staggering, I caught myself, then raced on.

He was forty, maybe fifty feet ahead. Younger than me and making better choices in footwear, he was at a distinct advantage. If he made it to the end of the alley where it opened at the *Trocadéro*, I'd lose him.

Sensing me behind him, he grabbed anything that was loose, garbage bins, flats with bits of rotting vegetables, broken-down cardboard boxes, and threw them into my path. With a kick or a push or a quick dart to the side, I avoided most of them. The others bounced off my thighs as I ran past. But his tactic did slow me down. The distance between us grew.

I put my head down, running through the detritus he tossed in my path.

My breathing ragged, I sucked in air, willing myself to run faster. Pain greeted each step. I gritted my teeth against it. I was closing the distance.

He glanced back, a wild look in his eye. His face was crimson, his breathing as ragged as my own.

Twenty feet now.

The sound of traffic grew louder. Up ahead, the *Trocadéro* flung traffic around in a circle, with each car gaining speed as the drivers jockeyed, positioning for their exit. I'd have ten feet of sidewalk, maybe fifteen, before we both would be fed into the vehicular melee like wood into a chipper.

Not much room to stop or turn.

The light of the opening ahead. The rush of traffic rose.

Fifteen feet.

I wasn't going to catch him in time.

He burst through into the light. Ten feet. Almost close enough to throw myself at him. But not quite.

Like a panicked deer, head down, he kept running.

This time of year, people had found shelter from the cold. The sidewalk was empty.

A furtive glance. Measuring my options.

A couple caught my eye. Familiar as they bent toward each other heads together, as they sat at a small table at the café on the corner. His hair curled softly, dark but not too. A classic profile. Turning-head handsome. A blue scarf knotted at his neck and tucked into the vee in his jacket. She was sultry and upset. Leaning toward him. Head tilted down. A wounded animal. He touched her cheek. I knew them. One of them intimately. Or so I thought.

Jean-Charles.

Emma Moreau.

The cars rushed around the traffic circle.

The dishwasher didn't slow down. A klaxon horn. The squealing of tires. The crunch of metal. Someone shouted. Maybe me? The couple looked up, startled. Our eyes met.

An odd thud that hit a visceral note, yanking me back.

A car swerved toward me.

A moment of realization.

I leaped.

CHAPTER TWELVE

"*L*UCKY?" THE voice, male. "Lucky, are you okay? Talk to me."

Jean-Charles. Where was I? Why did he sound so scared? I struggled to remember. I tried to move, to open my eyes. Nothing seemed to work.

Breathe, Lucky. Breathe.

I focused on calm, on breathing slowly, on trying to feel, to remember.

Christophe! His face swam before me. Scared. Worried. *Someone must tell him I'm okay!*

The warmth of adrenaline flooded through me. My eyes flew open. Blinking rapidly, I brought Jean-Charles into focus. Worried, just like his son. I managed to grab his lapel with one hand. "Call home. Tell Christophe I'm okay." My voice didn't sound like mine.

"But you are not okay." Jean-Charles could adopt the wrong emotion in any situation—it was one of his best things.

Pragmatism in the face of panic didn't work for me. "Do it."

He knew when to argue and when to just suck it up. Smart man, he pulled out his phone.

A sea of faces all looking down at me circled at the edges of my periphery. Someone said something about calling the police and an ambulance.

I worked myself to one elbow. The world swam then righted. "I'm okay. Give me a minute." More wishful thinking than truth. My body was numb, quiet with shock. That would change.

Another voice in French, another one I recognized. This one I didn't trust. "I am the police."

Emma Moreau. And Jean-Charles.

I remembered.

How long had I been out? I analyzed the faces staring at me. Most looked concerned. One looked terrified. The driver, I'd bet. He wrung his hands and muttered for anyone who would listen, "I dodged the man. It was instinct." Tears still streaked his face, so I couldn't have been out long.

They'd been here together, Jean-Charles and his "old friend." Perhaps at one of the cafés ringing the *Trocadéro*. I hoped not at my favorite, *Carette*.

"She was right there," the driver continued as he wrung his hands. "Nothing I could do."

Except maybe run over the bad guy instead of the good guy next time, I thought. He clearly didn't have Dorothy's instincts when it came to dropping houses...or cars...on people. "Where is the man who ran into traffic?" I actually managed most of that in French as I tested my feet. They moved. A good sign.

The somber look from the faces in the crowd, not a good sign.

A man close to me winced. "A bus."

"Dead?"

"*Oui.*"

He held out a hand and helped pull me to a seated position. "You can move, *oui?*"

I wiggled, gingerly testing all the various parts. My head

throbbed, but everything responded, albeit reluctantly. I touched the epicenter of the pain on my temple. Hell of a goose egg. Above me, I heard Jean-Charles ask for Christophe. Finally, the man had seen a glimmer of truth—do what I ask; it's more expedient that way. Especially if he wanted me to do something.

As I tried to rise, Jean-Charles put a hand on my shoulder, stopping me. He pressed the phone to his chest. "Just a minute and I will help you." Then he returned to speak into the phone. "Yes, she is here. Everything is fine. Not to worry." He listened, flicking glances my way. "You want to talk to her? That is not—"

I snatched the phone from him and took a deep breath. "Christophe, honey, I'm so sorry to worry you. I'm fine." His words tumbled over each other. I waited until he'd finished. "I know I don't sound like myself. I had to run very far. That's why I had your father call you." He calmed down. "I love you, too," I said, then relinquished the phone to his father.

He said a hasty goodbye, then pocketed the device. "Here, let me help you."

The circle of people widened as he eased me to a standing position. "Are you sure nothing is broken?"

A bit wobbly, I was thankful for his steadying arm around my waist as he guided me to a café table behind a glassine curtain and next to a heater. With each step, my feet sang out, reminding me of the punishment they'd taken. Various body parts chimed in on the chorus. "Nothing broken. One hell of a headache, but I feel pretty lucky that's the worst of it." As I put my right foot down, the heel of my shoe snapped off. I sagged against the solid chest of Jean-Charles. "One dead pair of truly righteous shoes. Add that to the list. And I'll never get the oil and grime out of this coat. In fact, given how the whole day has gone, I think I'll burn the whole outfit as an offering to the Goddess of Good Luck, who clearly has a beef with me. Although, for what, I can't fathom." I knew I was babbling but could do little to stop the run-on words. Maybe a bit of shock kicking in. Where on the Stress Scale of Bad Shit being hit by a car fit was anybody's guess, but it packed a wallop. And then there was the whole impending marriage thing—I knew that was on there. And then the relationship thing, which sounds the same but was different, that was on there, too. Ditto a close relative with a serious health issue. I had two. According to that scale, I was pretty sure I was bumping up against the "might shit a cold purple Twinkie" category.

"You will be very sore tomorrow." Jean-Charles turned me and eased me into a chair.

He fussed over me a bit, brushing down my coat where he could. He plucked at a bit of dark green. Wrinkling his nose, he held it aloft and squinted at it.

"Yes, it's what you think. Something rotten."

He flicked it away, then took the seat across from me. Two Champagne flutes, one of them empty, one nearly so, rose damningly between us. An empty bottle, upended, poked from an ice bucket next to Jean-Charles.

"Am I interrupting?"

"It's not what it looks like." He looked like he wished he could run. Of course, that would be throwing in the guilty-as-hell towel.

"It's exactly what it looks like." Emotion tugged at the half-healed scar across my heart that Teddie had left. Love and anger, hurt, sharp and fresh, leaked out. Betrayal, red-hot, seared through me. Once bitten and all of that. Trust, once broken, would it always be a Humpty-Dumpty for me? Would I mistrust everyone? Guard my heart with such vigilance that no one could get in?

Blinking back emotion that would only cloud my thinking, I tried to remember that jumping to conclusions usually ended in a fatal leap off the High Cliff of Paranoia. Despite appearances, it could all be innocent.

Old friends. Or flame rekindled?

Just last night I'd broken bread with my former lover. *Perspective, Lucky. Perspective.*

I sucked in a ragged breath. Right now, I had a serious beef with dainty, sultry, manipulative Emma Moreau, but it wasn't about Jean-Charles. And my beef with him had more to do with respect and honesty and little to do with jealousy. At the very least I deserved to know...all of it. Only then could we find the bedrock on which to build a solid life.

"How are you even alive?" Jean-Charles had to steady his glass with both hands as he took a sip then offered me one.

I was grateful for even the last dollop.

"I could have lost you." His adrenaline levels were falling fast —I knew the signs. Reality crept in, and possibilities of different outcomes had him climbing the stress ladder right behind me. "Quite frankly, you are the most confounding woman, but without you, life would be so boring, and my heart would not be whole."

His words punched right through the case of righteous Indignation I was building. What did my father always ask me when I had a serious case of twisted knickers? Are you building a case or building a bridge?

"Reflexes. That's all I can tell you. And some seriously great guardian angels." At his raised eyebrow, I nodded. "I'm seriously into angels. I *know* they exist. Don't ask me how, but I do. Ever since I was little, fourth grade maybe. Now as to the whole story about some fat, white guy sitting on a cloud making rules about my life—that's a bit sketchy. God or whatever you choose to call him is bigger than that. My theory. Religion has killed more people on this planet than everything else. We need to get over it and realize we're all simply talking about goodness. All of us. And my goodness isn't any better than anybody's and vice versa."

"So, you think angels saved you? We need to get that bump on your head checked out." His smile told me he was teasing, so I stepped down the whole Battle that Couldn't Be Won thing.

"Does it matter? It makes me feel good. And I'm here, aren't I? Perhaps when I shouldn't be."

"Yes." The seriousness returned to his face. I loved the way it sharpened his features and made him look even sexier. I wasn't so fond of the mansplaining that indubitably would follow. "So, tell me"—he signaled the waiter to bring another bottle—"how did you come to be chasing a man down the alley and into the *Trocadéro?*"

"Yes, this I would like to know as well." Emma Moreau joined us, taking the remaining seat as Jean-Charles pulled me around closer to him. He snaked an arm around my shoulders.

I wondered who he was trying to deliver a message to—me, Emma, or himself.

I eyed my adversary. Underestimating the *commissaire* would be unwise. As a local, she already had a leg up. Her history with the Bouclets and the Laurents gave her insight and allies I lacked. And being a member of the Judicial Police gave her a flush when I was holding a W.H.I.P.

Assaulting a police officer. Getting hit by a car. Chasing a man to his death. And finding myself holding a cap pistol in a duel to the death. Could today get any better?

Jean-Charles painted on a smile. Emma didn't bother.

Something niggled at me as Emma waited for my response. Something important, but I couldn't find its storage spot in my scrambled brain. A deep breath. Another. I worked for calm, closing my eyes. Then it hit me. "As you were leaving last night with Sinjin and Desiree, I saw you speaking with the dead man at the Bouclets'."

That took a bit of her bounce. "Who?"

After a quick glance, I hooked a finger over my shoulder toward the now-shrouded body. The police had rerouted traffic, and an ambulance sounded in the distance. "Him. He called to you from the doorway."

Her eyes flicked from side to side as she scrambled for an answer. "He told me Desiree took Sinjin to the wine cellar."

"What did Desiree say?"

Emma regained her footing. "I'm not at liberty to say."

One of those phrases used by the police to stonewall us mere citizens.

"I'm assuming you searched Victor's house?"

"The man had no I.D. We have no idea who he really was, much less where he lived."

Apparently, there was info she was at liberty to tell me, which had my antennae up. Something in her tone told me she knew more than she wanted me to know. "And his employer? Could he offer any insight?"

"Paul Bay? He'd never heard of him."

The waiter had yet to clear the table. From the remnants, it appeared Jean-Charles and Emma had shared an omelet, some flaky pastries, and the Champagne I'd noticed before. "I'm crashing a private party?"

My light tone didn't fool Jean-Charles. His smile slipped away. "Lucky."

Deciding offense was the best strategy, I turned to face *Commissaire* Moreau. "How dare you?"

Her face reddened. "We are old friends. Surely you are not that insecure?"

I waved that away with a chuckle. "I'm sorry; I wasn't clear. Your history is just that. We all have one. But Mr. Desai?"

Jean-Charles pulled on my shoulder. "Who?"

"I'm not talking to you. I'm asking your 'old friend' here why, and on whose authority, she put a tail on me."

Jean-Charles's hand dropped from my shoulder. He sucked in a breath which sounded a lot like indignation. Maybe he could dig himself out of his hole with me after all. "Emma! Did you do such a thing?"

"It seemed prudent." Her gaze darted from side to side like a scared rabbit. "She has been involved in a lot of murders."

His eyes turned dark and stormy. I knew what that meant: run. "By that metric, so have you." His voice was low, vibrating with emotion. Yep, I was right, indignation.

I allowed myself a tiny gloat. The man *could* ride to my defense. Maybe my knight's steed was a small pony and not a fearsome white stallion, but it was something. After the day I'd had, I'd take it.

The waiter delivered the Champagne, and I settled in to enjoy an altercation that did not require my input. All I'd had to do was light the fuse. As a tactic, it bore remembering. Usually a frontal assault kind of gal, I was warming to the idea of defeat by outflanking my opponent.

"It is my job," Emma huffed. Her excuse fell short. "Sinjin Smythe-Gordon is being held on suspicion of murder. He implicated you."

Remembering she didn't know the man like I did, I resisted rolling my eyes. "If he told you I was Father Christmas would you believe him? Surely, you've heard of a little thing called proof? I grant you, he's guilty of something. You could probably hold him if there is such a thing as felony lying. As for me, you got nothing." That last bit was more bluster than bullshit. Trumping up some reason to haul me to the hoosegow for interrogation wouldn't challenge even the fair *commissaire*'s skimpy skills.

"Emma, the Prosecuting Judge would never have approved such a thing based on that," Jean-Charles continued, working up a serious case of righteous indignation. "This is smelling like a personal vendetta. You cannot use your powers this way. I have told you before, you must always play by the rules. That is the only way to win."

From Jean-Charles's reaction, I guessed the *commissaire* had committed some rather large breach of protocol; otherwise, she'd be parrying every attack with a bit more vigor. France, despite appearances, protected civil liberties with way more enthusiasm than the Americans who had a camera in every bedroom and on every corner, who used phones and facial recognition to keep track of us all. National security, my ass. It was a power play, pure and simple. As a culture, we'd given up so many liberties in the name of safety. Yet, we had mass shootings so numerous we no longer responded with outrage. So, exactly how well was all that working out?

And he'd had to have this discussion with her before? That just rubbed me all over with warm fuzzies.

Emma squirmed like a castigated schoolchild as she fumed. Her anger found a target. She leaned across the table, catching my hand in hers. "You will be very careful. If you stick one finger across the line, I will cut it off."

"Toe."

"What?"

"Toe across the line."

She thought about carrying her bluff further; I could see it in the way she ground her teeth.

Jean-Charles stepped in, stopping her from completely making a fool of herself by tilting at the wrong windmill. "Emma! You will stop, now! Lucky is not part of this problem." Emma wilted under his scowl. "You will stay out of her way, or the judge will hear about your...miscalculations." He'd chosen the word carefully. "The local police in Las Vegas count on Lucky's inside knowledge to help in investigations. You'd be wise to do the same."

Well *that* was going to make her like me *so* much more.

He should've stopped while he had his nose in front, inches from the finish line.

What I would've given to have been a fly on the wall eavesdropping on their little *tête-à-tête* before I crashed the party. From his tone and her bright eyes and quivering chin, all was not as I had assumed. I waited for the silence to get uncomfortably awkward; then I dove in. "Have you found the wine?"

Neither gave me their attention. I knew the answer anyway.

Locked in some sort of battle that had its origin in the past, they glared at each other across the tiny table. Too late, I realized I was in the middle—always an awkward position but a familiar one. "Okay, no wine. And Desiree? Where is she?" I asked before one of them picked up a knife and did something they'd regret.

Emma took a few moments and several deep breaths before she tore her eyes from my betrothed to glare at me. "She is home while we decide if we will charge her with a crime."

"I might be able to add a bit on that one." The comment sounded smug, but I didn't feel a bit happy about the little stinkbomb I was about to toss to my fiancé. But it did have the effect of defusing the escalating emotion.

"The man I was chasing," I twisted around to look squarely at Jean-Charles. "He worked in your parents' kitchen." As I swiveled to look at him, a man, just visible over his shoulder, caught my eye. Dark hair, high cheekbones, radiating a confident swagger. A tumbler fell into place. *An inside job, he'd said.* "I believe he worked with Mr. Smythe-Gordon as his inside man. Desiree was complicit. She even showed Sinjin the location of the cellar."

"That is not true!" Jean-Charles stiffened against my back. "What is it? What do you see?" He tried to turn to follow my gaze.

I snapped my mouth closed. "Nothing. Nothing at all. Just got lost there for a moment. My head is still spinning," I lied.

"Understandable. Are you sure you don't need to go back to the hotel?"

"I'm good." What were we talking about? Oh yes, the thieves

and an inside job. "And you have been gone from here for a long time." Not to mention he was also seriously into magical thinking when it came to his family. Guilty of the same transgression, I couldn't cast the first stone. "Your father met with Enzo Laurent in the wine cellar on a regular basis. If it was a secret, then more than the family knew."

I glanced over his shoulder again. The man was gone.

A stunned silence reverberated for a few moments. When he broke it, his voice was soft with defeat. "I do not know what to say."

"Well, the dead man won't be saying anything either. Do you know anything about him?"

"Only that my mother hired him based on a recommendation from Enzo Laurent."

Was Enzo Laurent the kind of guy who would pay any attention to a dishwasher in his kitchen? "We need to convince your sister to do some serious singing."

"How do you know this about my sister and the man you were chasing?"

"Someone saw them. They told me." I prayed he wouldn't ask me who. I wouldn't tell him, but that would derail the whole conversation.

"You were at my parents' house without me?" Spoken like a true control freak, he made that sound like a transgression.

Not well-versed in the nuances of Parisian social protocol, I'd probably committed enough sins to be banished to social purgatory, which, to this social pariah, actually sounded like a one-way trip to the beach in January. "Yes, just now. That's how I flushed the guy in the kitchen and ended up bird-dogging him here."

"Why were you there?"

"To talk with your father."

"He is not well."

189

"He'll be dead if his daughter goes to jail and we don't recover that wine."

Acceptance reverberated in his silence. Two points for the home team. "Did you see my sister?"

I kept my expression impassive. "No. Both she and your father need to fess up, and quickly, before this thing escalates along with the body count."

"My father?" Jean-Charles frowned at my casting aspersions on a family member.

"You need to have a discussion with him."

"About what?"

"I don't know, but he does. And the minute he tells you, you better tell me. No more playing hide-and-seek with the truth. It's all the cards on the table from here on out. Got it?"

Unused to anyone getting in his face, he breathed in sharply through his nose.

"Think carefully before you speak."

He breathed out slowly until I thought he might pass out. "I will speak to him."

Emma had said nothing as she licked her wounds and watched Jean-Charles and me. She couldn't really hear what we were saying, but she probably caught the gist from our postures.

She gave me a smug look. Looking for a puppy to kick, she pounced. "What were you doing in the Kléber Metro trying to go through a tunnel access door?"

"Your officer finding me was pretty convenient. Was he following me as well?" A long shot.

Her sudden silence betrayed her shock. I had a feeling she was a better cop than she appeared to be. Emotions. Getting invested in the outcome screwed with competency.

"Emma?" Jean-Charles's question held an accusation.

"I have my team watching for her, for reports of a tall, arrogant American woman sticking her nose in where it will get cut off." She made a slicing motion with her hand.

"You are picking the wrong fight, Emma." Jean-Charles had his back up for sure.

While we still had the telling-me-the-whole-story thing to work on, I didn't think we had any issues with Emma Moreau, at least not between the two of us. She was working hard to get between me and my freedom, but that was my fight. "Look, *Commissaire*, you can mess with me all you want, but it's not going to get you any closer to the killer or to finding that wine. Your choice, but you're wasting assets and risking your career. Is a personal vendetta worth it?"

She still looked ready to spit nails. "What did you speak with Enzo Laurent about?"

"Ask him. Now, what do you know about the wine? I'm assuming you didn't find it." Thankfully Jean-Charles refrained from giving me a war on two fronts, at least not in front of his *old* friend.

"I will. Enzo will tell me." Her attitude lost a bit of bluster at my lack of intimidation. With her back against the wall, she decided to toss a few morsels to the mongrel at her feet. "My team traced the wine deeper into the sewers, but they were clever in the path they took. With the water and some..." She asked Jean-Charles for a translation.

"Cement."

"Yes, this. Together they made it impossible to follow exactly where they went."

"Don't you have a map of the sewers? They had to bring the wine up somewhere."

"We followed them as far as the river where they went under, through a telecom tunnel. On the other side, the tunnel opens to the whole catacomb network. Nobody knows for sure exactly where all those tunnels go. It is a very good place to hide —dark, confusing, and dangerous in places."

"And the license plate on the black sedan parked behind M. Fabrice's?"

"A wild bird chase—"

"Goose."

If looks could kill, I'd been drawn, quartered, and spread across the back forty. "The license number M. Fabrice gave us was registered to a red Fiat in the Nineteenth. The owner was home all night, the car with him."

I leaned back. Jean-Charles nuzzled my ear—a good sign, as long as he didn't pull a Mike Tyson. "I'm familiar with tunnels. The storm drains under Vegas stretch for over three hundred maze-like miles. One thing I learned, even if the maps are outdated, *somebody* knows where all the passages go."

Despite the Champagne, she looked like she needed a drink. "It is illegal to go there."

"Even better." A bit of confidence crept in. "Even Eve couldn't resist the Forbidden Fruit."

Emma's phone jangled and danced on the table. She grabbed it with a practiced swipe. "*Oui?*" Her face reddened and her mouth puckered as she listened. "What do you mean he escaped? No one dances out of the jail." She turned her back to us as if the movement would block our interest and the conversation.

I stifled a laugh. More than half of me expected this. No, not just anyone, but a particular dark-haired, flamboyant, bad-boy pirate I knew who made his living out of avoiding consequences.

Jean-Charles looked lost. "Sinjin," I mouthed to him. Understanding bloomed, quickly replaced by anger. "And Desiree?" he mouthed back.

I shook my head. "She wasn't home," I mouthed back.

A moment of confusion, then understanding dawned.

We both had that sinking feeling. Desiree and her bad choices. And Sinjin with his smooth manners and matinee looks could convince even the most skeptical that he was a good choice...until he proved he wasn't. Reeling from two disastrous relationships, Desiree was ripe for the picking.

What the hell had she done? And could I pull her bacon from the fire this time? Could anyone? Should we? Without consequences how would she learn?

We both continued eavesdropping on the *commissaire's* conversation. "He must've had help. Did anyone come to see him?" She paused, listening, then her eyes flicked to Jean-Charles.

"There's your answer." I put my hand over his.

He threw back the rest of his Champagne, then placed the glass on the table with so much force I thought the stem would break. It didn't. "My sister. If there is trouble, she will find it."

"Don't be too hard on her. When it comes to women, Sinjin Smythe-Gordon is the proof to Mesmer's theory of Animal Magnetism."

"Really?" Looking for a fight, he let an accusatory tone slip into the question.

Way too smart to pick up that gauntlet, I realized my words held the seeds of self-incrimination. "Experience is an antidote to his charm. I've met far better." I pulled his arm around me until I could feel his breath on my cheek.

"Really?" he whispered.

"I didn't exactly sit at home waiting for you to drop in my lap. And, don't forget, I was raised in a whorehouse."

Emma had ended the call and stared at us, her head swiveling from one to the other like a spectator at a tennis match. "Whorehouse. What is this?"

"Exactly what it sounds like." I shut her down with a frown. "So Sinjin is on the lam and Desiree is helping him."

"I am not sure of this 'lam,' but he is free. A woman matching Desiree's description visited him just before he disappeared. We don't have *proof...*" she enunciated the word with a slight eye-roll for my benefit, "...but the implication is clear. We must find them both."

"Guilty by implication, it's a thing here?" I know, sticking my thumb in the gaping wound in her pride, but, well, I had an excuse not to be my best self at the moment. Being on the wrong end of a fight with a Peugeot was excuse enough. The woman had me wishing on a star that I could find proof of *her* guilt. Rather female of me, which didn't make me proud. But I couldn't shake the feeling she was mixed up in all of this some-how. "Oh, I wouldn't waste your time beating the bistros. He'll show up."

She leaned back and crossed her arms, giving my exposed legs a quick glance of irritation. "Why do you think that?"

"He needs help, and I'm the only real friend he has. Desiree is beautiful and can simper, but I can get things done."

"You seem confident."

While I was pretty sure I was right, confident might be over-stating, but I decided to go with it. "The wine thieves double-crossed him. I have a feeling he needs that wine, or his ass is in a crack." Knowing Sinjin, he'd played both ends against the middle and the wine was the key. Without it, he'd piss off some very bad folks—I'd bet my last dollar on that.

The temptation to just let it all go, to not help anyone find the wine or solve the crime washed over me. For once, Sinjin would get what was coming to him. But then, so would the Bouclets, and Desiree, as misguided as she was, needed help. I couldn't let her hang for a murder she didn't commit, or even a jailbreak she probably did. Was there a twelve-step program to cure the compunction to save everyone from themselves? If so, I needed a long residency.

"Sinjin likes control. Don't we all. Here in France, he is out of his control zone. He'll look for someone he thinks he can manipulate, or at least convince to help him. He already has Desiree dangling on his every glance. But he needs someone else, someone who can walk the walk and hang with those who talk the talk in his world."

"You?" She still looked skeptical.

I could see her wheels turning. I'd bet a mint she thought this looked like a good chance to catch me red-handed. Such a gift I have—cultivating low friends in high places. "If you can think of any other candidates, I'll gladly give up my spot at the head of the line."

"Does she always talk like this?" Emma asked Jean-Charles.

"Yes. It is her way to keep the madness at bay."

I tried to twist around to give him some stink-eye, but he held me tight. "And your Sinjin has much to learn if he thinks he can best you at a game of bluffing." His words were meant to mollify.

I didn't share his confidence. To think I could pull it off again was pushing my luck, not that I had any choice. The key would be to teach him a lesson and not be left holding the loot when *le flic* showed up. But before Sinjin roped me into any ill-conceived plan, I had to figure out what was going on, who was behind it, and where they might have stashed a king's ransom in fancy wine. "I need to figure out where they went in the underground, or where they might have gone. Maybe from that, we can extrapolate what they did with the wine."

Jean-Charles whispered in my ear, his breath soft and sweet. "I know just who you need to talk with."

One of the officers on the scene beckoned to Emma, who clearly was tiring of our game of verbal thrust and parry. Which worked out—I'd had enough of her dodge and weave and attacks on my character. She was hiding something; I could feel it. Maybe it was just a serious case of the-one-who-got-away. Time would tell.

I pulled Jean-Charles's arms as tight as possible around me, wincing as the anesthetic properties of the adrenaline abated. "You sound so sexy when you're all concerned and helpful."

"You like this?" He lowered his voice even further, making me laugh, which hurt.

"Okay, we can talk with this person if you think he can help. Then I will need a very hot bath with someone to scrub my back. Then I am thinking some medicinal makeup sex, very gentle makeup sex."

"You always have the best ideas."

CHAPTER THIRTEEN

I CLUNG to the loop to keep my balance on the Metro train as it hurtled through the tunnels. Each jostle reminded me I'd suffered a collision with a large metal projectile. My head pounded. My body ached in places I didn't know possible. It hurt to breathe. I thought perhaps a rib or two might be bruised or dislocated or broken or whatever happens to ribs to make each breath torture. I'd done the best I could to clean my coat. The stockings were a complete loss, as were the shoes. I'd scored a pair of flats in a shop on Avenue Kléber as we'd headed for the Metro. There I'd pulled myself together as best I could with damp cloths in the restroom. For a gal who'd cheated death, I thought I'd come through rather brilliantly.

A few of my fellow Metro passengers thought otherwise as they shot me curious looks.

Jean-Charles hung onto the loop next to mine. The rest of the passengers, some seated, some standing, all disinterested in those around them, stared at their phones or blankly through the windows—another day in the bank. Occasional lights strobed in the darkness as we flashed by. The air was heavy and dank and smelled of adventure. I loved the subways, any subway —well, okay, not the ones in Tokyo where people jammed in so tight you literally couldn't breathe, and, at my height, I could see over the heads of the short men to see the comic-book porn they were absorbing. I never quite got that—sex with comic book figures? How did that titillate? But the Paris Metro had a gentrified, Old-World shabby chic to it that contrasted with occasional glaring modernization. "Where are we going?"

"Not far. Near the Sorbonne. It is quite the game for the young people to traverse the catacombs." He shouted over the clatter of the train.

"To see how far they can get without getting caught." I remembered many a scary night as a stupid college kid wandering the drainage tunnels under Vegas. We took great delight in thumbing our noses at authority. Big bad-asses that we were, we often found ourselves running from the denizens of the dark who called the drains home and who fiercely protected their turf. The adrenaline jolt had become addictive— a character flaw I was aware of but curiously incapable of mitigating.

"Don't even think about it," Jean-Charles said, reading my mind.

I pressed a hand to my chest, gently. The ribs howled, stealing my breath. I glossed over the pain. Ignoring it would make it go away, right? "*Moi?* I would never. Aren't you worried about your sister?"

"I'm serious." He looked it, too, not that that made a bit of difference. "And don't try to distract me with talk of Desiree. All these years she has been flying slowly toward a crash site. Perhaps today is the day she learns the limits of her charms. You need to be taught a lesson as well."

"Yes, us uppity women need to be put in our place." I gave him a fake smile. When would men stop beating their chests and start being partners rather than protectors? He couldn't watch me 24/7, and somebody had to find that wine. For some reason, my gut told me Emma Moreau wouldn't be hell-bent on that angle...she had a killer to catch. The wine and the murder were related, but she'd work her angle, and I'd work mine.

"You will be the death of me. A nice turn of phrase." He sobered. "But my sister might actually put my father in the grave."

"I would say you will die a happy man, but it is not the truth, and I don't mean to be a problem. You must let me be me. Let me do what I need to do. I'm not so dumb. Look, I've made it this far without some man saving my bacon. Maybe someday I'll overplay it, get cocky, but not today. And not tomorrow."

He waffled and let me have my way...for now.

For that I was grateful. I didn't need a fight, couldn't stomach it, quite frankly. In a moment of infrequent clarity, I realized the whole saving-my-world-as-I-knew-it-from-the-forces-of-evil was getting super old. Yes, I overstated my importance—but that was the key to conjuring my superpowers, such as they were. I wore self-delusion like a personal Cloak of Invincibility. But when I got home, maybe I'd find a new job, cut back the tilting at windmills. A nice dream. But for dreams to come true, they have to start somewhere. "Who does Emma hate?"

He reared back in surprise. "Why do you think she hates anyone?"

"Come on. She wears it like a comfortable sweater."

He stared out the window for a bit, his eyes unfocused. "There are people who are fighters, and people who are victims, or define themselves as such."

"Emma is a victim?" A *commissaire* in the police department didn't scream victim to me.

"Of life."

"Ah, she aspired to loftier positions. And marrying it would be an expedient way to achieve it. Sounds more like a predator than a victim."

Jean-Charles arched his eyebrows in surprise. "She is harmless."

"Like a spider."

"You two drew a line in the sand the moment you met."

There was some truth there. "But that doesn't mean it's not warranted. How did your cozy little Champagne confab come about?"

"She wanted to tell me what she found out about the wine theft."

"And did she?"

The look on his face told me all I needed to know. She'd maneuvered him into a compromising situation, and he'd fallen for it. Not that most men wouldn't. Some lessons are learned the hard way. "Former lovers transitioning to friends, a battle most don't survive. Take it from one who's suffered the wounds of friendly fire." Before he could offer a lame excuse or an explanation that would make me think less of him, I asked, "Who are we going to see?"

"Pepper Kirkland."

"My mother had a Peter O'Toole fetish. Pepper's parents must have been Stan Lee fans." I turned my eyes skyward. "Rest in peace, Mr. Lee." I resumed my diatribe. "I'm sure Pepper would agree we need to bring back originality, but some of us suffer when those who love us try to fit our size ten feet into size four shoes."

Jean-Charles chewed on his lip as his face squinched in concentration. "Sometimes you talk, and I am completely lost. I do not have this problem with anyone else."

"*Iron Man.* Pepper is the name of Tony Stark's assistant. But her last name is Potts, not Kirkland. I'm sorta glad about that. Weird shit happens in the Stark household."

Jean-Charles clamped his mouth shut, which had been hanging open.

I had him back on his heels, a proud moment. "We're a young country. Movie references are all the history we have. Is your Pepper American? Male or female?"

A gamer, he pulled himself together. Thankful for a question he could answer, his expression relaxed. "American, although he came to Paris to study music after college and stayed. And he's most decidedly male, a rather refined specimen, or so I've been told. He teaches at the American University and studies French wine for his Masters of Wine. A brilliant oenologist."

"But he feels a bit constrained in the dusty, musty Old-World reality of Bordeaux, Burgundy, and academia?" I liked this kid already. No doubt we would get on swimmingly.

"He's taken a shine to urban spelunking, I believe they call it. But he doesn't partake; rather, he maps the tunnels. Others take photos and draw diagrams, and Pep turns those scribblings into beautiful maps. I'm sure he'll tell you all about it. Beautiful women bring out the storyteller in him."

"Urban spelunking?" The words rolled around inside my imagination. I felt one side of my mouth curl. "I've been looking for a hobby."

"No!" He said it with such force a few passengers looked up from their mental masturbation devices.

When they realized no blood would be spilled, they quickly lost interest, returning to the pleasure at hand, so to speak. That metaphor was getting the best of my imagination. I needed to leave them to their own devices. Unable to help myself, I chuckled—a bit of merriment in a dismal day. My ribs protested, but I felt better.

Urban spelunking. Who could resist? "You said so yourself, all work and no play makes me rather dull."

"It's illegal." His tone had lost its playful lilt. I couldn't imagine why.

"And your point?" I feigned innocence. If I couldn't torture another metaphor to please me, then I could at least tug on his chain for a bit.

"My mother..."

"Will love me if I save her daughter, reclaim the lost wine, and refurbish the family name." I neglected to mention she would see me shot at dawn if I failed, but we both knew it. So what was the point? Speaking the words made them real. I liked my version of the story better, so I left it at that. A bit of willful manifesting, if that wasn't redundant.

The train slowed. Passengers pushing toward the door paused our verbal back-and-forth, leaving me on the upswing, at least for now. Reality was, I'd do what I wanted, and Jean-Charles could choose to bail me out or not.

I found going up the stairs was far less painful than the going-down part. The night had deepened when we climbed from the bowels to once again breathe fresh air. This part of Paris was just unfolding, embracing the night. Filled with a mix of locals, students, and a few tourists who knew Paris was best in the winter, the streets teemed with energy. The bookstores, the cafés in the alleyways only open at night, the bars and night-clubs still slumbering yet as the night was a bit too young for that kind of merriment; the place beat like the heart of the city. My favorite arrondissement by far. My whole being thrummed with life. I grabbed Jean-Charles's hand with both of my own. "In a perfect world, *this* is where I would live."

"We can live here." He said it quietly, without emotion, so perhaps I wouldn't realize it was the first skirmish in the war of putting two very full, very demanding lives together.

"Life is far from perfect." I didn't let that thought dim my enjoyment of the spectacle of life in the Latin Quarter.

"If you lived here, you would drink too much, eat too much, and get no sleep." Jean-Charles tried to lighten his mood.

"Sounds like home already." The dance of humanity caught in the throes of merriment whirled around me, reminding me of Vegas in so many ways. Maybe that's what drew me. "Where are we going to find your friend?"

"First, let me buy a bottle of wine. With Pep, it is best to come bearing gifts. He will expect it." Jean-Charles tugged me down an alleyway, then through a low door into a grotto. "Watch your head," he said, just in time for me to duck.

With brick-lined walls and a barrel ceiling, the place reminded me of a wine cave. With sconces on the walls and dim lighting, it even had that musty, fruity, old grape juice smell. The floor was dirt as if someone had excavated just enough space under his house to have a wine shop. As the ceiling sloped to meet the walls, I had to duck to get close to the wine.

"What is this place?" I whispered to myself. The window, all one square foot of it, hadn't seen a cleaning since the French Revolution. Wood planks held together with metal fittings served as a door. Stout and solid, it had probably withheld the heathen horde when appropriate. No sign. Not even faded gilded lettering. Nothing gave a hint as to this place or the treasures within.

Unlike M. Fabrice's store, this one lacked the rows and rows of cases of wine stacked like cordwood for the winter. Here the wine was curated, special bottles displayed like works of fine art. Jean-Charles negotiated with the proprietor, an elfish man who looked like he belonged in this Hobbit-hole, while I drank it all in, afraid to touch anything, staggered by the prices and the rare wine.

With his purchase tucked under his arm, Jean-Charles appeared at my side. "Ready?"

"Did you have to give them a secret password, knock three times and tell them you'd rather take a bullet than drink California wines to get in?"

"Almost. It is a place for those who truly appreciate good wine. A place where we can barter for very special wines, trade amongst ourselves. You see, really expensive wines are not like art. The wine collectors don't own the wine because of its value. They own it to someday drink it, savor it, and share it."

"Holy shit, he has a bottle of Domain de la Romanée-Conti that must be like a hundred grand."

"Twice that." He gently steered me by the elbow toward the door. "Needless to say, I chose something less...gaudy."

"I'd love to taste that wine someday."

"It is spectacular."

"But drinking it would be like carving up the Mona Lisa and giving each of your friends a piece," I muttered, knowing it wasn't quite the same. Great wine was transcendent, and in consuming it, in relishing the experience, you were infused with a bit of its magic.

Jean-Charles squeezed my hand but didn't argue. He knew the artist in me understood, but the capitalist was appalled. In America, we have secret bars, speakeasies, holdovers from the days of Prohibition, that the younger crowd thinks are great fun. The lure of being one of the ones in the know. Leave it to the French to have secret wine stores where refined appreciation gains entry.

We timed our entrance back into the flow of people—matching the speed of the crowd, while it didn't ensure you wouldn't get trampled, it helped. "Come, this way." He led me farther into the maze of alleyways away from the bustle. Shops still occupied the lower floors, but as the streets quieted a bit, I noticed lights shining behind shutters on the upper floors. Jean-Charles took an alley to our right that was so dark I didn't even notice it was there. A narrow passageway really, barely wide enough for us to walk single-file. "Perhaps I should have brought light bulbs. Pep never remembers to replace the burnt ones."

"Keeps guests away." I trailed behind Jean-Charles, keeping a hand on his jacket. If I wobbled, my shoulder brushed the wall. As we moved deeper into the alley, the darkness closed in. Cramped spaces gave me the willies. And cramped places with only one way out pushed me to the edge of hyperventilation. "Is this a dead end?"

"No, we can always climb out." He gestured to the narrow ladders, most of them accordioned over our heads.

Not exactly what I wanted to hear, given the rib thing—and my right knee was swelling a bit and hot to the touch—but at least I wasn't searching the trash bins for a brown paper bag.

"Do you have any aspirin? I've got a thumper—no food, little sleep, and getting up close and personal with a scrappy little Peugeot have taken their toll."

He held up the bottle. "Wine, it is the best for everything that hurts."

I wondered if that included scraped-up hearts, but I didn't think that would be an appropriate question since mine was the heart in question.

The narrow space captured sound like an echo chamber, projecting the hum of the street party a few short blocks away. The distinct aroma of curry drifted down from an apartment above. Faint whispers of light played with the shadows, pushing them back enough to see outlines, but not enough to navigate. Or see danger if it hid here. "Are you sure it's safe?"

"I'm sure we can handle what life throws at us."

"I agree, but only if it has a nose and I can get some leverage behind my elbow."

He chuckled, a warm sound holding back the darkness. "You must have faith."

"How do you trust the good when so much shit has happened?" The cover of darkness, the lack of meaningful eye contact, both conspired to give me enough false courage for difficult questions.

"That, my love, is one of your best charms. You keep punching away at the fences. This is how you say it, no?"

A mixed idiom. In a French accent. I tingled all over. That was even more fun than a mixed metaphor. "I don't think so. Either you mean I keep swinging for the fences, a baseball analogy, or I keep climbing back into the ring, a boxing reference."

"This is it." He stopped at a rickety set of stairs that looked like a fire escape. "These are his stairs."

This set unfurled from above so the bottom step floated a bit above the ground, reachable, but a big step in a tight skirt. "You consider these stairs?" The whole contraption looked like a trap to catch the larcenous looking for a computer to pawn.

Jean-Charles put both hands on the railing and gave it a shake. "If not stairs, what then would you call it?"

"A code violation." Despite the insult, the stairs gave a grinding rattle and not only held together but stayed affixed to the wall, both minor miracles. I peered upward into the darkness. A faint glow outlined a lone window at the top of the stairs. "And that is the front entrance?"

"Of course not. There is a street entrance, but, according to Pep, from the beginning, the lift never worked. This is the only other way. And I think the boxing reference is the one I wanted. Seems to match your personality better."

Despite resisting the prick of guilt, I couldn't argue. Well, I could, but what would be the point? I didn't even feel inclined to argue tort law, shyster attorneys, and the staircase that was a sure accident waiting to happen. Could the battle with the car have knocked some normal into me?

"Will you be okay to travel the stairs?" Concern crept into his voice.

"If I go slowly." He only knew about the aches and pains and the headache. If he found out about the ribs, we'd be on the way to the hospital. Time I couldn't give right now—unless, of course, a lung collapsed, or I did.

"We really should see about your head. Closed-head injuries..."

Killed Natasha Richardson, Liam Neeson's beautiful wife. I knew that. But again, the time thing. "If I start getting wonky, then we'll go."

"How will I know?" He tried to keep a straight face but failed.

Frankly, I thought he had a point. And I didn't have an answer.

"Be careful here," Jean-Charles added with the Pavlovian instincts of a parent as he tested the first step. "This is treacherous in the daylight. In the dark, it's murderous."

I hoped not—we'd had more than our share of that in the last twenty-four hours. The flashlight function on my iPhone lit up with one swipe, illuminating the alley like a poacher spotting deer. We both cringed against the onslaught. "Better?"

He shaded his eyes and blinked rapidly. "I don't know. No wonder interrogators love those things."

"They do? iPhones? Remind me to buy more Apple stock."

"I am joking," he said, missing my grin. Finally, he could open his eyes without them tearing. "Follow me." The stairs held as they took his weight. They bent, and they groaned, but they didn't buckle.

Jean-Charles eased upward as I tried to steady the whole contraption from the bottom. Two substantial humans might be more than one thin metal jungle gym could handle, so I waited. Tonight was not the night to test the lofty reputation of the French medical system. Besides, as I angled the light upwards, illuminating the stairs for Jean-Charles's safety, I had a great view of his ass.

At the top, he rapped on the window. In short order the shutters opened, and a male face mooned in the window. Bearded, shaggy-haired, a pipe in one corner of a curved mouth. The window sash flew upwards. "Well I'll be goddamned." A meaty paw reached out and half-dragged Jean-Charles through the opening. "JC! What the hell are you doing here?" He reached up to close the window. "Colder than a witch's tit out there."

"Wait, I've brought a friend."

CHAPTER FOURTEEN

HE MAN who I assumed to be Pepper Kirkland stuck his head out the window. I waved. "Well, I'll be double-goddamned. A female."

Every woman of some experience knows there is a fine line between flattery and lasciviousness. Pepper Kirkland didn't strike me as the flattering type. Men, so clueless about other men and how they approach women.

"Come, come!" he beckoned me up. "All the cold air is finding its way inside, and my radiator is once again wheezing."

After the first tentative step, I gained my footing. Taking one step at a time, trying to keep balanced over my feet so I didn't have to use my hands to steady myself, I climbed to the top. He reached out to pull me through, but at my raised hands, he backed off. "I can manage it, I think. Thank you."

Putting my butt on the sill, I took a deep breath, tightening my stomach against the pain, then swung my legs over, protecting my dignity by holding my skirt tight to my legs. To make sure the rest of me followed, I had to duck. The pain had me seeing stars.

Perhaps in deference to my gender, perhaps a shred of a

long-forgotten bit of chivalry. Pepper Kirkland grabbed my elbow, steadying me as I slipped off the sill, landing on my feet, then taking a large step to save my balance.

"Only a seven-point-five, my dear." Pepper Kirkland eyed me with a glint in his eye. Most men thought the habit charming; most women found it off-putting.

"Gymnastics isn't my sport." I tried to tug down my skirt, but bending, even slightly, felt like a knife between the ribs.

"Leave it. You are stunning." With his pipe clamped tightly, he spoke through his teeth. "And clever."

Clearly, he needed glasses, but definitely having lost the dewy glow of youth, I took compliments where I found them. "Thank you. Clever I'll claim." Still, I pushed at the delicate bit of silk. What *had* I been thinking?

A big bear of a man, Pepper Kirkland appeared of indeterminate age. The gray in his longish brown hair indicated he might be in his fifties, maybe? I couldn't tell, but he certainly wasn't the student I expected. He wore khakis and a button-down, no socks, and scuffed penny loafers. His whole presentation screamed American in a place where most tried to hide it.

While Pepper Kirkland's eyes only flicked over my legs, they latched onto the bottle Jean-Charles lifted. "I've brought refreshments."

"What have you here?" If he'd had a tail, he would've wagged it. He doffed a pair of wire-rims and leaned in for a closer look.

While he inspected the bottle, I used the lack of attention to give the apartment a once-over. A studio with a neatly made cot pushed against the far wall. The blanket of sturdy green wool. Army issue. One lone, rather flat pillow. The kitchenette consisted of a hot plate, a microwave, a French press, and a stained sink. No dirty dishes or empty pizza boxes with yesterday's pie moldering inside. One set of plates with a coffee mug overturned dried on a towel. Several wine glasses waited. He was used to company. The room smelled of exotic spices, cardamom, saffron and paprika, cumin and pepper. Moroccan spices. The thought of a good Tajine or Bissara had my mouth watering but my stomach roiling. I'd been to Morocco once. Against my wishes, a friend had eaten his fill of street meat in the Souks. He'd damn near died. Ran through a month's cycle of antibiotics and wasn't right again for several more months. Lesson learned. Despite what my mother said, he proved there were some lessons I could learn vicariously.

Various antique maps, some framed, some just tacked up, adorned the walls.

The large wooden desk had the gravitas of a lawyer's—no, a senior partner's—desk. An accountant's lamp with its green light shield arced over the work area. One large map filled the surface, edge to edge. It matched one of the ones tacked to the walls and lit with the reverence accorded a lesser work of one of the Masters. Wandering lines intersecting, branching, some wider than others, some with missing sections, all notated meticulously in print too tiny for me to read from here. One sheaf of papers splayed open across the map on his desk—hand-written notes, several photographs. Bookshelves lined all the rest of the available wall space, the shelves holding an array of books covering wine and mapmaking with a whole section devoted to languages, mainly the Romance languages, but a smattering of others got a bit of shelf space. A few tomes dealing with music theory rounded out the collection.

One thing I loved about Europe that I found missing in the States was an emphasis on learning. Not learning for a particular purpose but learning as the sole goal—to experience the human condition more fully. Maybe that became incumbent with the weight of a long and varied history. Or maybe Americans were too busy making money to wonder why...or, even to wonder at all.

While Pep and JC cooed over the bottle like a prized pet, I went in search of a restroom. With the whole of the apartment encapsulated in the one room, I was presented with a game-show choice of doors. "Sorry to interrupt, but is the loo behind door number two or door number three?"

Pepper looked at me over his glasses. His eyes were a vibrant green. How had I missed that? "Second door there. Not much privacy. A step up, so be careful."

"The economy and ingenuity are impressive."

"Yes, the room is small, the owner unresponsive, but the rate is very palatable, especially for this neighborhood."

With their cramped quarters, foul air, and exorbitant prices, urban mazes never much appealed, but there was no denying the energy and the power. In fact, it was intoxicating. Guess that explained all the indignities the denizens suffered to live the high-density lifestyle.

I stepped through the door and immediately was very happy I had eased my way in. The whole bathroom, sink, commode, and shower fit into an area smaller than the galley kitchen in my first apartment. A tiny sink the size one might find on a smallish yacht protruded from the wall; an equally minuscule medicine cabinet hung above it. The cabinet made it impossible to lean over the sink. Instead, I had to bend backward and thrust my hands under the trickle of cold water. Never one to study myself in the mirror, I nevertheless took a quick gander. Not too scary. I patted at my hair that curled, and not in a nice way, in the unfamiliar humidity. And I swiped at the dark bits under my eyes. The cold had dabbed some color to my cheeks, so all was not lost.

I had to wiggle a squirm with barely enough room to maneuver. In fact, silly as the space was, it impressed me with its efficiency—not a design component I associated with the French. And I could see now why they oohed and ahhed over the vast spaces in the U.S. allotted to such things. Once we'd had a client at the hotel who demanded another room as the bathroom in her room measured one square foot smaller than our brochure touted. Only now did I appreciate the significance of that missing square foot.

Careful not to make any noise, I opened the medicine cabinet to search for aspirin or anything to help the pain. I shook three from a bottle, swallowing them dry. Then I unspooled a long section of surgical tape and wrapped it as tight as I dared around the ribs. After the application of three sections of tape, I could breathe a bit easier.

As I opened the door, the low handle reminded me of the step-down. That would be potentially lethal in the staggering wee small hours.

JC and Pep had their heads together. If Pep only knew how much Jean-Charles hated that nickname. He thought the whole American need to familiarize everyone's name as if they were children, true-loves at first blush, or friends from the first meeting was a subtle way to disrespect that person. With my name, I never suffered that indignity—many others but not that one—but I agreed.

Jean-Charles meticulously decanted the blood-red liquid and Pep watched with ill-concealed lust. Since neither man acknowledged my return, I felt free to amuse myself with scanning the book titles and inching closer to the maps.

"Your calf. That's a nasty scar."

I turned at the unspoken question to find Pep staring at my leg. He shifted his gaze higher, not quite to my eyes, but he did make an effort. I gave him points for that, not many, but a few. "Hmm." Careful not to move my torso overmuch, I angled my calf so I could see the back of it. Red and angry, the welt chastised me, although I'd mostly forgotten it.

"It looks like a jellyfish sting." Another question cloaked as a statement in the local custom.

"Bullet." I gave him a sweet smile.

Horror flicked across his features. "That tragedy in Vegas?"

His question brought back the searing memories from that

day—a crazy gunman, fifty-eight lives lost. The city would never be the same. Yes, it was stronger, the population more united, more invested in their home and each other, but it would never be the same. Neither would I. "No, my mother," I said, lost in the horror. Friends of mine had run for their lives. Most had made it.

"Your mother shot you?" While he seemed to accept the possibility in a gunned-up America, his voice rose on a note of incredulity.

"What?" I blinked and focused. Not back in Vegas. "Oh, no, sorry. She's not much of a shot, but she does inspire homicidal tendencies. I got in the way."

It took him a minute to absorb that. "I think I'd like your mother," he announced with finality.

"Haven't met a man who didn't. Even the man with the gun."

His pipe cold, he tapped out the ashes, then pressed some new tobacco in the bowl, touching it with a flame as he drew air through the stem. "For sure the man with the gun. Love is a powerful emotion. Turns to hate like that." He snapped his fingers.

Pretty cynical. There was a story there, perhaps many stories. But I couldn't shoulder their weight tonight.

Pep returned to focus on the wine but this time with a bit of distraction as he pulled and pulled to light his pipe properly. "Be gentle with it, JC. It's been waiting for us for a long time. Have you savored great wine, Ms. O'Toole?"

"Lucky, please." I waved away another question I saw forming. "My mother, she has a sense of humor. And, yes, rarely, but I have."

"Then you understand?"

I felt like I was being asked to perform the secret handshake of The Cult of Wine Worship. Bluffing, I nodded. Unfortunately, I didn't have quite the palate or the stomach for thousand-dollar bottles of wine. Drinking them seemed a sin, a mortal sin when sharing them with me. But Jean-Charles seemed more than willing to fund the cost of my continuing education, so who was I to argue?

"It will need a bit of time to open." Jean-Charles set the decanter on the tiny French bistro table set with china and silver for one.

Waiting on the wine and with no real distraction, we had time to fill with small talk to ease everyone to the critical topic. Inane chatter, second cousin to bullshit, resided in my wheelhouse. One of the perks of dealing with perpetually pissed-off people—tired, hung-over, or on the wrong end of a long run at the tables, they all expected me to make their world better. I flipped the switch and launched in. "I can't believe you go in and out of this place every day, probably multiple times a day, through that window and up and down that insult of a fire escape."

Pep raised his eyebrows. "Me? Of course not. Proper gentleman that I am, I use the lift and the front door."

Jean-Charles whirled on him. "You told me the lift doesn't work."

"Yes, well." Pep moved the mountain of his shoulders as if shifting the weight of subterfuge. "Sometimes it's fun to take the starch out of you French snobs who often think just a tad too much of yourselves. Especially those of you at the top of the Bordeaux heap."

A laugh burbled up from somewhere deep and visceral, overcoming the wretched day, the blistering headache, the piercing pain of my ribs. Holding my ribs tight in a bear hug, I let the laugh burst forth, not that I could've stopped it. Part genuine mirth, part a middle-finger to the bad day, it rolled in consuming waves until tears leaked from the corners of my eyes. My head! My ribs! My God, the pain! But I couldn't stop.

At first a bit appalled, the men finally caught the bug and joined in until tears ran freely. Like a wave crashing on the shore, the laugh broke, finally allowing me to breathe. I dabbed at the tears with the back of a knuckle.

And I revised my original impression of Pepper Kirkland. The more I knew about him, the more he seemed like a man with an active mind with no real outlets, so mischief amused him. A kindred spirit...well, not the active mind bit...even well-oiled, my gears still ground. But I did love a bit of good mischief. "Mr. Kirkland, I like your style."

"Professor Kirkland," he gasped, "but call me Pep. I noticed a bit of blood there on your elbow. And a scrape on your knee. And the hint of blue at the hairline at your temple. You've fought your battles today, haven't you?"

"A few." Unsure how far to go with my tale of misadventure, I looked to Jean-Charles for guidance. He seemed unconcerned that I might cast aspersions. But I respected secrets...and reputation. Besides, the jury was out on the Bouclets and their culpability, so what I knew was more gossip than fact...for now. I took the high road. "I broke a young man's nose today. I'm not proud of it."

Shock registered on Jean-Charles's face. "Mr. Desai? Emma's...friend?"

"I guess, in the excitement, I forgot to mention it." He knew the man had followed me.

"You broke his nose?"

I patted my elbow and shrugged. "I didn't know...he knew Emma."

Pep slapped Jean-Charles on the back. "I'm sure he deserved it. Your lady doesn't look like one to go off half-cocked."

Appearances...so deceiving.

Pep focused on me, and I saw a lecture coming on. I tried not to sigh. I think I was successful. If I wasn't, it didn't slow him down.

"Through the years, I often was propositioned for a fight, most of the time with good cause." Pep smiled at the history lesson. "Somewhere along the way, perhaps it was my last overnight in the Gulag, I learned one doesn't have to break noses to win."

Jean-Charles gave me a pointed stare, which I ignored. "Having a size and strength advantage helps. How exactly did you plan your day today to avoid being sexually assaulted?"

"Avoid it?" He laughed. "I would welcome it." His attempt at a joke fell like a three-day-old helium balloon. His smile fled in light of his unreceptive audience. "I'm sorry, very poor taste."

"Women have to be watching, planning, and prepared to defend themselves always. It's a fact of life. I learned the lesson well in my mother's whorehouse. Unfortunately, most men had more manners there than they do in the anonymity of life."

"Well played. Very well played indeed. Most men can't understand what it means to always be preyed upon because of a physical disadvantage, and we all could use some reminding. So, thank you."

I took that as an apology, a rather eloquent apology. "Unfortunately, Mr. Desai's reminder came in the form of a broken nose." In retrospect, I felt horrible about that. But, going in, how was I to know? "What do you teach?"

Both men seemed grateful for the segue. "Music, mostly. But mapmaking is my passion. Mapmaking and wine."

"At the moment," Jean-Charles teased having regained his stride quickly.

So, I was right about Pepper Kirkland. And there was a lesson in his words somewhere. Perhaps he was right, and the best offense was a misdirection play. Grist for the mental strategy mill. Being a bit more selective as to the noses I broke would for sure help with the guilt struggles, not to mention the potential incarcerations.

Equivocating, I kept rolling through the small talk toward my ultimate destination. "I'm a bit shallow when it comes to music. I'm partial to musical theater—pretty people, singing and dancing and falling in love." The happily-ever-after part I left out. Post-Teddie, it seemed more of a pipe dream than a possibility. "I know the words to every song written by Oscar Hammerstein and scored by Richard Rodgers, but that is the extent." I felt a flush rise in my cheeks. "A bit like only liking Impressionist art, I know. But I have little time for a deep dive into the esoterica of the arts."

"A shame, but knowing what you like is always a very good start." A pull on his pipe, then he released the smoke, tilting his head back so the smoke drifted harmlessly toward the ceiling. If he judged me, he hid it well. "Art is personal. What touches my heart might rebuff you. To me, the Impressionists, as well as Rodgers and Hammerstein speak to our hearts, the romantic in us. To deny that connection would…"

"Make her very cross," Jean-Charles chimed in. "And you are right; she is a woman of strong opinion. She knows what she likes."

"Only in the easy, non-threatening aspects." For a nanosecond, I inspected where I had failed in the knowing. The list was endless, so many places. But perhaps knowledge was gained only through trying and failing. That I had down. My father had said so many times, "If I only knew then what I know now." Perhaps that's what he meant.

My father!

A dagger of fear took my breath. I glanced at my watch. The doctors would be doing rounds now back in Vegas. I needed to speak with them.

After a nanosecond, I stopped myself from reaching for my phone. In talking with them I sought only information. They would do their job with or without my fear. Here, drawing out Professor Kirkland, I sought answers.

I graced him with all the interest I could muster. "I am intrigued by your mapmaking." I looped a hand through his arm. The movement, even so slight, had me sucking in a quick gasp. He didn't seem to notice, although Jean-Charles's look sharpened. "You have a fascination with the catacombs." I focused on the professor, brushing aside Jean-Charles's concern. "Would you show me what you're working on?"

Years of practice went into my ability to keep a straight face while asking a man to show me his etchings. Even though the skill went unappreciated by the current audience, that didn't diminish my flare of pride when he preened like a rooster ready to crow. My gloat was momentary. He eyed me with a practiced stare that missed nothing. "What is your interest? These tunnels are very dangerous. It is possible to get lost and never be found. Your family will never know what happened to you."

"Oh, they'll know. They'll know I died of stupidity, which is not how I intend to leave this planet." I decided that the fact I committed it on a regular basis wasn't pertinent to my success here, so I left it out. Just the sort of thing I accused Jean-Charles of, lying by omission. But this was different, wasn't it? How would my death by stupidity in the catacombs affect Pep? Just the sort of high moral ground I wanted to skirt at the moment. However, I promised myself I wouldn't go into the catacombs unprepared. "I'm not stupid, at least not at the moment and never about this." There, no omission, no lie.

My decidedly biased self-assessment mollified him.

Jean-Charles gave me a quick nod over Pep's shoulder, giving me the go-ahead. A few minutes was all it took to fill him in on the wine heist, rekindling his enthusiasm in helping. As he warmed up, but before he dove in, I squeezed his arm. "I must tell you; one man has already died."

"Well then, we must be clever. And you must not be stupid." In a few short minutes, not only had I gauged Pep, but he'd also returned the favor. Sucking on his pipe, he turned to the map, studying it for a moment, his eyes following various paths. As he pointed to a spot, he released a stream of smoke, minty and smooth. "This is your parents' flat, no?" He flicked a glance to catch Jean-Charles's nod, then returned to the map. "And Lucky, you said the *commissaire* told you her team followed the trail to the river?"

"So she said."

Something in my tone must've telegraphed my uncertainty. "You don't trust her?" Pep asked.

Curiously, Jean-Charles remained mute.

"I truly don't know. I've no reason not to believe her other than I get the sense she's playing both ends against the middle."

Pep raised a finger, an odd Sherlockian mannerism. "Facts are only one aspect. Instinct, intuition, they are warnings we should not ignore."

"To be honest, I could just be having a rather embarrassing fit of female jealousy. The *commissaire* seems rather fond of Jean-Charles, and their relationship is not...professional. A bit of pissed-off lurks in there as well—she had me tailed today."

"The kid whose nose you broke?" Amusement lifted his mouth into a wide grin.

"Nothing like getting off to a good start with the local constabulary."

"She was wrong to have you tailed. This is a serious thing in France."

"It's an everyday thing in the U.S. The people in power abuse it relentlessly."

"I've been keeping up with the news from home. But, here, the police cannot do such a thing on their own. Unless lives are at immediate risk, that sort of thing."

"That's why Lucky isn't in jail," Jean-Charles added, not as an explanation but as a warning. The man could never pass a dead horse without beating it.

Not that he would influence my decisions but, in the interest of mollifying him, I pretended to give the poor animal a kick or two myself. "Loud and clear, my love. I'm making a concerted effort here to be transparent. I don't think jealousy or irritation is driving my opinion, but in the interest of getting it all out on the table so we can solve this, and I can get home to an ailing father and an increasingly frantic mother, I offer them as possibilities."

"There is nothing between us, Lucky, other than some history." Jean-Charles seemed to want to have that conversation now.

"Not the time or the place, Jean-Charles." Airing dirty laundry wasn't going to help us right now. "I know you had some sort of a teenage crush."

"Before Juliet, yes. My parents found Emma unsuitable."

"Ah yes, the winemaker's daughter. Almost as bad as the chauffeur's daughter, I presume?" My tone got a chuckle from Pep. We shared American righteous indignation at the biases of the landed gentry. Even though Enzo had told me my supposition was false, I was curious as to what Jean-Charles would say.

"I don't know if that factored into it. We were young, impetuous. Neither knew the expectations that would befall us." He paused. The memory held pain. "We took matters in our own hands. We got as far as the border. The guards summoned my father and grandfather. That was the end of it."

"For you perhaps." I'd be willing to bet he might think that was where it all ended, but the sting of being found unworthy probably still resonated through the Moreaus.

Watch your back—my interpretation of Enzo Laurent's camouflaged warning.

"Besides, she switched her affections to Enzo. Not until a bit later, though."

I felt my eyebrows climb skyward. "Really?" Any port in a storm—the girl had been desperate to climb the social ladder. "Isn't he much older?"

Jean-Charles pursed his lips and shook his head. "Not so much."

"I'm assuming he rebuffed her?"

"Enzo is an avowed bachelor, but I don't keep up with his conquests, so who's to say. Emma's been vying for one or the other of us since we were old enough to feel the surge of hormones. Perhaps before. She is a woman, after all."

Not only a woman, but a woman scorned—one of the most dangerous creatures on the planet. "She is also the chief *commissaire* assigned to this case."

"And as such, she must tread carefully."

If one can cover their own tracks, must they worry about where they step? Learning the answer to that the hard way would put a big damper on my *joie de vivre.* Best to remain wary.

"All of this is terribly salacious, and I'd love to hear more," Pep Kirkland interrupted. "But let's focus on the heist. Perhaps we can narrow down where the perpetrators came from and where they might have gone." He locked those green eyes on me. "That's what you want to know, isn't it?"

"For starters." I focused on the map, placing my finger on the location of Jean-Charles's family's home. "This is the house, but we walked a bit through a tunnel to get to the wine room, didn't we?"

Jean-Charles joined me at the map, his shoulder touching mine. Would I always feel the heat of his touch?

He took a moment to orient himself. "Yes, a hundred meters to the south, southeast."

"That makes a difference." Pep traced a path in that direction, mentally measuring the distance. With a red X, he marked the spot. "Let's see what that tells us."

"According to this map, there isn't anything underneath that location." Trails gone cold were not what I needed right now.

"This is a base map showing what we know for sure. On the north side of the river, we have mainly sewers." He traced a thin black arc. "This is the main line. It runs close to the Bouclet property." He grabbed a black marker from the desk drawer, then traced as he talked, I presumed for my benefit. "Sometimes in the past, there were secret tunnels for more nefarious purposes, smuggling, burying the dead, hiding things that might prove embarrassing if found, that sort of thing. While not known for confrontation, the French are rather good at subterfuge. Many of these spaces were used during the Resistance, for instance. None of them are mapped. We glean their locations from personal knowledge and anecdotes. Historical mentions in diaries, that sort of thing. As you can see, the Bouclets' tunnel has remained undetected."

"Until now."

"There is no need to disclose it widely. But, I must point out, someone already knew about it."

"Of course. I'm working that angle." Jean-Charles's eyes widened. "Okay, *was* working that angle. You could say I reached a dead end." No, I wasn't above trotting out that groan-worthy old saw when I needed a smile.

Jean-Charles didn't share my amusement. Of course, he'd witnessed the man die and had seen his broken body. I'd been tangling with that pesky Peugeot and saw little, remembering even less.

"So how did the thieves put all this together?" I asked Pep. "Would these maps appear together anywhere other than here in your office?"

"No. No, they are mine. And they stay here."

"Who else has seen them?"

"No one. When I have company, I put them away. You both were unexpected, and I trust Jean-Charles. He would have no reason to want any of this knowledge and no motivation to use it for improper purposes."

"Anybody else you trust?"

"Only a few of the cataphiles. And even then, I don't let them see the whole map or all the information I've collected. When I began this project, it did dawn on me the catacombs and the other tunnels could be used like alleys in the suburbs of America."

"As great ingress and egress paths for criminals."

"And now my fears have been realized." A look of defeat rearranged his features.

Cynicism, I knew it well. "The cataphiles are the people who collect information in the catacombs for you?"

"Yes, some of my students are cataphiles. The whole movement started at the Sorbonne long before I showed up."

I arched an eyebrow.

"They are musicians and performers, a bit on the bohemian side. They use the spaces as performance halls, party rooms, and the like."

"A very student-like thing to do." Such a parallel between Paris and the storm drains under Vegas, except the Vegas tunnels served as homes for those who had none, not performing halls for kids on a lark. "And the cops? They don't care?"

"On the contrary. The police have a special squadron, the E.R.I.C. Some call them the catacops. I think they actually heighten the appeal rather than detract from it."

"That whole risk-reward thing?"

"Indeed. Not only is it highly illegal, but it's also quite dangerous. Getting lost is but one of the potential perils. There are sections with neatly finished rooms, mortared bricks, spiral staircases, beautiful archways, with walls adorned in street art. But, in other sections, the support is lacking and it's possible, although not terribly frequent, to have cave-ins."

"In the city?" Talk about putting a cool twist on the whole Florida sinkhole problem.

"Yes, in the 1870s sections of a street would just drop. People died. Quite frankly it sounds like a wild form of Russian roulette."

"And now?"

"They say the catacombs are safe, but who is to say? The network is extensive, old, some parts blocking access to others. And much of the sewers become a raging torrent when it rains, so drowning is a possibility. We lost someone down there recently. Not to drowning though." He paused, giving me a pointed look. "He went in alone, unprepared." He waited to see if I got the lesson.

"You lost him to stupidity."

"Precisely." He pulled on his pipe, but it had gone cold. "Blast!" He rapped the bowl on the edge of an ashtray, dislodging the few ashes that remained. "Jean-Charles, hasn't that wine reached its time yet?" As an American of a certain age, Pep and I smiled at his oblique reference to an old wine commercial in the States.

Jean-Charles chose a glass and poured himself a taste of wine.

I needed to keep both men focused on the path I worked to lead them down. "While sitting in the middle of the Mojave, one of the world's driest places, it's also possible to die of drowning the same way in structures very similar under Las Vegas."

"Then you can appreciate the danger," Pep continued, still looking for his wine. "Fueled by morbid curiosity of the ossuaries, most think that was the only purpose of the catacombs and that they are the only tunnels under Paris. They actually began as quarries from which came the stone used to build the grand buildings lining the Seine. In addition, there are also sewers, canals, the tunnels for the Metro and other utilities—there are even some reservoirs."

"It sounds vast. I had no idea."

"Hundreds and hundreds of kilometers, and, to complicate matters, various arms of the network were built at varying depths."

"How much is mapped?"

225

Pep watched Jean-Charles sip the wine from a glass with a large bowl.

Jean-Charles sighed. "It is all you hoped." He proffered the glass to Pep. "Would you like to test it?"

The big man licked his lips but deferred. "You're the expert." He turned back to the map and my question. "Hard to say. The original drawings, made by the quarrymen themselves, burned in the fire that leveled the Hôtel de Ville in 1871. Over one hundred years of meticulous records turned to ash. Since then, the mapmaking is more of a cobbling together of various renderings through the years. To compound the difficulty, over the course of time, cataphiles built interconnections between all the different systems. This greatly expands the network, but many of the interconnections are hidden."

"Yeah, the threat of a firing squad usually squelches initiative."

"It is ready," Jean-Charles announced, then drained the last of his taste of wine. "Perhaps it will open a bit more, but it is lovely."

Wine was not at the top of my priority list, but I appeared to be the lone holdout. I touched Pep on the arm, keeping his attention. "Okay, so you said this map is just what you know." An open-ended question I hoped Pep would leap to close. My window of opportunity was closing fast with Jean-Charles waving rare wine under his nose.

As I hoped, my question held Pep's attention. His competing passions improved my odds. "Yes, I've made the map in layers." He pulled several sheets of tracing paper from a wide drawer, the uppermost of many, each only a few inches deep, in a chest tucked out of sight in the corner. "These show what we know, what we can extrapolate, and what we expect." Three sheets for three different levels of knowledge. He tacked them together over the original map. First, he dropped one, letting it drift over the map. It added more tunnels, these marked in orange. The original tunnels in black still showed through. "These are the sewers and utility tunnels. You see how this branch passes very close to the Bouclets' private tunnel?"

Jean-Charles returned with a glass of wine for each of us. He handed me mine, kept one for himself, and put Pep's on the desk.

"Where is the location of the entrance Desiree identified again?" Pep eyed the wine, but showed amazing restraint, preferring to finish his explanation.

"In the Metro station under Avenue Kléber."

"Walk me to it." He dropped the additional layer over the two already displayed. The other two plats still showed through, so the network grew with each sheet, adding tunnels in differing colors. I recognized this as an overlay of the subway tunnels. His finger moved as I described my path to the door by the Picasso advertisement. He nodded, his lips moving as he built the scenario. "Okay, that works." He traced it out. "They made it to here, right?" He'd moved through the sewer, past the Bouclets' to the river.

"According to the *commissaire*."

"Good, good." He stepped back as he let the last map fall. He picked up his wine, holding it to the light, then swirling it. "Impressive," he said to Jean-Charles.

"Focus, please. You need to finish the story. Messing with Lucky, leading her on, dragging this out, you're risking life and limb."

"First, some much-needed sustenance; it is a worthy price to pay." He stuck his nose inside the bowl of the glass and breathed deeply. "Jesus."

Jean-Charles looked like he was enjoying the whole power play going on. I patted my elbow, cocking it slightly, erasing his smile. "You wouldn't."

"I'm desperate."

"Pep, the wine deserves your full attention. Perhaps you could let Lucky off the hook before we partake."

Pep set his glass down with a smile. "An old man has his amusements."

"You need a spank"—remembering my first impression and how they are often right, I changed tactics—"scolding."

"My schoolmaster gave it his best which only served to solidify my resistance. But you, my dear, are too charming to resist." Only ingrained, perfunctory charm infused his words, avoiding smarmy altogether. "Okay, look. You can get under the river here. There are not many places, but this is one. It is a telecom tunnel. And from there, your thieves had access to the entire ancient labyrinth."

I let out my breath in a long, steady stream, mostly to keep from wiping the smirk off his face. "You led me on."

"Not at all. Perhaps it might be difficult to pinpoint the exact location your thieves chose as a lair, but we can narrow it down."

"You think they're still in there?" That surprised me. I figured they'd be long gone.

"Yes, in the catacombs proper. In the sewers and utility tunnels on the Right Bank, the location of the Bouclets' house, the egress points are too public. Most of them open into areas with cameras monitored by the police."

"Like the Metro?"

"Yes. While we are averse to tailing people, we spy on them all day long with millions of cameras around the city."

"Vegas, too. It seems so wrong, yet so justifiable at the same time."

"Depends, doesn't it, on how they use the information?"

"And what is collected in the first place."

"Right now, the cameras work in our favor, narrowing the scope of your search. The place to store the wine would be in one of the lesser rooms in the catacombs, too small to be of interest to the cataphiles with their large gatherings but of sufficient size to warehouse some wine. It's the perfect place. The temperature never wavers from 14 degrees."

"But they still have the problem of getting all the wine out."

He angled a look at me. "Who's to say they want to take the whole lot out at once? Both the Resistance and the Nazis used the catacombs to move and store their black-market goods, food, arms, and such, parsing them out when it was to their advantage."

"Okay." I took my glass as I struggled to find a reason to store private wine in the not-so-private catacombs. What was their game? "Let's say you're right. How do I get down there without getting lost?"

"Lucky, no," Jean-Charles started, but without much vigor as if accepting defeat already.

"Don't bother, JC. Your lady has a mind of her own and a strong independent streak."

For a moment there I thought he was going to add a strong death wish to my list of personal shortcomings, which might have been true to an outsider, but I certainly wouldn't characterize myself that way. My personal lackings revolved around a serious Don Quixote complex to right the unrightable wrongs and all of that. Not a bad goal.

"First, my dear, you'll need a map." Pep handed me personal-sized renditions of the wall map and its overlays.

"Thank you. May I have two sets, please?"

"Of course." He handed me the thicker base map, licked his fingers, and then peeled off another set of the parchment-thin paper overlays. "You'll need one other thing." He grasped my hand in his.

"What's that?" I asked, almost afraid of the answer.

"A guide." He bent over his desk and scrawled a name on a scrap of paper. "Her name is Gillian. She plays the violin like an angel."

Did angels play violins? I didn't know. My bet would be on the harp if she were, in fact, an angel. But she only played like one. As a cataphile, she probably lacked angel credentials. My kind of gal.

"There is a problem, though. Tonight is the opening of a new, limited-run show in Montmartre. *Two Americans*. Sold out for months. She is in the orchestra and quite thrilled, but she is out of pocket, I'm afraid, and I have no idea where exactly the show opens."

"*Two Americans*? You're sure?"

"Quite. I've been rehearsing with her for weeks."

I rolled my eyes at the kismet of it all. The tickets Teddie and Jordan had given me remained zipped into the side pocket of my bag. Pep angled his head to read the print. "Two tickets for the opening tonight. *Two Americans. A Musical Revue.* You must've had these for weeks."

"Even better. I have low friends in high places. I love it when a plan shows up." I glanced at my watch. "Curtain up in an hour. We'd better get a move on."

CHAPTER FIFTEEN

*T*HE NIGHT closed around us with a shivering chill. Jean-Charles and I paused on the front step of Pep's building. As I cinched my jacket tight once again, he seemed unaffected by the night air. This time, we'd ridden down in style in the lift and exited the building through its beautiful arched doorway just like we were somebody, or somebodies...whatever.

"I need to go see about my sister. If my father gets wind..." Jean-Charles started in unnecessarily. "My sister will be the death of him. His favorite, she has been a disappointment."

"Expectations can be killer." The rebuke sounded odd in my voice—not like me at all. And hadn't Jordan fed me the same line not too long ago? Maybe not in so many words, but the sentiment was the same. The Hotel Raphael Bar, as I recalled. Last night? It seemed like at least a light-year or two—I'd certainly aged noticeably in the interim. "I need to tell you something."

The tone in my voice commanded his attention.

"Remember when I told you that you needed to speak to your father about something he and Enzo Laurent had cooked up?" He nodded. "Well, they just might have stepped over the line in protecting their interests."

"How do you mean?"

"I don't know. Your father had a coughing fit before I could pull the answer out of him. But I think they might have broken a few of the wine world ten commandments or something."

He blinked for a minute, interpreting and processing. "Why do you think this?"

"According to your father, Victor Martin was an undercover cop for the folks who make all the rules in Bordeaux."

"And if he and Enzo…"

"They would have a motive in the murder." I put the exclamation point on a thought he didn't want to have.

"I need to get to my family." He jammed his hands in his pockets and scanned the street for a taxi, as if forgetting they didn't stop for mere mortals. No, they made us find them in their appointed queues.

Nary a car moved in the darkness, much less a taxi. "Any ideas?"

He ignored me, which I took to mean no.

Standing on the curb of a not-so-well-traveled street, freezing my choochillala in my short skirt and skimpy French lingerie, I was losing my smile. Putting a finger in the side of my mouth, I whistled.

"That doesn't work here." Jean-Charles took my elbow. "We need to go find the taxi stand," he said, steering me toward an exit from the rabbit-warren neighborhood.

I remained rooted—the man had to know by now how much I hated to be pushed, steered, prodded, or otherwise guided in any way, shape or form. Recently we had initiated the Imminent Death Rule—okay, *I* had put the rule in place…with everyone. And it went like this: I could do what I wanted, go where I wanted to go, drive as fast as I dared, leap from tall buildings in a single bound, and nobody could say a word. No advice, no opinions, no warnings, nothing, nada, zilch…unless they thought I was in danger of imminent death. Then they needed to sing loud and clear. So far, enforcement was an issue, but baby steps. Retraining adults was a Herculean task. Some days, I was up to it. Others, I simply pouted.

I whistled one more time.

"I'm telling you; it won't work." Jean-Charles tugged on my elbow.

A black sedan with a Taxi light illuminated whistled to a stop in front of us. I opened the back door with a flourish and a shallow bow, imitating Paolo, the Babylon's head chauffeur. "Patience, my love. And if you believe, then anything is possible."

"With those legs? For sure." Jean-Charles folded himself into the back of the cab. I followed and leaned back as he gave the cabbie directions to his family home on Avenue Kléber. Some of the cabbies spoke English, most of them understood English, but all of them wanted to punish anyone who dared use such a crass language, so I kept my mouth shut and enjoyed the ride.

"I'm sorry you will be missing the show." Jean-Charles put a hand on my knee, his skin warm against my cold flesh. "We will find this person tomorrow. But, my family, you understand."

"Perfectly. Go easy on your sister, okay? Assuming you find her." Men were so interesting. It never occurred to him I would go to the show whether he wanted to come or not. His decision, his dictate, controlled my actions. What had he been smoking?

Arguing would only solidify his resolve and make my escape more difficult, so I stared out the window at the sights passing by. As luck would have it, the cabbie took us over the Alexander III, my favorite bridge, and up the *Champs Élysées*. Past the fancy stores, the restaurants that a true Parisian wouldn't be caught dead in, one turn around the *Arc de Triomphe* to prove today was not our day to die, then an elegant exit onto Avenue Kléber and a refined stop in front of the Bouclets' address.

Jean-Charles paid while I shivered. "You take care of your family. I'm heading to the hotel."

He gave me a perfunctory kiss. "Don't stay up for me. I'll be late."

"And let me know what your father says," I added to Jean-Charles's back. He didn't turn. "He likes me, but that goes just so far. Intimate secrets are a bit outside my need-to-know status with your family at the moment."

I watched as he hurried up the steps. The butler, who'd been waiting at the door, ushered him inside. They both disappeared behind the heavy door without a backward glance.

The hotel wasn't far. And I hadn't lied—I'd stop there, but just to change my clothes. Montmartre wasn't a designer kind of place. And I had no intention of freezing my ass off.

TEN MINUTES, MAX...OKAY TWENTY—THE RIBS SLOWED ME DOWN —and I'd donned a pair of elegant wool slacks, a silk shirt, a leather jacket and my fur coat. I know, very non-PC, and it made me feel bad...sometimes. I'd inherited the coat—the animals had made the ultimate sacrifice decades ago. Justifying at its finest, I know. But, damn, it was cold!

Even on short notice, the front desk had secured a private sedan for me. Thankfully, the driver exhibited discretion, only doing as I asked and not offering any unsolicited advice. He also handled English without a sneer. Montmartre wasn't the best place for a lady to go unescorted at night, or so I'd been told. Good thing I was no lady. I smiled at the old joke, enjoying the truth it held.

Montmartre was home to the world-famous *Folies Bergère*, a classic French cabaret, slightly naughty, often topless, and always titillating. Now, there were other "peep" shows and nude reviews that melded into my perception of the whole Montmartre area. A taste of Vegas in a city of refinement. I didn't like it particularly. No need to sully the incredible beauty of Paris.

Of course, the *Sacré-Coeur* Basilica, one of the most beautiful buildings in all of Paris, lorded over everyone from high on the hill. The Catholics referred to it as a minor basilica. As such, I felt a kinship—I was just a minor human, often trying to accomplish major human feats. Built on pagan ground where druids and Romans had worshipped, the basilica now housed one variation of the Christian sect. The religious turnover appealed to me. Should anyone begin to think their religion was the enduring one, or the only "right" one, all they had to do was look at history to be disabused of that notion. Of course, someday we could get a God-O-Gram, and we'd know who was right and who was wrong. But for now, maybe muddling along trying to be nice, non-judgmental, and helpful might get me at least a quick interview with St. Peter or whoever was in charge of the keys to the Kingdom. Not that it was a goal. I just wanted to leave the world better for me having been here, and I'd let Eternity take care of itself.

And tonight's mission, fraught with personal peril as it was —I'd be on Teddie's turf—would push my guardian angels to the max.

"It's just down the side street there," the driver said in heavily accented, flawless English as he motioned to the front. "I'm afraid they have the street blocked off. The show is quite popular already. Tonight was the opening, I think. So many famous people here for it." I could stay in France just to listen to the locals speak English. I mean, the French was enough of a turn-on, but English? With a French accent? Mesmerizing.

"I'll hoof it from here."

He glanced at me in the rearview. "Are you certain?"

He eased to stop a block or two away from the theater on the main theater drag of Montmartre. Even from this distance, the marquee flashed like a Broadway beacon. Large, red letters spelled out "Two Americans" in lights so bright they could be read from space. Very fitting for the two Americans involved. The luminaries in attendance had attracted quite a crowd.

For some reason, the night felt colder this time as I charged into it, hurrying toward an ultimate resolution I couldn't identify, chasing a thousand problems that unfortunately I could. Hell, I didn't know where to start, much less where I'd end up.

Although, Teddie's show and the enigmatic Gillian the cataphile gave me an interim destination and a mission.

Life—it had taken what should be the happiest time and showed me its flip side. Jesus, I felt a Charles Dickens moment coming on. *It was the best of times; it was the worst of times...*

I'd enjoyed that book until I'd finally understood it.

The thought of the inevitable long-distance thing in my future...if there was a future with Jean-Charles...exhausted me. How long was the flight from Vegas to Paris? The few stolen days I might find would be spent on a plane. His family needed him. Mine needed me. We were like the proverbial split baby. This problem needed two to solve, so I focused on the ones I might have a chance of shining light on while flying solo.

History had taught me the Yellow Brick Road usually started with what I already knew.

Even I confused myself with the rampant *Wizard of Oz* references. Did I feel like a stranger in a strange land? Did I really just want to go home? Or had I arrived in time to drop a house on a bad witch? Or maybe I just needed a Teddie twelve-step program to clear my head and get my life back on track.

I cinched my belt tighter, girding my loins as it were, and in a way that wouldn't get me arrested, cringing as the belt I tied to hold my fur coat closed hit a rib, then braced for a dash through the cold.

Okay, focus, Lucky. Focus. According to just about everybody, we had a bunch of very expensive wine stolen from a location known to only a few. An inventory of the stash would be helpful. That I could get. And getting a bead on who knew what might be nice. I needed an insider for that.

Sinjin Smythe-Gordon was up to his perfect ass in skullduggery. Was he a good witch or a bad witch? Time would tell. And Desiree. Her picker was so bad, maybe a good strategy would be just to follow her and let her lead me to the worst apple in the barrel. Of course, bad didn't equate to guilty. Details. That's where the Devil lived, right? And Jean-Charles. He might or might not be feeding me information only when it was convenient. Innocent until proven guilty and all of that, but we had a serious come-to-Jesus talk in our near future. And Jean-Louis and Enzo Laurent, bound by money and hate and some secret that threatened to blow everything to hell and back. And then the Liu connection. Hadn't Sinjin trotted out some impossible foreign name as a counterfeiter? But there was a Liu involved; I knew that. And then there was Emma, fueled by hate, trapped in victimhood. How much would she risk to win whatever it was she wanted?

And so back to the stolen wine. We knew the what, when, and where. I sorta had an idea as to why. But the who was still eluding me. And the where. Where had they stashed all that wine? Beaten into submission, I stopped. Two ladies behind me muttered something that I didn't quite get but understood as they slammed on the brakes then knifed around me. The crowd behind had time to adjust and now parted like the Red Sea sparing Moses and his people.

A man bumped into me. Catching me by the shoulders, he stepped around and continued on with a *"pardon,"* completely unaware how close he'd come to an elbow to his nose.

My adrenaline, already high, spiked, making my heart leap. Pulling my coat tight in the front, clutching it closed with a fist, I took a moment to catalog those around me. Women and men hurrying, everyone with a place to go. A few couples ambling, lost in each other. The bite of jealousy nipped. Grass is greener, but a bit of time to enjoy some of the joys present in my life would be nice. Did I stay busy to avoid the difficult questions, or was my life truly as peripatetic as a child enraptured by all the possibilities?

Why couldn't I stop thinking and start living?

I stepped into a doorway and took a good long look at everyone, trying to focus.

The rules were different, the language often inscrutable, but underneath it all people were people. Good, bad, most of us somewhere in between and fighting the urge to slip to the dark side. To win this game, I needed to ignore the differences, focus on the similarities, and if I stepped across the line, ask for forgiveness later.

Lately, too many men had caught me with my pants down, as it were. My game needed upping in the worst way.

Much like when in Vegas, I took comfort in the normal. Normal for Paris would have to do. I ignored the differences, finding the common threads that linked all of humanity. The crowd in front of the theater looked much like a hometown crowd all twisting and turning and hoping for a glimpse of a luminary. Leaning through a tiny gap between a large man and his diminutive wife, I waved my ticket at the security guard tasked with determining who was worthy and who was not. He gave me a glare to let me know I was hopelessly late, then waved me through. The lobby was empty. I could hear the beginning strains as the orchestra warmed up.

An usher hurried me inside the theater with a whispered French something. I think he told me the show would start any moment. The chords of the orchestra segued from the mixed warmup, settling into the strains of something I recognized— one of Oscar Hammerstein's finest.

The lights already dimmed, my eyes needed a moment to adjust.

Someone touched my elbow and whispered *"Billet?"* With a

quick glance at my ticket illuminated by a flash from a penlight, he escorted me down the center aisle. Fourth-row center, best seats in the house. And like New Yorkers, the Parisians already seated displayed their displeasure at being crawled over as I made my way to a better seat than theirs.

Needing an escape and longing for the familiarity of home, I relaxed into the music. Teddie and Jordan, each a brilliant song-and-dance man in his own right, wove magic together. From the opening, they held the audience spellbound. Of course, familiar Broadway show tunes helped, at least for me.

I surrendered myself to their brilliance.

When the lights came up, signaling intermission, the audience groaned in disappointment. I refrained, but I was shocked by how quickly two hours had passed.

Pep had said Gillian played the violin.

Leaning over the railing, I scanned the orchestra pit. A red-headed pixie, Gillian looked like a child handling a grown-up instrument, albeit with expert precision. The dichotomy appealed. Curious—she didn't look like a habitual criminal. Gesturing wildly, I caught her attention. "May I have a moment?"

Cradling her violin, she wiggled through the forest of chairs and music stands to arrive under me. "Are you Lucky? Professor Kirkland asked me to help you," she said in a lilting Irish brogue.

Okay, the guy did have some class that ran deep. His introduction smoothed my intro. "Listen to my story; that's all I ask." Drawing innocents into an already deadly game wasn't my style. Help was in short supply, for sure, but I had to be able to live with myself after everything unraveled in due course. "After you digest it all, then you decide whether you want to get involved."

She smiled slowly at first, and then her smile grew wider as "of-course-I-will" triumphed over "I-really-shouldn't." Sisters separated by an accent. "Meet me backstage after the show. We don't have time now." Her fellow musicians began filtering back into the pit, retaking their seats, as if to prove her point. "I'll make sure the guard lets you back. Go to that door over there." She pointed to a door to the right of the stage. "I'll have a little over an hour between shows. Teddie will let us use his ante-room off his dressing room. He's cool. Will that work?"

Cool indeed. "Perfectly. Thanks."

As the lights dimmed, I retook my seat, managing to avoid crawling over some of society's best in the process. Settling back, I let the music capture me once again, keeping the dread of anticipation at bay. *Teddie.*

By the time the crowd had filtered out of the theater and I'd made my way to the indicated door, the guard was scanning the crowd looking for me. "Madam Lucky?" he asked as he spied me.

Even my name sounded better in accented English. "*Oui.*" A meager effort, but an effort nonetheless. As he ushered me backstage, he gave me a nod of appreciation. Gillian waited stage left, chatting with Jordan, who registered my approach before she did.

"Lucky, my love! You came!" Still in stage makeup, he looked a garish rendition of himself...not that that was a bad thing. Always handsome and magnetic, no matter, Jordan turned all heads wherever he went. What would that be like? Probably not nearly as good as it seemed. He wrapped me in a bear hug, then made a big show of kissing me on each cheek.

"It's me. No need to give me the Hollywood version." I kissed him back. Old friends made life manageable. And somehow his familiar presence in this unfamiliar place made me feel better. I clung to him a bit longer than necessary, which he tolerated with kindness.

"How did you like the show?" he asked once I'd pulled myself together.

"Magic. You both totally slayed it."

"You two know each other?" Gillian asked, unable to hide her hint of jealousy.

"Friends forever," I said. "We go way back. Back before Jordan Marsh became *Jordan Marsh*."

"Oh, honey," Jordan took my arm, "remember you've been sworn to secrecy. Come. Teddie will be apoplectic if we don't show up soon."

"I'm here to speak with Gillian." How did anyone learn to deal with a former lover who had stolen their heart then shattered it...and who now regretted it. Or so he said. Could trust ever be rebuilt?

He glanced at Gillian who waited like an expectant puppy. "Okay." He fixed me with a stare. "But don't leave without saying goodbye. We have a show at midnight." One more kiss, then he upped the wattage of his smile and turned to work the room. A show must have patrons. Patrons must be pandered to. An enduring rule of live theater. Jordan had mastered the art.

"Where would you like to talk?" I asked Gillian. "We could use a bit more privacy." Jordan had left us stranded in the middle of the stage surrounded by a sea of people.

Gillian wrung her hands. "You know Jordan?"

"Hmmm." We'd established that. I felt no desire to elaborate.

"Teddie, too?"

"I gave him his start in Vegas." The truth, as far as it went.

"He's...amazing," she gushed.

"In every way," I deadpanned, which got a second look.

She blushed. Pink made her porcelain skin even more perfect. "I'm a bit star-struck."

"He puts on his pants one leg at a time just like the rest of us; trust me on that one." I was desperate to talk about stolen wine and hiding places in the catacombs, and here I was fielding lobs from a love-struck kid who had a thing for my former lover. Her obvious lust had me going, for sure. Right now, did I want

Teddie or did I simply not want anyone else to have him? Was I really so disappointing?

Finally, the light dawned on the kid. "I'm sure. Sorry. Come this way. There's a place we can speak privately." She led me through a maze of knee-knockers, racks of costumes, rows of feather boas and headpieces, a bit of Vegas in Paris and the detritus of a show. My imagination had me smelling greasepaint and hearing the hiss of hot lights. The theater held magic—a slice of life, yet a complete escape. The door to the room she chose was unmarked but adjacent to another door stenciled simply, "Teddie K." Kowalski was his legal surname. In Vegas, he'd been the Great Teddie Divine, Vegas's foremost female impersonator. To me, he was none of those things; yet, he had been everything.

Ancient history my heart had not forgotten.

I cringed when she opened the door, but the room was empty. A table with four chairs sat in the middle. Racks with labeled costumes lined the walls. No Teddie. Thank God.

I pulled the maps from my bag, careful not to tear them. I took one set and folded the other one and put it in a side-pocket inside my Birkin. "Nice bag," Gillian said with an appreciative smile.

"A gift."

"Sweet. I need to find me a guy like that."

I bit down on a smile. "My father."

She didn't miss a beat. "Is he married?"

"Quite."

She shrugged as she pressed the maps out on the table.

Gillian and I hunched over them. "Professor Kirkland." Gillian touched one of the maps, tracing the lines, her voice soft and kind. "He's an odd duck, harmless and sweet. And meticulous."

Nice to know the professor wasn't one of the predators who seemed to be everywhere these days. "Yes. I'm grateful for his help. Did he tell you what I need?" In the bright light from the lone overhead bulb, the maps looked like foreign squiggles, communication from aliens, the landmarks unfamiliar. The odds of my success slipped to minuscule—I couldn't even get my bearings, much less a grasp of the lay of the land.

Sleep would help. And food.

"Only that you are looking for a place in the catacombs where someone might hide a rather large cache of wine without drawing attention. Where they could come and go at will and with ease. And, on occasion, they could transport some of the wine to the surface and not cause undue interest." She scanned the map with the intensity of a treasure hunter finally being shown the X marking the spot.

"That about covers it."

"Show me where they got to before the police lost them." She glanced up, the schoolgirl gone, the woman firmly in control.

I turned the maps to orient myself. Still, it took me a moment. Starting at the Kléber Metro, I worked through the overlays to arrive at the Seine where the trail went cold. "Here."

She chewed on her lip as the wheels turned.

If Teddie had indulged, it was easy to see why. Gillian was part ingénue and part competent woman, an intoxicating mix of neediness and resilience...or so I'd heard others described that way. I'd never been any kind of intoxicating mix—incendiary, maybe, but that was the best I could hope for. And at my advanced state of almost-maturity, that was as good as it would get.

"Look." She pulled my attention back with a touch on my hand. "From that point, they could get under the river easily through this telecom tunnel." She folded back the single overlay to look only at the map of the ancient network underneath. "Then, there's a step-through here, narrow, but it would be possible to pass the wine through."

"Where?" I squinted but couldn't make out what she referred to.

"It's here. Professor Kirkland doesn't have it on his map." She found a kohl pencil in Teddie's makeup kit, then drew in the short connection on the map. "From there you end up in the catacombs under Saint-Sulpice."

"Okay. Where does that leave us?"

"The egress here is a manhole. It pops up in a block filled with restaurants, quiet, not well traveled. I've used it myself many times. No cameras. No police." She rubbed her wrist. "Well, only once."

I thought of the streets of New York, my only experience with streets above and subterranean spaces below covered by metal grates that opened in the sidewalks. The cases of produce and wine handed to those below by the delivery guys. A perfect cover. "So you can climb out of there, maybe bring a few bottles of wine, and anybody who saw you might think the restaurants had a storage area down there. They wouldn't think that was part of the catacombs." A door slammed. Close enough to shake the walls. I jumped. What the hell was the matter with me? I didn't need to dig deep to find the answer. Hurt, alone in a strange land with those around me acting strangely, I was vulnerable, desperate for kindness. A perfect setup for disaster. Neediness would torpedo my future. Hell, neediness torpedoed everything.

"It's a great setup and a great hiding place." Gillian nodded, unaware or unbothered by my internal war with my weaknesses.

"Can you pinpoint where they might choose to hide their stash? It needs to be a relatively large space." I visually measured the room we stood in. "This size would do, but larger would be better. And it would need to be out of the way where normal cataphiles wouldn't wander in."

"They wouldn't carry the wine any farther than they had to."
She glanced up for my agreement.

We were thinking along the same lines.

"I know this section pretty well." She smiled at a memory.
"One time, this boy…" She trailed off as a hint of pink crept into
her porcelain skin. "He was beautiful. And when he sang…" She
fisted her hands together at her heart. "He could take you away."

When Teddie sang he made me feel that way…or he used to.
"He took you into the catacombs?"

She nodded, her eyes bright, caught in the memory. "Yes, my
first time…for everything. We dropped down one block south of
the manhole I pointed out here." She pointed again to the spot.

"Saint-Sulpice."

"Yes. In the short step-through between the two. No one
goes down it. A covering shields the entrance. Half the tunnel
caved in not too long ago, but there is a way past. Once you go
through, the tunnel opens up, and there are several branches off
the main tunnel. Some have amazing rooms, plenty large
enough for the wine."

"That is great! Show me." I pointed to her marking. "The
step-through is here. Where would you hide the wine, if you
were an international thief?"

"That second room there." She pointed to the map, and I
made a mental X-marks-the-spot. "But don't miss the step-
through. If you do, you'll be wandering in a maze." She pointed
to a blank section on the map. "As you can see, the tunnels in
here haven't been mapped. They're a maze and very dangerous.
You likely won't get out unless someone comes looking for you."

"Will you mark it so I can't miss it?" Death by stupidity was
not part of my plan, sketchy as it was.

She made a thick black line where the step-through would
be, then circled it. "Don't miss it. If you do…"

"Death awaits." I pulled out a chair and sank into it. My head throbbed with a sugar low. My body was starved for food and rest. My brain functioned like an engine running on fumes.

"Worse, the step-through is pretty shaky. The supports have not been touched in centuries. They were not restored in the last major renovation several centuries ago."

"Terrific." For insurance, I pulled the second map out of my purse and made a large black X over the part I didn't want to go wandering in.

"Very easy to trigger a cave-in," she added as if I could avoid the implication.

Jordan stuck his head in. "You guys finishing up? Gillian, you need some food. You'll need to be in your chair in twenty."

"Thanks." She put a hand on my arm. "I can go with you. You should not go alone."

I tried to sound brave, but I probably only managed foolish. "I can't ask you to do that. This is dangerous—far more than just cave-ins and such. It's my fight." Jesus, now I sounded like I was the ill-fated protagonist in a spaghetti western. I carefully folded the maps into a tiny rectangle. The case on my phone popped off easily, and I secreted the maps behind it as I pressed it back into place.

"Call me if you change your mind…and you should." She pressed a slip of paper into my hand then sidled by Jordan and disappeared through the door.

I hadn't even said thank you.

I eyed Jordan, weighing the odds of getting past him without sacrificing blood or dignity. Not good. "I don't want to do what you want me to do." Curiously, I was fresh out of fight. I'd run smack into my limit as to the number of loved ones I could fight with at any given moment. "Okay, let's do this."

He gripped my hand so tightly I couldn't extract it. "Be kind, Lucky. Just a moment, no more."

"You really think he's contrite?" I whispered.

"He's devastated. But what I think doesn't matter." He gave

my hand a pat and refused to relinquish it. Instead, he held me rooted to the spot so I couldn't flee.

Fight or flight was big for me, strong in its lure. Since I didn't have a fight, flight seemed almost irresistible. "Trust—"

"Is ultimately a choice, whether it's been broken or not. People learn, they grow. But whether they deserve a second chance? That's up to you." He pulled me past set pieces raised or pushed out of the way. Although the cast was small—a few characters and an ensemble of dancers—many remained on stage, still in costume, to greet excited friends, family, and benefactors. Many stopped Jordan for a word, a quick handshake. He gave each of them the moment they wanted. Not that I would ever be that in demand, but I took notes anyway. Making each person you met feel special was a good gift to have. Gillian intercepted us and trailed behind, darting and dancing on ballet-slipper-clad feet, trying to catch every word.

"Teddie's dressing room is back there," I said, pointing behind us.

"He's waiting in mine." Jordan's dressing room was the last one at the far end of a dark hall. Closed doors on either side, stenciled with names, marked other dressing rooms. Jordan disengaged at the entrance to the hallway. "Don't be long. We don't have a lot of time. The show will start soon."

I shot him a serious side-eye. Given the choice, I'd take like zero time, and we all could be happy…well, most of us anyway. The set of his jaw told me that wasn't an option. Catching Gillian, who lurked on his periphery as if she'd been waiting for him, with an arm around her shoulders, he stepped back and disappeared into the melee of people, now thinning as curtain time approached.

Taking a deep breath, I fisted my hand. Before I could knock, the door flew open.

Teddie.

His makeup only half refreshed, his eyes wide, his mouth

curved into a determined smile, he held the door, sagging slightly in a James Dean affectation. Whether it was intentional or not was anybody's guess. The cynic in me said yes. The former lover said no. It was a draw. And there he stood, with his spiky blonde hair, big baby blues, and enough memories to melt the hardest heart.

"Hey." Faced with the stuff of my fears, I felt my fear evaporate. We'd been best friends. That was the part I so desperately missed.

He stepped aside, motioning me inside. His Adam's apple bobbed as he swallowed hard. "I've practiced this a million times, and now that it's here, you're here..." He ground to an insecure halt. Not like him at all.

"We used to be able to talk about everything." I didn't intend it as a recrimination, and thankfully it didn't sound like one, hidden as it was in sadness and a bit of hopelessness. "Your show is great." Safer ground.

"Jordan's a pro. I've learned a lot."

So many ways that could be taken. I left it as it was, not reading anything into it. "Are you enjoying being a song-and-dance man as opposed to a rock star?"

He motioned me to a chair. I waved it away. "I'll stand, thanks."

"I was always a song-and-dance man, whether in a gown channeling Cher or as myself belting out one of your favorite songs."

"*I'm Gonna Wash that Man Right Outta My Hair?*" The minute I said it, I regretted it. "Sorry. I'll stop. Time to move on. Beating a dead horse never made any distance." Antsy, I tugged at a pink feather boa, slithering it off its hook then wrapping it around my neck—a tangible reminder of home.

"Are we a dead horse?"

The fate of my future hinged on my response. I resisted that idea. Ran from that reality. But either I had to put the hurt to bed or take him to mine. I took a deep breath.

The door burst open. A brief vision. A man. Didn't know him. Followed by another. The first raised a gun and fired. A nanosecond to cringe. A sting. I whirled to reach for Teddie.

The world went dark.

CHAPTER SIXTEEN

"MISS?" A voice, soft and insistent. A push on my arm. "Miss!"

I shifted away from the pressure. My head exploded.

Or maybe I just wished it would. The throbbing pain telescoped my vision and focused my anger. With both eyes open, I could focus if I fought the pain. *Damn!*

"Miss, we are here." Again, that semi-sweet disembodied voice. I wanted to kill her. I slammed my hands over my ears. A serious hangover but I never remembered drinking. If one thing pissed me off, it was pain without the pleasure.

I swiveled then reared back, trying to bring the face that swam in front of me into focus. "Aspirin." My voice sounded like I'd spent the last week in the Mojave with no map and no water, on the verge of death and homicide.

"Yes, miss." The face disappeared, thankfully taking the voice with it before I did anything rash.

Which, at this moment, was a bit of a pipe dream. My muscles refused to work properly with a lag time between thought and action as if my neural network had lost bandwidth. 5G thoughts on an EDGE network. But the lack of prodding gave me a moment to try to absorb my surroundings, which meant bridging a huge disconnect. Last thing I remembered? Let's start there. Jordan's dressing room. Teddie.

I grabbed the arms of the seat and looked around. Teddie. Where was Teddie?

Right next to me, as it turned out. Out like a light.

I punched his shoulder. Not hard as I knew the pain that could inflict—on me and my ribs. "Teddie," I hissed. "Wake up."

He groaned. Even before full consciousness, his hands moved to cradle his head. "Dear God in Heaven," he muttered, his words slurred. "I hope to hell a comparable level of pleasure preceded this much pain. If it didn't, then justifiable homicide will follow."

"My sentiments exactly."

Okay, he was alive. Next question: where were we?

Windows. A center aisle. Slight movement rocked my seat. Buildings slid past outside. A train. We were on a fucking train. That was going to make getting home at a reasonable hour a tad difficult. My anger flared anew, cutting the pain.

The voice returned. "Here, miss. I brought water as well. How many tablets?"

Closing one eye allowed me to focus a bit better. I gave her a long look. The attendant, a bottle of aspirin on a tray accompanied by a bottle of Evian. "Half the bottle for me. The other half for my companion." Quick movement—hell, any movement—hurt, so I slowly tilted my head ever so slightly toward Teddie as I kept my torso rigid.

"The water? Half for you, half for him?" Her frown didn't even pinch her perfect skin. A pox on her...for many reasons, none of which were her fault.

Shaking my head wasn't as painful if I kept it centered over my neck. "The aspirin."

"You can't mean...that is not wise."

I snagged the bottle and shook out enough aspirin to make

my blood as thin as India ink. Maybe that way it could pass through the capillaries in my head without killing me with excruciation. Tossing back the pills with half the bottle of water, I then extended the remaining aspirin to Teddie, who eyed me with returning clarity.

"Where the hell *are* we?" he asked as he choked down the remaining aspirin and drained the water.

"Bordeaux," the attendant said, smiling sweetly. "Your friends said not to awaken you until we got here."

"Did you see our *friends?*" I asked.

"No. This is a private car attached to the regular train. A special rental. I had only thirty minutes to get to the station when they called. When I arrived, you both were already here. One of my colleagues gave me the message to leave you alone. I'll collect your things." She moved out of sight.

I levered myself to a standing position—well, as close as bum ribs and what felt to be a full-body bruise would allow me.

"What's the matter with you? Hunched over like that you remind me of the old crone with the apple in Sleeping Beauty."

"*Snow White.* You're slipping." I chalked his faulty memory up to the drugs. "I did a stint as a hood ornament on a Peugeot."

He laughed, then sobered. "Seriously?"

I shrugged. "Been an interesting trip so far."

"You need to take it easy." He actually sounded serious.

"I will. But only until presented with the chance to squeeze the life out of the asshole who drugged us and put us on this train." I surveyed the rest of the car, which was more difficult than it sounded. Keeping my neck rigid, my head aligned with it, I kept the headache to just below homicidal levels. But then I had to turn at the waist to look around me, which caused the ribs to take a stab at jutting through my skin. With every fifteen degrees I turned, I renegotiated a pain truce between the warring body parts, which slowed down my information gathering.

Near as I could tolerate, we were the only passengers, not that I expected any different. "Well played, even on the fly," I muttered to myself.

"What was that?" Teddie, his pupils dilated by the adrenaline kick of the pain, was fighting through it.

I braced myself against the seat as the train slowed even further. "I'm sorry you got caught up in this mess. I understand grabbing me. I've been ruffling a few feathers. But why bring you along? You're nothing but a witness with nothing to add."

"Please, don't pander to my ego. I'm a man; I can take it."

I shot him some side-eye. "Calling it as I see it." What I didn't tell him was his presence here worried me. Of course, I had no idea who had orchestrated this little game, although I had my suspicions. "Look." I leaned across, making sure to get his attention. "Two people have already died, one murdered. This isn't some lark in the park. At the first opportunity, I need to get you on a train back to Paris."

"Jordan must be having kittens about now."

The show!

Teddie was a no-show for the late show.

And that was bound to get some attention.

So why alert the world to our disappearance?

Unless the kidnapper wanted the world to know.

What game was he playing?

"What happened to the other guy?" Teddie asked, jerking me out of my reverie.

"What other guy?"

"You said two people died; one was murdered."

"The other one ran into traffic, ended up picking a bus to tangle with."

Teddie grimaced. "Why'd he run into traffic?"

The attendant saved me from an awkward, painful moment. "Ma'am, your driver is here." She stood at a respectful distance, her gloved hands clasped in front of her.

Teddie, his faculties returning, nudged me with an elbow. I gritted my teeth against the pain. Clearly, he had no intention of leaving without me. "We could make a run for it," he suggested.

"Oh, but where would be the fun in that?"

As promised, a liveried man waited, his hat tucked under his arm, his black suit pressed to a knife edge, his expression absent. When he saw us, he nodded and turned, expecting us to follow. Our footfalls echoed in the empty station. Not too many leaving Paris for a late nightcap in Bordeaux.

I steered Teddie ninety degrees to the right toward an exit down a short hallway.

"What are you doing?" he hissed.

"Testing our boundaries."

As I thought, two men moved in, like cowboys herding recalcitrant calves. We moved away from their menace and fell back in trail behind the driver, who so kindly had waited for us. Two others closed in from behind him. Five of them. Two of us. Okay, considering Teddie's skills, one and a half. With my diminished capabilities at the moment, together we were down to one, or one-half. Five to one-half. We could make a scene and test the odds, maybe recruit some to our cause, which we would need. But there was the whole no-one-around thing, so a scene might be a bit of a dud as a strategy.

The man who...summoned...us counted on curiosity to keep us in line, but he'd hedged his bets.

And he'd read my bio. Curiosity was my Kryptonite. All the story threads in this intricate personal tapestry...deception, betrayal, death...whatever. God, it sounded perfect for Shakespeare...and me. I'd heard most everyone's piece of the story, or enough of them to get an idea. However, one was missing.

If my hunch was right, not for long.

Teddie leaned in. "Does this happen to you often?"

"With alarming regularity," I admitted, and I was surprised to find I didn't begrudge that fact, nor shy from its implications. Problem solving required diving down some rat holes. In doing so, occasionally one encountered a rat.

"I'm not sure how I feel about that."

Great, now both men vying for my heart were having second thoughts, put off by my competence. That's what it was, really. Often, when thinking about competent women, men didn't consider that competence could cross over into what they considered to be their domain—rough, tumble, and a bit sketchy...if not downright dangerous. When would men learn that women were like racehorses; the harder the men pulled on the bit, the harder the women ran? "I'm not sure how I feel about it either."

"That's a lie," Teddie said as he opened the glass door for me and we stepped into the night. "You feel just fine about it."

Damn. The guy did so get me. "And that's what bothers you."

"Only when the bullets start flying."

"This isn't Chicago. This is France where firearms are considered decorative. And personal firearms vulgar."

The driver held open the back door of a black Audi. What was it with black cars in this country? I slid into the back. The driver motioned Teddie to take the front. Divide and conquer. Still, he'd improved our odds, although I'd bet his friends weren't far behind.

Bordeaux was buttoned up for the night, which was too bad. Known as a well-kept secret alternative to Paris, the city reminded me of Paris before it got so full of itself, before it got so that everywhere you turned someone was accosting you to buy some pot metal hot-pink miniature of the Eiffel Tower. Of course, here in Bordeaux wine reigned supreme—which might have been part of the appeal. I much preferred a vertical flight to an hour revisiting Monet. And it was easy to draw a parallel with the white limestone buildings in the center part of town. None of that was in evidence tonight.

The sidewalks had been rolled up, the storefronts dark, the restaurants long past dinner, even by French standards, which were late, but not nearly as late as the Spanish, who dragged themselves in as Americans left for work. Few lights burned behind curtains in the apartments above on the outskirts of town.

Whoever had summoned us either burned the midnight oil or wanted no witnesses.

Within minutes we'd left the comfort of town, of knowing someone might hear us if we screamed. The night deepened. The scent of damp, verdant ground filtered in where Teddie had lowered his window a few inches. A set of headlights followed us out of town. The reinforcements from the train station.

I leaned forward to whisper in Teddie's outside ear. The lock release was missing from the back door. I smoothed my hand up the upper panel on the passenger door bedside Teddie. Missing as well. I guessed very few willingly accepted our host's invitations. "I'm feeling a bit bad about not encouraging you to make a run for it."

"Five against two, assuming there were two guys on each of our flanks," he said out of the side of his mouth, sounding for all the world like Humphrey Bogart. "Doable, but we probably wouldn't have made it."

We weren't fooling the driver. He kept flicking interest our way, but he let us talk.

"We should've split up. The goons would've followed me."

"As if I would let that happen. Give it a rest. I graduated from the School of Hard Knocks; I can handle myself."

Who was he kidding? He was a Beacon Hill blue blood. But according to the tabloids, he *had* spent hours beating back his adoring fans, so I let him have his fantasy. I relaxed back into the seat and waited. Nothing I loved more than being taken for a ride. I'd get my pound of flesh, but not before I figured out what was going on.

Whoever waited for us wanted something, most likely from me. And he'd gone through the trouble of bringing Teddie, whose absence most likely had everyone, police included, beating the bushes.

Why?

Outside the window, the night raced past. Lost in thought, I hardly noticed, paying no attention to the twists and turns we took other than to note we followed the river to the north. Darkness swallowed any real landmarks. So, back to my question: why go to all the trouble of making a very public snatch and grab sure to raise an alarm?

Who would be angry if Teddie had disappeared?

Jordan. Everyone in the show. Ticket holders. That was a dead end. I couldn't imagine a connection between that group and a wine heist.

Okay, slightly different question: who would be angry if Teddie and I disappeared together?

Jean-Charles, of course. Teddie pushed a special button for him. So, if Jean-Charles was stupid enough to do the jealousy thing, then where did that leave me? On the outside looking in. My French friends would abandon me. My participation in the heist and murder would be over.

I must be one hell of a burr under someone's saddle to warrant a kidnapping and such a public one at that.

Crossing my arms, I allowed myself a moment to gloat.

Somebody wanted me out of the picture.

Things were definitely looking up.

A CHÂTEAU LOOMED AT THE END OF A LONG, TREE-LINED GRAVEL lane. In the darkness, I didn't see it as much as I felt its presence.

The many windows caught the moonlight, glinting, mocking, yet few lights flickered.

"This place gives me the creeps," Teddie whispered over his shoulder. "It's like a place some deformed genius would live."

"France getting to you, is it?"

"Whatever happened to wine, women, and song?" he muttered as he leaned forward, craning to see more through the trees. "Do you think they have a dungeon?"

"A wine cellar, for sure."

"You really know how to bust a guy's fantasy, don't you?"

Leave it to Teddie to burden his lines with staggering subtext. "You worked that hard for *that* line?" The verbal base-ball bat left me curiously unmoved as I focused on the house as it filled the windscreen.

The car crunched to a stop on the gravel drive as it curved in front of the entrance. The door clicked, and I tried the handle. It opened, letting in a rush of cold and damp. Trading silk Versace for functional wool had been the right choice—probably my only one in the recent past.

A flight of eight brick steps led to the imposing wooden door. At least twenty feet high and half as wide with metal fittings and a large pull on one side, the thing was suited to holding back the heathens, which, somehow seemed appropriate as Teddie joined me before the imposing entrance.

He took in the acres of solid wood. "Seriously? I'm thinking there ought to be a sign that reads 'nobody gets to see the Wizard, not nobody, not no how.'"

"Great. I need the guy with the ax, and they sent the strawman with no brain." I held my ground as someone on the other side threw the bolt.

The door squealed open, revealing a huge foyer and a man that God had molded not in his image but in a Charles Addams imaginative one. Macabre yet somehow droll as if he'd stepped out of a *New Yorker* comic cell. He wore a black coat and lace-up boots. His dark hair slicked back only accentuated his high fore-head and closely-set tiny eyes. The red slash of his lips, the only wound of color in a bloodless visage.

Without a word, he stepped aside, inviting us in.

I looked for a hump.

"Lovely." Teddie strode through the door, his chest stuck out like a shield.

He got points for being the first into the breach, but not many.

A crystal chandelier that would rival any in Vegas—even the one at Aria—hung over a large round hall. Ancient Persian rugs covered the stone floor. Glass-enclosed, temperature-controlled cases held a dizzying display of wine. Even my limited knowl-edge recognized some of the most prized labels. I bent down for a closer look.

"I see you've found my wine." The voice was deep, unexpect-edly so. The man was trim and dapper in a silk smoking jacket, black slacks, and slippers. He had a slightly foreign look but worked hard to overcome it.

"You've made it a showpiece. Hard to avoid...Mr. Liu." I rose to my full height which was several inches more than his. "We would've accepted an invitation. You needn't have gone to all the trouble to drug us, kidnap us. Such a bother, I would think." My head still pounded a bit, keeping the edge of my anger sharp. I couldn't imagine the fuss Jordan would be raising back in Paris, so I didn't think about it.

He nodded as he pressed a hand to his chest in a slight bow. "At your service. And, my apologies. It's all part of the game." He gestured to the cases. "Impressive, no?"

Game? One man was dead—several others on the brink of war. Despite wanting to choke the explanation out of him, I stifled myself and followed his lead. "You've clearly spent years collecting."

Teddie fell into step. "There are some rather obscure wines

here," he said as if he had a clue what he was talking about.

We both were talking through our hats. What I liked was a far cry from what was considered exceptional. "You seem to have focused on the Bouclet Family Vineyards." One case held a vast array of their varietals in what I assumed were the best vintages. I bent to examine the bottles more closely. "These are the Estate Laurent vintages, aren't they?"

"The best of the best."

I bent again. Row after row of Estate Laurent, a bottle for each year. Except for one. A dark ring showed where a bottle should be. The light coat of dust around it showed it had been there. "And this one?"

He bent down to examine the space. "What the hell?" he muttered, the color rising in his face. "It was…" He straightened, working for composure. "That is for the '94, a rare vintage. One of the most highly valued wines in the world." He seemed a bit shaken as he looked at the empty spot. He forced a smile "But it is still lacking from my collection. It is impossible to get except from private collections at auction."

I wondered why he felt the need to lie. "You favor the Bouclet wine?"

"Not just the Bouclets, but most of the *Grand cru* houses. They are all represented here." Regaining his stride, Frank Liu spread his arms wide. "This is my love letter to the best wine in the world."

"A class to which you think you belong."

He had a Jekyll and Hyde moment as his composure slipped, letting the venal side show. "Not think. I *know* I belong; my wine is of equal quality. Now and for the past three decades, the wine made from our estate grapes rivals the very best of Bordeaux."

"Keep ahead of the pack for three centuries, and then you might get some recognition."

His eyes narrowed, and I could see the meanness there. "What is old is not necessarily good."

Hadn't I said something along those lines recently? If I did, I retracted it. Staying at the top of the game for that long *did* mean something. As long as the race wasn't rigged. "You think the Bouclets and the Laurents are using their influence to keep their wine in and yours out."

Mr. Liu eyed his wine with the look of the losing team eyeing the trophy. "You know what they say about absolute power."

"That is merely a theory, and it must be proven."

He flashed me a mean little smile that made me shiver. "Or overcome."

When had the Rules of Fair Play been expanded to include lying, innuendo, misstating, finger-pointing, and all the other things I used to get punished for as a kid? Now, grown-ups used them with impunity to wage trials by media. And you'd better draw first blood. First impressions, even if later invalidated, always stuck with an alarming resonance—like a case of poison ivy that wouldn't go away.

Clasping his hands behind his back, he strolled along the displays. "These are just a few of my bottles, and not necessarily the most prestigious. I rotate them for my pleasure. I have probably over one-hundred-million dollars invested in my collection."

"Which is your favorite?"

"Oh, I don't drink it. I'm a Scotch man myself. I enjoy owning what others want."

"And you want to be what others can't be." A pretender to the throne of Bordeaux. An insult to every man and woman who lived, breathed, and died for the grapes, for the wine they made. Not only that, but in hiding the wine behind glass, in sequestering it in perfectly controlled environments, in paying a king's ransom for a single bottle, he removed wine from being for the people. And in doing so, he robbed the wine of its warmth, of its reason.

261

Maybe a bit overwrought, but something about the whole business just pissed me off.

Nobody had ever told the Frank Lius of the world that you could buy it, but without the work, you can't be it. In a searing bit of insight, I understood what it was the Bouclets, the Laurents, and those like them were fighting so hard to protect— that joy of working so hard, giving so much, sacrificing untold hours, risking everything to claw your way to perfection.

So human. So satisfying. So difficult.

"So, what's the game? Divide and conquer?"

"In chaos lies opportunity."

Jesus, the guy wanted to go all Confucius on me. "You fancy yourself a disruptor?" I hated that current bit of tech jargon. As if disrupting was always a good thing. "And murder? How do you feel about that?"

His gloat slipped. "Murder?" He swallowed hard.

"Victor Martin?"

He shook his head. "I don't know him."

"He was marinated in a barrel of some of that wine there." I pointed to the Bouclet case. "Estate Laurent."

"That's a pity." It wasn't clear whether the pity he imagined was the demise of Victor Martin or the loss of the wine.

I pulled out my phone and scrolled to the blurry photo Sinjin had on his phone. "This is Victor Martin." I thrust the phone in front of him. "Now do you recognize him?"

Frank Liu squinted at the grainy image. "It is not a good picture, but I know this man." He looked me in the eye. "He is a private *commissaire*, a private detective, I think you call them."

"How do you know this?"

"I hired him."

"Because of the allegations you have leveled against two of the major châteaus." It wasn't a question, and he didn't interpret it as such.

"Yes, it turned out to be true. The man there," he lifted his chin toward my phone, "his real name is Claude Simon. He found proof of collusion between Jean-Louis Bouclet and Enzo Laurent."

"What kind of collusion?"

"Price, distribution, and a concerted effort to keep other châteaus out of the highest ranking."

If that were true, the implications would be disastrous for both houses. "What did Victor...Claude...do? He came to you first, I assume?"

"Yes."

"And then?"

"I sent him as my emissary to both men with a compromise."

"They let you in, or you turn them in." He didn't need to tell me I was right. "They turned you down." How could those two pompous asses be so ignorant? In the question, I'd provided the answer.

"No, not at all."

"What?" My shock must've registered, causing Mr. Liu to give me a tight smile.

"They said they would talk and get back to me. Understand, the proof is unassailable."

I'd reserve judgment. Everyone in this game made bluffing an art form. "Do you have it?"

A tic worked in his cheek as he looked away.

"You don't, do you? Victor...Claude was too smart. He knew his information would keep him alive, so he kept it safe."

"He was playing with the wrong man." Liu sounded like a man who knew how to eliminate his enemies.

"Did you kill him?"

His laugh broke the tension. "On the contrary, I needed him alive. I needed what he had." He shrugged. "After I got it, no promises."

Far easier to play tough than be tough. "When did Claude expect to hear from Laurent or Jean-Louis?"

"Yesterday. Claude told me he would be meeting with Laurent and would get back to me. I've been waiting to hear from him."

"But he ended up dead."

"I didn't know that until you told me."

"Why am I here?"

"We'll get to that." Mr. Liu motioned behind me. "Perhaps some wine after your long journey?" He waited for a moment as his steward placed three glasses on a sideboard. Expecting us, he'd taken the liberty to decant a red, presumably a Bordeaux.

"With the headache I have, it couldn't hurt." The aspirin had cut the pain, but it still packed a punch.

"I am sorry for this. I did not think you both would come if you had a choice." He motioned the steward away, then poured the wine himself, extending a glass to Teddie first, then to me.

Teddie waited for my nod before he took it. We both waited for Mr. Liu to sample it before tasting. Even to my uncultured palate, this was primo juice. He'd broken out the good stuff to butter us up. He wanted something. I should've known—there wasn't one man in my life who didn't.

"Very nice," I said, waiting for his move. But my patience long exhausted and my curiosity waning, I wouldn't wait for long.

He gave me a nod then turned to peruse his collection. "I'm sure you are curious as to why I asked you to come."

Teddie rolled his eyes. I figured quibbling wouldn't get me what I wanted to know, so I resisted and motioned for him to let it go. His internal war seemed harder than mine. I guessed I could understand—I'd missed a night of sleep; he'd disappointed several thousand theatergoers, pissed off a promoter, and cost his partner and himself countless Euros and endless goodwill. I'd have to make it up to him. I hadn't a clue how.

"I understand my connection to your personal vendetta with the Bouclets and the Laurents."

"Yes, you seem to have the ear of both families."

An interesting assumption, but I didn't disabuse him of the notion. "But Teddie?"

"He is important to you."

Both men turned their attention my way. I did my best to ignore them. One was easier than the other. This was a game; Mr. Liu had said so himself. How then would be the best way to play it? I worked for composure. "You are mistaken. He is nothing more than a former fling." How I managed that with a straight face and a calm voice, I'll never know.

"Remind me to never play poker with you, Ms. O'Toole." Mr. Liu poured himself some more wine. Seeing Teddie's and my glasses still full, he didn't offer us any. "Come, enjoy the wine. It is some of the best."

Teddie complied, drinking his a bit too fast. Yep, we both had a bad feeling about this.

"Ms. O'Toole." Frank Liu once again commanded my attention. "In your position with the hotel, your life is played out online. Your actions tell everyone of your intentions. You may be able to fool yourself. And perhaps Jean-Charles."

His assessment circled too close to the truth. "Would you get to the point?"

"Yes, of course. I have caused you discomfort." His pleasure broke through in a smile.

Game-playing wasn't my strong suit—I tried to not beat myself up too much for my transparent performance. "And your point?"

"I want you to deliver a message to Enzo Laurent and Jean-Charles." He smiled a benign smile that turned my heart to ice. "I want you to tell them to admit my winery to the *Premier Cru.*"

"Or?"

"You will never see your Mr. Kowalski again."

CHAPTER SEVENTEEN

*T*HE DRIVER who had brought us here sidled in behind the wheel as Liu's goons shoved me in the passenger seat of the same car. The man knew great wine, but he had a lot to learn about hospitality.

Liu leaned in. "You do as I say and everything will be fine," he said, then he slammed the door and retreated up the front steps.

The driver and me. One on one. And with the guy within reach. Seemed a bit overconfident on Mr. Liu's part—especially if my life was such an open book.

These were odds I could work with. As I pushed myself to a seated position and struggled to get my bearings, the door behind the driver eased open.

I didn't need to look at the figure who climbed in behind the driver. "I was wondering when you'd show up."

Sinjin, staying low to avoid detection, pressed a gun to the back of the driver's head. "Drive like everything is normal."

Frank Liu watched us from the front door, so I looked straight ahead.

The driver weighed his options for a moment. Sinjin pressed

his advantage. The driver eased his foot off the brake, letting the car roll forward, inching away from the house and Mr. Liu's view.

Two against one.

"Aren't you glad I showed up?" Sinjin asked with a typical male sense of indispensability.

"Overkill, but it is nice to have someone to talk to."

"Someday, you will give me my proper due."

"Oh, for sure. You can count on it." We each imagined diametric scenarios—that I knew—and it made me smile.

Sinjin bought into his own fantasy. "You are, quite frankly, the most difficult woman to pin down." He stayed low so no one could see him.

"You pinched that bottle, didn't you?" I stared straight ahead so Frank Liu wouldn't think anything amiss...or more amiss than being drugged and kidnapped, which I sorta seemed to have more energy about than he did. Someday, I'd teach him the error of his assumptions.

"Pinched? I'm offended," he said, oozing pride.

"Very clever, but you've made a powerful enemy."

Sinjin didn't seem overly bothered. "Tell him to take a number." Noticing the driver was a bit unenthusiastic in his job, Sinjin pushed the gun through the small space between the back of the seat and the headrest. No doubt the driver could feel its cold threat at the top of his spine. "Drive. Act normal."

"Frank Liu seemed a bit shaken that the '94 estate Laurent was missing. It had been there—dust had settled around the bottle, leaving a circle in its absence. So, if not pinched, how would you characterize your being in possession of the bottle?" I was assuming, but it was a pretty safe assumption.

"I reacquired what was mine."

Assumption confirmed. "Yours?" I didn't know the exact value of that bottle, but I knew it sold for prices rivaling

Domaine de la Romanée Conti, so it had to be serious six figures.

The driver eased us down the long curving driveway until night protected us from view. Sinjin popped up, taking the seat behind the driver, his gun still nestled against the man's spine.

I didn't need to look at Sinjin to see him waffling—that whole love-hate relationship he had with the truth.

"Let me go out on a limb here," I said as the driver wheeled us right onto a blacktop road barely wide enough for one car, let alone two. Night disguised us. I swiveled to look behind. No one followed. Another bit of misogynistic arrogance. Sometimes men made it way too easy. "I'm betting you stole that wine from someone in Hong Kong, someone with fewer scruples and more power than you. You've probably stolen wine from him before. Probably a lot of it. But he's vastly wealthy with a huge wine inventory, so he never noticed. Until you took the wrong bottle—three of them, to be exact." Out of sight of the chateau, I swiveled to look at him. "How'm I doing?"

The driver let off the gas. Sinjin pressed the gun in farther. "Drive. To Paris."

"You've got most of it." Sinjin didn't elaborate, goading me to finish the story.

"Okay. But there was a complication. I'm betting you had both sides of the deal, didn't you? You sold it to him, then stole it to resell. He discovered the theft. You couldn't return it to him, which is all he asked, because the bottles were fakes." I swiveled around for another look at Sinjin. "You needed the real stuff, so that's why you got in with the wine thieves. There were more than three bottles of the vintage you were looking for squirreled away in the Bouclets' wine cellar. But the thieves double-crossed you. Without that wine to deliver to your Hong Kong heavy, your ass is a grape. How'm I doing now? Any better?"

"A bit coarse and lacking nuance, but accurate."

As my feeble brain struggled to keep up, I turned back to face forward, one eye on the road, one ear on Sinjin. A sign flashed by in a blur as the headlights caught it. "That was the turnoff for the A-10 to Paris." I swiveled around to catch it behind us. My ribs screamed. I ignored them. Time to retake the upper hand.

I cocked my elbow and let it fly as I turned back around, uncoiling myself. My aim impeccable, I caught the driver on the nose. A fine mist of blood coated the inside of the windscreen. Instinctively, he cupped his nose, keeping one hand on the wheel.

For good measure, Sinjin cold-cocked him with the pistol.

I grabbed the wheel as the car swerved. Careful not to over-control, I kept the car on the road...barely.

The driver sagged against the door. Sinjin reached forward along the driver's door, popping it open. Without a moment of remorse, I shoved, and the driver tumbled into the darkness. I slipped over to take the wheel. "There. Much better."

"We're a good team." Sinjin leaned over, his chin almost on my shoulder.

I reached a hand back, palm up. "The gun?"

His breath hissed in my ear and warmed my cheek. "We're on the same side of this fight."

He'd be wrong about that in the end, but I didn't disabuse him of the notion. "Then, as the weaker sex, I should have the firepower to even the odds."

"What a bunch of malarkey," he said with a chuckle, but he handed over the gun, which I stuffed in my waistband.

His acquiescence told me two things: he needed something from me, and he had another gun. "The wine?"

This time he didn't put up a fight, handing the bottle over. I nestled it under the front seat. After snagging my phone, I put it in my pocket and stuffed my bag in beside the wine. "You made sure Liu knew the wine was fake, didn't you?"

Sinjin sighed. "You hold me in such low esteem." His voice held hurt.

My gut told me I was in over my head. To lie that well…that was championship stuff, and I barely made the B Team. "Cut the bullshit. You figured he would take care of the counterfeiters, giving you a bit of vicarious revenge. "You told him, didn't you? That the bottle was a fake."

"Seemed a good way to get both ends playing against the middle."

"While you did a snatch-and-grab."

"I take care of people who set me up." The threat speared through the simple phrase.

He'd work with me as long as it suited him. I had what he needed, and that meant I'd stay out of his sights…for now. "I have a feeling there's a lot more of the fake stuff floating around than you realize. Why'd you steal Mr. Liu's bottle? It's a fake and worth nothing." I held up a hand, stopping the reply I saw forming. "The world of fine wine collecting is small; the big players know one another. He threatened to go to the Hong Kong guy and offer you for the bounty of a favor."

"As of now, the man in Hong Kong doesn't have proof that I tried to swindle him. He only knows I pinched the wine to resell. If I make the deal right, he might forgive me. But if he knew the original was fake…"

"You'd be fish food." Curiously, right now the thought left me remarkably unmoved. "Where'd you get the fakes?"

"From a wine merchant in Paris. He thinks he is transacting business in obscurity, hiding his digital footprint under many layers of misdirection."

My heart sank. "Fabrice." It made sense. Who better to get the fake stuff into wine collections than the guy who sold the real stuff?

"Playing with the big boys of Bordeaux and getting caught in the crossfire can have a serious negative impact on the bottom line," Sinjin explained. "Some guys get creative. Counterfeiting fine wine is a multi-billion-dollar business these days. The window is closing as collectors are wising up, but many wine collections will prove to be worth far less than assumed."

"And far less than they cost. Does he know you've fingered him?"

"No."

Of course, he'd be saving that little tidbit to use as leverage when he needed it. "So Fabrice is unaware his secret is out?"

"Far as I know."

"How did you ferret out Fabrice?" Even though I knew the answer—I'd seen his digital operation firsthand. I asked to keep him bragging while I plotted.

"As you know, I have many resources."

"A major player on the dark web, I have no doubt." He didn't argue. "Any idea where Fabrice gets his inventory?"

"Locally sourced, best I could tell. But I haven't found the source yet."

"You mean you haven't followed Liu to the source yet."

"A good CEO knows how to delegate."

"Right." I slowed then made a U-turn. "We have to go back."

"You can't be serious! I barely escaped with my life! The man may keep his henchmen out of sight, but he has an army back there."

"He has Teddie."

"The bloke who got shot in the thigh in Macau?"

The memory arced through me in a searing bolt of what-ifs. "Yeah."

"But you are to marry another."

So simple, yet so not. I resisted diving down that personal rabbit hole. "Shouldn't we call the police?"

"They would be of little help. I think they'd be reluctant to bother an esteemed citizen this late at night. Teddie's not missing. And you have no proof he's being kept against his will."

"And there's the whole issue of you being a fugitive. But I agree. Not to mention, it'd take too long."

Sinjin relaxed a bit, knowing I wouldn't be summoning the police. After all, he was on the lam. Would accepting his help be aiding and abetting? Who knew? At this point, who cared?

With both hands on the wheel, I squinted into the darkness. What I'd give for a little light. Feeling a bit more confident, I wheeled into the next curve.

A figure loomed in the middle of the road, waving his arms wildly.

"Shit!"

The headlights hit him.

"The damn driver!" Sinjin shouted.

Guess he hadn't witnessed the U-turn.

I jammed on the gas counting on him to jump. He did...at the last minute. I may have clipped him on the thigh.

"Brutal." Sinjin still underestimated me.

"You know what they say about love and war." I barreled into the night, driven by my imagination and the horrors Frank Liu could inflict on Teddie. Not sure why he would, but the mere possibility was enough to have me seeing red.

"And which one is this? Love? Or war?"

"Both. You don't get it, do you? Even if it were you back there with Frank Liu and his goons instead of Teddie, I wouldn't leave you."

"You'd risk life and limb to rescue me?" He clearly hadn't contemplated that possibility.

"Of course."

After a bit of silence, during which I wondered if I'd feel the cold prod of the business end of whatever pistol Sinjin still concealed, he slithered over the seat and secured himself beside me. "Well, I've never been one to turn my back on love, nor run from war."

His complicity confirmed he needed something from me.

Still in the dark, but not clueless, I figured he needed that wine in the worst way. And he thought I was his ticket to finding it. Misplaced confidence or out of options? Either way, I could count on him just so far.

But I had an advantage—I knew what he wanted. "That was you at the *Trocadéro*, wasn't it?" We both knew the answer.

Amazingly, he didn't try to shine me on. "Yep, that guy was my inside man."

"The scout for the thieves. You'd said a kitchen guy was instrumental in a previous theft. I believe you said his name was Jai Ling Ping."

"Right. My inside man. You killed my shot there."

"I didn't..." My voice rose an octave as I stepped into the trap. Quickly, I pulled my foot out. "You make me sound like a bad journalist killing the lead."

"A good analogy."

"The three previous thefts in Bordeaux you mentioned? Did you make that up on the fly, or were they real?"

"Very real." His look challenged me. He had the connections I needed, but he would make me work for them.

"And the houses that were robbed, would they be the same three that just signed new distribution agreements with the Laurent Company?"

"Very good." Sinjin seemed pleased but not surprised. "The Bouclets were the last of the *Grand Cru* houses with any affiliation to Laurent. I thought they might be the next target. A long shot, but I guessed right."

"So, you put three and three together and got five. For a cut of the action, you'd set it up."

He didn't confirm or deny, but he didn't have to. I could answer the question myself. "What about Victor Martin?" I didn't use his real name, wondering instead if Sinjin knew it. "You said he was part of the theft ring."

"I thought so, at first. That's why I followed him from the

Bouclets. Pots and pans started flying in the kitchen; he took off. Curious, I followed him. Desiree caught me at the front of the house. I told her to go inside, to leave this one alone."

"And she did as you told her?" I couldn't keep the incredulity out of my voice.

"As far as I know. She didn't follow us; that I know. She couldn't. We were moving too fast for high heels."

"Heels are a male conspiracy, designed to cause great pain and to slow us down. All so the poor Y-chromosome afflicted can have a hope of keeping up. Where did Victor go?"

"I felt sure he'd join his compatriots in the tunnels, but he didn't head down to the entrance through the Metro. He ran to the *Trocadéro* then across the bridge. I let him go."

"You had to get back to help steal the wine."

"And we both know how that turned out."

At least he had a bit of humor about it, but he didn't fool me. He'd ditch me once I'd given him what he wanted. "And you still need that wine. Any idea what Victor was up to at the Bouclets'?"

"I had the impression he was waiting for someone."

"Who?"

"Don't know."

"And now you are here because the counterfeiters left you hanging out to dry. Before you knew about them, you unwittingly sold their product as legit to very scary people. Now you're stealing it back so Liu can't throw you on the pyre, and then you're risking life and limb to get your hands on the real stuff to make it all right."

"A bit of a mess, for sure."

"Some are tidier than others." This one was threatening to blow up in Sinjin's face. As much as there was about him to distrust, there was also something noble. "These guys must be something to scare you," I thought out loud as I peered through the windshield. We weren't far. The château loomed on the hill to our left, the turnoff a hundred yards ahead, maybe less. I slowed, looking for a place to pull over, preferably with a tangle of bushes or a copse of trees to hide the stolen vehicle.

"I am but a humble thief. These guys elevate carving off body parts to an art form."

A realization dawned leaving a cold ball in my stomach. "Is Liu hooked in with the Hong Kong outfit? He has Teddie. I need to know." I squeezed the steering wheel and pushed aside thoughts of torture. "If Liu even so much as touches Teddie, he's a dead man."

"Agreed. But he won't. He's just a rich guy from Singapore who wants the cache of owning a fancy Bordeaux chateau." His words lacked the gravitas of truth.

"He's more than just some rich dude, isn't he? A benign wannabe wouldn't have had you going to the risk of stealing that wine to get him to smoke out and exterminate the counterfeiters."

He didn't have a lie that would trump the truth.

"Damn." Two against God knew what. Careful of a ditch along the side of the road, I pulled over as far as I could. "We hoof it from here."

Sinjin pulled a small automatic from a calf holster, confirming my reading of his character. "You've got one already chambered." He worked the slide, chambering a round in his gun. "We should be good to go."

I killed the engine and the lights. The silence that enveloped us had an ominous emptiness to it. The clock in the dash had read almost two. This time of year, the sunrise came late, giving us several hours. But if we took that long it wouldn't bode well for success. "Give me the layout." He'd pinched the wine and, as a pro, he hadn't taken the task lightly. He had to have a schematic of the property.

He leaned across me staring up at the target. "We're in a bit of luck. Much of the property is under renovations and blocked off."

"And open to the outside?"

"Unfortunately, no. I shimmied in through a small window in the dungeon."

That word did all kinds of bad things to my nerves. "Dungeon?"

He turned, his face inches from mine, and gave me a smile. "Sorry, no. The basement."

"Cute." With an elbow to his chest I shoved him away. "Any idea where they might hold Teddie?"

"Why are they holding him?"

Not wanting to give Sinjin any more information than absolutely necessary to ensure his assistance, I thought through my answer. "To make sure I do what Mr. Liu wants me to do."

Crossing his arms, Sinjin leaned a shoulder against the passenger door. "And what have they tasked you with?"

"I'm just supposed to deliver his offer to Jean-Charles and Enzo Laurent. If they let him in the top club, he'll call off the dogs."

Sinjin cocked his head and looked right through me to my soul. "And you have no intention of doing as he asks."

"Whether I do or I don't won't make any difference; the hounds have been unleashed."

"But you don't like being dangled on a puppet master's string."

"No more than you." We both were in the same boat, although on opposite sides of the law. An interesting synchronicity.

"So, we go in the same way." Sinjin wrenched on the door handle, opening the door on his side.

Just like a man to go all bossy. "No."

He paused, one foot out. "No?"

"The missing bottle of Estate Laurent surprised Mr. Liu. He'll be looking for the way you got in."

"There are no other easy entry points. The rest require climbing walls and trellises and bounding from balcony to balcony. Only Shakespeare thought that reasonable."

"There is one other."

The light dawned. "You can't be serious."

"Yep, we go in through the front door. They will not be expecting that." If they were expecting me to return at all, which I doubted. And Mr. Liu had no idea that the thief and I were acquainted and would form an alliance. "If we have any hope of succeeding, we must keep surprise on our side."

"You're the right woman for the job, then." He didn't sound miffed, only slightly amused...very slightly amused. "Before we jump off the cliff, let me ask you one question: do you have any idea where the missing wine is? When they snuffed Victor, the trail went cold."

"You know, you could save yourself a lot of trouble and just give the Hong Kong heavy his money back."

Sinjin's eyes widened at the affront. "I'm afraid it's too late for that. He's lost face. Nothing will restore it except my head on a pike."

Ah, the money was gone.

"Only a bottle of the real juice will save your ass."

"Two, to be exact. And you just happen to have a bead on them." He stuck out his hand. "I'll help you get your friend, and then you tell me where the wine is. Deal?"

"I can get my friend myself." I popped my door open, pocketed the keys, and started to get out. On second thought, I reached back and inserted the keys back in the ignition.

Sinjin pulled me back. "Okay, name it. What do you want?"

I pulled my leg back inside and closed the door—the night was cold, and I was chilled enough at the prospect of the adventure ahead. "You help me get Teddie, and then we go to Paris together. I find the wine, and you buy however many bottles you need from the Bouclets. They might even give you one if you help find the killer and thus the thieves."

"Buy it? With what? I am but a poor pirate."

"Who works in finance and already banked serious green for three bottles of what the buyer thought was the true Estate Laurent '94." I shrugged. "It's my deal, or you go back to Hong Kong, hat in hand, to throw yourself on the mercy of the Triad."

"You've been bingeing on James Bond again, haven't you?"

Someone yanked the driver's-side door out of my hand, throwing it open and stifling my satisfied gloat.

My adrenaline red-lined.

I didn't even look. Still angled to step out the door, I pulled my knees to my chest. Leaning back, I kicked my feet out as hard as I could.

A dark figure grunted.

Knifing at the waist, I dove out the door, driving my shoulder into the shadowy figure.

I landed on top of him. Palming the gun, I hit him across the cheek.

He went limp underneath me.

Breathing like a runner at the finish line, I straddled him while the world righted.

I shifted to the right to let the light from the open car door behind me shine on my attacker.

The driver.

"Damn, the guy has taken ten years off my life tonight."

"You should've run him over." Sinjin loomed over me.

"So helpful you are." I pulled the sash from my overcoat and offered it to him. "Will you? I don't want this guy to crash our party again." I backed off the guy and stood while Sinjin did the honors.

A few minutes and he had the guy trussed up like a calf at the rodeo finals.

"Nice."

"Let's go." The play slipped from his voice as his expression sobered.

I let him lead. Double-checking my phone was still on silent, I stuffed it in my pocket.

Puffing a bit from our dash through the night, Sinjin eyed the large lock on the front door. "You don't happen to know how to pick a lock, do you?"

I elbowed him aside. "Some bad guy you are." I eyed the stained-glass panels to the side of the door. They looked old, the lead joints white with the crust of age. I pressed one, then another, testing the give until I found the right one. "Do you have anything sharp?" I asked Sinjin, who hung over my shoulder like a vulture.

A pocket knife materialized. "Some bad guy you are," he mimicked.

"Point made." So far, our little game was a draw. I scraped at the lead, which flaked off in my hand. Quickly, I'd released three sides of the small pane of glass. I worked the knife through one of the joints, then pried the glass loose. Once I could get my fingers behind it, I took a good grasp and worked it until I could pull it out. I handed it back to Sinjin so we could pop it back in after opening the door. Putting one eye to the hole, I scanned the foyer. I couldn't see it all, but the part I could see looked empty. I then put my ear to hole and listened. No voices. No footsteps. Only then did I stick my hand, followed by my arm, through the hole. Bending my elbow, I angled for a grip on the knob. My fingers barely reached. "Why do Europeans always put the damn doorknob in the middle of the door?" I muttered to myself.

"To keep the unworthy from breaking in," Sinjin whispered in my ear.

I twisted. The lock clicked open. And the door eased inward. "We must be clean of heart. We're in."

CHAPTER EIGHTEEN

$\mathcal{B}$EFORE WORKING the latch, which looked built to squeak, I peered through the hole left by the glass pane I'd removed. Luckily, a couple more gave way easily. Together they gave me a complete view of the foyer and a clear shot three-quarters up the spiral staircase.

"All clear." I slowly pressed on the handle and held my breath. If anyone lurked at the top of the stairs or was coming down, they'd sound the alarm. Putting my ear to the hole, I listened. No sounds of movement. The risk/reward played out, so I went with it.

I'd been wrong about the latch. It worked silently but the hinges squeaked. I eased the door open wide enough to angle a look. Nobody. With Sinjin so close, I could feel the heat of his excitement. I slipped through then bolted to hide under the curve of the staircase.

Sinjin tucked in beside me, our shoulders touching, his breath hot on my cheek. "I'm having a déjà vu experience. Mind if I take the lead?"

"Where do you think he's holding Teddie?"

He motioned to our left. "That way. The renovation area. No prying eyes."

As good a bet as any, so I let him run with it, thankful he hadn't said where there was no one to hear Teddie scream. To be honest, the whole empty, ancient chateau thing had my imagination on overdrive. And dungeon imagery was apparently the flavor of the day. I lifted my chin signaling Sinjin to lead, then fell in behind him.

Teddie had to be okay. If not, I'd have to live with the fact that I left. Yes, I didn't intend to go far, only far enough to circle back to gain surprise. But still.

We'd slunk as far as the far hallway when a bell sounded behind us.

The doorbell!

We froze.

An angry banging followed. Footsteps sounded behind us hurrying our direction. Then bellowing. "Coming!"

Frank Liu with a case of redass.

Had someone been banging on my door at oh-dark-hundred, anger would not have been my knee-jerk. Stroking out maybe, but not anger.

Sinjin grabbed the handle of the nearest door, tugged it open and threw me in. He dove in behind me, leaving the door open a crack. The coat closet, barely large enough for two, if we were seriously friendly. "Sorry." His whisper, so soft it bordered on telepathic. In the dark, Sinjin's hand found personal territory.

"Let's see who is paying a wee-dark-hour's visit to Mr. Liu, if we can." I matched his volume.

Maneuvering in the tight space took some effrontery. Since we were both the same height, for both of us to see, one had to go high, and one low. Somehow, I thought it obvious, but I had to elbow Sinjin in the stomach to gain the high spot.

Mr. Liu, in a red velvet smoking jacket no less, and embroidered slippers to match, strode into view.

Instinctively I shrank back. Sinjin flinched as I stepped back on his foot.

"Sorry. We're even," I barely whispered.

The hinges creaked. Momentarily the door blocked the person outside. Hushed voices, angry.

"Come in before someone sees you." Mr. Liu stepped back.

Emma Moreau charged into the foyer, an aura of anger rippling around her.

Sinjin clasped a hand over my mouth, stifling the gasp he knew would be coming. He was right! What was the good *commissaire* doing here? And at this time of the wee morning? Sinjin took his hand away, but I had nothing to say. Instead, we both cocked an ear.

"I told you never to come here." Frank Liu's voice vibrated with lethal intensity. He lowered his head as he looked at her, a bull timing his charge. "You make the wine. Leave the rest to me."

She makes the wine.

The tumblers dropped into place. The daughter of the wine-maker. Of course!

To be honest, I should've seen it coming. Through the decades, Emma most likely picked up at least enough from her father to make bad wine. And her father most likely amassed quite a wine collection, much of it worth a small fortune now, all of it verified and beyond reproach. With the counterfeit stuff muddying the waters, the price for the legit stuff would skyrocket, a fortune Emma would inherit. Knowing her, she probably had plans to hasten that event. How petty of me. She was only a counterfeiter...killer took it to a whole other level. Was she capable? Given the right circumstances, we all were.

"Yes," Emma said, a waver in her voice. "But someone has *died*, Frank. That wasn't part of the deal." She paced and daggered glances at Mr. Liu. "I'm a *cop*, for chrissake!"

"And a criminal. You should've thought of that before." He tsked. "Such delicate sensibilities."

I could almost feel the slap of reality as it walloped *Commissaire* Moreau.

Slippery slope. Give a nail to a man like Liu, and he'd crucify you.

"We've been unable to identify him," Emma huffed, her voice tight. "But he was stuffed in a barrel then our wine poured in on top of him." She stopped and grabbed Liu by the lapels. "Someone knows, Frank."

More know than you think, dearie. Emma Moreau had never quite passed my smell test. But I'd doubted myself, thinking jealousy could've put me on the wrong scent. Apparently, I was better than that. Good to know.

A door closed upstairs, echoing through the cavernous foyer. Mr. Liu grabbed Emma's arm. "Come, let's go into the library. It's much too public out here." Their voices faded, then disappeared as the door shut.

We waited a few more moments. I didn't dare breathe, much less move.

Emma Moreau!

"Holy shit!" I whispered as Sinjin poked his head through the doorway.

"All clear." He offered me his hand, which I ignored. "Having a cop in your pocket makes being a bad guy sooo much easier."

"You should know." I elbowed past him. "Come, we must find Teddie and get out of here." Sinjin tugged me quickly into the hallway we'd approached before. Logic tempered the need for revenge burning through me. "We can get her later. Find the proof to nail her with but find Teddie first."

"Do you think Liu might kill her?" Sinjin's eyes narrowed. I bet his brain sounded like one of those irritating GPS units when you failed to follow the route...recalculating, recalculating.

"That depends on how much of the fake juice she's already made. Whoever killed Claude, Victor, whatever his name is, used the whole inventory of fake juice at M. Fabrice's to give him a bath."

"Without that wine, they don't have a plan."

"Not a workable one, for sure. Liu needs Emma to make the wine. She's the winemaker's daughter, after all." I put a hand on his arm. "Let's go find that evidence. And we'd better hurry before Emma beats feet."

THE HOUSE WAS EVEN LARGER THAN IT LOOKED FROM THE outside. After an interminable amount of time sneaking through hallways, listening, testing the air for the hint of raw wine, Sinjin pulled me into an alcove. "If we're going to find Teddie and get out of here before morning, we've got to divide and conquer."

"I don't trust you." I was too tired, too scared, too angry to sugarcoat the truth.

"What am I going to do?" He opened his arms wide. "Take Teddie?"

"Not out of the realm of possibilities." I didn't put it past him to use Teddie as a bargaining chip. "But burning the place down and everything inside with it is more your style."

He pursed his lips. "Not a bad idea. But it'd take more than a couple of sticks to rub together, which is all I can hope for at this point. Besides, the damned thing is mostly stone."

"And we're wasting time arguing," I said, huffing a bit. "Which way do you want to go?"

He pointed down the hallway and to the left.

"Fine, I'll go that way. You go right."

He grinned, then loped off as if he knew that's exactly what I would do. I couldn't decide whether I hated him or liked him far too much for my own safety. We were both fellow acolytes kneeling at the altar of Opportunity in Chaos. Why just once couldn't I actually be on top of my game when the Fates called on me to have my best?

Turning left at the intersection took me farther into the back of the house. The hallways narrowed, the light dimmed. Dust coated the wainscoting; tarps covered the floors. The silence of Sinjin's absence reverberated through me, sparking adrenaline hits. My stomach churned.

Bad guys worked at night.

But these guys weren't making wine, not in the traditional sense. I'd been approaching this all wrong, listening for large equipment, sniffing for the smell of grape juice. This stuff would be made in a lab. Cheap juice doctored to look like the real stuff. I grabbed the knob of the door to my right, then put my ear to it. Willing my heart to slow, I listened. Nothing, like the countless ones before it. Twisting the knob, I put my shoulder to the door. Moonlight outlined the window on the far side of the dark room. I didn't bother with trying to open the sash. Instead, I took my elbow to it, the sleeve of my coat protecting skin from glass. A large sliver of glass sliced through the fur of my coat, but only nicked the skin underneath. After pulling any slivers remaining in the frame, I slithered out through the window opening. My feet sank into soft dirt. In the diffuse moonlight, I could see a vast lawn sloping away from the house toward the vineyards, which rose in tangled rows up the slight hills backdropping the property. Only things missing were a pool and some cabana boys.

Hunched over, I ran through the darkness, aiming for a small grouping of bushes. I tucked in behind them, then grabbed some branches to move them so I could see the full length of the back of the house.

I was looking for a light. The living areas on the middle two floors shone brightly. If Mr. Liu didn't sleep, nobody slept, I guessed. The fourth floor was dark. Most of the ground floor as well. I could figure out which window was the library—that light still burned. The kitchen and entertaining areas would be in the far wing that stretched out of sight to my right. That left the wing in front of me. I'd searched the first half of it to no avail.

But the windows in the other half were all dark.

As my eyes adjusted better to the darkness, I thought I could see a faint glow through one of the windows. Five windows separated it from the window I'd crawled out of. Without a better target, I headed back to the house, slithered through my window, then continued down the hall, counting the rooms— two windows to a room. I paused at the third door and listened.

Only a faint hum. No sounds of movement.

I pressed the handle. The lock clicked open.

My heart pounded in my ears. Normally not a gun gal, I decided this might be a good time. I pulled Sinjin's pistol that I'd pocketed and checked the chamber. Empty. I popped the clip. Empty.

A round had been chambered, my ass! He'd lied, and I'd been fool enough to trust him.

But I did appreciate his style—robbery was one thing. Letting blood, altogether another.

I tucked the gun back in my waistband. Holding my breath, I eased the door open. The hum of machinery was the only sound to greet me. The light I'd seen came from the panels on various pieces of equipment dotted along the walls. Coolers I could identify. The rest, not so much. A high lab table ringed the room. Another rose in the middle. Several stools tucked up under the table overhang. Neat and tidy.

I'd always thought of crime as messy.

Was this part of a criminal enterprise? Most wineries had labs. This could be legit—Mr. Liu actually did make wine under his own label. The fact that it was in the house away from the wine-making operations struck me as a bit unusual, but not beyond the realm.

I needed proof, a link to the fake wine.

I could see a few bottles of wine through the glass-fronted cooler. After checking for some sort of alarm, I eased the door open. The light clicked on, and I flinched against its brightness. Feeling in the glare of a spotlight, I hurried. The bottles lacked labels or anything to identify them other than scrawled numbers. Not immediately helpful. I grabbed a bottle.

Scuffling sounded in the far corner. I dropped down, using the lab table in the middle of the room as protection. More scuffling. Then what sounded like someone trying to say something. Unintelligible words.

As if they'd been gagged.

Teddie!

The scuffing and muttering grew louder, more insistent now.

I fought the urge to make a beeline. Instead, on the off-chance someone else waited in the darkness, I moved around the opposite side of the lab table, working my way to the back of the room. At the end, I knelt, then peeked my head around.

Teddie! Trussed up like a Thanksgiving turkey. And madder than a wet hen.

Still, I eased ever so slowly in his direction. Surely, he wouldn't be making so much noise if danger lurked. Catching sight of me, his eyes widened, and he nodded his head.

Coast was clear.

I dropped to my knees beside him and worked his gag loose.

"That fucking pirate!" He sprayed spittle with his anger.

"Sinjin." I wasn't surprised. Hell, I wasn't even angry. He'd found Teddie, left him where he knew I'd find him, then took off to get the jump on me. The ease with which he did all of that let me know he'd known exactly where he was going, where Liu held Teddie. He'd led me on a wild-goose chase to ditch me.

That part did piss me off a bit. But at least the man was consistent. At least I knew what I'd get with him. At least I knew what angle he worked. All the other members of the Y-chromosome set weren't quite as straightforward.

"We have to hurry." Teddie wriggled his hands free, then helped me release his feet.

I pulled him to his feet. He looked none the worse for wear. "Why?"

He leveled those baby blues. "Did you happen to see the trip wire just inside the door?" My crestfallen look was enough to galvanize him to action. He grabbed my hand. "We're going to have company soon."

We'd made it to the room where I'd broken the window when footsteps beating a staccato rhythm heading our way sounded in front of us. Lots of footsteps. I grabbed Teddie's hand and tugged him into the room. "Out the window, then run like hell." He bolted for the window while I tucked a chair under the doorknob. It wouldn't hold for long, but hopefully for long enough.

He was ten feet ahead of me when I dropped to the ground. They were at the door, loud banging as they worked against the chair. With each bang, the legs of the chairs squeaked across the wooden floor, letting go by inches at a time. I tucked my chin and ran.

As I passed the bushes that had secreted me before, I tossed the bottle of wine into the middle, hoping its landing place would hide it. If Mr. Liu noticed its absence, then perhaps he would think I'd taken it with me. In fact, lacking unassailable proof at the moment and knowing he'd work to cover his tracks —assuming Teddie and I made it back whole and of sound mind —that bottle would be the ace up my sleeve. A lot of ifs and a long way to go.

The first bullet whizzed by my ear. Too close for comfort with only a hiss to announce its passage.

Night-vision scopes on silenced rifles—essential equipment at every winery I knew.

I caught up with Teddie and pulled him to the left toward the shadow of a large building. "We're screwed if we can't find something to hide behind." The second bullet hissed by.

"Too much moonlight?" Teddie gasped as he ran.

"Night-vision scopes."

He didn't waste his breath on an expletive. "Why are they missing?"

That question had been bothering me as well. "Herding us maybe?"

With few options, we let them.

The building, erected of wood, had bars on the windows but a wooden door with only a crossbar securing it. The lock hung open.

I tossed the crossbar back, yanked the door open and hurled myself inside, gaining momentum as I went.

Twenty feet inside Mr. Liu waited, flanked by Emma Moreau on one side and a goon with a gun on the other.

I didn't even slow down. Three strides and I launched myself at the goon, who froze in surprise. With one hand, I pushed up on the barrel of the gun before our bodies collided. For once I was happy with my bulk, which matched or bettered his. He fell backwards into the shadows. His shot went wild into the rafters. My weight fell on him, forcing his breath out in a whoosh. Sinjin's gun skittered from my waistband, landing just out of reach. I rolled off the goon, then lunged for the gun. He grabbed my arm. The silk lining of my coat let me slip my arm just far enough. My hand closed on metal. I palmed the gun. With one knee under me, I torqued my body, then pushed and swung. The butt took him right in the temple. His eyes rolled back.

I sprung off him and whirled.

Teddie, God bless him, had followed my lead. He was astride

Emma Moreau. She put up a fight. Hard to say who was winning. He had her hands pinned, but she was working a leg around to pull him off.

Frank Liu? Where was he? He rushed from the darkness, hand held high. Metal glinted in his hand. I jumped out of the shadows, catching him as he swung for Teddie's head.

"Hit her, goddamnit!" I shouted at Teddie. There was a time and a place for the Rules of Gender Engagement.

His fist connected with her jaw as I landed on top of Liu. "Get the door." The goon squad had to be almost here.

Frank rolled me off. I kept rolling then sprang to my feet. I lunged for him, tackling him at his midsection and driving him back. With legs churning like a running back, I drove him backward, gaining speed. He slammed into the far wall.

Behind us, I heard the inside crossbar slam into place and the lock click shut as the first goon hit the door. "Get down, Teddie!"

I grabbed Liu by his lapels and swung him around, his back to the door, his face to mine. His eyes grew wide when I ducked behind him, holding him up as a shield.

"Noooo!"

The goon squad outside opened fire. Liu's body jumped with each strike.

None of the bullets pierced him fully. The door, then his flesh, were enough to slow then stop the bullets. I felt a singe of pain as one missed him and grazed my calf.

Blood trickled out of the side of his mouth as the rain of bullets stopped. When I let go, his body fell motionless.

I motioned Teddie farther into the building. He followed without a word. What I'd presumed was the building housing the winemaking operations actually was the equipment shed. Keeping down, we snaked through a collection of tractors, backhoes, and other farm equipment. "There has to be a farm truck in here somewhere."

I was beginning to lose hope when I spied it. A Ford, which made me smile. And sitting at the end with nothing blocking it. Now, if the keys were in it. I peered inside. Oh, Lady Luck was working overtime. "Get in." I yanked open the door as Teddie settled in the passenger seat. The goons had gone disturbingly quiet. "Duck down and hold on." With my hand on the ignition, I turned to him. "I'm sorry."

"Are you kidding? Best night ever." He managed a high-wattage grin. Adrenaline—best drug ever.

I turned the key. The engine caught. I stomped on the accelerator.

CHAPTER NINETEEN

*T*HE ANCIENT wooden door shattered when we hit it. The truck bounded into the night. The tires found traction, and we hurtled forward. I flicked on the lights.

Men lined up in front of us, firearms at the ready.

A couple got off shots before we plowed into the phalanx. Bodies flew. Men screamed.

Then silence.

I raced into the night, bouncing over uneven ground. Once beyond rifle range, I cranked the wheel hard to the left. We careened around the side of the house and skidded through a rose garden before tires hit gravel. "Stay down," I barked as Teddie righted himself.

The truck skidded as I cranked to the right. The back tires lost traction, throwing gravel. I backed off the gas, then hit it again. This time they caught. We lurched forward as the front door burst open. The inside security detail—no rifles, just pistols—flowed into the driveway. Bullets thumped into the metal behind us. A moment more and we were out of range.

The engine roared as I pushed its top speed. All tires stayed inflated and rolling. No passengers perforated. About as good as I could've hoped for.

At the end of the drive, I took a right, following the route the driver had taken us on before.

We sped by the copse of trees I'd parked beside before. The lump of the driver's body edged the ditch by the road.

The car was gone.

Yep, Sinjin Smythe-Gordon was a creature of habit. I was counting on it.

"You okay?" I asked Teddie as my blood pressure slowly dipped toward normal.

He rolled down the window and stuck his face in the stream of cold air that rushed in. "Is this what you do when you're not with me?" His words rode the wind, breathy and excited.

"I do a lot of things." I squinted into the darkness. The cutoff to Paris wasn't far.

"You were amazing back there."

I caught the glint in his eyes as he turned to look at me in a new light. So not good. "Not amazing. Pissed and scared."

"Either way, you're a bad-ass—a force to be reckoned with."

That much he got right. At the last minute, I caught the tiny sign for the turnoff in the glare of the headlights and yanked hard right. The force caught Teddie unaware. His face landed in my lap as I righted the truck and accelerated onto the autoroute headed north.

Teddie scrambled back to his seat facing forward. If I could see it, I'd bet there was a hint of red in his cheeks. The guy could bluff a good game. Calling him on it usually had him backing up. "Well, remind me not to piss you off."

As if. We both knew he could do that without really trying.

Luck was still holding. My phone nestled deep in my pocket. "Here, take the wheel for a minute."

Teddie moved over and steered while I glared at my home screen. So many messages and missed calls I'd never get through them all. Bottom line was somebody missed me. Okay, a lot of somebodies. Guess I'd never turned the thing off silent. For some odd reason, chasing through the night, it never dawned on me that anyone would notice my absence. Jean-Charles wouldn't have been looking for me, thinking I was asleep.

Guess Jordan sounded the alarm.

"Who're you calling?" Teddie's breath was warm on my cheek as he leaned a bit closer than he had to.

"Jean-Charles. Jordan must've found him. They've been blowing up my phone."

"You're not calling the police?"

"Next." I hit Jean-Charles's speed-dial. Romeo was one. Teddie two, then Jean-Charles. I'd never gotten around to changing the order.

He answered before it had time to ring. "Lucky?"

The worry in his voice hit my heart. "I'm fine. All in one piece."

"Oh thank God!" We both took a deep breath. He spoke first. "What happened?"

I took the wheel back from Teddie and settled in to tell the story, for his benefit and Teddie's. I talked while the country-side, hidden in the shadows, slipped past. Every now and then, the moonlight would glint off a chateau on a hill above or a window in a farmhouse close to the road. Teddie had left the window down. The slap of the cold helped keep me awake. The scent of nature calmed my soul. Humans would come and go, but the earth would remain steadfast, solid, weathering the ugly and embracing the beautiful.

After a night filled with ugly, I took solace in that.

No one interrupted as I told my story, what I could remember, anyway. Finally, I wound down.

"Emma and Frank Liu are counterfeiting Chateau Bouclet wine?"

"Were. Frank Liu is dead. Don't ask, but I didn't kill him." I played a part for sure, but I didn't pull the triggers that launched the bullets that stopped his heart.

"Dead?"

"Him or me, but I'll explain later. We need to get the police out there." Emma Moreau no longer qualified. "If anyone is still at Liu's place, which I doubt, they'll spin the story to put the blame on me. They'll say Teddie and I trespassed, then we ran. You can make it up from there."

"And Emma?"

"When we left, I didn't see a car in the driveway. I assume she made a hasty retreat and is somewhere covering her tracks, licking her wounds, and whatever other cliché applies."

"If Liu and Emma were counterfeiting wine..."

"The part of their conversation I heard led me to believe that to be true, yes. Nothing I saw at the chateau proved it though. The rather large security team employed by Mr. Liu indicated he had something to hide rather than something to protect."

"So, you don't have any proof?" His voice lost its vigor.

I knew how he felt. "Not of counterfeiting. Of attempted murder, the bullet holes in the truck should get the conversation started, but then, they could always claim we were trespassers. Hell, we're motoring toward you in a truck I stole from Liu's equipment shed. Sinjin took the car, which, come to think of it, technically qualifies as stolen too." I left out the part about running over the driver. Jean-Charles had had more than he could stand already. "I do have an ace in the hole. Not sure it will pan out, but I think I've covered my bets."

"I sure hope so."

"Not nearly so much as me. It's my mug that's going to be gracing the police intake book."

He didn't argue. He didn't offer the use of his family's political capital. "Where are you now?"

"In the car with Teddie. He's fine, by the way. We're heading your way." Teddie gave me a lopsided grin. The warmth of that old familiarity nestled in next to my heart. I had no idea what to do with it. My heart jumped around like a flea in a frying pan. Of course, all my body parts seemed to have minds of their own, so no surprise, really.

"Yes, about Teddie. What was his role in all of this?" The phrasing implied Jean-Charles had already drawn a Snidely Whiplash mustache on Teddie.

"Leverage."

"Really? How so?" Disbelief dripped from every word.

"So I would deliver his ultimatum to you. And I think, perhaps to have you doing exactly what you're doing." I blinked my eyes, which had started to tear with exhaustion.

"And what is that?"

"Doubting me." He didn't ask about the ultimatum, which was fine. Frank Liu's death rendered it moot anyway. I decided I'd had enough. "I'm tired. We're heading for the Raphael. I need a bath, some food, and some sleep." With that, I terminated the call and tried to summon some energy to call the police.

Teddie wisely stared out the window.

I couldn't decide if this whole lack of communication thing with Jean-Charles was cultural or personal. When in France, had he donned the mantle of landed gentry who peered down their noses at hardscrabble upstarts like me? Or had something changed between us and I'd missed it entirely? So now he felt the need to bludgeon me with distance and disdain? Or was I simply feeling the discomfort of the misplaced and the displaced? Could I just take Christophe and go home? Did people stay in relationships for the kids? I knew they stayed in marriages...

The cloud of exhaustion fuzzied everything.

"Why don't you let me drive?" Teddie's question was soft with concern.

I eased to the side of the road. With the engine running, Teddie and I did a musical chairs bit to change seats. Teddie

adjusted his seat position and the mirrors, checking them twice
—a habit that set my teeth on edge. I was more of an on-the-fly
kind of adjuster. He signaled, of course, to the nonexistent traffic, then merged onto the autoroute. We'd be lucky to hit
cruising speed by the time we reached Paris—still a couple of
hours away...if I drove.

Adding homicide to the laundry list of my offenses so far
would only get the police all lathered up. To avoid such an even-
tuality, I ignored Teddie's scraping away at my last raw nerve
and I relaunched my phone to summon the cavalry. This was
going to be rare.

I pressed the phone to my ear as Teddie did his best Fred
Flinstone. Getting up to speed was going to take a while. Yabba
dabba do.

A brisk female voice answered, her French clipped and delicious. "Yes, *Commissaire* Desai, please." I listened for a moment.
"Yes, this is very important. Wake him up." If I had any hope of
staying free, single, and above the age of consent, I needed
someone on the inside to run interference. The only friend I
had right now was the kid whose nose I'd flattened. The cosmic
message lurking in that factoid hit me between the eyes, but I
had no idea what to do about it.

"I'll patch him in. He's not happy." The brisk Frenchie's tone
brooked no reply.

Soon a voice, grumpy and husky with sleep, answered with
what sounded like run-on French.

I stumbled into an explanation in English. "This is Lucky
O'Toole. Remember me?"

Silence, then he laughed.

I took that as a good sign. "Is English okay?" I didn't have
enough ergs left to try the whole thing in French.

"In Paris, it is never okay, but I understand. So tell me what
is wrong."

For the second time this evening I launched into a recitation of my dismal evening. When I got to the part about Emma Moreau, I left it all out. I was short on proof and long on pissed-off with a hint of jealous. Not the best fuel to fire logic. And, even though I could be petty, I wasn't the kind to make unfounded accusations because they made me feel good.

A long pause greeted the end of my sordid tale. I was getting used to it.

"Mr. Liu is dead?"

"He sure looked it, but, as I was next on the menu, I didn't stick around to confirm."

"His security force shot him?"

"Through the door. They couldn't see who they were shooting. They were aiming for me."

"Any idea why?"

"Mr. Liu was up to his ass in alligators." I stopped, knowing that would do a fly-by. "He used his chateau for legitimacy to cover most likely a myriad of criminal enterprises. I stuck my nose where it wasn't appreciated."

He groaned. The whole nose thing was a sore subject. "You really should perhaps keep more to your own business?"

"Then what would you do in the middle of the night?"

Another chuckle. "Where are you now?"

"Driving a stolen truck full of bullet holes heading back to Paris."

This time the silence was longer. "I am without words."

"Escape vehicle. Only one available."

"Understandable," he said, sounding like he didn't understand at all. "Do you need assistance?"

"Nope, only for you to catch the bad guys and tie them to the killing of the man at M. Fabrice's." I hadn't bothered to mention M. Fabrice's hand in all of this. I didn't have the heart. At the heart of it, M. Fabrice was an emasculated man, now with nothing to lose and no one to hurt, finally working up the courage for revenge. His timing sucked, but, well, revenge usually was best left to the Fates. I had no idea what to do about M. Fabrice.

Relief brightened Sam Desai's voice. "I have friends in Bordeaux. I'll get them out to Chateau Shasay."

"Will you meet them there?"

"*Oui.* It will be best if I tell them your story."

I'd made the right choice of accomplice. "Call me when you get there. I hid something that might be of interest. Not sure, but I have a gut feeling."

After he rang off, I held the phone for a moment. I'd set things in motion. I'd just have to wait and see how it all shook out. Patience, so not even a minor virtue of mine.

I put my seat back as far as it would go—not far in a Ford pickup—and closed my eyes. My ribs ached, but the adrenaline redlining for the past hour or so had taken care of the headache.

"It's over," Teddie sighed.

I had no idea exactly what he referred to—his comment could apply to several adventures in my current life.

"Hmmm," I offered—the only noncommittal reply I could think of. As the adrenaline abated, sleep rushed into the void.

The last thing I remembered was Teddie saying, "It'll all be okay, honey. You got this."

Why did everyone think I had all the answers?

One day, perhaps as soon as I feared, they'd all see behind the curtain.

MY EYES POPPED OPEN WHEN WE HIT THE EDGE OF TOWN. "ARE you staying at the Raphael as well?" Jordan shared my floor. I hoped to hell Teddie didn't also.

"Bunking with Jordan." Teddie's grin was starting to fray around the edges.

Oh joy. Watching the scenery, I looked for landmarks and

tried to get my bearings. Finally, I saw something I recognized. The Eiffel Tower, of course. Triangulating off it, I plotted a course or at least pointed out a general direction.

Teddie ignored me. "I know how to get there." He eased into the left lane and took the next corner, heading into the old part of Paris.

"You do? Without a map?"

"I studied music here for several years." He glanced at me. "You may think you know everything about me, but there are a few mysteries."

He knew curiosity was my Kryptonite. Today I didn't have the energy. "I'm sure many more than a few."

I tried not to think about all I didn't know as I watched Teddie navigate the narrow streets and the traffic like an expert. As I suspected, twenty miles an hour was his sweet spot. Before I knew it, he was making the U-turn onto the small side street that carried hotel traffic, protecting their guests as they entered and exited cars from the faster traffic on Avenue Kléber. Ever discreet and impossible to startle, the valet greeted us with a smile as he opened my door and offered me a hand. I took it with a smile. "Keep it close, please. The police will want to impound it. The bullet holes you see." I waited for the words to hit. His eyes widened as he scanned the vehicle. "They're evidence." With that, I pressed my elbows to my sides, stabilizing my ribs, painted on a nonchalant expression, and sashayed up the steps thankful I'd finally made an impact.

Always good to leave them guessing.

Pauline manned the desk. "Good morning, Ms. O'Toole." She didn't miss a beat.

Of course, I'd left my blood-splattered coat in the truck. The police would want that, too, I suspected. "Good morning. What time is it?" My sleep in the truck had been sound and the dreams vivid. I was still working my way back to full cognition, such as it was. Somewhere between the drugs, the bullets, and the blood I'd lost track of life and time.

"Almost six. The sun will be coming up soon."

Oh, how I wished I'd be going down for the count. "Thank you." For some reason, the elevator wasn't waiting on the first floor. I pressed the button and leaned against the wall to wait. I didn't have to wait long. Through the glass doors, as the car descended, first a pair of slippered feet, then silk-pajamaed legs appeared, followed by the rest of Jordan, also sheathed in silk and radiating worry mixed with relief. He started before the doors even opened. "Lucky, my *Gawd*! What the *Hell*? I've been apoplectic with worry. Teddie didn't give me details, but it sounds like you've been through the wringer."

If he had all the details, he would've stroked out. "It's been a night."

Teddie pressed in behind me as I moved Jordan into the elevator. "We're fine, Jordan." With hands on my shoulders, he maneuvered me in and pressed the fifth-floor button. "I'm sorry about the show."

"No worries. Not your fault. I extended us a couple of nights and gave the audience tickets. They were despondent without you." Jordan clung to my arm. "I couldn't bear to lose you. You're my connection to myself."

"That's about the nicest thing anyone could say. I'm too mean to die; you know that." The doors opened, spitting us into the hallway.

In front of my door, Jordan released my arm and gave me a quick buss on the cheek. He lingered in a hug, then turned to motor on toward his room. "Come, Teddie. Let's leave the woman in peace. Besides, you have to tell me *everything* before I'll let you sleep." He didn't look back as he disappeared inside his suite.

"Guess he knew who was the softest touch." I turned and ran smack into a solid chest.

Teddie grabbed my shoulders and moved in close in a cloud of Old Spice cologne.

Funny how scents triggered memories.

"I knew you'd come back for me." He clamped his mouth over mine, capturing me in a serious, sensual kiss.

My knees weakened, just a little—a moment as my senses reeled.

My knees snapped straight, and I snapped to my senses. With two hands to his chest, I shoved him away. Reeling back, I let fly. The slap left a red mark on his cheek and a hurt look in his eyes.

"Way overstepping. You lost the right to do that when you left me for another."

"I apologized. I was wrong. We both know that. Didn't you feel it? It's still there." Anger replaced the hurt I'd heard before when we'd had this discussion.

I felt it. I would always feel it. But that didn't mean he was the right guy for me.

"Well, that was interesting." Jean-Charles stepped out of the elevator. He'd seen everything through those damned glass doors.

"What is it with the accusation? It's like your default. I'm guilty until proven innocent." I was shouting; I couldn't help it. A toxic cocktail of fatigue, fear, anger, and hurt had my head spinning, my mouth spewing, and my body shaking. "Well, I am so over that. If you don't believe in me, if your default isn't to protect me but to accuse me, then I want no part of it." I ripped the ring from my finger and hurled it at him. "Take this and go home. I'm sure your mother has your room ready." I whirled on Teddie. "And you, grow up. Figure out what you really want and stop chasing what you can't have." With that, I slid my card into the slot, bolted through the door, and slammed it on the only two men I'd ever loved.

CHAPTER TWENTY

"*W*OW."

My eyes flew open, and I bolted upright from my position, leaning against the door where I'd been trying, unsuccessfully, to push away the what-have-I-dones. I felt bad, yet relieved. Above all, I felt completely drained, exhausted to the core.

"Romeo! Shit. You scared the life out of me. What are you doing here? Why didn't anyone tell me?" I pressed a hand over my chest. My heart threatened to jump out of my chest.

"You sent a plane for me." He looked pressed and polished and ready to go—well, except for the cowlick that stood up straight from the crown of his head. His eyes were bright, his smile high-wattage. "That, by the way, was epic. Did you like have a script or something?"

So not what I needed. I opened my arm wide, gesturing toward the closed door and the hallway beyond. "I don't know what I just did. And whatever it was, it could've been the stupidest thing ever."

Romeo gave me a smile that made him look wise beyond his

years. "What you just did was to demand those simpering idiots raise their game, so they are worthy of you."

"What?" The word came out in a whisper.

"You are the *crème de la crème* as they say in these parts. Any guy who wants to hook his wagon to your team is going to have to measure up in a big way. Neither of those yahoos is even lifting a finger to rise to the occasion. If they don't, they are out of the running. Demand the best, Lucky. You *are* the best."

I wrapped him in a bear hug and fought back tears. Sometimes, students really were the best teachers. I let him go before it got super-embarrassing. "Can I quote you on that?"

"I'll even crow it from the highest mountaintop, and you won't even have to pay me."

That made us both laugh, dimming the heat of the spotlight on me.

"I'm so glad you're here." I sank into the nearest chair, suddenly too tired to walk another step.

"Breakfast is on its way. Two pots of coffee." Romeo joined me, pulling his chair closer so we could talk without expending what little energy reserves I had left.

"Now, I'm even happier you're here." My brain spinning from, well, everything, I tried to slow it for a moment. There was something I needed to ask Romeo. "Oh, is Chitza still in jail? I mean like physically present behind bars?" All I needed was for Jean-Charles's murderous ex-half-sister-in-law to show up with a sharpened sword and several axes to grind.

"I spoke with her myself."

That took one player out of the list of potential murderers.

"This is some room." He eyed the spiral staircase leading to the second floor. "Bigger than my apartment."

"Mine, too."

Romeo placed his hands carefully, one on each arm of the chair, like a kid afraid to touch anything.

"Kid, you can't hurt anything here. And, if you do, they'll

charge it to the Babylon. Relax. Even in a Gulfstream, it's a long way between Vegas and here. I don't know about yours, but no matter how cushy the ride, my body revolts against being hurtled through the air. You gotta be exhausted."

"Not sure. Excited, amped, but underneath it the dark void of sleep is calling."

"You captured trans-atlantic travel perfectly."

"I'm sorry I got here too late."

"Too late for what?" I kicked off one shoe, then the other. That took all the energy I had. My ribs complained, but my feet were happy.

"Catching the killer." He still didn't move, but at least he seemed to be breathing.

"Oh, we haven't caught the killer."

"But I thought…"

"We busted a counterfeit ring, but I'm pretty sure the killer is still out there." The clues were there, pinging around. I knew how to put the pieces together, but I couldn't make sense of it all through the fog of adrenaline withdrawal.

"What makes you think that?"

God love him, Romeo would make me walk through the clues until they made sense. I pushed myself up in the chair. Before I could begin, a knock sounded. Coffee might be the jump start I needed.

"You sit." The kid popped out of his chair. "Allow me."

"Gladly."

The aroma of fully-leaded serious European coffee started my engine. The fog thinned.

Romeo handed me a cup. "Cream no sugar."

The kid's attention to detail hit my heart. "Thanks." I cradled the cup like it was part of my last meal. I waited until he'd settled with his own cup of steaming joe, then I brought him up to speed, hitting the high points.

Once I wound down, he worked his way through a second

cup of coffee while he processed. "You sure Liu wasn't the killer? Or Moreau?"

"Neither had a beef with the man we first knew as Victor Martin. His real name is Claude Simon. Apparently, he was some sort of undercover investigator. Whether legit or not, I don't know. Haven't gotten that far. But he had proof of collusion between Jean-Charles's father and another man, Enzo Laurent, to keep the pecking order in Bordeaux in place. No new blood and they're left running the show. Tons of money involved. Liu wanted it as leverage to change the hierarchy and get his chateau into the highest level. Emma Moreau had no idea who Victor/Claude was. I saw her face when she looked at him. So why would either of them kill him *and* steep him in a whole bunch of what I bet is their own counterfeit wine?"

"And Sinjin?" Romeo shook his head. "That guy is a piece of work. Aren't you worried he's got the jump on you and will find the wine and take what he wants before you get there?"

"No." I felt one corner of my mouth lift. "I got that covered."

"Tell me about the counterfeit wine. How are you going to prove that?" Romeo leaned forward, cradling his dainty cup.

"I'm not. You are."

"The bottle you had me bring." He took a sip of coffee, which drained the cup, then stared into the bottom of it. "Don't they have mugs here?"

"Please, how crass." I stuck my empty cup out for a refill. "Keep your hand on the pot; I am far from fully-caffeinated. As you surmised, I need you to take the bottle you brought and the one from the murder scene to an oenological testing expert. They will be able to tell if the wine is the same, and hopefully, they will be able to identify where the juice came from."

"Seriously?"

"If the French winemakers are as advanced as the Americans. As valuable as the Bordeaux grapes are, I bet they've mapped all of them. The test relates to the DNA. I'm not sure, but I think it's possible to trace the wine to specific grapes and then match them to regional grapes already mapped."

"I had no idea." He loomed over me with the coffeepot at the ready.

Even though the coffee was hot, I drained the tiny cup, then accepted a refill. "Wine may present as art, but there is serious science involved." I leaned back into the embrace of the wing-back chair as the caffeine worked its wonders. "You'll need to get one of the bottles out of evidence held by the local police."

"I can do that."

Expecting an argument, I raised an eyebrow.

"You'd be surprised what one can accomplish with Google translate and a badge."

"Any chance you have a spare?"

"Badge?" He scoffed.

"You could deputize me."

He pursed his lips and looked like he was considering my suggestion. "Good call on Nigel Wilde, by the way."

Okay, well, guess not. No pinning a badge to my breast for me. Probably a good thing. "Poison?"

"Aconite."

"See, I do good police work."

"No denying that, but I didn't bring a spare badge."

His sorrowful look made me want to give him another hug, but that would embarrass us both.

Romeo didn't retake his seat. Instead, feeling bolder, he wandered around the suite. The windows called to him. "You are one for the views."

I joined him to drink in the perfectly framed view of the Eiffel Tower. "Being able to see into the distance makes me feel free, optimistic, in a way."

"How big the world is and how small our problems really are." The morning light highlighted the wisdom and worry etched into his previously fresh-faced features.

"Good way to put it. Or maybe with a view I have more visible escape routes." The early light bathed the city in pink. The white stone of the buildings absorbed it until they glowed.

"Wow," Romeo whispered.

"Magic." With the city bathed in the fresh start to a new day, I couldn't shake the feeling I was missing something, something big. All the questions circled back to the murder of Claude Simon aka Victor Martin. An undercover investigator, or so Liu said. First impressions of Victor screamed petty hood, but Vegas had taught me well that appearances most often deflected the truth.

Why kill him?

By his own admission, Liu didn't yet have the evidence he'd paid for of collusion between Laurent and Jean-Louis. Of course, that could have been a self-serving admission to deflect suspicion. Regardless, even if he already had all he paid for, there was no reason to kill Victor. In making a public accusation, Liu already had let the news loose. So, if he didn't kill Victor, could Emma Moreau have done it? There was no evidence Victor knew of the counterfeit operation. Even if he had, as a police officer, Emma would be acutely aware of the difference between faking wine and killing someone. Emma was dislikable but not stupid.

So, who else would have a beef with Victor?

If there was solid proof behind Liu's smoke and mirrors, then Jean-Louis and Enzo Laurent moved right to the top of the suspect list. In his final months, and too weak to spend much time out of bed, Jean-Louis masquerading as a killer was unlikely. If the truth came to light, he'd be dead soon. Of course, that reasoning also worked if he had in fact killed Victor. Still, I didn't see him as the killer. But I left the possibility open.

Then there was Enzo Laurent, a bit of a wild card.

M. Fabrice placed Enzo at the scene of the murder—well, Enzo's car anyway.

"Oh!"

I startled Romeo enough that a bit of coffee sloshed out of his cup. "What?" One look at me and his expression changed. "You know who the killer is, don't you?"

"What time is it?" Oh man, the tumblers fell into place.

"Almost seven, I think. My watch is still on Vegas time. It's nine hours' difference, right? Ahead or behind?"

"Ahead here." For the first time since I arrived, I felt like I wore my own skin. I topped my cup, then headed toward the stairs and the bedroom suite upstairs. "First, a shower, then to catch a killer."

THE BUSTLING WARMTH OF MY FAVORITE BREAKFAST PLACE IN ALL of Paris, *Carette*, welcomed me inside. A quick scan told me my Navy-shower and quick change had been worth it—I was the first to arrive. One other couple had ventured out this early on a cold winter's morning. They occupied a table in the back, away from the door. I took one of the two-tops along the banquet lining the front window so I could see him coming, and so no one could overhear our conversation. My view was partially obscured but was the best unless I sat in the enclosed porch. To me, that was too exposed. This was a good compromise. Besides, the young man who I had chased to his death died mere feet from where I sat. Any closer would be too difficult, the memories too real. He'd been Sinjin's mole in the counterfeit ring. Maybe he'd been a good guy. Maybe he'd been the one who sold out Sinjin. Either way, he'd been young enough to pay his debt to society and then live a good life.

"You should order the scrambled eggs; they are always perfect."

Lost in my memories and guilt, I jumped at the sound of the deep voice above me. Some cop I'd be—Romeo was right to deflect my desire to be deputized. "What? Not the renowned pastries?"

Enzo Laurent eased into the chair across from me. He looked disheveled as if he'd had little sleep and too much worry. Bags sagged under eyes that held a blank, haunted look.

"Thank you for coming." I motioned to the server who rushed right over. "Coffee?" I asked Enzo.

"Champagne. The best you have. Two glasses."

The server's smile bloomed. "*Oui, monsieur.*"

"I hope that's okay," he said as he snapped open his napkin and laid it across his lap. "Like I said, the eggs are wonderful, the croissants, divine."

"I'd like my eggs with ham, please."

When the server returned, he ordered, then shooed her away as he did the honors with the Champagne. He eased the cork free with a quiet pop, then reached to fill my flute. "I was surprised to get your text. Very few people have my cell number."

"Madame Bouclet gave it to me. I needed to reach you without any interference."

He took a sip of the Champagne before he answered. "This is very nice. You will like it. Jeanne has always been a great friend."

"She told me. I'm sorry for all of you."

His forced smile fled. "Yes, it has been…"

"Living hell?"

He drank his Champagne with the vigor of a man finding an oasis after days in the desert. "Worse."

I leaned across, placing my hand on top of his. "You're being blackmailed, aren't you?"

His hand jumped underneath mine. He licked his lips and his eyes darted to see who might be listening.

"It's okay. Nobody is interested in our conversation. I can help you." I released his hand.

"Nobody can help me. If I don't do what's been asked…" He

ran a hand through his hair and settled back in his chair. "How do you know of the blackmail?"

We both fell silent as another couple pushed through the door. They eyed the tables near us, but I shooed them away. They muttered—something about my lineage—but they did as I asked.

"I wasn't sure, not until just now. But it makes sense."

The server saw an opening to deliver our food, bowls of steaming scrambled eggs and a plate piled high with croissants.

"Guess I look as hungry as I am." I shoveled in a bite, then groaned. The eggs perfectly cooked yet soft, the ham sliced into thin slivers—a total food orgasm. I waited a few more spoonsful before continuing the story. "Let me try to put this together. You tell me if I'm right." A sip of bracing Champagne, then I dove in. "Your assistant, Daria, has been with you a long, long time. So long that she runs every aspect of your life, knows all your secrets…bore you a child."

He winced as if I'd slapped him. "Guillaume."

"He suffers from a genetic disorder, the same one that took your brother at a young age." A guess, but a good one.

"My brother's death, it tore my heart. When I found out I could carry the same gene, I vowed never to have children. I couldn't deny Jeanne the chance at motherhood. She argued with me, but I would not relent. I made the right choice; I know this." He pushed at his eggs but didn't eat.

"Then Daria told you she was with child." I ripped into a croissant. Flaky, rich, and oh-my-God wonderful.

"I was furious, demanded she end it. This is a very Catholic country. It would have been difficult but not impossible."

"She refused."

"And my worst fears were realized." He threw back the Champagne remaining in his flute. "Do you have any idea what it is like to watch a child die?"

"I can't imagine." I thought of Christophe, his happy face,

his unconditional love, his gentle touch, the soft ripple of his laughter. I couldn't imagine living through his death. "Daria wanted you to accept him as your heir. You have no other children. French inheritance laws would give him half your estate, at least. Once he died, she could inherit it from Guillaume."

"I refused, of course. My cousin's son shows much interest and ability in not only wine but the business of wine. He will make a good partner to the Bouclets and their heirs. A good steward of our combined legacies. Guillaume will die, just like my brother. And I'd rather die before Daria inherited any of my estate."

"But Guillaume's health took a turn for the worse; time is short. Daria is running out of opportunities to convince you, so she upped her game."

"In this digital world, she can *be* me."

"And she has. First, in fabricating signed documents showing illegal collusion between you and Jean-Charles and telling Frank Liu about it. She didn't count on Liu calling her bluff and hiring Victor Martin to look into it."

"But he was good and found her so-called evidence."

The more I thought about it, the more I realized there must've been something real underneath it all, something that had Enzo and Jean-Louis running scared, something Daria knew about. Of course, hitting Enzo with my suspicions would only make an enemy of this wary ally, so I kept my suppositions to myself. "Yes, and she killed him. She put him in a barrel of counterfeit wine to throw off the authorities. To make them think this whole thing was about fake wine when it really was about blackmail."

"How did she know the wine was fake?"

"At first, when she had it delivered from M. Fabrice's shop, framing the order as originating with you, I don't think she did. But she poisoned the wine and then sent it to Jean-Charles's restaurant at my hotel in Vegas. Nigel Wilde was the recipient, and he called foul in a most public way."

"So she used the rest to steep Victor and put us all off the scent." Enzo picked up a fork and swirled his eggs around but didn't eat any. "Nobody died in Vegas, did they?"

"No, I caught it early. Really sheer luck or Nigel Wilde would've been a goner."

"Not a huge loss..." The hint of a grin as he worked for a joke.

"Yes, agreed, but the law..."

He waved the idea away. "Oh, I know. It doesn't lessen the punishment even if society is better off."

"The Nigel Wilde thing was brilliant. He'd crow to the moon that the wine was fake." Yeah, I could see the whole story now. "Then she stole all of Jean-Louis's wine, something counterfeiters would do. Supply and demand and all of that. Even though she had planned to steal it all along, the theft worked into her cover-up."

"She planned the theft?" Enzo looked wounded more than pissed.

"She's been using her inside knowledge to be a very bad girl."

He didn't ask for more. What he knew had already deflated him.

"I thought the theft would kill Jean-Louis."

"It might yet. We need to find that wine."

"One thing I can't figure out is how Daria knew about the wine cellar. The entrance is hidden in Jean-Louis's office. No one knows about it. I never breathed a word."

"Her son. He used to play there. Knew every nook and cranny, Madame Bouclet told me."

"I never knew." Enzo seemed to be happy he somehow wasn't at fault.

"The night he died Victor Martin was waiting for you outside the kitchen door at the Bouclets'."

"Yes, Daria sent him to make sure I told Jean-Louis about all of it."

"Jean-Louis threw you out."

"He couldn't believe I had been so dumb. He didn't understand. He has a brilliant wife to help him in his work." His pain was palpable.

"And the man you tangled with in the kitchen?"

"I didn't know him. He was in a tux. Long black hair. Handsome, I think a woman would say. Exotic looking."

Sinjin. As I thought. That's where he picked up Victor Martin. He must've been there to meet with his mole. The theft was imminent. "I know the man."

"And Emma? Why would she do such a thing?" Hurt let the air out of him.

"You knew about her? That's why you tried to warn me?" The final piece.

"Yes, but I still don't understand why."

"Woman scorned. Greed. Who knows? I guess you'll have to ask her."

"I don't think you can help me." He stared at his food in distaste.

We finished our meal in silence. Enzo paid, I was too slow to win in a fight for the bill. "Let's walk," I said as I bundled up and headed for the door. "I'm at the Raphael, so it isn't far."

The chill cut right through me as we rounded the corner heading back toward the hotel. We'd made it a few blocks before Enzo spoke. "How are we going to get her?" he asked.

"We'll have to convince the police to bring her in for questioning." Or force her into doing something stupid. Neither seemed like fool-proof plans.

"I've been such a fool."

"Yes, you have," a woman said before I could answer. She stepped in beside me. A scarf wrapped around her head and covered the lower half of her face. She pressed the barrel of a gun into my side.

Daria.

Help had arrived—proving there is no fool like a gloating fool. She was a candidate for the stupid criminal show, but she didn't realize it yet.

"How...?" Color rose in Enzo's cheeks.

"I get your text messages on the computer. You forget, I know all your passwords, everything." She didn't gloat; she merely stated a fact, comfortable in having the upper hand.

"Daria, haven't I given you enough?" Enzo crumpled in defeat.

"Money," she spat. "My son deserves your name, your position."

"My estate."

"Guillaume is dying. Time is short. You both must come with me."

I nodded to Enzo. "She has a gun." We needed to get her alone, out of the public eye. Find the wine. *Come on, Enzo, play along. I got this.*

As if he'd heard me, Enzo capitulated. "Daria, I will do anything you want, but you must let Lucky go."

CHAPTER TWENTY-ONE

*D*ARIA ESCORTED us into a waiting car.
Enzo took the front. I slipped in beside Daria in the back.

I patted the phone in my pocket. Yep, still there. If I'd guessed right, she'd trek us through the sewers and catacombs to the wine stash where she would have Enzo sign a declaration of parenthood.

Daria was crazy but efficient. Although, her plan left out the whole Victor/Claude angle. If I could figure it out, so could someone else.

A good thing as I wasn't too sure whether I'd be singing later or someone might be crying at my funeral.

Daria kept the gun trained on my side. "Make any move I don't like, Enzo, and Lucky's done."

The driver kept flicking glances in the rearview. Dead eyes.

We crossed the *Pont de l'Alma* then snaked our way through the Seventh. On the other side of Les Invalides, he took Boulevard Saint-Germain, then angled south on *Rue Bonaparte*, closing in on St. Sulpice. The driver pulled into a side street barely wide enough for one car and stopped.

Gillian had been right.

He put the car in park, then stepped around the front of the car. Bending, he tugged at a handle flush with the narrow sidewalk, opening a trap door. Then he retook his position behind the wheel. Again, a flash of those dead eyes. Well, he wouldn't be any help, but he wasn't going to decrease my odds by joining his boss in this little underground trek either.

Foot traffic was nonexistent. No help there.

"You first." Daria used the gun concealed in the long sleeve of her coat to gesture Enzo over to the hole. "Remember, you so much as flinch..."

Enzo acknowledged her threat with a tired wave as he grabbed the handrail and disappeared down the steps.

"You next." She prodded me with the gun.

I stifled the urge to break her arm. But she was the quickest route to that wine. I started down. Virtually complete, the darkness of the catacombs seemed almost tangible. When I reached the bottom, I could barely see Enzo in the thin beam of muted daylight angling through the trap door. The damp air held a hint of death and decay. The walls of the narrow tunnel were cool to the touch and scarred with the tool marks of the quarrymen who had dug them out centuries ago. The bones of two million souls found their final resting place down here. I felt the pain of the unremembered, the chill of their presence.

Enzo eased in next to me, lifting his chin in suggestion as Daria's feet appeared. She bent down, the gun pointed at my chest. "Don't even think about it." The gun never wavered as she finished her descent. With one hand, she raked back her scarf, exposing a small headlamp which she pulled lower on her forehead and flicked on. "That way." She motioned straight ahead into the darkness.

Enzo took the lead with me behind, Daria's gun in my ribs, her breath heavy behind me. Her light bobbing as she walked barely pierced the darkness. As we walked, I worked to remember our path. One hundred steps. A hard right. A wider tunnel. Bones tossed like pick-up sticks. Some we had to step over. This part of the catacombs bore little resemblance to the carefully curated public section with its lights, endless stairs up and down, and meticulously piled femurs and skulls, some arranged in patterns like hearts. Here the bones were piled willy-nilly. Some femurs, a few skulls, but mainly the lesser bones that didn't lend themselves to tidy, artistic stacking. The whole thing had me feeling Death breathing down my neck.

Not today, asshole.

I counted my steps and visualized our path on Professor Kirkland's map with Gillian's markings. We should be getting close to the step-through.

Seventy-five steps from the corner, Daria barked, "Stop."

I felt the slight brush of air from my left.

Daria pulled a couple of beams back, letting them fall. The last one fell, exposing a narrow step-through. No one would've seen this unless they knew it was there. So tight, it was more like a slip-through. Enzo and I would both have to sidle through. Wraithlike, Daria wouldn't have the same trouble. "You go." With a waggle of the gun, she urged Enzo through.

He pulled in his breath and angled into the opening. Still, I had to give him a little push before he popped through. Holding my breath was enough to get me through, picking up some dirty smudges along the way. Daria, as expected, slipped through unsullied.

From this point, the danger increased as did Gillian's guess-work as to which room might hold the treasure we sought.

Hence my tolerance of Daria.

In this section, the going was slower. We had to step over fallen supports, piles of bones, rocks; you name it. The roof lowered here enough that I had to crouch. Enzo too. He'd started to limp, his breathing heavy.

Again, I counted steps. This time I added turnoffs to the

count. They wouldn't have gone far, not with all that wine. We'd passed three turnoffs and gotten two hundred steps in when Daria said, "Left here."

I wondered if the Nazis used this step-through and abandoned branch. Evil lurked here. Or my imagination worked overtime. Either way, I was pretty creeped out and pissed beyond seeing red.

Fifty more steps and I felt rather than saw the walls of the tunnel move away as the space opened up, becoming less cramped, the air less stale, the sounds we made echoing rather than reverberating around us. Behind me, Daria flipped a switch and we were blinded by light.

Blinking as my eyes teared, I whirled. A quick blink. I steeled myself against the pain, then launched myself into the woman who had turned slightly to hit the lights. She wasn't as stupid as Liu and his goons. Of course, she didn't suffer from male arrogance and their pathological underestimation of the fairer sex.

I caught her with my shoulder. A glancing blow, staggering. Landing on all fours, I ignored the screaming of my ribs. I pulled my knees underneath me. My hand found something hard, round.

A bone.

I fought the recoil and grabbed it. Pushing with all I had, I bounded toward Daria, raising the bone high. As she brought the gun around to bear, I pulled down. The bone caught her across the forearm. The gun fell, and I kicked it to the side. The dirt of the floor obscured its final resting spot.

"*Mano a mano*, bitch."

A moment of hesitation, then she faded back and ran into the tunnel through which we'd come. "Stay here," I barked to Enzo as I lunged to follow Daria. "It's dark, and you have no light. I'll be back."

I dove into the darkness. Harder going this time as I followed the bobbing light in front of me. Fueled by adrenaline and running on fury, I ignored the pain of the knee-knockers, ignored the danger of putting my weight on the decaying supports, ignored my body bruised and battered. Some of the supports shifted, raining dirt. But they held.

The light closer now, Daria's ragged breathing reverberated. Mine joined hers, but anger trumped fear. The woman was mine.

I ran crouched over, my hands feeling for things in the dark to trip me. Higher than expected, one caught my foot. I fell hard, but kept my legs churning. Pain streaked through my chest taking my breath. The thought to take out one of the supports occurred to me, but I dismissed it. That could trigger a cave-in and trap us all.

The light disappeared. She'd taken the turn, but she'd gone right. I swung my arms up like a left-handed batter. As I made the turn, I swung. The bone shattered as it hit flesh. Breath left in a whoosh.

Taking a play out of my playbook, Daria had killed the light and waited to pounce. Ten feet from me, the light popped on as she ran. My swing hadn't stopped her, but it had slowed her down. I put my head down and churned as fast as I could make my legs go. I needed to stop her before the main tunnel. There, she'd have much less bulk to carry on tired legs and no impediments.

She slowed to take the next turn. I kept churning. Expecting a right, I was surprised when she took a left, working her way deeper into the maze. She was too far ahead. All I could do was follow as she made turn after turn, two right, a left, another right, followed by two lefts.

Remember Lucky. Remember.

At each turn, I made up a little ground. After the sixth turn, I launched myself at her. I tackled her around the waist. My bulk drove her into the far wall, her body absorbing the blow. I let off, then drove her into the stone again. This time the sound of her skull hitting rock made a satisfying meaty thunk. She sagged. I let her fall.

Standing over her with my breath searing my throat, I let out a yell of satisfaction. Her belt worked nicely, binding her hands together, then tying them to her feet. My handiwork might not make the National Finals Rodeo, but they'd keep her here long enough. I tore the light from her head, then popped the back off my phone. The rectangle of paper was still there. As I unfolded it, I whispered, "Now that was two lefts, a right, a left, two rights…"

MY SCOUTING SKILLS HADN'T LET ME DOWN. I BLINKED AGAINST the light, but this time I'd been prepared, easing in slowly so as not to be blinded. Enzo stood in the middle of a large, exquisite stone room. The barreled ceiling gave the illusion of space. The arches above the doorways allowed folks like me to get through without ducking too much. Columns supported the ceiling and murals of performers in bright costumes decorated the walls.

He turned when I walked in. "It's all here. Every bottle. If you hadn't returned, I would've died a happy man. Some of this wine is so rare I've not had an opportunity to taste it."

I could picture him, the wine keeping him alive, muting the pain of life as he waited for the release of Death.

"Rather prosaic, but a bit over the top, don't you think?" I looked at all the wine. It seemed inconsequential to a non-oenophile like me. But what trouble it had caused. I didn't want to know the final body count.

God willing, one wouldn't be Jean-Louis.

"Come, we need to call the police. Then you need to talk with Jean-Louis. I'll make sure Daria is turned over to someone other than Emma Moreau."

He let me lead him out. "How did you find your way back?"

"It wasn't that hard. I counted turns, but I had a back-up in case I got lost." I showed him the bit of paper, then held it out for him to see. "A map."

"Impressive."

"I knew I'd be looking for the wine down here. But I never thought I'd be chasing a killer." I thought of the other map. I needed to hurry.

Once up the ladder into the daylight, I handed my phone to Enzo. "My French is sketchy. Could you get the phone number for a Professor Kirkland?"

A minute of rapid-fire French and he had it. He pressed it into my phone then handed it to me. "I'll call the police."

Pep answered just as I pressed the phone to my ear. "Professor, Lucky O'Toole here. How fast can you scramble the underground spelunkers?"

THE SPELUNKERS ARRIVED AS THE POLICE WERE TIDYING UP. THEY screeched off in a blaze of self-importance and howling sirens.

I'd used my map to fetch Daria, taking along three beefy uniforms to secure her. She hadn't put up a fight. Three squares and exercise time was a far cry better than death by starvation lost in the catacombs—if she didn't go mad first.

Gillian led a gang of five all outfitted with maps, headlamps, and backpacks with food and water.

"You know that part of the catacombs you said to not go into?"

She smiled. "We're going in, aren't we?"

"Yes, we have someone to find."

This time, surrounded by spelunking experts and armed with sustenance, light, and maps...and minus the gun in my ribs...I felt a lot better, the creep-factor diminished by a factor of ten at least. My crew was focused, professional. They snapped photos—the breadcrumbs to lead us out—and spoke little. Occasionally, we'd pause to call.

"Sinjin?" We took turns shouting.

As we worked our way deeper and deeper into uncharted territory, my confidence started to wane. Knowing him as I did, I'd left the other map in my bag in the car at Liu's. I figured Sinjin would bolt at a point where I couldn't follow him. He'd go through my stuff, find the map—the one I'd put a large X on. Of course, the X was in the wrong spot, leading him into the unmapped section. All planned. The risks weighed.

Now, had it worked?

We kept moving, calling. Nothing. We checked side tunnels as far as they went, then back to the main tunnel leading us deeper. We'd scrambled over partial collapses and been careful to avoid triggering any others.

"Professor Kirkland knows where we've gone, right?" Why it took me this long to ask, I don't know.

"Yeah," Gillian said. "Told him myself. Even marked the map. I thought he was going to hyperventilate. We also have one of those transponders they use in avalanches. It probably won't transmit through this much rock, but it'll help if someone comes after us."

If. I didn't like the sound of that, but, then again, I was a stickler for proper semantics.

After I don't know how long, we stopped for some water and a few bites of sandwich, which the kids kindly shared.

"Most would've lost courage by now and stopped," one of the young men remarked through a mouthful of sandwich.

"I don't think I could live with myself if he is in here and we stop too soon. Could we go a bit farther?"

The tunnels had narrowed, the ceiling lower now. They were much like the tunnels on the other side of the step-through. Thankfully, no bones. Even the guys ditching them hadn't come this far.

Terrific.

"It's really not much farther," a voice from the back sang out. A short, wiry, ginger-headed young man. "There's a cave-in up a bit. It's not safe to go any further, even if we could."

"You've been here before?"

"Once. By mistake. It's pretty bad in here. Very unstable."

Ah, confidence restored. "I noticed. Takes a bit of the fun out of it."

We pressed on. "The cave-in blocking the tunnel is just there." He flashed his light, illuminating the path ahead.

And captured the smiling mug of Sinjin Smythe-Gordon. "Lucky, old girl, you cut it rather close. A bit longer and I would've been a goner."

CHAPTER TWENTY-TWO

*C*RISIS OVER, I was left to pick up of the shattered bits of my life.

First, to find out how shattered.

My mother answered before I heard a ring on my end. "Lucky! Where are you?"

"Hotel Raphael. I need a bath in the worst way. Maybe two. Then I'm coming home." I stared through the window at the Eiffel Tower. I'd always love Paris, no matter the heartbreak.

"I see." She sobered. "Are you okay?"

"Curiously, I haven't felt this much like me in a long time." That much was true. I felt in control of me. I didn't feel the need to run around making everyone happy. Most problems weren't mine to solve. Such a new idea! I wasn't sure what to do with the freedom. "How's father?"

I gripped the phone tight, bracing for the worst, hoping for the best.

"He's fine. They never found the bleeder they expected, but his iron levels have stabilized."

"What caused the drop?"

"They don't know, but they aren't concerned. His strength is rebounding. They're letting him come home tomorrow. I'm so relieved."

Overcome, I couldn't talk for a moment. He wasn't dying—well, not any faster than the rest of us. I'd lose him someday, but not as soon as Jean-Charles would lose his father. "That makes two of us," I said, then cleared my throat. "How are Frankie and Sammie?" My voice regained its strength.

"Last night they slept through the night for the first time! I didn't get a wink. I was up and down all night long checking to make sure they were still breathing."

"As I understand it, part of the deal." Somehow the thought of my mother being all motherly weakened my wariness.

"I'd forgotten." She'd gone all breathy. "I'm one of the walking dead. Speaking of, how did things work out in Paris?"

That was such a complicated question. The police had carted off Sinjin and Daria. With no penalty for perjury in France, I had no doubt Sinjin would be a free man any time now, if he wasn't already. Daria could lie to the moon and back, but she wasn't going to wiggle out of this one, especially as lacking in charm as she was. Romeo would report back soon. And the men in my life? Disappointments, both of them. To be honest, I was disappointed in me, too. Buying into fantasy only gave reality an open invitation to bite you on the ass.

I considered myself bitten.

And all I really wanted right now was a long, steaming bath. "It's been interesting. Jean-Charles's father is dying."

"Is that why you're coming home alone?" She'd inferred as much from my use of the singular. Typically, her aim wasn't this close to the bull's-eye.

"Mostly. We both have large business interests that require our souls. We need to work on that...and a few other things."

"And Teddie?"

How could I answer that when I had no answer?

"I see." Mona read enough in my silence. She'd jump to

conclusions, and telling her not to would only confirm a quick leap. "And that incredible ring?"

Ah, there was the mercenary Mona I knew and feared. "Mother, let it go. I've got this. My heart; my life."

"Sure, honey. Just worried about you."

And my ring, but I didn't cast aspersions on her few hints of maternal concern. Maybe this was the beginning of a new chapter for each of us. "I'll let you know my ETA when I get on board and have a flight plan."

"I love you, Lucky. Come home soon."

"You, too, Mom." Why were the words so hard when the sentiment was real?

THE WATER HAD REACHED THE PERFECT TEMPERATURE, AND I slipped into the bath. The tape around my torso had been a bear to remove. It had left raw patches where it had taken a scrape of skin with it. They hurt like hell, but to be honest, they were the least of the insults. A quick look in the mirror as I'd passed confirmed all manner of purple, blue, and red splotches on my body. That was the surface stuff. In addition, my knee was a bit grumpy and my ribs took affront at every breath I dared take.

The hot water hurt the raw spots but soothed everything else. All the bumps and bruises had dulled to an acceptable ache when I heard the bell, then the door open and close. I'd resisted the Siren call of Champagne, so it couldn't be the waitstaff. Must be the housekeepers. I folded one of the plush bath sheets into a puffy pillow and stuffed it behind my head as water lapped my chin. Absolute bliss.

"Lucky?"

Jean-Charles. So much for the perfect bath.

"Can we talk later?" I kept my eyes closed. I didn't want to look at him. For sure, I didn't want to touch him. And I didn't want him to touch me—I don't think there was one square inch that hadn't suffered some abuse. For the second time, I was thankful the Raphael believed bubbles made a perfect bath. They hid the damage from Jean-Charles. That would be a conversation I didn't have the strength for.

"Now would be best. But not long, I promise."

Somehow, I knew I wouldn't have a say in this.

"How are you feeling?"

That was new. "About what?"

"Your body. I believe it collided with a car."

I didn't dare move. Breathing hurt. I hurt in places I didn't know I even had. But, curiously, the collision might have actually knocked some sense into me. Time would tell. "I think your body treats being hit by a car in the same way it treats childbirth. Apparently, there is some sort of chemical your body secretes that allows ligaments and tendons to stretch beyond their normal, so it is possible to survive."

"How do you know this?" Jean-Charles managed to ask after a long pause.

"You know my mother; she doesn't have a filter."

He cleared his throat, which meant he was at a loss and something difficult was coming. "I think we need to find a place to work from now, assuming you want to." He had moved closer.

I didn't want to, not now. Hanging onto hurt and anger seemed like a better choice, less painful. But that really wasn't true; I knew that. Anger only hurt the one who carried it. "I like the Vegas you much better than the stuffy, entitled Parisian, heir to a fortune and a legacy."

"Me, too."

That got my eyes open. He crouched by the tub—close, but not too close, keeping a distance so a spark couldn't fly. The toll of the last few days had dimmed his brightness. It had most likely left all of us a bit diminished.

"Vegas is a fantasy; you tell me that all the time. And it's true. There I am able to be who I want to be without all the obligations and expectations I leave here. I thought I could move beyond everything here, run it from afar. I guess I thought my parents would live long enough for me to be happy."

My turn for a long pause. Legacies aren't all they're cracked up to be. "It was good, wasn't it?"

"I'll never be able to listen to *Thomas the Tank Engine* again without…"

"I know." While playing the theme song to *Thomas the Tank Engine*, we'd about herniated ourselves having animal sex in the bathroom. "But a lifetime isn't built on that."

"No, but it was a great start."

I matched his smile at the warm memory. "We have two very complicated lives that are pulling us in opposite directions. A long-distance marriage isn't what either of us wants." I waited for his confirmation. "We have a lot to figure out. Neither of us knows right now how all of this will shake out. Your father is dying. Your mother is strong but brokenhearted. My father is weak. I don't think he will ever regain the vigor he had before. When they go, what will life look like for us?"

"All questions with no answers."

"Somehow we both have to figure out how to honor ourselves and our own dreams and, yet, also honor the legacy of our families."

"The balance, I do not know. But I do know I love you."

I closed my eyes and looked deep, deep inside. "I love you, too," I whispered, the truth tearing at me.

"Then perhaps that is where we could start?"

"Yes." With my foot, I twisted the tap to add more hot water. A woman of extremes, I didn't do tepid, or average, or mediocre, nor did I settle. At least the new me didn't.

"You have some other choices to make."

He furrowed his brow. "I do?"

"First, your father. I don't have proof, mind you, but there must be some truth to the collusion angle between him and Laurent."

"They are old men desperate to hold onto their power in a world where good wine is made all over the globe. I wouldn't put it past them. Why do you say this?"

"I think Daria killed Victor because he found out the truth and he threatened to hang out both Enzo and your father to dry. This would threaten the value of the estate Daria worked so hard to inherit. In fact, it might do enough damage to Laurent's reputation that it could render his business irrelevant. And the way she killed Victor, with the counterfeit wine poured over him? That was meant to throw everyone off. Initially, we all thought he was involved in the theft and fake wine, not the collusion angle. I think the reverse is true."

"You have no proof of the collusion?"

"No, but I bet it's somewhere. It may be Daria's trump card. Be careful. And do what you have to do to get the truth out of your father. Trust me on this one. My father thinks nothing of skirting the law to his advantage when the stakes are high enough. It's like being in charge of a two-year-old who can drive. The carnage can be immeasurable."

"Thank you for caring enough to tell me. I am on the inside. So much emotion. So many things I don't want to believe."

"I understand. But, when on the ropes, we are all capable of doing things we never thought we could...or would. Hopefully, we have loved ones around to remind us that values are far more important than financial gain."

"And sometimes the hurt runs too deep, and the years are too many."

So, this thing between Jean-Louis and Enzo was more personal than business. Not my problem. I didn't rule the world. "And you need to think about Emma and M. Fabrice. We don't have much proof, none if Sinjin and I don't breathe a word of what we overheard at Liu's."

"You would do that?"

"As I said, sometimes good people do bad things. There will be a punishment; there always is. But that doesn't mean I have to deliver it. This is your turf. These are your people. You decide." Yep, for sure I was sick. Me. Always tilting at windmills in the name of truth, justice, and the American Way.

Maybe maturity brought compassion.

As much as I'd like to deny it, we all lived somewhere in the gray. Oh, sure, underneath all of it was a solid base of right and wrong but understanding and wisdom should make them less harsh.

At a loss, Jean-Charles pushed himself to his feet. "My parents, they want you to come by before you go. And Christophe..."

"Oh, Jean-Charles. Christophe. I can't."

He accepted that and turned to go.

I stopped him. "Yes. Yes, I can. I can't be that cruel, no matter the personal cost."

He smiled at me as if he'd known my ultimate choice all along. "I'll tell them to expect you...?"

"Give me an hour."

"Keep it running," I said to the driver as I let myself out of the back. On the sidewalk, I felt like no time and yet a lifetime had passed since I'd looked up at the façade of the Bouclets' house with the same trepidation.

Once again, the same butler greeted me at the door. This time he smiled, fleeting as it was. The more things change...

He escorted me to the elevator and pressed the button for

the second floor. "The family is expecting you." Still on the outside. Maybe that's where I belonged.

As the doors opened, Christophe launched himself at me, hugging my knees. I maneuvered him out of the elevator, then squatted down so we were eye-to-eye. I hid my gasp of pain. Who knew ribs were integral to every tiny motion? "Hey, big guy. Can you look at me?"

He'd been crying. He fought against the tears that welled again.

"It's okay to cry. Some things hurt. This is one of them."

"*Papa* told me why you have to go and why we have to stay. *Grand-père* is very sick, and *Papa* has much to do here."

"I have some of the same problems in Vegas."

"I know." His lip quivered.

I couldn't look at that beautiful face all scrunched in pain. I stood then, took a deep breath, then swooped him up, placing him on my hip. A victory that I didn't cry out from the stab in my ribs. "It'll be okay. You like it here. Sara will let you cook. I bet she'll even help you make happy face pancakes."

"But she's not you."

Jean-Charles stepped out of a room halfway down the hall.

"You'll come visit," Christophe insisted.

As we came within hearing distance of Jean-Charles, I said, "Maybe your father will bring you to see me, or maybe he'll let you fly all on your own to see me."

Jean-Charles looked slightly traumatized at the thought.

"There's a direct flight." I didn't know if that would make the thought of one's child alone in a thin metal tube hurtling across the ocean any easier to bear. But I thought probably not.

"*Papa?*"

"You will see Lucky. Don't worry about that." He held his arms open. "Here, let Lucky go see your grandparents. We'll wait for her here."

I shot him a questioning look.

"Their request."

Just like before, the room was too warm by far. Madame Bouclet sat in a chair pulled as close as possible to her husband's bedside. She clutched his hand. Jean-Louis looked a bit uncomfortable at all the fuss. Unlike before, this time he had some color and some vibrancy. Someone had taped gauze over his wound. His eyes even had a hint of sparkle. His hand wavered as he held it out to me.

His skin was cool to the touch when I took his hand in both of my own.

"I'm am a lucky man to be flanked by two formidable women."

Madame Bouclet gave me a warm smile. "Thank you. You found the wine, and you brought my husband back." Her eyes held the rest that she didn't say. "If only for a while."

"I'm so glad you are doing much better." I squeezed Jean-Louis's hand.

"You are to blame."

I smiled at his unwitting choice of words. "Then I am honored."

"Jean-Charles, he loves you. And Christophe..." He rolled his eyes and gave me an energetic *boof!* "I know you are needed in Vegas, for many of the same reasons Jean-Charles feels compelled to stay here."

"Life has a way of working out." I turned to Madame Bouclet. "If you let it."

She gave me a nod. The choice would be Jean-Charles's. I didn't expect her to be able to completely avoid guilting him into staying—zebras and stripes, and all of that—but at least she'd try.

"You have restored our legacy," Jean-Louis said, his breathing now a bit labored. Too much excitement, dwindling strength. "We must do something for you in return for this great gift."

"No, thank you. It's sorta what I do...did...do. Solving problems is my superpower."

"Regardless, there must be something. We insist." He glanced at his wife who joined in his conviction. "Please?"

I could see it was terribly important to them both. I thought for a moment. "You know, there is one thing..."

THE PLANE WAITED ON THE TARMAC, THE PILOTS WALKING around it, making their final checks. A guard waved the car through the gate in the chain link fence. A pilot rushed over to grab my luggage from the trunk. I stepped around to greet him. "You're not one of our normal crew."

"No, ma'am. The crew needed their mandatory rest."

I'd forgotten Romeo had just arrived. "Right. Quick turn."

"Yes, ma'am."

I contemplated the luxury of a long ride home, by myself, with no internet, when a man peeked his head out of the doorway and waved.

Sinjin Smythe-Gordon.

I shook my head. "You are like an ugly growth on my ass."

He sauntered down the steps looking anything but. "The police graciously denied me room and board. I am free to go."

"But you still have a very large problem, and this plane is your ticket away and your haven from danger." Sinjin had worked hard to earn my cynicism. I didn't see any reason to deny him of it.

He opened his arms wide, amping up the charm factor until he practically glowed. "Lucky, you wound me to the core."

Yep, I can confirm, I am immune. "Don't waste it on me." His shiner had turned a deep purple fading to greens and yellows at the edges. "Enzo gave you that shiner, didn't he?"

Sinjin stepped to the side as the pilot eased past him with my suitcase. "Yeah, as I said, I was there to meet with my mole. Things got hairy when he burst into the kitchen and went at it with the old man."

"Jean-Louis."

"Yes. Jean-Louis."

"But you were in the tunnels. Jean-Louis said he surprised you there."

"Can you think of a more private place to meet?"

"That night it was a bit crowded. Jean-Louis followed you to the kitchen, the easiest escape route, where you encountered Laurent." I didn't need him to confirm. "What are you planning on doing about the Hong Kong problem?" I asked before he answered my first observation. They would eventually hunt him down and whatever ensued would be painful.

He smiled and shrugged. "I'll figure something out."

"So, you don't want a ride with me?"

"I would not put you in that position. These men who are following me are ruthless. They care nothing about…collateral damage. Not to mention, they wouldn't hesitate to use you against me."

"Ah, so you have a warm spot for me, do you?" The man knew no end to the game-playing. "Is that why you are here?"

He could tell I was joking. "No, I wanted to say goodbye. You have bested me twice. Impressive."

"And third time's your charm?"

"Could be. Who's to say? But it was brilliant leaving that map for me to find. You knew I'd look through your things looking for any clue to where that wine was. All I needed were two bottles."

"Worth a fortune. And they didn't belong to you." I reached into the back seat of the car. I pulled two bottles of Estate Laurent that Jean-Louis and Jeanne had gladly given me. "Would these be the bottles you seek?" I'd felt bad asking in a way for such an expensive recompense, but they were glad to do it. Especially when I told them Sinjin's life hung in the balance.

He stepped closer. As he looked at the bottles, he practically vibrated with need. Putting his hands behind his back, he stepped back. "Where'd you get those?"

He didn't trust himself either. "From the Bouclets. A reward, so to speak. They belong to me."

He eyed me for a moment. "Curious those were the two bottles they selected."

"Isn't it?" I reached back into the car, relinquishing a bottle for a moment while I hooked my Birkin over my arm before grabbing the bottle again. Over Sinjin's shoulder, the pilot gave me the all-ready sign.

"It's time for me to go."

Sinjin took another step back. "Yes, well then. You are a formidable adversary. Until next time."

Feeling a bit like a creep but enjoying it immensely, I walked toward the stairs. I'd made it halfway up when I turned. Sinjin hadn't moved. Taking my time, I stepped back down. "Okay, here's the deal. I am not your adversary. You think you need to strong-arm people into helping you. You never give anyone a chance to rise to the occasion. I know you do bad things for good reasons. I get that. I will help. Just don't ever leave me holding the bag again. We win together. Or we lose together. If the goal is worth it, I'm in."

"I've never had a partner. I have trust issues."

I laughed. "Man, you are looking at the poster child for trust issues. If I can learn to trust you, then..." I held the bottles higher. "But I'm not asking to be your partner. I'm just saying should the need arise..."

"You drive a hard bargain."

I extended the bottles then pulled them back. "What did you do with the money you got from selling what turned out to be counterfeit wine to the Hong Kong creep?"

He dug a toe in the tarmac. "There is a nun who is helping the girls in Macau who are forced to sell themselves. They need shelter, safety, and education."

"A name." Like I said, trust didn't come easy to me.

"Sister Margaret at the St. Sidney School."

"There's no St. Sidney." Not a Catholic, I couldn't be certain, but I was pretty sure.

"One of the lesser saints, actually, but the name refers to Sidney Ho. He gave the funding for the original building."

I thrust the bottles at him with a laugh. "Do not sell these or I will kill you myself. Make it right with the Hong Kong dude. The world needs a man with a Robin Hood complex."

"Are you sure?" The waver in his voice told me how much my gesture meant.

"And stay out of jail. Hard to do good from there."

"You told me you would have risked your life to come back for me. I didn't believe you."

"I don't know where you came from or what your story is, but people can be good if you let them. Now, this emotional stuff is making me all nervous. Are you sure you don't need a ride?"

"I have a game set up in Monte Carlo."

"I bet you do."

"But I need to go to Hong Kong first."

"A bit out of my way."

He shrugged.

"But I need a break. And some sleep. A trip home in a round-about way would be just the thing."

"Seriously?" He seemed incredulous.

"Your ass is a grape the longer it takes you to get to Hong Kong. With my pull with the FBI there, maybe I can get you an escort. The guy who wants your head pretends to be legit, right?"

"Totally." His smile started to bloom as he thought about it.

"Then it could work?"

"You don't mind?"

"Of course not, but I need to let the pilots know there is a change of plans. They'll have to work on a route with stops and clearances. May take a bit."

He hooked his arm through mine. "Not to worry. I put one of your bottles of Champagne on ice. Great choice, by the way."

For a player, he'd played me perfectly. I let him have his win.

We'd made it halfway up when sirens sounded behind us. Sinjin flinched.

"You aren't running from the law, are you?" I don't know why I didn't think to ask. Perhaps I held his skills in too high a regard.

"No. Daria, Desiree, and I convinced the police of my innocence."

"Impressive, as you are the least innocent man I know. And Liu is dead so he can't complain about the theft of the wine. What about Desiree?"

"The police will let her family deal with her. She helped an innocent man." He couldn't help the grin that leaked through.

"But she still broke the law." Truthfully, Desiree needed some counseling, and some love. Jail wouldn't give her either.

A black sedan, a rotating light attached to its roof wheeled through the gate and skidded to a stop. Romeo bounded out of the passenger side. "I'm glad I caught you. I know I said I'd stay, but Sam has it covered."

Sam Desai stepped out of the driver's side. "You left quite the mess at Chateau Shasay. But you did warn me."

I waited for the ax to drop.

"But your friend Theodore confirmed your story."

"And the security force?"

"Long gone. They'll take some chasing down."

"I know you are up to the challenge. And Emma Moreau?"

His face fell. "I'm afraid she took her own life."

"Oh. That wasn't the way out."

"With her father's position compromised, her family's reputation sullied, her career in shambles, and prison with many people she was responsible for putting there in her future, I think she saw it as the only way out."

"Then whether the wine is counterfeit and where it came from is moot."

"I have the bottles—the one Detective Romeo brought, the ones we have in evidence, and the bottle you hid. They may confirm what we already think we know."

"I'd like that." I extended my hand. "Thank you. And I'm sorry about the nose. But maybe you shouldn't try tailing anybody again, at least not without more practice."

"A good lesson."

"You didn't?" Romeo couldn't keep the awe out of his voice.

"I gave her no choice." Sam rode to my defense, but none was necessary; Romeo wouldn't believe him anyway.

"Kid," I said to Romeo, "you should stay in Paris. Let Sam show you around. It's an amazing city."

"Yes, the City of Love." He smiled as he brought up our old disagreement. "If I'm going to experience this place, it will be with Brandy's hand in mine."

My young Romeo was such a romantic. I threw an arm around his shoulders. "Kid, I think this is the beginning of a beautiful friendship." I'd said it before, but it bore repeating. Besides, even I couldn't resist stealing a great line like that. "Come, gentlemen, adventure awaits."

THE END OF ONE ADVENTURE,
THE BEGINNING OF ANOTHER….

Thank you so much for going on a Lucky adventure with me. I
hope you enjoyed the ride.

As you may know, reviews are SUPER helpful. They not only help potential readers make a choice, but they also help me win coveted spots on various advertising platforms.

So, if you would please, do me the favor of leaving a review at the outlet of your choice.

NEXT UP FOR LUCKY...

Read a short excerpt below

CHAPTER ONE

"ALMOST HOME, miss." The First Officer peeked his head through the open doorway of the small office off the largest bedroom in the back of the plane. "I'll need you up front and belted in for landing."

"Thank you." I shut down the computer and my efforts to try to catch up on what had been going on in Vegas while I'd been gone. My name is Lucky O'Toole and for the last two weeks or more I'd been ignoring my responsibilities as the vice president of customer relations for the Babylon Group, the owner of multiple properties in Vegas and one of the primo Strip properties. Not that a couple of hours over the Pacific would get me up to speed, but it might help me hit the ground running.

I reached to flip off the satellite television showing a live feed of the local news. The face on the screen stopped me. My best friend, Flash Gordon, newshound extraordinaire, reporting from a local party—not her usual beat. As the sun was out, it looked like the party was earlier this afternoon. I glanced at my watch.

Just after midnight.

In the feed, Flash interviewed another buddy of mine Jordan Marsh, Hollywood heartthrob. They were promoting the Concours d'Elegance, a fancy car party starting soon, so I didn't bother with the sound. Next to Jordan, attempting to squeeze into a sliver of importance, bobbed a man I didn't know—tall, thin, graying temples and a smile that would have most smart men grabbing their wives and daughters. There was one in every crowd. I shook my head and snapped off the TV. That was Vegas right there: fancy cars, celebrity cachet, and a regular Joe soaking it up for the weekend, perhaps pretending an importance he didn't have.

The pilots pulled back power and started our descent as I buckled in.

The lights of Las Vegas spread across the valley below—thousands of pinpoints in the desert darkness. At ten thousand feet, the plane skimmed over the Sunrise Mountains then started the drop to final approach—the end of a very long trip. Along the way, I'd left broken hearts, numerous bodies, and perhaps some sanity in my wake.

It struck me that a few short weeks ago, I'd started out heading west and had kept going until I'd come full circle.

Home again.

Odd when the beginning can be the end. Sort of like that old joke: when do you leave home to get home? Guess my life resembled a game of baseball.

Hadn't struck out yet, but I couldn't shake the feeling that the damage I'd left behind wasn't going to stay in my rearview.

The plane that now carried me home, one of the Babylon's G650s, certainly had made a clean getaway all the easier. I thought I'd left each country with the approval and most likely the enthusiasm of the local constabularies, but I wasn't entirely sure. At some point it would be my luck to land on the wrong side of a modern-day Avert. Despite the body count, there'd been only one near fatality on the side of truth, justice and all of that—one of the fractured hearts was mine.

Thankfully, my body had survived. Most of the time I was grateful for that.

I pressed my nose to the window as the pilot banked the plane lining up on final approach. Landing to the north put the Strip on the left side of the plane. The lights beckoned with a false promise of fun. Oh, don't get me wrong; for most who came here, the city delivered.

But not for me.

As the Chief Problem Solver of the Babylon Group (my business card reads Vice President of Customer Relations, but let's be real), it was my job to keep the Vegas magic burning bright for all who stepped across the threshold of one of our properties. Consequently, I'd seen behind the curtain. And once you see the levers and gears, the magic isn't quite as...magical.

For me, Vegas was not a holiday, not one last toot with my BFFs before the impending stranglehold of marriage, nor did it provide even a simple weekend fantasy to offset the drag of real life.

No. Vegas *was* my real life.

My home.

And it was no fantasy.

Like everybody else, I lived with my problems lurking with the dust bunnies under the pieces of large furniture and whispering from the shadows. But unlike everyone else, I didn't have Vegas in which to offload them, not even for the weekend.

I leaned back in my seat and closed my eyes contemplating exactly where to begin my reentry, how to solve a few of the looming problems, but I hadn't a clue. I'd left a beautiful young girl killed on my watch in London, a broken engagement in

Paris, and a slew of bodies and unanswered questions in Bordeaux. I'd delivered a Hong Kong financier on the run from some very scary Triad enforcers to Monte Carlo with only the slimmest chance to right a wrong and save his own hide. But those paled in the light of my worst problem. My father, the head and heart of the Babylon Group, still struggled to recover from a bullet to the chest. My mother couldn't...or wouldn't... tell me how sick he really was.

If he died it would change everything.

Between you and me, I found adulting to be a cruel hoax perpetrated on happy children. I once was a happy child...I think. But that little slice of Norman Rockwell (the *only* slice of Norman Rockwell in my childhood) was so far in my rearview it had vanished in the haze.

"Glad to be back?" A familiar voice knifed through my little bit of dirty laundry airing. Detective Romeo.

For a moment I'd forgotten about him—my personal Sir Galahad who had ridden to my rescue. (His take. I let him have the fantasy.) He'd arrived in Paris as I touched a match to the fuse and fireworks lit the sky. He'd stayed to help me pick up the pieces, then caught a ride home...via Monte Carlo.

While he was my secret weapon in the Las Vegas Metropolitan Police Department—Metro to us locals—he was just a kid. Although, tonight, he looked way more world-weary than his years would allow. In fact, he looked as tired as I felt, despite the now mashed lei around his neck, the white Plumeria blossoms starting to brown—we'd stopped for fuel in Hawaii and had done the whole customs and island thing. At the time, I'd resented the time it had taken but was grateful now we'd done it.

Romeo blinked at me, clearly expecting some kind of response—I couldn't remember to what. Dark circles underslung his red eyes. The hint of worry lines bracketed his mouth and radiated from the corners of his eyes. Somewhere over

Indonesia he'd stopped worrying about straightening his tie or combing his hair. The flag of a cowlick sprung from the crown of his head.

I resisted the urge to brush it flat.

A hint of sympathy lit the blue of his eyes, faded by lack of sleep. "You left a lot of shit back there. Home must feel good." His attempt to make me feel better was appreciated but fell short of the mark. Not his fault. For some reason I wasn't feeling the homecoming joy.

Must home feel good? Did it? Jet lagged and heartbroken, and more than a little panicked, I didn't have an answer for him. In fact, I didn't have any answers period—heck of a place for a professional problem solver. The only answer I could give him was a shrug.

As the wheels kissed the runway, he turned to look at the Strip out the window that still held my nose print. "Pretty amazing, isn't it?" He was still young enough to be awestruck.

"One constant in a sea of change." Too tired to muster a grin at the irony—if Vegas stood for anything it was change, even if only for a weekend—I pulled my phone out of my bag and powered it up. A few seconds of silence, no more, and texts pinged like the ringing of a come-to-dinner bell but without eliciting the same salivating anticipation.

Romeo and I both looked at the offending device.

"Damn," he said. "You must be important." His smile told me he thought so.

I wasn't so sure. "Being the one who stops the proverbial buck makes me popular, but I'm not so sure about important."

Miss P, the head of customer relations for the Babylon Casino Hotel, our most exquisite, over-the-top Strip property and my right-hand man, caught me before I had a chance to begin to tackle the texts. I answered her call on the second ring. "Have you been bugging the FAA again?"

"I have a copy of your flight plan."

One more bit of proof that I could indeed run but not hide. "Along with a detailed transcript of my last visit to my therapist."

"You don't have a therapist."

"An oversight soon to be corrected."

"Riiiight." She knew me well. Whining was my go-to when pressure mounted. Sharing my innermost thoughts with a stranger didn't promise the same immediate gratification. "Can we talk now, without the whine?"

"Oh, if you insist." As the plane slowed to a taxi, Romeo pushed himself up and disappeared toward the back. I took his place at the window, working to draw energy from the wattage outside. I'd been told the Strip could be seen from a galaxy far, far, away. As I blinked against its brightness, I believed it. "Whatcha got?" The lure of a problem that perhaps I could actually solve tickled me. The old happy-to-be-home tingle shivered through me—a faint shiver, but there.

"I'm sorry to do this to you, but we've got a dead guy."

A dead guy! Oh yeah. Right in my wheelhouse. As I tucked the phone between my shoulder and ear and pushed up my sleeves, I resisted pondering what that said about my life. "How fresh?"

"Still warm."

"Where?"

"Delivery bay seven. Police are on their way. Jerry's pulling the security feed. You know the drill."

I did. Death was the flip side of the fun and frivolity in Vegas. Like all the properties, we had our share. But a dead guy in a delivery bay raised questions. He couldn't be explained away like a tapped-out gambler deciding to go out in a blaze of idiocy, or a panicked john shoving a roughed-up woman under a bed, or one of the millions of private negotiations that went on all over town going bad. "I've got Romeo with me."

"Paolo is on his way to get you."

"Thanks. Anything else I need to know?"

"Oh, we've got the full complement of crazy this weekend, but I can fill you in later." Miss P sounded tired. Little wonder— Vegas was a nonstop mischief shop and we were the proprietors. No doubt, my Paris respite with its lure of a normal life with a normal schedule had eroded my 24/7 skills. Although there had been the guy stuffed in a barrel of wine and then the shootout in Bordeaux. Maybe I wasn't as rusty as I feared. Besides, fire tempers steel and this one would be hot, even by Vegas standards.

"Did my father get home safely from the hospital?"

"Yes." Her tone turned guarded.

"I'm really surprised they discharged him so soon. A good sign, don't you think?"

A pause. "They didn't."

"They didn't what?" I asked, sitting up a bit straighter. This rat was stinking to high heaven.

"He left. They didn't discharge him."

"He just walked out of the hospital?" That sounded so much like my father.

"He said he had to talk to you. It's important."

"He's okay, right?"

"Resting comfortably according to your mother."

No one was ever comfortable in my mother's presence, least of all her family, but I took the words at face value for comfort. "Okay, dead guy first on the list, my father second."

I disconnected without waiting for a reply, then tossed my phone on the seat next to me. "Am I lucky or what?" I said to no one in particular.

Romeo plopped back down in the seat across from me looking all spit and polished, his eyes bright with anticipation. "People get shot for saying that in your presence." He watched me; his brows stitched together with worry.

I shot him a bit of slitty-eye. Unchastised, he grinned. Of

course, he had a beautiful fiancée who would be very glad to see him—that could sure scrape away the travel grime. I hated to dim his wattage, but I needed his help. "Your homecoming will have to wait. We've got a bit of a problem."

I filled him in on the few details I had.

A puppy eyeing a bone, he perked up. If he had a damn tail... A look of grown-up competence replaced his slobberdog. Personally, I liked the slobberdog better. It reminded me of the aw-gee-whiz kid he'd been when we first met. Now he was Grasshopper all grown up and ready to snatch the stone from my hand. He pulled out his notepad and pencil, then shot me a half-smile. "A dead guy, you say? Welcome home."

Home. I took a deep breath. A dead guy in the delivery bay and all manner of craziness yet to be discovered and waiting to be dealt with.

Problems to solve, magic to preserve. The old sizzle burned stronger just under the surface.

Home.

Yes, it was good to be back.

As the plane rolled to a stop and the pilots shut down the engines, Romeo jumped up to help the First Officer lower the stairs. Once the stairs had descended, they both stepped aside to let me go first.

"We'll call for your car, Ms. O'Toole. I believe one is waiting in the parking lot." The First Officer held out his hand. Fresh-faced, his cheeks devoid of stubble, his hair still wet from a recent combing—heck, even his shirt was pressed, and his pants still held a crease—he looked as if he could go around the globe again. Of course, he also looked like high school was still in his future. I wasn't sure when they allowed mere children to fly, but somehow, I'd missed it.

"Watch the first step, it's bigger than you think."

Even though the idea that he would think I needed help rankled, I put my hand in his. "Thank you," I said, surprising myself with the hint of sincerity. Romeo coughed behind me. "Manners, Grasshopper," I hissed over my shoulder.

The reference did a fly-by right past the First Officer as he continued without a hitch. "We'll grab your luggage," he said with the perfunctory tone of an order shaped like a suggestion. Jean-Charles had an irritating way of doing the same thing.

Jean-Charles.

"Are you French?" I asked the young officer as I paused at the top of the stairs.

Romeo sniggered behind me.

"No, ma'am. I'm from Idaho."

And cursed with a Y-chromosome, I thought. From the bland smile on his face, I hadn't given word to my thoughts for once in my life, for which I was profoundly grateful.

"I don't have time to wait for you to fetch my luggage. Would you send it later?" I charged down the steps, in too much of a hurry to wait for his answer. I folded a coat over my arm and took the stairs as quickly as I could with a tired, folded-up body and balky parts. Why was it so easy to sit but so hard to unbend and move again? Even my brain was having a hard time spooling up. The cold slap of wind provided the wake-up call I needed.

Late spring in Vegas was a mercurial thing. Clouds scudded low capturing the light and reflecting a multihued but mostly pink glow. The sting of a wind-driven pellet or two stung my cheeks. Water of any sort occupied a spot on the endangered species list here in the middle of the Mojave, so rain, or more precisely, corn snow, would likely cause citywide wonderment.

I welcomed anything that hinted of a season other than unblinking sunshine and skin-melting heat. Tonight snow, but tomorrow could be sunbathing weather. Nobody could forecast it, least of all the weathermen.

A low, dark limo with the Babylon logo scrawled in hot pink down the side stopped at the bottom of the stairs. The pink had been my idea. I still liked it. My father tolerated it but occasionally, when he thought I was out of earshot, did grudgingly admit it had a certain flair. We made a good team, father and daughter —cut from the same cloth but with a chromosomal orientation that differed yet complemented.

Paolo, the Babylon's head chauffeur, jumped out of the driver's side, smashing his chauffeur's hat on his head as he greeted me with a smile that hinted at his normal wattage but seemed dimmed, perhaps by the demands of a weekend already spooling at a high RPM. "Miss Lucky!" He opened the back door with a flourish. "Welcome home!" Paolo always spoke in exclamation points, something that used to bother me. Not tonight. Not anymore.

Life held precious few superlatives.

My lungs did a happy dance as I paused, breathing in the cold and damp. A few lungsful, then I dove inside.

"The Babylon. Step on it." I'd always wanted to say that, but tonight it didn't make me smile. Romeo barely had enough time to scramble in next to me before Paolo threw the car in gear and hit the gas.

The acceleration threw Romeo back against the seat. "Shit!" Apparently, he hadn't graduated to five letters from four as I'd been trying to do as I navigated my former fiancé's, Jean-Charles's, turf. French society frowned on such common vulgarity.

Turns out common was sorta where I lived. Growing up in a whorehouse didn't prepare one for navigating the halls of palaces filled with the intrigue, backstabbing, and head lopping —the whispers of kings and queens long dead. I pursed my lips as I pondered that. On second thought, maybe it did.

"My sentiments," I said, embracing Romeo's base assessment. As I watched the scenery race by and tried not to think about the number of tourists we endangered, I wondered just how much my parents and Miss P hadn't told me. I glanced at the rearview to catch Paolo's eyes bracketed by worry, taking quick peeks to check on me. "What is it, Paolo?" Surely, he wouldn't know any details about my father...or the dead guy—for me, a toss-up in importance. Duty or family—wasn't that a historical choice suffered by many through the annals? Just carve my name next to Gandhi, who gave up sex with his wife to best serve his people. Okay, not Gandhi. Maybe Richard the Lion-heart or Alfred the Great.

"I picked up Mr. Teddie yesterday," Paolo said, his usual verve wilting to a whisper at the end.

Romeo swiveled a look as I absorbed the punch.

"See." I held my arms out wide, "all I have to do is think about sex and his name comes up." Obviously, my self-censor had taken a break. Of course, that presupposed I had any sort of filter. If I did, we weren't terribly well-acquainted.

That left Romeo struggling to keep up as red crept up his cheeks. "You were thinking about sex?"

"An odd thing, I know, all things considered. I won't explain how I got there. Besides they say men have a sexual thought every seven seconds. I'm merely trying to keep up."

"Lowering your personal expectations, I should think." Romeo coughed and straightened his tie, angling for a look in the side mirror—a thinly cloaked attempt to avoid my slitty-eye.

Paolo's eyes held the hint of the smile I could not see.

I eyed Romeo. Yes, the student had truly become the teacher. "Indeed. I will endeavor to up my game." What was it they said? Women who wanted to be equal to men weren't very ambitious. In a rare show of self-regulation, I kept that to myself.

"Mr. Teddie is here because of his show..." Paolo added. "He asked if you'd gotten home."

His show! Of course! I'd forgotten. My father, in a flagrant if rare break with family loyalty, had booked Teddie into the theater at the Babylon. In addition to being a super-hot, super-virile man whose voice would make the Pied Piper jealous—especially if he was interested in luring women instead of children—Teddie was also Vegas's foremost female impersonator. Yes, the first man I'd given my heart to not only looked better in a dress than I did, but he also had daddy issues. I'd snatched my heart back...well, after he'd cut me loose...but I'd left a piece of it behind. Guess that's how it worked with love. If I were the great Poohbah of the Universe, I'd change that. That way the aftermath of a failed love affair would be a bit less devastating—not that there was any risk I'd ever assume that throne.

"And what did you tell him?" I asked Paolo, who was spending far too much time nervously glancing at my reflection rather than at the road in front of him.

Paolo slunk down a bit in his seat which made him all but disappear, not exactly comforting.

"I told him you'd be home tonight." He dropped even lower.

I inched toward the edge of the seat and leaned over the front. "I hope from down there you can see more than I can from back here." People and buildings, signs and cars passed by outside the window in an alarming blur.

"Not so much."

I reached over the seat and pulled him up by the shoulder of his jacket, reinstalling him to where I was pretty sure he could at least see through the steering wheel. "My whereabouts aren't a secret." Not that I wanted Teddie anywhere within eyesight until I figured out how to handle all my mixed emotions. Did I love him? Sure. Did I trust him? Not on your life. Could love exist without trust or did it become something else? Once broken could it ever be repaired, or was it forever lost? Could those questions even be answered?

"Terrific." I wondered if the show was the only reason he was here. Part of me wished it so. The other part wasn't so sure.

Romeo touched me on the arm. "It'll be okay."

Teddie and I had dodged bullets together in France. Bonding through bullets didn't sound like the glue to hold a relationship together. And there was still that bit where Teddie had thrown me over for some young songbird and the huge ego boost. Now he was back and singing a different tune. Still sounded a bit off-key to me.

"Okay?" I arched an eyebrow at the young detective who, to his merit, didn't wilt. "One way or the other." There was a tiny continuum between homicide and rekindled love. Where Teddie and I would fall was anybody's guess. "Come on kid, let's go solve some problems. Remember, no matter how shallow life gets, it's nice to be needed."

"Somehow, between you and me, I think we're looking for mental health in all the wrong places."

End of Sample
To continue reading, be sure to pick up *Lucky Enough* at your favorite retailer.

ALSO BY DEBORAH COONTS

The Lucky O'Toole Vegas Adventure Series

Wanna Get Lucky? (Book 1)

Lucky Stiff (Book 2)

So Damn Lucky (Book 3)

Lucky Bastard (Book 4)

Lucky Catch (Book 5)

Lucky Break (Book 6)

Lucky the Hard Way (Book 7)

Lucky Ride (Book 8)

Lucky Score (Book 9)

Lucky Ce Soir (Book 10)

Lucky Enough (Book 11)

Other Lucky O'Toole Books

The Housewife Assassin Gets Lucky

(Co-written with Josie Brown, author of the Housewife Assassin series)

Lucky O'Toole Original Novellas

Lucky in Love (Novella 1)

Lucky Bang (Novella 2)

Lucky Now and Then (Novella 3)

Lucky Flash (Novella 4)

The Brinda Rose Humorous Mystery Series

90 Days to Score (Book 1)

The Kate Sawyer Medical Thriller Series

After Me (Book 1)

Deadfall (Book 2)

Other Novels

Deep Water (romantic suspense)

Crushed (women's fiction)

ABOUT THE AUTHOR

Deborah Coonts swears she was switched at birth. Coming from a family of homebodies, Deborah is the odd woman out, happiest with a passport, a high-limit credit card, her computer, and changing scenery outside her window. Goaded by an insatiable curiosity, she flies airplanes, rides motorcycles, travels the world, and pretends to be more of a badass than she probably is. Deborah is the author of the Lucky O'Toole Vegas Adventure series, a romantic mystery romp through Sin City. *Wanna Get Lucky?*, the first in the series, was a *New York Times* Notable Crime Novel and a double RITA™ Award Finalist. She has also penned the Kate Sawyer Medical Thriller series, the Brinda Rose Humorous Mystery series, as well as a couple of stand-alones. Although often on an adventure, you can always track her down at:

www.deborahcoonts.com
deborah@deborahcoonts.com

facebook.com/deborahcoonts
twitter.com/DeborahCoonts
instagram.com/deborahcoonts
pinterest.com/debcoonts
bookbub.com/authors/deborah-coonts
amazon.com/author/debcoonts
goodreads.com/DeborahCoonts

CPSIA information can be obtained
at www.ICGtesting.com
Printed in the USA
LVHW091245081121
702755LV00001B/2